INVASION

An Abaddon Books™ Publication
www.abaddonbooks.com
abaddon@rebellion.co.uk

First published in 2016 by Abaddon Books™,
Rebellion Intellectual Property Limited,
Riverside House, Osney Mead, Oxford, OX2 0ES, UK.

10 9 8 7 6 5 4 3 2 1

By Anne Tibbets and Malcolm Cross,
writing as Addison Gunn

Editors: Jonathan Oliver & David Moore
Cover Art: Edouard Groult
Design: Sam Gretton & Oz Osborne
Marketing and PR: Rob Power
Head of Books and Comics Publishing: Ben Smith
Creative Director and CEO: Jason Kingsley
Chief Technical Officer: Chris Kingsley

Extinction Biome created by
Malcolm Cross and David Thomas Moore

ISBN: 978-1-78108-388-8 (UK)
ISBN: 978-1-78108-389-5 (US)

EXTINCTION BIOME
INVASION

ADDISON GUNN

ABADDON
BOOKS

WWW.ABADDONBOOKS.COM

OPERATION HONSHU WOLF

DEAD PIGEONS WERE scattered across the streets and sidewalks in a threadbare carpet, baked dry, almost mummified by the heat in a matter of days. Say what you wanted about global warming and climate change: at least it had finally solved New York's pigeon problem.

Sweat trickled down Alex Miller's nose, despite the armoured limousine's air conditioning.

Something the size of a Great Dane nosed through the crumbling bed of bones and feathers with its misshapen skull. The creature seemed to be all teeth, all jaw, built from evolution's pre-mammalian leftovers. Ridges of bone knobbled its skull, leaving the creature's leathery face looking warty and distended. It peeled its lips back, revealing snakelike fangs, and snatched something small and squealing from amidst the pigeons—it looked like a particularly long-bodied rat, but rats didn't have armour-plated skulls like prehistoric fish.

The terror-jaw whipped the little thing side-to-side, muscular neck straining, and with one last flick the rat-thing's spine snapped and the squeals ended. It looked back, as if for approval, toward Miller's target—a dirty, scruffy, ungroomed white man in his late thirties.

You couldn't *tame* the new wildlife. Everyone knew that—the damn things were as wild as lions, and a damn sight older—but that didn't seem to matter to the target. He was *filthy*, with some kind of scabrous orange growth crawling up his shoulder.

Gingerly, Miller reached up and scratched his nose, safe behind the limo's locked doors and parked in the shade of an alleyway. He had no desire whatsoever to grab the target, but there weren't any other untried options on the table, and a hostage exchange wouldn't work if Miller didn't take hostages...

Miller leaned forward in his seat, pulling his Gallican .45 from its concealed holster under the back of his Louis Vuitton suit jacket. He hesitated, glancing across the limousine at du Trieux. "When this goes wrong, you be ready to pull my ass out of the fire."

Du Trieux nodded seriously. Morland, behind her in the back seat, gripped his shotgun more tightly. Miller knew he could rely on du Trieux in a pinch—she was a French-Nigerian ex-*jihadiyya,* who fought back in the early '30s to liberate Syria from Daesh and the rest of the false caliphate. She could be a cool-headed killer if she needed to be. But Morland? Morland was a *kid*, barely twenty, from the south of England. Sure, the 'kid' was an imposing six-foot-eight, but that didn't change the way his hands were sweating. No experience at all—which was why Morland was in the limo, while the team's second Englishman was on his own with a rifle on a rooftop.

Miller tapped his earpiece. "Doyle? Get ready to kill the dog."

"*It really isn't a dog,*" Doyle replied, his clipped Oxford English buzzing through the earpiece's low-bandwidth encryption. "*On target.*"

Miller gnawed his lip, hovering a fingertip over the door's lock. "Trix, you take the wheel. Morland, be ready to receive the hostage." In other words, stay in the back seat and don't shoot anybody.

The kid just about melted in relief.

Miller shared a look with du Trieux, and got out of the limo's sweet air conditioning and into the oppressive heat. And the *smell*, Jesus. Maybe parking in an alleyway hadn't been such a good idea. He clicked the door shut.

The terror-jaw out in the street jerked up, alert, twisting its head side-to-side, presenting its ears—fissures in its skull—to search for the origin of the sound. It saw Miller and bared its teeth. As he approached, leaving the stink of the alleyway for the stench of the street, it ducked its head and raised its rump, like a cat ready to leap. The abduction target twisted around, lifting his shaggy hair out of his eyes.

"Doyle?" Miller asked, finger on his earpiece, panic edging into his voice.

The shot tore open the asphalt inches from the terror-jaw's forepaw. The animal backed up with a startled jolt, looking up toward the source of thunder... and then bounded for Miller, jaws wide.

"Doyle!"

"*Sorry, not at my best.*"

Miller got off two shots with the Gallican—a double tap, centre mass at the charging animal, but broken bones and blood hardly impeded the thing. Its wet throat was scarlet behind the grille of its fangs, ravenous, *eager*. Miller reflexively pushed his gun out at the terror-jaw, heart skipping a beat, then spasming as something hammered the creature's head sideways. Blood was everywhere.

The creature fell, twitching, and didn't rise.

Doyle's second shot.

The only other time Miller had seen a terror-jaw from this close was around two years ago. His dad called, complaining about seeing weird things out on the ranch. At first Miller had figured it was just nerves, his parents weren't used to rural life, they should've taken their retirement in the suburbs. Then he visited and saw a sickly little creature that one of the cows had stepped on.

Back then, four years after he'd left the army, the creatures of the Archaeobiome were still a scientific curiosity—it seemed that the entire ecology slumbered over hundreds of thousands, maybe millions of years. Researchers had called it a kind of migration, through time rather than space. Instead of travelling from place to place in search of food, the creatures just laid eggs or hibernated over millennia until droughts ended and deserts turned to jungles. Nobody had seriously considered whether or not the reawakening ecology could be some kind of threat. Why would they? At that point the biggest terror-jaws anyone knew about were *maybe* the size of a cat.

Now, two years on and a healthy chunk into Miller's sixth year as a bodyguard, the only thing unusual about the massive beast lying twisted and broken in front of him was that it had a collar around its tree-trunk neck.

"You shot my dog." The abduction target fell to his knees in dismay, crushing a desiccated pigeon-corpse. He plucked at the terror-jaw's gnarled, leathery forefoot as though it were a puppy's paw. "Why'd you shoot my dog?"

"Stay there," Miller snapped, lifting the Gallican. "Just stay right there, and put your hands on your head." He forced himself to relax his grip, stop trembling.

The man slowly raised his arms. "What are you? Some kind of cop?"

Miller didn't answer, stepping around the cooling body to get behind the guy. The abduction target *stank*, and the longer he looked at Miller, the more disgust crawled into his eyes.

Oh, it was obvious the guy was a commune-member. Infected with the parasite. It wasn't the orange rash infesting his skin—though that kind of thing was common in Infected communes—it was the smell, the terror-jaw, the look in his eye.

"How'd you do it?" Miller asked, bundling up the guy's wrists in a set of zip-tie cuffs.

"Do what?" He watched Miller from the corner of his eye, part afraid, part *angry*.

"The terror-jaw. How'd you get a collar on it?" Had the terror-jaw been infected too? Could the Archaean Parasite jump species?

"Dunno. It was eating our trash." The guy shrugged. "Hey, Blondie. These are too tight."

"Don't call me that. I'm not even all that blonde," he muttered. It had been months since his barber shop had closed; his highlights were almost gone.

"So what's your name?"

"You don't need to know that."

"Guess I don't. I'm Nick." The prisoner laughed, a slow, rising laugh that ended in a racking cough. He hunched forwards on his knees in front of Miller, spluttering and drooling. "They're gonna come and get me, you know. I can smell them," he wheezed. "They heard the shots."

"Don't care," Miller grunted, hauling Nick to his feet. The man's sweat stained the cuff of Miller's suit jacket—it was light silk, just bearable in the heat. And now it was stained, and where the hell was Miller going to find a dry cleaner? He shook out his wrist, grunting. "Where's Lester Allen?"

"Who?"

"The BioGen scientist your commune abducted." Miller shoved Nick into a shuffling walk, and tapped his earpiece. "Trix? Follow us."

"*Oui,*" du Trieux responded.

Every few steps Nick stopped to look back at Miller and the limousine crawling along after them.

"The scientist? You mean the guy who tried to *poison us*?"

"Nobody's trying to poison you people."

"Of course they are. They put drugs in the food aid packages—they're trying to kill us, trying to destroy our *gift!*" Nick shambled forward, turning to glare one last time. "*You're* trying to do it. The ungifted."

"Uninfected," Miller corrected.

Nick was more right than he knew. A completely separate subsidiary of Schaeffer-Yeager International was responsible for distributing the famine aid packages, but the CEO had insisted that every package contain a supply of anti-parasitics. It was a matter of principle, but one that had spooked the Infected into burning soup kitchens and aid stations across the city.

The lucidity drained out of Nick with each step closer to the commune's territory. He stopped focussing on the ground, on the tightness of his handcuffs, and instead followed a little girl hiding behind a trash can with his gaze. After she was sure Nick and Miller had seen her, she ran away with a long hooting cry.

They melted out of the buildings like a troop of apes on the savannah. Roused by the alarm call, they slipped from doorways and appeared at corners. A lanky man, a wide-set woman, an old white man in a decades-faded Tea Party Republican shirt. There was a hipsterish guy with an old shotgun and a bedraggled beard, and two women nervously walking hand in hand as they came to investigate.

With each new arrival, Nick stopped being Nick, and bit by bit became part of the mob.

The crowd forming in front of Miller were a multicultural mingling of black and white, old and young. And they looked at Miller the way a spooked Doberman watches a stranger touching her puppies.

"Hey!" Miller yelled. "I have your guy hostage. Talk to me."

One woman blinked owlishly at him, then another, then Nick, twisting around with his cuffed hands at his back, then the girl, then a tall black man... their focus of attention flooding across the mob in a wave, until every single one of them was standing still, staring at Miller intently. Just staring and breathing. They made half-vocalized nonsense sounds at the edge of understanding, muttered pieces of words, a constant murmuring babble that grew louder as they advanced.

Miller backed away a step. "Who's in charge?"

They laughed at him.

All of them.

From Nick the hostage to the little girl hiding back at her trash can, every single one of them began laughing and stopped laughing within seconds of each other, even those who'd been well out of earshot of what he'd said.

"Nobody—" "Nobod—" "—ody's in—" "Nobody's—" "Nobo—" "—body's—"

The chorus of answers spilled over, the mob talking across itself, unable to get the words out, stammering and stopping and starting over until they stopped trying to speak. The mob didn't speak with one voice—it spoke with a hundred.

Sweat trickled down the back of Miller's spine.

Consensus pushed one of the Infected from the front of the milling group, a guy not out of his college years. He spread his hands awkwardly, smiling as if he'd been caught unexpectedly on camera. "Nobody's in charge!" he called after getting a good twenty feet away from anyone else—far enough he couldn't see his friends, just Nick. Half-consciously he held his hands behind his back, mimicking Nick's cuffs. "We're all just going with it."

A susurration of 'yeahs' and 'uh huhs' bubbled through the crowd, even Nick nodding along under Miller's gun.

"*You okay, Miller?*" du Trieux asked, voice faint in Miller's earpiece.

Miller reached up, as if scratching his ear, and hit the earpiece's push-to-talk clicker twice—the acknowledgement signal.

"I—we—just want our guy back, okay? Lester Allen, the BioGen scientist your commune took. Is he okay? Still alive? Nobody has to get hurt."

"You mean the poisoner? You're with him? Nobody's hurt anybody except you corporate freaks! Take your drug cloud machines and fuck off!" The spokesman's anger rippled through the crowd like a Mexican wave.

"We *haven't* been using aerosol dispersed drugs," Miller protested, forcing down the fear-driven impulse to lift his gun and point it at the crowd edging in around him. "Lester works for BioGen, he's only interested in agriculture, air quality, that fungus that started the New Dust Bowl, trying to *stop* it; we have nothing to do with medicine of any—"

The mob roared as one, an impassable press of bodies.

"Don't give us tha—" "—lying scum—" "—course you did—" "—children can't—" "—pumping poison into—"

Miller switched tactics. He jammed the Gallican's barrel into the back of Nick's skull and roared back at them as loud as he could. "Shut up! Shut *up* or I'll kill Nick!"

Nick heard him; the others, probably not. But Nick's fear bled over into them somehow— pheromones, parasite-overstimulated sympathies, it didn't matter. Whatever the mechanism was, the entire mob shuffled back a half-step, as though Miller were pointing the gun at *them*.

"Who's Nick?" one caught near the front asked.

They didn't recognise his name, but when Miller ground the gun into Nick's greasy hair, they cared. They cared like it was their best friend, their brother, their son.

"It's okay," the new spokesman said, hands up placatingly, drifting carefully towards Miller. "Lester's just fine. It's all cool, you don't have to hold a gun to our guy's head."

Miller bit back a laugh. "Yes, I do."

"No, you don't." He spoke as if Miller was the crazy, dangerous one.

"No? I think I do."

Another step forward, and the spokesman stopped, hands up, fearful as if the gun were on him, not Nick. "It's all cool, man. Lester's fine, he's cool, he's *gifted* now."

Miller's jaw tensed. "He's what?"

"He's right here," a voice from the mob said, stepping forward with Lester Allen. Miller recognised him, bald spot and all, from the briefing's employee records, but Lester looked feverish and sweaty, wearing a torn green T-shirt.

Lester stumbled forward a step, a second. He stood, staring at the spokesman, at Nick. Bewildered, overstimulated.

"Lester Allen? I'm Alex Miller, I'm here to take you home."

"I want to go home," Lester murmured, flinching away from the closest of the mob as they began to repeat what he said. He covered his ears, stumbling away from them in fright. "Home!" he screeched.

"Ho—" "—oa—" "—mmmh!"

Miller shoved Nick to the ground, then pounced forward and grabbed Lester's shirt with one hand, pointing the Gallican .45 at every face in sight with the other. He hauled Lester backward and hissed, "Where's your phone? You have your phone?"

Lester patted his pocket dumbly, half hauled it out, and Miller stripped the phone from him, shoving it away inside his jacket.

"Trix!" Miller called. "Exit, now."

"What's going on?" one of the mob called, the

last clear voice before a murmuring mass of noise erupted from them, stammering half-sounds, guttural ape cries. The sentries—those watching from the edges of the crowd—pointed and called as the limo neared.

It rolled near-silently, electric wheels purring to a halt directly behind Lester and Miller.

Miller backed away, shielding Lester, and like an oiled machine Morland opened the door behind him, pulling Lester inside with a yelp of surprise.

The Infected mob watched Miller holster the Gallican in his inside-waistband holster, smooth out the lines of his jacket, and slip into the limousine's driver-side door, Trix having already crawled into the back.

Closing the door on the crowd and the blistering heat should have made the interior of the air-conditioned limousine into a blissful sanctuary. What Miller hadn't counted on was Lester's smell. He was almost as bad as Nick.

And now, Lester was panicking.

"Who are you?" he screamed in du Trieux's face, before Morland yanked him back down to the seat. "*What* are you?"

Miller had heard about this. The Infected shared so many more cues of body language and scent that, to them, an uninfected human ceased to be entirely human. The uninfected belonged in the 'uncanny valley': mechanical dolls, unnatural homonculi. A mockery of what was familiar, and instinctively repulsive.

Morland smothered Lester against the back seat with du Trieux's help, while Miller leaned back and handed Trix her bagged syringe and phial.

"I don't like this! Who are you? Why aren't I going home? I want to go home!"

"We're Schaeffer-Yeager's bodyguards. We're *taking* you home!" du Trieux snapped.

"I don't work for Schaeffer-Yeager, I work for BioGen—"

"Schaeffer-Yeager International *owns* Biogen. We're your friends, everything's alright!"

Miller settled himself into the driver's seat, glanced once at the rear-view mirror, disengaged the automatic and steered the limousine around one of the mob members in the street. He tapped his earpiece. "Doyle. You good to get out on your own?"

"Should do. Although you should know: there are more running your way."

"More?"

"I think the Infected called in for help."

In the back seat, Lester stopped fighting for a moment, panting. "W-what's that for?" he asked, pale and tense under Morland's grip, staring at the syringe with dinner-plate eyes.

"We're giving you Firbenzol," du Trieux snapped.

Lester's eyes widened. He knew the anti-parasitic drug by name, and he didn't seem to want it, struggling to lash out at her from the midst of Morland's bear-hug.

Du Trieux quickly, and very professionally, drew

a measure of the drug from the phial, gazing at the syringe contemplatively as she held it up and squeezed the air bubbles back into the phial. She gestured, and Morland pinned Lester tighter, prompting a strangled yelp from the man. Du Trieux jabbed the needle into the meat of his shoulder. Lester struggled, twisted— God knew how she did it, but du Trieux got the full dose into him and pulled the needle free without him snapping it off in his flesh.

One of the mob, loping alongside the limousine, yelled as if they'd seen the syringe and didn't like it any more than Lester did.

He clawed at his shoulder as if du Trieux had injected him with acid, his eyes growing ever more droopy.

Morland kept Lester down, pinning his arms to his chest. "Miller!"

"I see them," Miller replied, swinging the steering wheel round, guiding the limousine up onto the sidewalk, speeding up past a clump of the crowd emerging from a side street.

Doyle was right. More and more of the Infected were coming out of alleyways and buildings—a brewing riot.

Behind them, the mob was following in fits and starts, jogging, sprinting after them. Someone banged on the limo's back end when Miller was forced to slow down and swerve around an idiot trying to catch all two tons of the limousine with his hands.

"Dammit, Miller! They're trying the doors!" Morland shouted.

Miller angled for the last gap ahead he could see, and stomped on the pedal.

Scarlet lights ignited, the car bawled, *"Emergency Stop! Alert. Emergenc—"*

"Get the override," du Trieux screamed. "Miller, override the safeties!"

Miller already had. But even if the limo's automatic braking system was disengaged, he wasn't about to run over children. Miller wrenched the wheel to the side, teeth gritted, and slowed to avoid running headlong into a wall. The second he was clear, he started pumping on the pedal as if the electric vehicle still had gas to be metered out, staring at the filthy people climbing over the limousine's hood. A little boy clambered up the car, stamping on the limousine's armoured roof with hollow thuds, while a teenager started pounding on the windshield with a brick.

He nudged a woman out of the way with the limousine's fender, rolling the wheel side to side, but the mass of humanity was too thick. Eventually the pounding fists ceased sliding past, and they all but held the limo in place. Each time he punched the accelerator, the car nudged forward, and then the crowd physically pushed it back.

Their screams were strangely hollow, distant through the armour.

"They can't get in, can they?" Morland asked, nervous.

"I don't think so."

Du Trieux finished trussing up Lester's limp arms behind him with a set of zip-tie cuffs, started on his legs.

The crowd parted briefly, and Miller tried to push the mob aside, only for the windshield to be covered in beating hands, hammering fists of all colours... an elderly gentleman helped hoist up a stop sign torn physically out of the ground, two younger people taking the post and stabbing the jagged end into the windshield like workers with shovels.

The windshield glass's upper laminate layer spiderwebbed, and began to chip away.

Miller floored the manual-drive pedal again, again, but the vehicle wouldn't move, grimacing Infected pushing at the back when he tried reversing it. The mob literally pulled the limousine deeper inside itself, the wheels scraping sideways with a hellish rubber-on-concrete growl.

They couldn't escape.

The steady *schunk* of the stop sign into the windshield was joined by the shriek of metal as someone took a pry-bar to one of the limo's door seams, and over it all, Lester mewling for help in a drugged haze.

Miller flipped open his phone's casing, told it to dial work, and pulled his Gallican back out, setting the handgun on his lap.

"Miller?"

"Cobalt-1, this is Cobalt-2." Miller flattened the drive pedal again, and the crowd lunged, pushing the car sideways until the wheels thudded against the curb. "An Infected riot's brewing. The limo can't move and they're trying to get in."

"*Fuck.*" Brandon Lewis, head of Cobalt-1, had

been resolving to quit swearing for years. Today clearly wasn't the day, though. *"Motherfucking son of a bitch, Miller. This is not what I need to hear. How many are there?"*

It was as easy as putting on the camera and holding the phone against the side-window. Miller got it up just in time for someone to smash a divot out of the armoured glass. Faintly, Miller heard a rising chant of "Kill the poisoners!"

"Lots." Miller cleared his throat, bringing the phone back to his ear. "We need help. Immediate help. Tear gas, riot squad, whatever's left of the NYPD, I don't care, Lewis. Get us out of here."

"I don't think there's anything of the NYPD left." Lewis hesitated. *"I'll get Bob Harris on the horn. We'll bring in Bayonet if we need to."*

"Roger that," Miller murmured, wiping his face.

Miller silently watched one of the mob bring up a shotgun and unload it at him, point blank. The buckshot rebounded back at the shooter off the glass, where the pellets hadn't embedded in the chipped upper laminate, causing screams and howls and blood to cover the windshield.

Miller's phone rang. Robert Harris, head of site, personnel, and executive security for Schaeffer-Yeager International, was on the other end of the line. *"You have Allen?"*

"Yeah. He's been infected like we thought." Miller risked a glance back, wincing at the distant crunch of glass behind him. They were almost halfway through the rear window's two-inch laminate.

"You have his research? His phone?"

Miller checked inside his jacket, pulling it free. Last year's Apple phablet, but Miller didn't think it'd be worth telling Harris that Lester's phone was from the competition. "Yeah. Secured as requested."

"Okay. Send me what you can. It's critical—"

"Can't." Miller thumbed the phone's power button again. The screen flashed a drained battery symbol. "Dead, no charge."

Harris was silent for a moment. *"Stay in the vehicle. Don't open the windows, nothing. You hear me?"*

Armoured limos didn't *have* windows that opened; they were built in place. But Harris had never done any field work. Miller didn't bother explaining. "I hear you."

"Sit tight," Harris said, and cut the connection.

A glance back over the interior of the limousine, the light entering the vehicle strobing as hammering hands rose and fell, and Miller realized it was the last place he ever wanted to be.

"Doyle, you seeing this?" Miller asked, cupping his ear.

"Afraid not," Doyle replied. *"Thought it best to get the hell out while I could. I'm in my car and en route back home."*

"Mob's got us."

The mob's pounding seemed to be growing steadier.

"I'll be back in a tick."

"No, don't turn around. Then we'll have to haul you out of this, too."

"Bloody hell! Look at that!"

"What?" Miller glanced back at Morland and du Trieux, who were staring bloodlessly out at one of the Infected standing on the trunk. He'd set down his crowbar, and was gazing up into the sky. Miller realised all of the Infected had stopped to look, but somehow the steady thumping was only growing louder.

It wasn't the mob's pounding.

Help arrived. It screamed with turbofan engines and battered the ear with the bassy chop of rotor blades. An attack helicopter. Ugly, armoured, fresh off the assembly line in unpainted grey primer and serial numbers, gunpods and missiles glistening and fresh as it banked across the rooftops above. It slowed, then fired.

Tracer rounds cut into the ground, streaking flares in alternating red and orange, 20mm anti-armour explosive shells chewing the street surface to splinters, punching straight through the mass of humanity and tearing into the rock beneath without regard for their lives. Rippling blasts raced back and forth across the mob like a kid pissing on the snow, beating them down and tearing limbs from bodies, crippling blasts leaving nothing but blood and bone where there had been *people* an instant before.

The screaming of humanity was overpowering. Blood and tissue fogged the nearside window, and fragments of concrete and metal rang off the windows, leaving dark pits in the scratched, spiderwebbed laminate.

The helicopter hovered in place, as if surveying what it had done. The aftermath's silence exposed screaming, crying terror. The street was a shifting mass of running bodies, dying bodies. Bodies, everywhere.

The second attack was shorter than the first, a roaring as God and Zeus ganged up on mortal men with exploding metal and thunder, tearing them down where they stood, precisely cutting them apart and tearing them away from the limousine as if they were nothing.

The echoes washed through the streets almost as swiftly as the blood filled the gutters. The limousine was painted with ragged splashes of gore and a sandblasting of metal splinters, broken limbs and gobbets of flesh, but what the crowd of Infected humanity had been unable to endure, the vehicle's armour had shrugged off without complaint.

Those who weren't dead, fled. Running ribbons of tracer fire punched through their backs, the only living things in sight left ruined and twitching, crawling messes of bloody limbs.

Near silently, Miller managed to get the limo rolling forward, rocking as its wheels rolled over lumpen mash and torn asphalt, levelling out as it fled, trailing bloody tracks behind it.

When they were clear, Miller opened the door a crack, leaned out, and threw up.

2

"*AND WHERE ARE the government in this? Where are the* police?"

The image on the screen bobbed unevenly, bad camera-work or shaking hands. Hsiung, unusually silent, picked up the remote control. No matter which channel she tried, it either displayed the same live scene from another angle, a flat blue screen, or a broken connection icon. The last surviving television station in New York, and it showed nothing but James Swift's perspiring face. His nose, his cheek, his eye, painful close-ups as his rage simmered over.

"*No one knows how many* citizens *of this city are dead, no one knows because it is impossible to* count," Swift growled, throwing back his head. "*Those who seek our* eradication, *those who have murdered us, have been left untouched by the sacred justice the freedoms our glorious country was* founded upon, *oh, yes.*" He nodded, and the camera bobbed in reflexive mimicry. No doubt,

Miller thought, it was an effort of willpower for the cameramen to avoid joining in with Swift's screed.

"*Their subsidiaries, WellBeechBeck and BioGen, toil to develop* poisons *for the terrible right hand of the corporate beast, seeking to* destroy *us, seeking to* destroy *the Archaean Gift, even while their left hand, the very military industrial complex itself, slaughters us* outright." He leered at the camera, all teeth and tongue. "*All in the name of* corporate interests. *Is this right? Is this* American?!" Swift demanded, gnashing at the lens, spittle at the corners of his mouth. "*Who does Schaeffer-Yeager's* genocide *profit? No one!*"

"Turn it off," Miller said, pinching at the bridge of his nose. This was the last fucking thing he needed in Cobalt's break room.

Hsiung glanced up, brief rebellion in her eyes, just on principle. If Miller didn't want to see it, she did. She clasped the remote tighter.

Doyle groaned, hands over his face. "At least turn it down."

Begrudgingly Hsiung complied.

"Thank you." Miller looked at the coffee machine for the dozenth time, but it was still heating up.

Hsiung stared at the screen, struggling to make sense of the unnatural camera angles and close-ups of Swift's sweating skin. "When did the Infected get Swift, anyway?"

"Oh, back when they were selling the parasite in bottled water. He fell in with the celebrity crowd," Mannon said, from the other end of the couch.

"That long ago?"

"He went quiet after falling in with the communes."

That would've been two, maybe three years ago? Miller's ex-girlfriend, Samantha, had wanted him to try 'Archaean Water' with her, back then. She'd bought into the celebrity fad endorsing it as a wonder-cure for troubled relationships.

It sounded great, didn't it? Water pulled out of a subglacial Antarctic lake, ultra-pure and natural, hidden beneath the ice for tens of thousands of years before global warming brought it near the surface. The early rumours about microscopic parasites in the stuff had dissuaded Miller from trying it just to patch things back up with Samantha, thank God. Maybe she'd ended up joining a commune?

It had seemed like a political thing, at first—living cooperatively, outside of the general economy. There were slums in the Bronx that had become the human equivalent of hives, the Infected living heel-to-toe, dozens of people to a room. The Infected hadn't wanted a cure, and by the time anyone had attempted to pass laws enforcing anti-parasitic drug treatments—years late, long after Schaeffer-Yeager had started providing the drugs free of charge wherever possible—too much of the population had been 'gifted' with the Archaean Parasite to do anything to stop it.

Communes had seemed like a good idea when the famines *really* started to get bad. Jimmy 'Eat The Poor' Swift had once been another Wall Street shark, one of L. Gray Matheson's—Schaeffer-

Yeager's CEO's—peers. He'd owned half of Queens. Then he'd sold out, joined the dirty hippies who'd been protesting capitalism's rise, and spent his considerable fortune feeding the city's Infected.

Good for some, but Miller remembered watching overfilled grocery carts trundling down the streets towards the communes while everyone else starved, courtesy Swift's fortune. Then, when Schaeffer-Yeager began its humanitarian campaign distributing anti-parasitic drugs and food, the communes had sent mobs to break up soup kitchens, burning trucks with the wrong logo no matter what they were carrying. It had been ugly then, but now...

While Swift spat fire on the screen, his words autocaptioned below, baying for the company's blood, the mobs were out on the streets rioting. Was it purely a social phenomenon, or was the parasite somehow defending itself, making the Infected attack those trying to cure them?

Then again, Miller mused, if they *were* treated, cured, they'd lose their communes, wouldn't they? It made sense if they were fighting to protect what they thought of as their families, didn't it?

On the screen, Swift called on the Army and the government and the police, what was left of them all, to strike Schaeffer-Yeager down in furious justice.

He was right. Why the hell weren't Miller and the rest in chains, with a summary execution for Robert Harris on the cards for calling down the helicopter strike?

When enough had finally dripped into the coffee

pot, Miller got up and filled two mugs, then put the pot back to catch the rest.

"Shouldn't do that. The first stuff's the best, you're stealing it," du Trieux muttered from the narrow card table behind the break room couch.

Miller shrugged. "At least you're not complaining about how Americans make their coffee anymore."

She grunted something guttural and French.

Coffee was hard to come by. They were scraping out old filters and adding a meagre amount from their dwindling supply of fresh coffee, mockingly calling it 'half-and-half.'

At one point, the Archaeobiome's 'novel' South American crop pests were considered someone else's problem—fairy-armadillo type creatures, though the pink-shelled little beasts weren't armadillos at all—but coffee drinkers, *serious* coffee drinkers, knew they were trouble long before the threat of the famines loomed.

The locust armadillos, *Pseudodasypus*, were little cynodonts—early precursors to mammals—which showed every sign of being straight out of the Triassic period, other than showing up out of nowhere in Colombian plantations around two years before. They'd arrived on his parents' ranch a year later, shortly before gnawing a swathe through the Midwest's cornfields. The biggest were three inches long, and to Miller they looked a lot like lizards with an armadillo shell. They even laid eggs, leathery little packets that shrank up like prunes in the sun.

The first hatching anyone witnessed had been out in Mexico, locust armadillo young crawling up out of the ground like tiny maggots, maybe two or three millimetres long—much smaller than later hatchlings from fresh eggs, something to do with how the Archaeobiome worked. Apparently the locust armadillos, along with most of the new wildlife, had been hiding out deep underground for close to thirty thousand years. Then they'd hatched tiny, grown up, and started reproducing. *Fast.*

That was if you believed the scientists who'd carbon dated the ancient eggs that hadn't hatched, anyway. A lot of people didn't, but a lot of people thought man-made global warming was a load of horse-shit because it still got cold in the winter.

The locust armadillo swarms had eaten every stalk of wheat within a hundred miles of his parents' ranch, but his dad hadn't been the one who told Miller about them. He hadn't learned about coffee and the locust armadillos from Brandon Lewis, either—the old man accepting the second cup of coffee when Miller joined him in the meeting room, at the far end of the table from the decision makers.

Over there, talking to Gray and Harris? There was the woman he'd heard about locust armadillos from, back when they were only ruining a couple of plantations. The woman that had, over a stretch of years, fed Miller every detail imaginable from the species of civet that shat the best coffee in Indonesia straight through to the exact difference between *espresso*, *restritto*, and *lungo*.

32

Jennifer Barrett.

Barrett wasn't just the company's top coffee maven. She was Schaeffer-Yeager's head of internal IT, and a delight to work close protection for. She understood that the weakest link in any chain of security were the people in it, and the sharkish, middle-aged woman didn't complain too hard when one of her bodyguards got her the wrong drink instead of letting her traipse through unsecured coffee shops. But even though she was understanding about security, anything else that rubbed her the wrong way was at risk of getting its throat ripped out.

Right now, her teeth were bared at Robert Harris, head of security and all around nice guy. You had to be a nice guy, didn't you, to call down a helicopter gunship on an unarmed crowd?

"It was necessary to preserve the life of one of our assets," Harris growled. "We had nothing else in the area and those *freaks* would have torn open the limousine if we'd waited any longer."

"Tear gas, stun grenades, painbeams, water cannons; there is riot control gear *on the books*," Barrett screeched, stabbing her finger onto the files displayed on a tablet in front of her. "There is *such a thing as proportionality, Bob!*"

"Proportionality? By the time the chopper arrived the howling mob was three blocks wide. Tens of goddamn *thousands!*" He thrust out his stubbled chin. Generally, he looked lean. Right now, despite having more than enough to eat, he looked starved and desperate. "I don't have a riot squad that can contain that, nobody does anymore! The non-lethal option wasn't an option."

In theory, Miller took orders from Harris. In practice, despite Miller heading Cobalt-2, his direct superior was head of Cobalt-1, Brandon Lewis. Harris may have dished out the orders, but he didn't know much about Cobalt's special-case personnel security role.

Lewis picked up his coffee after several moments listening to the big-wigs wig out at the far end of the board table, and shot a look at Miller. He put the coffee down without sipping any, rolled up his pantleg, and scratched at the stumps of his legs, the scars shockingly pink compared to the black skin of his thigh and hands. Lewis had been a marine, back in the Middle Eastern wars of the '10s, and gotten his legs taken off by an IED. After he'd gotten a decent set of prosthetics and learned to work on them, he'd gone right back on duty. Now in his sixties, his current prosthetics were about the best unpowered models available, springs and tensile cables providing a more than adequate replacement for his missing knees. But when Lewis got nervous, his stumps itched.

Miller slid in beside Lewis, and gingerly tried the half-and-half bastard coffee. He winced, and immediately regretted it.

"Bad?" Lewis asked, voice barely a whisper.

"Like somebody else drank it first, then pissed it through a burnt sneaker." Miller took a second sip anyway. He'd acclimatize to it soon enough.

Lewis glared down at his mug, steeled himself, and sipped. He immediately grimaced. "Had worse." Wiping at his mouth, he set the mug down. "Not for thirty years, but I've had worse."

"Trouble in paradise?" Miller asked quietly, glancing up the table.

"The President's trying to backpedal on his support for us. Bob Harris made the call on the helicopter, his balls are on the chopping block."

When the famine started running out of control, the company had relied heavily on having the President's ear. Sure, the Infected rioting and destroying soup kitchens made things tough, but without the government authorizing the mass movement of cargo and food across state lines, Schaeffer-Yeager would never have been able to help as much as it did. Now, of course, there wasn't much left to stop anyone from doing as they liked, but having a President bought and paid for by the company had been helpful.

The man who'd *actually* bought President Fredericks, not that Miller would ever say that to Gray's face, was looking calm and collected. But L. Gray Matheson always did.

There were two kinds of billionaires Miller had met in his life: the psychotics built on a foundation of poisonous ego, and the steely ones with ice in their veins. Gray was the steely kind, in public. With his kids—Miller usually provided live-in security for the family—he could warm up some.

Maybe, before the famines, there could have been

enough clout to quietly bury something like this. There had been armies of lobbyists on both sides of the aisle, and while Gray didn't directly own any of the media conglomerates, there was enough financial incestuousness to squash things. Now? Now there wasn't enough of a government left to authorize drilling in a national park.

There wasn't any law and order left in the continental United States. Even the National Guard had collapsed, since the famines had forced half of them to desert in search of food. And when a government couldn't even feed its armed forces, it sure as hell couldn't squelch a crime against humanity.

That's what the helicopter attack was, even if some wouldn't view the Infected as human.

"We. Had. To. Rescue. Our. *People!*" Harris roared from the table's opposite end, getting up and slamming his fists down. "The response was *legitimate!*"

Barrett was on her feet too, knuckles on the table, furious. "Stop trying to justify this, Bob. You didn't give a *shit* about 'our people,' you wanted BioGen's field research."

Harris blanched. "That's a baseless allegation."

"Whose department did you hand Lester Allen's phone to, Bob?" She bared teeth. "Of course I looked at what my guys pulled out of it. Why is genetic field analysis of air-trapped fungal spores worth killing that many people for?"

"This isn't going to stick in court. You can't pin this on me."

"This isn't *going* to court," Gray said, speaking up at last. "We're all friends here." Robust, in his mid-fifties, Gray spoke with a honey-warm burr. But, as Miller had seen many times before, Gray's voice could go from comforting purr to threatening growl in a flash. "There aren't any courts left to throw you in front of, Bob." There was that growl.

Harris sat down, slowly.

"So," Gray went on, "let's take it as given that your death sentence is *temporarily* suspended, and make the presumption that we're all working toward the same goals, whether we are *butchers*, bakers, or innocent, bystanding candlestick makers. Tell us, Bob. Why?"

Harris withered under Gray's gaze, realizing his boss didn't have his back to be friendly, but to be first one in with the knife. "Lester Allen's team weren't just tracking the spread of crop-killing Archaeobiome funguses," he admitted, at last.

"What were they doing, Bob?"

"Testing an aerosolized anti-parasitic drug called NAPA-33." Harris clawed his fingers over his face. "They loaded it into their air traps across the city, and dispersed it from there. It's designed to interfere with genetic replication in the parasite—we don't know if the drug works or not. Mixed in with the fungal genetic samples are samples his team pulled from the commune we were testing it on. It needs to get to what's left of BioGen."

"For God's sake," Barrett hissed. "You're talking about bioweapons."

"*Medicine!*" Harris roared. "This is *medicine!* The Infected are the biggest threat to humanity out there; if we don't stop them, *they're* the ones that will survive the famines, not *us!*"

"You can't test a fucking *genetic drug* on an unwilling population—"

Miller felt a chill in his gut. The Infected mob had been right. Dead right.

Gray lifted his hand, halting Barrett in her tracks. "Hold on there, Jen. The damage has already been done."

"Yes, Mr. Matheson." Compliantly, she sat down, but continued to glare at Harris.

"Bob's right, in a way. You *could* say this is a war." Gray glared at him. "Thank God we're not, though, Bob, because we *shoot* war criminals. However, these are hard times. We need soldiers, and every soldier needs something of the sociopath in him."

All three glanced down the table at Miller and Lewis. The weight of their gaze was uncomfortable.

"In hard times," Gray announced, as if making a presentation, "we need hard people to keep us safe, and there's two of ours. Now, Bob's fucked us over, gentlemen. What's left of the government can't prosecute us, or help us. The Infected are listening to old Jimmy Swift, with his axe to grind, and are sharpening axes of their own. Now what do we need to do to keep safe?"

Miller waited for Lewis to answer, but all he got in the silence was an elbow in his ribs. He jolted straight. "Uh, well. I would imagine that Mr. Harris would be better qualified, as head of security—"

"Having an imagination's a wonderful thing, Alex, but I don't want you to spin me a story." Gray folded his hands one over the other. "Bob's going to be busy cleaning up his mess. Ain't that right, Bob?"

"I'll get this squared away with BioGen," Harris murmured.

"So I ain't interested in what Bob's got to say right now. What's it gonna be, Alex?"

Miller glanced at Lewis for help, but the old warhorse just smiled at him. "Go on, son."

"Well. The communes have already demonstrated they're willing to attack us when we do nothing more offensive than distribute food and drugs. Currently a lot of our personnel are strung out across the city in their homes and the shelters we set up in offices. Running food and supplies to them is a mess already, let alone providing security to them with half the city after us.

"It'd be helpful if we could gather employees and their families into a central, defensible location…"

3

THE PROBLEM WITH suggestions is, the guy who makes them? That's the guy they pick to carry them out. At least, a week on, life was getting back to normal. Sort of. Miller was playing Armani again, anyway.

For nine months out of the year, most of Miller's time was spent watching over Gray's two children, James and Helen, along with Gray himself. Most of the time it was a light duty, letting him manage his team's training. He only handed off the family's round-the-clock protection to another security team when Cobalt had a special security situation to handle—like covering Barrett when intelligence had the Russian mob after her—or during the summer, when Gray sent the kids to live with their mother for their vacation. This summer, their vacation had been cut short, and they'd brought their mother home with them.

"James, Helen. Mrs. Williams." Miller pulled on his Armani smile, backing away from the passengers flowing off the plane. Strictly speaking he shouldn't have been in JFK Airport's disembarkation area, but with the TSA a thing of the past, rules were for bending. He gestured to Morland, and the baggage cart. "So glad the weather didn't affect your flight. If you'd like to give Morland your—"

"*Alex!*" Helen, recently fourteen, eyes grey as her father's, launched herself at Miller in a colossal bear hug.

"It's nice to see you too, Helen." Miller lost the Armani, but kept his smile.

She squeezed him tight, composed herself, stepped back, and pulled her candy-pink wheeled suitcase closer. "I missed you," she said, with far less enthusiasm, cultivating the standoffishness that was the mark of a true teenager.

Miller opened his arms to James, and the boy—nearly a man, *sixteen* now, Jesus—rolled his eyes before stepping into the hug. "Hey, Alex," he said, begrudgingly.

In theory, a close protection agent slipped into the role of the Armani to blend in with a high profile client's life, providing as little disruption and comment as possible. A heavily armed fashion accessory, in essence. Miller was widely regarded to be very, very good at it—his natural inclination for designer clothes and spa treatments helped him appear to be nothing more than a friend or member of the family's entourage—but sometimes, there was more to the job than being the Armani. Especially with the kids. Their dad was in his fifties, and Miller was a little young for a surrogate dad. Not quite thirty was perfect for a fun uncle, though. A fun uncle that carried guns and never ate with the rest of the family at the dinner table.

Mrs. Williams, formerly Matheson, daintily shook his hand when he offered it. "Been a long time, Alex."

"Yes. I was told Mr. Williams would be with you..." Her second husband, closer to her age—fortyish.

Mrs. Williams smiled tightly, almost wincing. "Harry's been missing two days." She ignored Helen's worried glance back at her, went on, almost babbling. "He didn't come home from work, the Army are looking into it, and they don't have a lot of time, but—"

Patting her shoulder, Miller nodded reassuringly. "I'm sure he's fine." Lying was easy, wasn't it? "We need to get y'all back to the Astoria Peninsula compound before the storm hits, so if you could follow me..."

Miller led them out to the Bravo—a military-style utility vehicle, somewhere between one of the old Humvees and an armoured personnel carrier, thanks to its uprated armour. StratDevCo manufactured them by the container load. This one had luxury fittings and a civilian paint-job, but after days of getting pelted with dust off the New Dustbowl— almost everything between Oklahoma to Iowa had been ruined by fungal blights—it looked like it'd been rolling in the mud. And there wouldn't be a chance to clean it off before the next load.

A dust storm was coming, a *real* dust storm.

The plane had barely come in ahead a hazy red-

and-tan wall that swallowed the western horizon and stretched up to the clouds. The storm was moving fast. Miller could feel the wind on his face as he waited to get into the Bravo, and he didn't like it. Du Trieux was shifting over to the passenger seat from the driver's, picking up an old Gilboa Viper II and laying it over her lap. She smiled at the kids, Mrs. Williams, and Morland in the back.

"Hey, what's that?" James asked, leaning forward—obligingly du Trieux lifted the weapon, a monstrous little thing, most easily described as a pair of assault rifles welded together side by side and remachined for a single stock and grip. "*Cool!*" James's eyes bugged out, but Mrs. Williams, realizing the implications, nervously settled back.

The new wildlife was getting friskier.

And bigger.

Miles later, caught in the urban sprawl, they found a terror-jaw picking through trash just off the corner of 109th Avenue and Lefferts Boulevard. It was the size of a horse. Big one. Clydesdale, maybe. Man-high at the shoulders.

Another terror-jaw picked its way between two abandoned looking houses, close-packed and double-storied. One turned its lumpen head to scan the Bravo, spurs and bone-ridges under the flesh giving it a decayed, ghoulish look. The other grinned at the car with a mouthful of dagger-like teeth that would've made a saber-toothed tiger back down in the day.

The one rumbled to the other, and the leathery creatures both trotted forward, dipping their heads to peer at the Bravo's narrow windshield contemplatively. A third joined them, bigger than the other two, stretching a little to lope over a garden fence, its miniscule nostrils flaring as it took a better look, as if it could see them all inside.

"Jesus. They don't get that big," James murmured authoritatively from the back. "They just don't."

Miller slowly and carefully backed the Bravo up, eyeing the houses to either side of the street. Not many cars around. He hoped the neighbourhood had all evacuated for somewhere else, with things that big prowling around. He headed down one sidestreet, and another, then he had to dog-leg the route around a known commune occupying the edge of Forest Park, and by the time they got anywhere near a straight route to the new compound, the dust storm hit.

It was like the hand of God passed over them, from the west to the east, left to right. The dust had seemed red, but the reddish haze of light lasted only a few moments before the full fury of the storm rolled over them, eating the sun with a howl of wind. Visibility dropped to thirty feet, then five, the headlights doing nothing more than creating murky blobs of tan and grey light in the murk. Thankfully the Bravo was fitted with smoke-piercing laser scanners. Even if Miller couldn't see, the car could, and he set it back to automatic drive.

"Everything's going to be fine," he said, leaning around the driver's seat. "We'll just be a little late getting you to the Astoria compound."

Helen was holding her nose. "What's that smell?"

"I'm sure it's just the dust, baby," Mrs. Williams said. "Could you turn on the air conditioning or something, Alex?"

The Bravo had something better than air conditioning—NBC grade HEPA/active carbon air filters. Miller toggled them on, just before he started to catch the scent too—something rotten, decaying. Mushrooms and, very faintly, the burning sting of ammonia. The filters cleared it quickly, thank God.

They didn't have the roads to themselves, even if the city seemed deserted in the murk. Just two intersections after their route straightened out, they encountered a knot of stalled traffic. Most of the cars were abandoned. A long queue led to the intersection—a chain of automatically driven vehicles had halted behind one empty car—but ahead of them were vehicles physically blocking both sides of the road. A few of the stopped cars' interiors were lit, passengers nervously looking ahead...

Miller craned his head and squinted through the fog, but couldn't see anything other than a blur of light.

"Trix?"

"*Oui?*" Du Trieux rested her thumb against the Gilboa's safety.

"Be ready to bail out after me." Miller smiled back at the kids. "This'll take just a moment." With that, he got out of the Bravo, slamming the door shut before too much of the roiling dust got in.

The smell hit him like a hammer. Rotting asparagus trapped at the bottom of a garbage bag with something acid and vile done to it, every fleck of dust in his mouth making him want to retch. His eyes watered uncontrollably, and each new breath felt like a bad idea. But Miller had survived the tear gas hut during basic training. During his four-year stretch, waiting for a war that never came, he and his squadmates had bet money on who'd make it longest in the hut without a mask on. It was the kind of dumb thing young men do, but Miller was glad for it now, struggling around to the Bravo's trunk and hammering on it until Morland or du Trieux popped it open from the control console.

Almost blind, Miller opened one of the panic-packs lined up next to the emergency medical kit, pulled out the gas-mask and mashed it against his face with one hand, taking clean breaths through the filters and coughing out whatever the shit in his lungs was while triggering the exhalation valves. After a few moments of spluttering and wheezing he was breathing clean again, and he took the time to finish securing the mask before grabbing one of the shotguns. The wind tugging unpredictably at his limbs, he made his way forward to take a better look at what had stopped them.

Shattered glass crunched under Miller's dress shoes. A multiple car pile-up in the middle of the next intersection. Six, maybe seven or eight cars; they were hard to count, they were too tangled. They must have been driven on manual, blind in the storm. First just two cars, then the third must have hit the mess, then the fourth behind it, and so on.

Now that he was close enough he could see what the other trapped drivers had been staring at. It wasn't the dead passengers, or the slinky, armour-faced rat-things clambering into the wrecks through shattered windows. It was the family that had gotten out of their car after its automatic driver stopped it.

The father, laying halfway across the opposite lane, was the only one Miller could bear looking at. He was still alive, barely. Twitching. Nose streaming with snot, vomit everywhere, convulsing like he'd been hit with some kind of nerve agent. What Miller first took for a light dusting of blood covering the dad's chin, where the snot was drying out, turned out to look more like scarlet threads of silk or lint. The beginnings of the cobweb-like shroud fungus that had been devastating the Midwest, triggering the New Dust Bowl by killing everything—*everything*—in the topsoil.

When its spores spread, even prairie dogs died en masse, effectively gassed in their burrows so their corpses could serve as fertilizer to feed the fungal growth.

Miller tore his eyes away from the dying family. Their youngest was already gone, and Miller had no idea what to do. Dialling 911 was a thing of the past.

Red specks of dust swirled around in front of the goggles of his gas mask, and Miller found himself slowly looking up to the black sky of the dust storm above. How many tons of dust were hanging in the wind over his head right now? How much of it was laced with shroud fungus?

No wonder the air was so foul.

One of the drivers nearby, safe in their car, banged on their windshield, yelling something Miller couldn't hear over the roar of the wind. Timidly, Miller stepped closer, holding the shotgun low, against his leg.

"What?" he yelled, not that they'd hear it through his mask.

She slapped the windshield again, pointed past the family's stopped car, her face frantic.

Miller turned around, he hadn't wanted to look. But someone was hunched over a child's body. A woman stood nearby, staring at Miller. Five people, in all. None of them were wearing gas masks. Some of them were coughing, spluttering, but none of them seemed to care about toxic fungal blooms. They were filthy, unwashed, slick with sweat. Swaying in unison.

The Infected.

"Why are you out of your car?" one called, her voice overrun by another asking, "Is it the Rapture?"

Just five of them weren't enough to start the chorus of moans, words colliding into a tangle of noise. But five of them were enough. One of them hefted a baseball bat to her shoulder.

"Is it the Rapture?" the other demanded again, her eyes wide. "The ungifted are dying. God hates them now. Is it the Rapture?"

"Trix?" Miller leaned his head to the side, lifting a hand to cover his earpiece and hold the transmit key.

"*Miller?*"

"Y'all are going to want to get out of the Bravo," he said, slowly, "without letting too much of this shit in, and grab a mask from the trunk. Then head up here with the Gilboa."

"Why are you wearing a mask?" one of the men demanded, stepping closer, then halting until the others caught up, stepping forward again... shambling forward, stop, go, stop, go.

"He's not gifted." "Ungifted?" "Why hasn't the Rapture taken him?"

Miller backed away a step, another, swinging the shotgun up to his shoulder as the Infected with the baseball bat came around to the front. The rapid click-slam of one of the Bravo's doors was followed by the sound of retching, which drew the small mob's attention for an instant. But only an instant.

Their eyes were raw, bloodshot. Probably from the dust more than the parasite infecting them.

Wheezing through her mask, du Trieux, ever dependable, loped out of the dust and blaze of the Bravo's headlights, rifle up. More than anything else, the two side-by-side barrels of the Gilboa Viper II looked *nasty*. A lot nastier than just some little shotgun.

The one with the baseball bat let it swing down to his feet, the group starting to shuffle backward. "You're supposed to be dead!" one of them howled. Another, all but spitting up tears, said, "You're supposed to be extinct. Like animals. We're the only ones meant to survive."

Before they disappeared into the dust entirely,

breaking into a run like a pack of defeated wolves, Miller's steel slipped entirely. His hands shook, the shotgun's barrel wobbling, and the sweat plastering his skin turned cold despite the heat.

"Miller?"

"Dial Northwind," he said into his earpiece, touching the 'phone' button. He marched towards the accident at the intersection, tapping back onto the Cobalt team circuit. "Trix, guard those bodies." He jerked his head in the direction of the family. A few were still twitching, but Miller doubted anything could be done.

"*How the fuck are the Infected breathing this shit?*" du Trieux asked, her voice lost to the dust and wind, audible only in his earpiece. "*A mouthful of it nearly made me throw up.*"

"I have no idea." The phone continued to ring in Miller's earpiece, then went to hold music. He got to the mangled wrecks, and had to stop to fiddle for a moment with the shotgun's flashlight. He eventually got it switched on and swung it to illuminate the interior of one of the wrecks, to see four rat-things sitting in the driver's lap gnawing their way into his guts. They looked up in shock, like dumb toads, blinded by the light and sitting stock still as blood dribbled off their leathery faces.

They weren't having any trouble breathing either. Apparently the Archaeobiome wildlife, and the Archaean Parasite, both got along with the lethal fungal blooms just fine.

Miller shifted his point of aim fractionally, and

blasted all four of them into the passenger seat with a single shot. A second shot ended their squealing. He did the same in the other wrecked cars, clearing them of the bastard little scavengers, and finished just as Northwind picked up his phone call.

UNTIL RECENTLY, CYCLOPS-NORTHWIND had nothing to do with civilian operations, and nothing to do with Miller. But, piece by piece, Schaeffer-Yeager was absorbing useful parts of its subsidiaries. Originally, Cyclops was part of StratDevCo's support and logistic services. Now Northwind, its communications satellite management department, had been sealed into the filtered, steel-shuttered concrete blockhouse of their private mission control centre somewhere in Arizona with an expanded set of responsibilities.

Tracing the spider's web of what the corporation owned and who it employed was a full time job in itself. Miller could, if he needed, ask Northwind to handle that for him, but not today. Miller knew *who* he needed, just not how to get in touch with them.

Forty minutes later, faster than some pizza deliveries he'd had, a pair of fire truck-sized emergency response vehicles shouldered through the traffic jam, pausing every so often to push abandoned vehicles off the road and onto the sidewalks. Boltman Oil and Chemical's in-house fast emergency intervention and response team—the Blue Bolts. They were trained to deal with industrial accidents, oil well fires, chemical spills. This was biological, but Miller's gamble that they were equipped to deal with that, too, paid off.

A team of four in firefighters' exoskeletal harnesses finished clearing the road, and a new convoy set off, trapped civilian vehicles following them through the streets to the Astoria Peninsula. Their refugee convoy was met by the light of arc-welders working through the dust—more Boltman engineers building a wall across the peninsula, straight down the middle of 12th Street to sever all access from the land.

The forty-foot-high gate, still under construction, was an impressive sight. Concrete reinforced pillars on either side linked into the compound wall, this section built from stacked interlocking concrete slabs pinned together with rebar. Rolling through, James's eyes bugged out. He pressed himself against the glass, staring at the flash of welders in the dust storm's dark. "*Cool!*"

Even if what really mattered to Miller was getting into shelter and safety, for a moment, he let part of himself be sixteen again, and leaned against the windows with James to stare as engineers rolled the half-constructed gate shut behind them, an imposing edifice out of a monster movie.

"Cool," Miller agreed. "Very cool." It was something the fun uncle, the Armani, would have said to his young wards.

Miller didn't think he'd get the chance to be the Armani, or the fun uncle, ever again.

4

FOR SIX HOURS the dust storm continued to reverse day into night. Nothing but roiling blackness outside, and the stink of fungal growth indoors. With the windows sealed it wasn't too bad—foul smelling but survivable. Some of the refugees came down with a cough, and the medics treating it almost caused a riot talking about an airborne infection. The doctors had to explain they meant a *lung* infection, fungal spores trying to colonize the lungs, not a *parasitic* infection.

The wind died down and the dust fell out of the air, barely in time for the sunset's light to reveal the East River's waters stained black and scarlet. It was still dangerous in places, especially where dust had piled up into drifts—walking through could kick up fresh fungal spores—but the storm hadn't been as apocalyptic as Miller had feared. Almost everyone seemed to be wheezing or coughing up dirty mucus through the night, but it appeared that almost everyone who'd been able to stay indoors had survived.

Outdoors, there were bodies in the streets. It wasn't as bad as the famine's first peak, just a few scattered bodies half-buried in the dust. Of course there was another explanation for the scarcity of corpses, one Miller did his best to ignore: the terror-jaws and the rat-things might have been scavenging during the storm.

Miller gently lifted his cup of tea, his reward for surviving the night through to the morning after, and sipped slowly.

"Why are you still in a suit, Alex?" Gray asked, lounging across the table from him.

The riverside plaza, white-tiled and beautiful, was all but abandoned. This side of the peninsula, Astoria Cove, stood in stark contrast to the housing projects on the south end. Both were packed with towering buildings, but on the Cove's end of the peninsula an apartment sold for tens of millions of dollars. The projects just a couple of blocks away were where the city sent the poor and elderly who couldn't afford to live anywhere else.

The barrier walls had swallowed both into one settlement, less than a fifth of a square mile, jutting out into the East River. The work hadn't stopped for the dust storm, and it hadn't stopped overnight. Stretches of wire fencing protected rolling concrete-printer trucks adding layer upon layer to growing segments of the wall, while Boltman Oil and Chemical engineers barricaded buildings and linked them into the wall's structure with sheet metal cladding.

The Cove was quiet but for the muted roar of power tools and engineers yelling instructions to each other, still wearing their gas masks loose around their necks in case the wind picked up. Someone had cleared the plaza, its white tiles polished, almost gleaming. It felt peaceful. Gray's kids were fiddling with their phones at another table, trying to connect to what was left of the internet.

It felt very different from the refugee quarantine sector, where Miller had been assisting with spot checks. Refugee numbers were picking up after the storm. The helicopter massacre had terrified people, Infected or not. Hardly anyone had wanted anything to do with the corporation after that. Now, desperation and fear—the dust, famine, the new animals—had forced them into the disorderly queues funnelling through the quarantine sector's chain-link fencing, waiting their turn to have their eyes examined with ophthalmoscopes for the parasite's cysts in scenes that made Miller think of a dystopian prison.

He'd looked out of place, in his Louis Vuitton suit. Why *was* he still wearing it?

Miller took another sip of tea. "There's a laundry on Fourth Street. Next to the hairdressers?" He set the cup down. "I managed to bribe them to do my suits for me, but it's not as though there's much to spend money on anymore, so..."

Gray laughed. "Now, you know that's not what I meant."

"The hairdressers are talking about opening up

again, apparently." Miller didn't bother looking up. "Lot of people around who need haircuts."

Gray kept laughing, shaking his head. "God*damn*, Alex. You going to get those bleached highlights again or something?"

"I'm nothing if not a slave to fashion. Besides, if I'm going to fit in with you, I need to look the part."

"There aren't going to be any more functions where my bodyguard'll need to pass for a Hollywood star nobody's heard of, Alex."

"Yet." He took another sip. "That nobody's heard of *yet*."

It was almost word for word something Billy said, once, when Miller had complained that the makeover had made him look like a knock-off movie star nobody ever heard of.

Not yet, Billy had said. Just not *yet*.

Miller wondered where Billy was, in all this. He knew Samantha had taken the water. Probably joined a commune.

His boss, at least, had his kids to gaze lovingly at, while taking another sip of tea.

"I want more oversight on what Bob's doing," Gray said.

"I'm guessing Mr. Harris doesn't have any more helicopters under his control."

Gray snorted. "More than I'm happy with him having. We pulled everything that we could off the production lines."

"The Army is going to shit a brick."

"So is every military we've got contracts with.

We're taking it all for ourselves, Alex." Calmly, Gray picked up one of the muffins from its bone china plate. Turned it over, and selected another. "Schaeffer-Yeager Aerospace, StratDevCo, everything. Unofficially, we're starting our own army."

Miller struggled to swallow that down. "This is getting out of hand," he said, eventually.

"God only knows how many thousands of people died in the dust yesterday, and you only think it's getting out of hand *now*, Alex?"

Stubbornly, Miller clung to the fact that there was such a thing as a dry cleaner again. "It's getting better," he murmured.

"Food's running out. Most of the refugees who are willing to join us are on the edge of starving to death." Gray nibbled cautiously on his muffin. "There are rumours of cannibalism. They have to be *desperate* to come to us, after we mowed down the Infected like that, but they are. You've seen them."

"The way *Harris* mowed them down," Miller snapped. "I had nothing to do with that."

"But you have killed, haven't you?" Gray dropped his voice, eyes cold. "You were a soldier."

"I never deployed," Miller said, quietly. "There weren't any wars while I was enlisted. I've used a Taser, but never been in a situation I *needed* to kill anyone."

"You could if you had to, couldn't you?" Gray leaned forward intently. "This isn't a theoretical question anymore, Alex. With everything out there."

"I could," Miller said, surer than he thought

he'd be, but not as confident about it as when he'd been swimming in the army's propaganda. "If the situation called for it."

"Good. Because I need you to be my soldier, Alex. *My* soldier. Not Bob's, not America's. *Mine*." Gray settled back down. "I won't let famine, the Infected, or *anything* take their future away from them," he said, nodding at his kids.

Miller looked over at them, but remained silent.

Helen was playing something on her phone, while her older brother continued to struggle with the spotty connection.

"Money might not buy much anymore, Alex, but I own more than just *money*. If there's going to be a better future for them—hell, *any* kind of future—I'm putting everything I have into defending it. You with me?"

Miller didn't even think before nodding. "Of course I am. You're like family."

Gray paused, just for a second. "Heard from your parents?"

Miller hesitated on answering. But Gray had the right to ask, after bankrolling his aunt's cancer treatments. "Before their internet cut out, they were doing okay. Well-stocked on all the essentials, and the storm cellar's pretty substantial. Steel door and all." Miller pushed the tea away, and rubbed at an eye. "I'm sure they're holding out fine."

"Me too. We'll see about sending someone out to check on them, when things settle a little around here."

Miller nodded his thanks.

"For now, I need you to take charge of one of Bob's projects, but you'll need to lose the suit, Alex. Switch over to something a little more practical and outdoorsy."

"What's the project?"

"Same as what you've been doing, really, picking them up from the airport." Gray nodded towards his kids. "Just a little more urgent. After that storm, we're worried about our own. Bob Harris has put together a list of critical personnel we want brought to the compound who are stuck in the city. Some are trapped in place, don't have transport, or just aren't answering their phones. You're going to go out and get them."

"Just bringing people in? I can wear my suit for that, Gray."

"Alex. Stop kidding yourself. It's going to hit a hundred and ten degrees at noon, and the streets are full of Infected, and those things with all the teeth." Calmly, Gray sipped his tea. "Ditch the designer suit. Dress like a soldier."

5

A TACTICAL VEST and urban camos weren't Miller's first choice for comfort—his clearest memory of pulling on BDUs and load-bearing equipment for the first time involved a lot of chafing—but despite the weight and heat, it was like stepping into an old set of well-loved shoes. Maybe his first few weeks in boot camp wearing this kind of thing had been uncomfortable, but he must have settled into it over the rest of his enlistment.

Sweat continued to pour down his face, and his hand rose in an old reflex before he knew what he was doing. Miller stopped, spooked, then simply let it happen, like scratching an itch. He tugged up the drinking tube on his water pouch, just like he had thousands of times before in his former life as a soldier. The water was tepid, but as it hit his mouth he discovered how thirsty he was, waiting in the shade of a dying tree for the next target of Robert Harris's Operation Honshū Wolf to answer their door.

So far everything had gone textbook, like the airport pickup. Miller had split his team in two, and across the morning they'd recovered around sixty civilians—all employees and their families—and whisked them past the queues of starving refugees seeking entry into the Astoria compound.

Now it was getting toward noon, and the shade under the fungally-blighted tree was shrinking away as the heat rose. Pinkish globs of fuzz covered the tree's leaves, dragging them down. A midsummer's autumn in the affluent part of the Bronx.

Miller pushed the doorbell for a fifth time and stepped back, glancing at the neighbouring houses. The mailbox in the brownstone to the left was choked, discoloured envelopes sticking out every which way.

It had been... three months, maybe, since the postal service shut down? Five? It was difficult to keep track of precisely when any given piece of civil life had dried out and crumbled away.

It was all deserted. Miller swore under his breath.

Du Trieux held the Gilboa low against her side. "What now? We go after the next target?"

"No. We find out what happened. I'll go get the pry-bar for the door."

But before Miller reached the Bravo, du Trieux tried the door handle and she called out, "Miller? It's unlocked."

Impossible. Maybe the rural neighbours at his parents' ranch would do it, but *nobody* left their doors unlocked in the city, no matter how affluent the neighbourhood.

Miller skipped the pry-bar, and unslung his M27 instead. The weapon was only slightly unfamiliar—a ruggedized, upgraded assault rifle that the Marines used to use with drum magazines as a lighter alternative to machine guns. Miller had grabbed it out of the armoury as the first thing he saw that he trusted to actually kill a terror-jaw, though he suspected he'd have to go through most of his ammunition if he wanted to be sure.

He edged up beside du Trieux, and shared a nod with her. She was familiar with entry procedures, and although it had been a long time since he'd practised this with anything bigger than a handgun, snugging the long M27 against his shoulder and preparing to palm the door open had a familiar feel.

"Mr. Baxter?" Miller called out. "Mrs. Baxter? We're coming inside..."

No one answered them as they cleared the house, room by room. Du Trieux took point with the shorter Gilboa—easier to swing around door frames—and Miller trailed after, the M27 short-stocked with its butt tucked over his shoulder at an angle. Not very accurate, but at this range and with a hundred and fifty rounds in the drum magazine, he didn't need to be.

Alphonse Baxter and his wife, Linda, both employees of Schaeffer-Yeager subsidiary DDLN Software, had left touches of their life throughout their home. Family pictures were everywhere. A mixed race couple, their children looked a little like they might have been du Trieux's kids to Miller's eye. The kid's toys littered their bedrooms, shockingly clean behind the closed doors after the dust-caked misery of the hall and living room. Two windows had been broken, either during the dust storm or before, and something that smelled of acid and decaying meat had been nesting in the shredded remnants of the living room sofa.

No sign of the Baxters. Their clothes were still in their dressers, luggage on top of wardrobes. The kids' things all seemed to be in place. Toothbrushes in the bathrooms. A pile of school things had been hastily dumped out in one of the children's bedrooms, though, and there were gaps in the ranks of stuffed animals arranged on a bed.

Maybe one of the kids had dumped out their school bag and left their access cards, binders and school tablet on the floor to save a few treasured toys before the family fled? But if they'd run, they'd run *quickly*. Mrs. Baxter either didn't seem to own jewellery, or she'd taken it with her. The car was missing from the garage, and a gun safe in the master bedroom was empty.

Empty, and unlocked. The gun safe *wouldn't* lock when Miller tried shutting it.

It didn't make sense. The house definitely had solar panels on the roof—useless under dust right now, sure, but they'd also have hydrogen fuel cells in the attic. And those were clearly still charged; the lights worked when Miller tried them.

But the gun safe was open. And so was the front door. The locks hadn't disengaged because of a fire, or a power outage—that was precisely why the building *had* fuel cells and solar power, one of the standard recommendations the company gave its staff. With always-on power, the security systems were always on. But the remote alarm link had failed, and the system logs were scrambled. Maybe some kind of error after internet connectivity had started cutting out?

"Looks like the Baxters were forced to evacuate their home about a week and a half ago," Miller said, fingertips pressed to his earpiece's transmit button.

"*How do you figure?*" the Northwind operator asked, on the other end of a satellite link.

"Mostly guessing. The security system's log is scrambled, but that's about how stinky the milk in the fridge is—and that's when the Infected started rioting after the massacre."

A moment's silence. "*Okay. You want the next pick-up target?*"

"Not yet. Can you tell me what the Baxters' emergency plan was?"

"*Uh. Give me a minute. Need to see if DDLN's servers are still online...*"

"If it's filed, there'll be a copy with S-Y internal security," Miller explained. "Somewhere under the employee protection plan files. You can use Cobalt's account to access it."

"*A moment while I try and pull that up...*"

Du Trieux was shuffling around the nesting site in the living room. It looked like some kind of colossal dog had shredded the couch upholstery and taken a shit in it.

"Anything?" Miller asked her.

She shook her head, poking at the mess with one booted toe. "Just... eggshells, I think."

"Eggshells?" Miller frowned, and came over for a closer look.

They weren't... shells, exactly. Not the hard fragments he'd expect from a chicken egg, at any rate; more like dry scar tissue. Thick, crusted, slightly flexible. A cluster of empty pods, flopping over each other and clustered like oversized fly eggs. The carpet underneath them was soaked, and stank.

"I think they're eggs, anyway," du Trieux said, a little hesitantly.

Near the broken windows there were tracks in the fallen dust, what Miller had taken to be rats or birds or something. But since the heatwave had killed off most of the city's birds, and the ancient creatures were eating the rats... that left *something* as the only viable answer.

Outside in the back yard what Miller might have assumed were mice or squirrels were nervously watching the house from the shrubbery. At a second look, even at a distance, even that *small*, the knobbled head and white glints of snake-like teeth were obvious. Terror-jaws, a couple of inches long.

"We should leave," Miller murmured.

"Yeah," du Trieux agreed. "Let's not be here when Mama gets home."

EMERGENCY PLANS WERE issued by Schaeffer-Yeager's internal security department to most executives and high-level staff, as well as those with access to material useful for industrial sabotage or at risk of extortion. The plans tended to be simple and short. Easy to remember, for when they came home to find the front door hanging open, or when someone broke in through a window at night. If there was a more substantial threat—terrorist attack, fire, natural disaster—a plan to keep the company's personnel safe until a security team could pick them up was helpful, sometimes lifesaving.

The plan Northwind found for the Baxters had been updated just two weeks before, and was simple as could be. Relocate immediately to a shelter in the WellBeechBeck Washington Heights office, and await retrieval by security team Sabre.

"That's bullshit," Miller said. "There *is* no Sabre."

"*Sabre is what's listed.*"

"We've got Stiletto, Switchblade, Bayonet and Dagger. The security teams are named after knives, not swords—who authored the last plan update?" Miller growled, twisting the Bravo's wheel. There was a little traffic at the bridges, cars nervously edging across in clumps. Not many drivers; half the city's mainline electricity was down, and liquid fuels and cars were even scarcer than electrics right now.

"*It's a numeric account with the internal security office. Forty-six, seventy-two.*" The voice from Northwind paused. "*Doesn't seem to have a user linked to it.*"

"Harris, maybe?" du Trieux asked. "Bob Harris's office is on the forty-sixth floor of Sexy Towers."

"*Don't* call it that in front of anybody important," Miller said, as if he'd never spent time coming up with ways to fill in the blank on the 'S-Y' logo plastered all over the Schaeffer-Yeager skyscraper.

The Northwind operator snorted back laughter. "*Is there anything else I can do for you?*"

"Not unless you can raise anyone at the Washington Heights office."

"*There's a landline, but it's disconnected.*"

"We're good, then."

"*Thanks for calling.*"

Northwind hung up on him, and Miller squinted at the GPS navigator. At least GPS still worked.

Du Trieux petted the Gilboa on her lap like it was an animal, staring out of the windows. "We should leave this to someone else and bring in the next target on the list."

"The Baxters are on the list. We go look. If we don't find them at the WBB office, we'll list them as missing and move on."

She nodded, scratching at the weapon's bulky receiver. "What do you think the Sabre thing's about?"

"Don't know," Miller said. "Maybe it's a placeholder name for drafting up emergency plans, just a typo that slipped through. 'Dear Mr. John Doe, upon triggering your personal alarm you will be met by team Sabre at the corner of Left and Right street...'"

"You don't really think that, do you?"

Miller kept his mouth shut, concentrating on the road and the GPS's audio navigation cues.

"Why the hell were the Baxters' locks all open? You don't think this is more of Harris's bullshit, do you?"

"I think my job's picking up the Baxters and taking them to safety." Miller checked the mirrors as he turned, glancing every which way and checking the Bravo's external cameras for signs of Infected or wildlife. "I'll leave the mysteries to Sherlock Holmes."

"But—"

"But nothing. We're armed, these Bravos can roll over landmines and IEDs without blinking, and if we run into trouble we can't get out of we can call in Doyle and Morland from their pick-ups. If the four of us can't handle it, I'm sure there are more of those fucking helicopters on standby somewhere." He glanced at her. "So one problem at a time. Our problem right now is figuring out where the hell the Baxters are."

Du Trieux nodded, lightly. "Don't like this, though."

"Me either," Miller replied. "I'd like it better if we had more guns and combat exoharnesses, but I'll settle for an open barber who does a decent hot towel shave."

She laughed, and stopped gripping the Gilboa quite so hard. "Is that all you miss? Hot shaves?"

"With just *that* much sandalwood oil," Miller said, gesturing. "Better than going to the spa. What do you miss?"

"Palm wine," she said, without hesitation. "My Nigerian cousins used to bring over *crates* of the stuff."

"Now, I thought good Muslims don't drink."

Du Trieux settled back, smirking. "But if I didn't drink I wouldn't be a very good Frenchwoman. *Oui*?"

Miller's turn to laugh. The lists of things they missed from before the famines and the heatwaves, from before all this *bullshit* started, were just about inexhaustible. In the right mood, going over it all brought back good memories, rather than the gloomy certainty that none of it would ever come by again. They reached cream cheese (du Trieux's) and gay stand-up comics (Miller's) when the sign for the 'WellBeechBeck Washington Heights' turn-off came into view ahead of them.

The medical company was one of Schaeffer-Yeager's largest subsidiaries, along with S-Y Aerospace. Ordinarily its assets would never be involved with protecting high-level personnel from an entity as minor as DDLN, but it was routine for these office buildings to be used as initial shelters for employees.

The fifteen-storey tower looked dead, nothing to be seen through the mirrored facade, no lights, but the building's internal systems were online when Miller tried connecting to them. He couldn't access the closed circuit cameras or any door-locks. Without a live internet connection for the building to authenticate him on, the best it could do was show him the login page and hang up.

While Miller was messing with technology, du Trieux looked at the building like a woman hunting guerrillas. When he told her that he didn't think anyone was home, she disagreed immediately, pointing out what she could see from her seat.

"See that pile of trash there? Fresh—some of it not yet covered by dust or fungus. That pit looks like a latrine, or somewhere to dump food scraps." She tapped into the Bravo's cameras, and zoomed in on something sticking out of one of the windows on a lower floor—a scorched-looking length of air conditioner duct.

"That's a chimney," she said. "They have a fire, maybe for cooking. This building is *very much* occupied."

Miller touched his earpiece. "Dial Cobalt-2-2," he told it.

Doyle, reliable as ever, picked up on the first ring. "*Miller?*"

"What's your status?"

"*Moving to drop off civilians at the compound.*"

Miller consulted the GPS navigator, and tried to figure out if its guess of a twenty-five minute ride between Astoria and his location would be accurate. Probably, but they were burning daylight. Wasting both his teams' time on this...

"Fuck it," Miller muttered. Better safe than sorry. "Doyle, we've got a big scary building to search, and I want more than two of us doing it. Get over here, and bring guns."

ONCE IN A while, channel-hopping as a child and wishing he had streaming video on demand instead of the cable TV provided by the Air Force base his dad had been stationed at, Miller used to stumble across these nature programs. They weren't documentaries, not like the dramatic ones on Discovery Channel where they got alligators to eat people in protective suits and hunted for giant sharks that were never quite so giant when they found them, but the shows were nice for having in the background while dicking around on social networks.

In the nature programs there was a scientist, or a biologist, always speaking in soft, hushed tones, as if they were frightened of startling what was on camera. And it was just... footage of animals, doing animal things. Sleeping, walking around, hunting, whatever. The footage was either from a hand camera or a drone, and somehow those shows turned a lion getting up and walking toward a jeep into the most terrifying moment in the world, way better than Discovery Channel's crazy sharks, because the sharks felt like something somebody made up for a monster movie, and lions on the savannah were *real*. And lions were so rare it was illegal to shoot them, so if they attacked, you just got eaten, and that was that.

Miller found himself talking to du Trieux in the same hushed tones, even though he had an M27 across his lap and the Bravo's armour could hold off RPGs, let alone the claws and teeth of the predators crossing the road a few blocks away. Not terror-jaws, something much bigger and stockier. They might have been nicknamed thugs? Miller wasn't sure if it really was a thug—a heavy-built scavenger that'd gnawed its way through Canada—he didn't think they got as big as what he saw in his binoculars. Even so, he wasn't too worried. Sure, maybe some of these Archaeobiome things had eaten T-rexes once upon a time, but so far as Miller knew, dinosaurs weren't built to handle IEDs.

Then again, even if these things weren't lions and Miller was very definitely allowed to blow them away, he didn't much like the idea of trying to take down something the size of a fucking *rhino* with rifle rounds.

"Do you think the people in there are hiding until nightfall?" du Trieux asked, matching his tone. "Perhaps the predators around here can't see too well."

Privately, Miller suspected it was the heat. The Bravo's interior fans were roaring away, but Miller didn't even want to guess what it must have been like to suffer outside for hours on end. The building's shade might have been all that was keeping the inhabitants alive.

"Maybe," he murmured, quickly changing the subject. "Doubt any decent local clubs open up until eight or nine, anyway." He glanced across the Bravo at her. "We could come back then, find dates. I call dibs on blondes and redheads. *Especially* blondes."

She hesitated, lifting an eyebrow. "Do I get first shot at blonde men, at least?"

"Hell, no. Not if they're short, anyhow."

Du Trieux snorted. "I hope it's okay to ask, but... You prefer men? Or women?"

"Both. Maybe a little pickier when it comes to men—if he doesn't take better care of his looks than I do, not too interested." Miller tapped the driver's wheel. "You? Men, women, both?"

"Just men."

"Really? Didn't someone say you were dating a Lebanese around the water cooler...?"

She near enough slapped him. "Don't you Americans know *any* countries other than ones you invade—" And then she saw his mock-serious expression, and laughed.

He left her to chuckle, and glanced through the windshield nervously.

"Why do you do that?" du Trieux asked.

"Do what?"

"Distract us with bullshit when things get serious."

Miller tapped his fingers on the wheel again, glancing around in hopes of spotting Doyle and Morland's Bravo. "You know I was in the Army, right?"

"Right."

"The closest I ever got to war was sitting around the base on rapid deployment alert. They'd line us up with all our gear, sometimes sit us in troop transport planes. It'd go on for weeks at a time whenever they held an election in Saudi Arabia, or if someone blew up an oil pipeline in Russia, or whatever." Miller chewed his lip. "It was like sitting with a guillotine hanging over us, day after day, and we were *begging* it to drop. There wasn't any other way to break the tension; bullshitting each other instead of thinking about—it's an instinct by now."

Du Trieux joined him in silently watching the building and streets for a while, lightly fingering her Gilboa.

"You remind me of Hasim," she said, eventually.

"Hasim?"

"A *jihadi* I met while we were liberating Syria from the false caliphate, the Daesh." She glanced at him uncertainly, but he didn't explode in war-on-terror speak and bigotry, so she went on. "Mostly, at camp, he sang songs that the Daesh would have executed him for. Not just because they were mocking, but because the Daesh think music is *evil*. All he wanted to do was sing. He didn't want to fight. Not really."

Miller nodded slightly, tapping away at the wheel to distract himself. "Yeah, I'm kind of a coward like that."

"Oh, Hasim wasn't a coward," du Trieux said. "He didn't *want* to fight, but he knew he must. Not out of vengeance for our brothers and sisters, like most of us there, but because it was the correct thing—the *right* thing—to do."

Miller's fingers stilled on the steering wheel.

"There isn't any shame in a fear of violence, Miller. This is what bravery is, isn't it? Overcoming fear to do what is right?"

He blinked at her. "I heard the soldier needs something of the sociopath in him."

She wrinkled her nose at him. "Men like that are good killers, but they are not good *men*, you understand?"

Miller looked away, thinking on what du Trieux

had said, and what Gray had said. "Maybe," he said quietly.

Du Trieux lapsed into silence after that, leaving Miller alone with his thoughts and she with hers.

As the minutes and heat wore on, the behemoth-sized thugs trotted away to find something weak or dead to eat. Eventually the streets were quiet and still, except for the movement of another Bravo rolling to a halt at a nearby intersection.

"*In position*," Doyle reported a moment later.

They brought the Bravos together, and sat in their air conditioning with the doors open for a quick briefing.

"We're looking for the Baxters. Their emergency plan directed them to evacuate here, their home's been abandoned at least a week." Miller passed the pad with Alphonse and Linda's pictures on it over to Doyle and Morland, letting them get a look. "Two kids. From family photos, their skin's a little lighter than their dad's, frizzy hair like his. The building's got *somebody* living in it, though we haven't seen any movement in the half-hour we've been here," he said. "Except for big-ass animals, but they cleared out."

Morland obliged them with a nervous glance around, as if he expected to be eaten at any moment. "Apparently scavengers are following the dust storms around," he said. "Looking for a free meal."

"Great," Miller muttered.

"Were any of our other pickups directed here?" Doyle asked.

"Don't think so. So far as I know, Switchblade cleared the last of the employee shelters a couple of days ago." Miller glanced at the building again, trying to find signs of life behind the building's mirrored glass. "We're only interested in the Baxters for now. If other employees are resident, we'll pass it up the chain and the executives can make the call."

A few sips of water later, and Cobalt-2 assembled on the lobby doors. Morland and Doyle in front with their shotguns—magazine-fed automatics laid out like oversized assault rifles—Miller and du Trieux behind.

This close, the tiny key reader, a plastic lozenge beside one of the door hinges, clearly displayed three blue lights. Unlocked. Doyle paused, S-Y master key software loaded on his phone, and glanced back at Miller.

It wasn't right. The Baxters' home was one thing, but an office block being used as a shelter? The lobby doors would be stronger than they looked— these buildings were designed to survive a car bomb detonated on the kerb; they could *easily* hold out the wildlife, if they were locked.

The doors swung open, and yielded to the shadowy darkness of the interior. The inner lobby doors, normally shut to hold in the building's air-conditioned atmosphere, were hanging wide open.

The smell hit Miller first. He could barely see— his eyes struggling to adapt to the building's cave-darkness after the sunlight outside—but he could *smell* body odour. Gym socks and stale urine, the subway in midsummer with hundreds of sweating people in close quarters. The unwashed smell of an Infected mob.

The lobby doors shut on their springs behind them with a *whoomph*, and everything seemed still. Dead.

The front desk was overturned, graffiti on the wall behind it, just to cement the horror movie atmosphere. No scrawled warnings, no creepy messages in blood, just neat orderly rows of childish stick figures holding hands. There was more crayon work further in, swirls and scribbles and crude animals along with a few more detailed pictures of cars and trees, as if adults had watched a couple of five-year-olds start drawing on the walls and had decided to join in.

Miller struggled with the impulse to cry out a greeting, beg the occupants to show their faces, but he held his tongue, directing his small team through the lobby and into the building's wings, checking meeting rooms one by one. In about half, the projectors' screens had been drawn over with more crayon work—definitely collaborations between adults and children, zoo animals and newer wildlife cavorting under oversized yellow suns.

The place seemed deserted, except for the fire escapes.

Piles of trash and furniture were stacked up behind the stairwell doors, completely barricaded. Not even an inch of give when Morland put his huge shoulder to the door and pushed. It seemed like a fire hazard, but nobody, *nobody*, would be making it upstairs without using the elevators. Thankfully, they worked. Sort of. The call buttons lit up, and the elevator panels accepted the master key, at least.

Miller hammered on the call button again, but the elevators refused to arrive.

"*Who are you?*"

"What?" Miller looked round, trying to find the source of the voice. "We're corporate-board-level security, who are you?"

"Over here," Doyle said, pointing at a panel on the wall. An intercom with a tiny screen, just barely lit.

The man on the display was shirtless, sweaty, his hair at all angles. Eyes wild. "*You're not them? The Infected?*" he demanded. "*You're employees like us?*"

"Yes, we are." Miller leaned in, pulling up his ID card from its clip on his chest to show the panel.

"*Oh... Okay. I'll go free the elevator and come down for you. Just, wait there. Okay? Wait there...*" He vanished from the screen, but the panel continued to display a wall.

"At least they're not infected," Morland said.

"Don't know about that," Miller muttered, clutching his M27 tighter.

The floor-number display above one of the elevator doors began slowly counting down.

The elevator pinged after a tense wait, and the shirtless man from the intercom—and his *stink*—emerged from within. He looked around nervously, chewing at his fingernails. "There aren't any Infected with you, are there?"

"No," Miller said, kindly as he could. "We're here to protect you from them. I'm Alex."

The man didn't answer at first, his eyes shuddering over each of their faces like a drug addict's, unable to focus on any particular feature without his eyes leaping away. For a moment Miller was afraid the poor guy was having a seizure, but he retreated into the elevator, pressing himself against the wall. "I-I'm George. Are you sure you're an employee like me?"

"Yes."

George didn't seem to believe him, shrinking into that corner of the elevator. "O-okay. You can come upstairs."

The elevator wasn't that tight a fit with five people, but it was uncomfortable. Dark. The buttons and display provided the only light, until Doyle flipped on his chest-rig flashlight. George flinched away from the light, looking a little ghoulish in the blue-tinged glow.

"Alright?" Doyle asked, thinly.

George huddled back, wretched and dishevelled. "It's fine. Just bright. Light hurts sometimes."

"Is that why the lights are out?"

George nodded, but didn't offer any further information. When they reached the fifth floor, he scurried out into the half-lit corridor—a little sunlight snaking through the building's corridors from the windows, catching dancing motes of dust and fairy-like gnats in the sunbeams—and pulled a piece of board through the elevator's doors, blocking them. All the elevators had been treated similarly—

in one lay an overturned filing cabinet, in another a pair of office chairs.

Pointing, Miller asked, "Why?"

"To keep us safe," George said, breathlessly turning the board over so as best to catch the door. "None of the locks work. They're all... all broken. When the Infected came, the doors opened for them. We blocked the elevators and barricaded the stairs, so they can't come back."

"The Infected were here?" Miller asked, wiping his eye. One of the gnats had flown into it, making his eye tear up.

"They bit us," George said, lifting his arm, displaying a recent crescent-shaped scab, before stopping nervously in the middle of the hall. "It's, it's all right now. The others were going to send us out, because we'd been bitten, but it's alright, we all like each other now..."

They were infected. They were *all* damn well infected.

Bit by bit they got the story out of George, how the building's security systems had failed during the riots. The building *did* have shelter supplies, and everything had locked up the way it was supposed to, up until the mob arrived, shortly after Jimmy Swift's broadcasts. Then the doors spilled open, and two security guards and a janitor had been killed— beaten to death. Others had been injured, many had been bitten. And the one thing missing from the supplies were anti-parasitic drugs.

The infection spread rapidly after that—the

cramped conditions, the lack of hygiene, the necessity of letting infected people handle foraged food. The parasite spread with most kinds of body-fluid contact. Saliva, sweat. Sex. The Infected's natural inclination to get along, to like one another, to think like each other, to be *affectionate*, had brought the mild cases in close contact with those so far gone they were starting to forget what language was for. Soon there weren't any mild cases left, thanks to the repeated reinfections.

"It's not so bad if they keep apart from each other," one of the last uninfected, Opal, a woman with an anti-parasitic drug implant, said. "They're still... people?" She said the word uncertainly. "When there's more than a few together, they... they get mob-minded."

Right now, in a dingy office, there was George and a teenaged girl, watching, swaying more or less in time with one another. "It's confusing," George said, gently.

"Can't stop thinking about what other people are doing, too many things to think about," the girl said. "It's easier if you shut—" "—shut your eyes, less to—" "—less to *think* about," they said, almost murmuring over each other's voices.

"But you're not like them?" Miller asked, hand resting against the stock of his slung M27. "You don't want to go and join their communes?"

"We're employees," George said, almost desperately. "They kill employees."

Early on, Opal explained, some of the newly

infected—uncomfortable with their uninfected former co-workers—had tried to escape, to join the mobs. They'd all promised to return if it was safe, but none had. Foraging parties sometimes disappeared, never just one or two, but entire groups. The remaining infected employees had convinced themselves that the communes had killed them—there was a strong strain of paranoia running through the group after the earlier attack.

Privately Miller suspected, and he could see that Opal shared his suspicion, that the Infected had run along with the communes and forgotten all about their fellow employees the moment mob-mindedness took over.

"It wasn't too bad, while more of us were still uninfected. Right now Alphonse and I aren't very popular," Opal said. "Apparently we don't smell right, but they know us and we're employees. That seems to matter more than what we smell like."

"We're the same, we're employees, we're the same, we work for the company..." George was rocking back and forth, the girl beside him similarly agitated.

"Alphonse? Alphonse *Baxter*?"

"That's right. He has the chip too—you know him?"

Miller looked back at his squad, then nodded fractionally. "We're here to take him and his family to safety."

Opal tugged at her chin nervously. "The rest won't like that."

* * *

"PLEASE, BABY, PLEASE, let me take it out..." Linda Baxter, considerably worse-for-wear after a week of exile, started to rock nervously in front of her husband.

Alphonse looked tired, defeated. The broken arm had something to do with that, but so did the way his children sat rooted beside their mother, joining her pleading with half-burbled whines more suited to toddlers.

Du Trieux was trying to guard the door, but failing. Curious employees were drifting after them, the news of Cobalt-2's arrival spreading rapidly up- and downstairs—the stairwells were only barricaded at the bottom floors, and were the only means of getting around with the elevators on lockdown.

Alphonse looked up first, surprised to see someone with a gun, and Linda's half-conscious rocking grew worse as she spotted George, his nervousness joining hers in a confused muddle.

"Mr. and Mrs. Baxter? We're here to take you and your children to safety."

"Oh, thank God—"

"We *are* safe," Linda snapped, drawing her husband's sling-bound arm toward her again, despite his wincing. She didn't seem to understand he was hurt, but she understood George's bubbling nerves *perfectly*. The two children watched owlishly, their faces twisting to match their mother's severe tone.

Gnats danced in the gloom along with the dust, fizzing along just above head level.

"Afe," the daughter murmured, words seemingly

having lost all meaning for the child, simply mimicking her mother's sounds.

"Don't listen to her," Alphonse begged, wrapping his good arm around the bad, leaning away from her wife. "Please, take us, we need to get out of here, it's been days—"

"Al, please, we need to take it out, we just need to cut it out and then you'll be alright, don't you see?" The woman lost all interest in the visitors, and reached for her husband's bad arm again. His right arm—the arm drug chips were usually implanted in.

George stumbled forward, falling to his knees nearby... caressing the air as if it were Alphonse's arm. The employees were in motion, and there wasn't anything du Trieux could do to keep them from shoving past her at the door. First one got past, then a second, pushing at her like drunks dealing with an unwelcome party-guest, all fumbles and knuckles.

Cobalt's mere presence was putting them on edge. George wasn't just afraid of them because they had guns; they were *strangers*, and they were uninfected. Revulsion at their presence was the last straw on the camel's back, and Miller realized it only as he spotted the situation spiralling out of control.

"We just need to tear it out..."

"Linda, no!" Alphonse struggled to stand, and she, and George, and the other employees, even the children, all pushed him back down. She leaned forward, gently pulling away the ragged remnants of his sleeve, and dipped as if to kiss his shoulder...

He screamed, and she bit him again, tearing at his shoulder with her teeth.

"Stop!" Miller yelled, hesitating with his rifle. He half-reached for the trigger, then made his choice—left the M27 to hang at his side as he tore George away, throwing the malnourished man to the floor and pushing Linda away from her husband.

The room exploded in panic. Maybe it had been George, maybe it was Linda's terror at being pulled away from her husband. Her lips bloody, she fought Miller, punching at him, kicking him—no, those were her children at his legs—screaming, "You're not one of us! You don't know, don't—"

Voices blotted her out, howls, anguish, anger. The only reason Miller could make her out at all—"You won't take him away!"—was because she was screaming right in his ear whilst trying to tear it off.

Morland, praise the oversized lug, caught the back of the door and started pushing it against the flow of the crowd. Doyle backed up towards a side door, du Trieux flanking him as they opened up a gap with their bodies.

Miller managed to half-throw Alphonse in their direction. Alphonse stumbled, Doyle caught him and they backed through. Du Trieux had her weapon up, ready to shoot.

God help him, Miller had tried to keep this from turning into an armed conflict, but he'd never figured on a woman spitting her husband's blood at him while her children tore at his legs. He hadn't wanted to take things this far, but he didn't see any other options.

He threw his elbow against her face, buying himself a moment's grace, and palmed a compact stun-gun from his belt rig.

It turned her into a hundred and forty pounds of seizuring muscle, and she fell, puking. Her children screamed, but Miller couldn't bring himself to use the weapon on them. He simply tottered, clutching at one Infected's back for support while pushing the stun-gun's electric probes against another.

Doyle cocked his shotgun and fired against the exterior wall—full-length plate glass windows— but the sound of shattering glass and gunfire did nothing to intimidate the Infected. There was a hate to their eyes, one that hadn't been there before.

It was, Miller dimly realized, between flashing arcs of blazing electrical light as he missed his target, like the kids who'd called him 'faggot' in high school for being willing to try dating another guy. It was like they'd never wanted to see him as human, and that one date out of a dozen let them flip a switch to look past his humanity and turn him into *vermin*.

They hadn't been violent in high school, though. Those two teenage boys had known that no matter how they felt, there were consequences— suspension, maybe worse.

The Infected didn't give a shit.

George charged Miller, the poor spindly man transformed into something entirely *other*, wearing Linda's feelings and the mob's hatred on a face not really suited to either. But Miller wasn't about to let him start gnawing off his ears.

The stun-gun crackled, and du Trieux was beating someone off Morland's back with the butt of her rifle as he tried to get away. Doyle had given up on warning shots and had backed up, switching magazines to rubber buckshot. The pellets— slightly larger than a toy gun's BB—stung across Miller's legs. The Baxter children screamed and collapsed, bruised and bleeding but not seriously injured.

A second shot of rubber pellets at chest height made the screaming Infected back off long enough for Miller's team to drag him through into the next room, and the Infected that followed them in before Morland managed to barricade the doors weren't too much trouble after they'd been zip-cuffed.

Miller did his best to concentrate on blocking off the side-room's other entrance, and to avoid thinking about the spots of blood on his pants from the children. Or any of what had just happened.

He certainly didn't focus on Baxter, hovering over his hog-tied wife and rocking like a nervous Infected, blood streaming from the gouge gnawed out of his shoulder.

"We gotta fucking lock this thing," Morland grunted, shoulders spread against the table tipped against the doorway—even with his weight it rocked against his back, rhythmically opening a crack and slamming shut amidst snatches of snarling and howling.

"Can't," du Trieux said, struggling with the room's building systems console.

Miller grunted, and started pushing another table towards the doorway. "Why not?"

"Somebody burnt out control access to the locks."

COBALT EVENTUALLY BARRICADED themselves in, and sheltered in place the way employees were supposed to in emergencies, waiting for the support of security team Bayonet to arrive. When they did, they took the building by storm with shock batons and Tasers, smoke and gas.

Cobalt's barricade had been effective enough that the Infected had started breaking through the relatively thin walls instead. They were still trying when Bayonet came in through the second floor with breaching charges and ladders, like medieval raiders.

Helicopters swept the early-evening sky, hacking the air into submission, and the roaming mobs of Infected fearfully avoided the area. The protection was going to be short-lived, though—the pilots were having trouble with their engines. Their air filters couldn't handle the fungus—already two out of the five overwatch choppers had turned back to base before their intakes clogged entirely.

With a satellite connection re-established, Miller stood in the building's security room, watching the Northwind operator on the conferencing screen—a young Chinese-American woman—work remotely on the building's systems. She was shaking her head.

"*We can't recover this without repairing each part of the system individually. The locks and cameras*

*have all had their wireless links burnt out—someone
used the reprogrammable circuits to short circuit
them with the power supply."*

Miller was vaguely familiar with the systems
involved. In the event of an intruder attacking a
building electronically, standard procedure was to
command locks to short out their antennae. It severed
them from the network, made them impossible
to hack without literally cutting into the locks and
soldering an access-port into the circuit boards.

But it was a last ditch option, to lock the doors and
ensure they stayed shut. Locking them open? While
mobs of the Infected were rioting across the city?

"I already know what happened, Northwind; the
part I want to know is who did it."

The Northwind operator kept shaking her head,
like she didn't want to believe it. *"It's that account
with the S-Y internal security department again.
Forty-six, seventy-two."*

Robert Harris.

6

L. Gʀᴀʏ Mᴀᴛʜᴇsᴏɴ put down the first printout and picked up the second. He scanned the emergency plan's instructions, and picked up the next, then the next... at last he simply flicked through them, only paying attention to the parts that changed. Name and address.

Nearly three hundred employees of various ranks and from various subsidiaries had been told to evacuate to the WellBeechBeck Washington Heights office block, and that security team Sabre would come to collect them.

Gray tapped his lip with the corner of the stacked sheets, gazing blankly at the surface of his desk, recently installed into his Astoria Cove office.

"I sent members of Switchblade to check a few of the employees' homes, along with the Baxters'. Their building systems all crashed shortly after the meeting with you, Barrett, and Harris, last week. Just after the helicopter incident." Miller crossed and uncrossed his legs uncomfortably—combat gear didn't feel right for talking with his boss. He should've gotten back into a suit.

"How many were in the building?"

"Eighty-seven. They'd been losing people at a fairly rapid rate. Three died during the operation. Heart attacks or suffocation, we think." Miller swallowed back bile. "The electroshock weapons. Some of them were too weak, malnourished." He shook his head. "I'm sorry."

Gray stuck out his jaw, tapping his face one last time. He didn't seem to be listening. "And where are they now?" He put down the papers.

"We cleared out one of the refugee quarantine blocks. They're in there for now."

There wasn't any real doubt, not to Miller, but Gray had to ask. "You're sure Bob's involved?"

"Yes."

"You don't have direct proof?"

Miller puffed out a breath. "That's why I'm here talking to you, Gray, instead of marching over to shoot the man myself. He deliberately isolated people, *our* people, in that building. And then he blew the damn locks so the Infected could tear into them. He wanted a captive Infected commune, probably for those fucking bioweapons of his."

"And the Baxters?" Gray asked, gently. "Why'd he put them on the Honshū Wolf list, then?"

Miller shook his head. "Only Alphonse was on the Honshū Wolf list. The emergency plan was addressed to his wife, I don't think he was supposed to be there."

Gray nodded, once. "I'll look into it. You get back to whatever you were doing, Alex. I'll let you know."

MILLER'S BODY COUNT rose from three, to four, to twenty-seven.

Sure, *he* hadn't killed those three unfortunates who'd died after being shock-stunned to the ground—that was Bayonet's work. Even so, he was responsible. He'd led the operation to go into that building, he'd called in Bayonet, it was his fault. The hundreds who'd been cut down by the helicopter, weeks before? That was on Harris's head; but this, *this* was on Miller's.

The living had been cleared away, but blood had pooled in the refugee quarantine cell, an expanse of chain-link fencing stapled to the concrete floor of a storehouse.

The fourth death on Miller's head was Opal Dernier's, also on the Honshū Wolf evacuations list, and also on the list for anti-parasitic drug implants. She had been lumped in with the rest of the captured Infected employees because Miller hadn't been alert enough to realize that she, like Alphonse, like the children, like the injured, needed special treatment.

The guard who'd been on duty explained it all to Miller, his face drained of blood.

At first, nothing had looked wrong. The Infected—and Opal—had been herded into the huge wire-mesh cells that kept the refugees in place through quarantine and testing. They'd sat around, stumbled—they were still all zip-tied, hands behind their backs as they'd shuffled around. Stinking, filthy, sweaty.

They mostly stood around in a single mass, but one or two, sometimes three, broke away from the pack and moved up to the far end every so often. Like they were searching for an escape from their mob, but only a temporary one. They always came back to join the huddle. Except for one prisoner, not that any of the guards had noticed.

Opal had been sitting in the corner, as far away from the main mob as she could get. She shouted at the guards for attention a few times, but the whole mob was shouting, mumbling, moaning. Like bird-song. Twittering tones and sounds that could almost have been musical, if they weren't made up from murmurs and howls and grunts. No one had heard her.

The longer they were in the cage, the more the mob's individual members wanted to escape it, to get respite from each other. And when too many were trying to find solitude, that's when things went sour.

The first Infected to get too close to Opal screamed at her, called her all kinds of filthy names, told her that she wasn't one of them, wasn't human, wasn't real—that same disgust Miller had seen when the mob was on the attack.

With one of their number disturbed, a second picked up on it soon enough, a third, a fourth, until the whole mob were screaming at Opal. But it didn't stop there. Their shared rage grew out of control, reflecting back at them from every face around them, until they simply charged Opal, crushing her against the fence with their weight and their shoulders and their xenophobic hatred.

And then, working with a single mind and near perfect coordination, sixty people pushed over the chain-link fence like bison trampling grass.

What was left of the wire fence was slick with blood, pieces of skin and hair caught in the weave. Her body lay, crumpled and bruised, her flesh raggedly cut by the mesh. Miller stepped back a little, keeping clear of the still-spreading pool.

Obviously she was dead.

So were the twenty-three Infected the guards had been forced to gun down before the mob within their midst had torn two of them apart—there had been more injured by gunfire, and by the Bayonet team that had re-secured the storehouse, but they were in a temporary infirmary. Only Opal, and the twenty-three, remained on the storehouse floor.

One of the Bayonet operatives, wearing a full-body exoskeleton that made him seem Herculean and inhuman behind his gas mask, awkwardly shook his head. "It was god-awful," he buzzed through his personal radio's external speaker, rather than leaving his voice muffled behind his mask. "Those Infected... they're all monsters."

HEADING UP TO Gray's office in the elevator, Miller pulled the Gallican from its holster again. Just to be sure it wasn't stuck in there—the belt rig was different from the little concealed holster he usually wore and he wasn't sure if he trusted it yet.

He drew back the slide, making sure there was a round chambered, set the safety back on, and reholstered the gun. Then he pulled it free, checking for snags, and let it drop back down again.

Miller had never *actually* shot anyone. Never *actually* killed anyone, not personally. It made sense he'd be nervous.

Holly Moulin, Gray's personal assistant, was at her desk. She looked up, smiling tightly. "You okay there, Mr. Miller? I'm afraid you can't go in," she said, with an awkward smile. "Mr. Matheson's in a confidential meeting—"

"Gray doesn't keep anything confidential from me," Miller snapped, pushing by.

"Mr. Miller! I know you have a special working relationship with Mr. Matheson, but—"

Miller ignored her, and pulled open the office door. Special enough that Miller could murder someone in front of Gray? Just have to see.

Shutting the door behind himself, Miller looked up to see Gray and Harris blinking at him. They hadn't expected to be disturbed from their meeting.

"Alex?" Gray asked.

"I'm killing Harris." Miller yanked the Gallican free, and nudged off the safety.

Robert Harris didn't seem to believe it. Looking at the gun, at Miller... at Gray, as if this were something the CEO would have to sign off on first, maybe after running it past the accountants.

"It's a complicated situation, Alex."

"No, it isn't. He ordered the helicopter attack, he released biological weapons on civilians, he turned innocents into *monsters*." Miller held up the gun. "Because of him, dozens more people died today."

"What happened, Alex?" Gray asked, gently.

"There was a riot in the refugee zone. Twenty-three, twenty-four... Jesus, that's not even counting the guards they killed. I can't even fucking count it. There are too many dead!"

"You're upset, Alex, I can see that..."

"This has to *stop*. Someone has to stop you, Mr. Harris. And nobody else will," Miller said, levelling the Gallican at him.

For a heartbeat, Miller registered Robert Harris's shocked recognition that Miller *meant* it, and then Gray stood in the line of fire. Miller looked at the gun, looked at where it was pointing, and took a step to the side, aiming at Harris's face.

"Don't. We need him." Calmly, Gray sidestepped with Miller. "It's a complicated situation," he repeated, firmly.

"How?" All the strength left his arm, and the Gallican dropped to his side. "How?" Miller begged. "He fucked us, Gray. He turned us into the enemy. Don't you understand that? We're the ones locking people into cages, poisoning people. *We're* the monsters. Because of him."

"We're not the bad guys, Alex. We're fighting to survive." Gray cocked his head ever so slightly. "That parasite's going to kill us all if we let it."

"The Infected aren't *evil!* They're sick, they need treatment—they're *people.*"

"And that's why we have to stop the parasite, Alex. Pass me that tablet you were showing me, Bob."

"Here," Harris said, passing it up.

"This," Gray said, coming in to stand beside Miller, "is a scan of one of those people's skulls. You see this row of little blobs?"

They started inside the eye. Small white marks, tiny pinpricks of light, were clumped around the retina—but they weren't the parasite-cysts the quarantine teams checked for with ophthalmoscopes. From the retina, a thin line of them seemed to be marching in single file through the little gap in the bone around the tear duct and into the sinuses, then the nose. From there they squeezed into holes pockmarking a plate of bone behind it, and then... they were right up against the brain, dozens of them.

"Yeah," Miller replied. "I see them."

"Those are wasp larvae."

"*Wasps?* In the guy's *brain?*"

"You probably met some yourself. Most are tiny little fuckers, not much more than an eighth of an inch long."

The gnats! "Fuck!" Miller whipped a knuckle to his eyes, scrubbing furiously. "I got one in my eye—"

"Hold on, there, *you're* probably fine," Gray said, taking Miller's shoulder. He leaned in, checking Miller's eye. "You blink? Eye watered?"

"Y-yeah," Miller stammered, glancing again at the

pad, the larvae in the guy's eyes and *brain*, laying on the desk.

"Damn little bastard probably didn't lay anything in you," Gray said. "But if you were infected with the Archaean Parasite? It'd be a whole other story."

Harris steepled his fingers. "The Infected don't blink the wasps away. According to the research, the parasite weakens the blink reflex and forces you to let the wasps lay as many eggs in you as they want. It's part of the life cycle."

Miller couldn't shake off the nagging *need* to find a doctor.

"The parasite is like toxoplasma, that thing in cat-shit. It can't reproduce properly in humans—it just splits up and divides, cloning itself. For it to *breed*, for the little single-celled fuckers to have *sex*, our best guess is that they have to get eaten by this wasp. Now, there's a lot we still don't understand about this thing," Harris went on, warming to his topic, "but the parasite *loves* living in your nerves. In your skin, in your gut, in your *brain*. And it wants to goddamn *feed* your skin, your gut, your *brain* to these wasps."

"Fuck," Miller whispered.

"I don't need to see eye-to-eye with you, Miller. And I ain't proud of what I've done." Harris drummed his fingers on the table. "But I don't think either of us wants this fucker eating our brains. But that's exactly what's going to happen, to *everybody*, if we don't deal with the Infected."

"You can't just, just..."

"Alex, it's okay." Gray took his shoulder. "This mess is a big old rock that's been flipped over, and we found a snake underneath. It's ugly, but we need the snake to kill the rats eating our food, you understand? We need Bob. We need to *survive*."

"Like hell we do!" Miller snapped. "*We* didn't survive, Gray! *We* weren't people who used biological weapons and rounded up refugees in wire cages, kicking half of them out for being too infected to make it worth bringing them in!"

Gray's face clouded, his eyes narrowing coldly. "They *burned* us, Alex. We gave people the drugs they needed in their aid packages, and they killed our truck drivers with Molotovs."

"That doesn't change what *he* did," Miller growled, clutching the handgun tighter, glaring at Harris.

"No," Gray agreed, "but—"

Whatever Gray was about to say was lost as Holly Moulin knocked once, sharply, and stuck her head through the door. "Mr. Matheson? Mr. Swift is on the phone for you? A conference call, with a Major General Stockman on the line…"

THE RECORDINGS PLAYED continuously over the decaying public television signal. James Swift in clean clothes, a lurid orange and pink crust of scabrous skin running from the side of his throat to beneath his collar. His hair had been brushed; he was smiling, calm. So was Major General Stockman, seated twelve feet away, man normal but for his greasy skin and hair. Somehow his uniform was keeping its creases.

"Hello? Jimmy?"

"*Gray. Been a long time since we've spoken.*" Swift smiled slowly, his mouth a narrow slash. "*I don't believe you know Major General Stockman.*"

"*I do not.*"

"*Mr. Matheson.*" Stockman smiled back at Swift, that same narrow smile. "*I regret to inform you that a warrant has been issued for you and your company board's arrest. I must ask you to surrender yourself and your corporation's assets* immediately."

The sweep of the camera, between Swift and Stockman seated so far apart, made it obvious they were being shot with an extreme zoom. The cameraman had to have been clear on the other side of the studio—everyone given their personal space, with enough separation to remain individuals.

Gray didn't answer immediately. On the other end of the line he'd been gesturing wildly at Holly to get back on the line and start recording the call, but the stony silence seemed to stretch out for a calm and measured eternity.

"*Could you clarify under whose authority that is?*"

"*My own,*" Stockman said, his jaw squaring. "*I am declaring martial law in the states of New York, New Jersey, Connecticut and Pennsylvania, and I warn you that my 11th Infantry Division is entering the city as we speak. Mr. Matheson, Schaeffer-Yeager International cannot outrun the laws of our fifty united states.*"

At this point the recording froze frame on Stockman's steely gaze, and cut out.

In his office, at about that point, Gray gritted his teeth and asked, "And which branch of the government ordered you to do so, Major General?"

Miller didn't hear the response, but Gray laughed out loud. "I'm sorry, but Jimmy's not an elected leader. Tell me, have you been following the National Emergency Presidential Directives? Specifically directive thirty-two?" A pause. "You haven't, have you? That's the one making it a felony for military personnel if they don't take their issued anti-parasitic drugs... No, Major-General, I believe what you're doing is staging a coup d'état against whatever shreds of governmental authority still exist."

Made sense that they wouldn't show that on TV.

That was roughly how it went down. Miller finished telling the other members of Cobalt about it in their new break room, while Lewis picked through old coffee filters in the hopes of finding one that almost qualified as fresh.

Du Trieux was painted over the back of one of the couches, while Doyle cleaned a rifle he'd had 3D-printed in metal and polymer, going over its blocky frame with sandpaper. Nobody asked the obvious question, while shaky footage on the television showed squads of ragged, scruffy-looking soldiers lurching in lockstep along a freeway while Bravos rolled back and forth behind them.

The Gallican was holstered, and loaded, and he still hadn't put the safety back on.

Miller would have to figure out what to do about Harris later, but right now, there were bigger problems. What the hell were they going to do with an Infected army coming for them?

Miller didn't know, but by the end of whatever the hell had just started, he didn't think he'd ever find an open dry cleaner again.

OPERATION WILD TARPAN

7

"You understand that every second we stay here, you're a target?"

L. Gray Matheson, CEO of Schaeffer-Yeager International and master of all he surveyed, shrugged off Miller's concerns with a gentle raise of the palm. "In a minute, Alex. I'm on the phone with the President."

At least, Miller thought, Gray wasn't calling the President 'Huck' again.

"Now then, Huck. Like I said, I'm having trouble with one of your boys..."

Miller slapped his palm over his face.

Gray ignored Miller, and turned to face the queues of unhappy civilians waiting for their turn at the aid truck. He put on a patrician smile, and waved. "Uh-huh. Well, I know Major General Stockman isn't following orders, Huck, but I need you to make that clear to what's left of the media." Somehow, and Miller didn't know how he did it, Gray could smile without any hint of it reaching his voice.

Downtown Brooklyn, just south of Trinity Park and east of Cadman Plaza, had a liberal sprinkling of what could almost have been normality.

There was a media team following Gray around with cameras, and Miller was back in his suit playing at being the Armani while the cameras were streaming footage over anaemic satellite links back to what was left of the rest of the country.

There were un-Infected civilians, looking like a considerably expanded population of the city's homeless, queuing for soup and aid packages provided by the generous corporation Schaeffer-Yeager, who'd even managed to restore electric power to the region.

Of course, the power was off the local solar grid, and with air conditioning growling away wherever anyone had it, there wouldn't be enough juice in the grid's fuel cells to last more than a few hours into the evening—but the press didn't need to know that.

In fact, there was a lot they hoped the media detail wouldn't notice. For one thing, du Trieux and Morland stood to one side with Miller's combat gear, ready for him to shrug off his suit the moment the cameras were out of sight. For another, before the cameras had started filming, Miller and the others had cleared the dead off the surrounding streets.

Emaciated corpses, literally skin and bones, where the starved had fallen in search for a morsel to eat, had lain scattered and rotting across the entire city block.

Some only looked dead, and were simply too weak to move. Volunteers had pulled them to a make-shift triage tent and were treating them with little packets of gloopy processed food that had been developed by WellBeechBeck for saving Ethiopian orphans, but the volunteers were hungry enough that some were shamelessly sucking a mouthful from the packets before serving the starving.

Further down the street, titan-birds had gorged themselves on bodies too mutilated for the troops to even try to move without a shovel. Doyle was blasting the bastard creatures every time one landed in search of a meal, in hopes of keeping them out of sight of the cameras. But the stench of the dead remained in the air.

The titan-birds, New York's newest residents, were hanging in the thermals between Brooklyn's towers, stretched out, their leathery wings ready to catch any slight breeze allowing the colossal birds to glide and swoop down in search of prey.

At this distance they looked a little like pale eagles. Close in, they were more like half-feathered pterosaurs—some kind of failed and archaic evolutionary off-shoot locked into the hibernation cycles of the Archaeobiome. They'd followed the dust storms into the city, and couldn't have arrived at a better time. Better for them, that is.

The flying monstrosities were intellectually on par with sauerkraut, Miller'd noticed, and didn't seem to understand that flapping into low-flying helicopters was a quick way to get slashed to pieces by the rotors. Unfortunately, the beasts ranged from a twenty- to a sixty-foot wingspan and helicopters didn't survive the encounters any better than the titan-birds did.

Helicopters just like the one a block away waiting to whisk Gray out of this hell-hole the second they were done.

"Uh-huh. Yeah." Gray turned away from the food trucks doling out aid parcels, two per person able to carry them, and idly traced the toe of his shoe over stringy weeds struggling up through a crack in the sidewalk. "I don't suppose you've got the manpower to stop Major General Stockman and his division, do you, Huck?" A pause. "No. I'm not suggesting— no, no you can't possibly deploy a nuclear weapon on home soil, Huck, I know that."

That morning, Major General Stockman had reiterated his demand for Schaeffer-Yeager International to stand down and surrender all its staff and assets to the custody of the U.S. Army.

Gray had... declined.

His actual words may have invoked something along the lines of 'you motherfucking Infected traitors aren't getting a fucking dime out of me,' but so far as Miller knew the contents of that conversation hadn't been made public, and like a good bodyguard who'd eavesdropped on more than he'd intended to, Miller did his best to forget about it.

Stockman was coming, though. Even if he'd decried the president, Huckabee Fredericks, as a corporate stooge with no more authority over the American people than the Queen of England, there was no military to stop him.

What remained of the legitimate U.S. military was in tatters. Army divisions were running off into the wilderness with the food aid packages they were supposed to distribute to civilians. Starving soldiers were deserting in droves, large chunks of the Midwest were depopulating as food ran out.

Depopulating, Miller mused. What a sanitized term for starving to death and fleeing for their lives with everything they could carry.

After finishing with the President, in the few seconds he had before getting back onto camera, Gray stood scowling hard enough the wrinkles showed through the cosmetic treatments.

"Gray?"

"You think anybody around here needs the furniture in those?" He jerked his chin toward the ramshackle aid tents.

"Possibly. Why?"

"I said those bastards weren't getting anything of mine, and I damn well meant it." Gray wiped his sweating forehead with a handkerchief, and looked down at the pink smears of foundation he'd scraped off in dismay. "Damnit."

Sometimes, being the Armani had more in common with being a gun-toting butler than anyone's mental image of a bodyguard. Miller unfolded a compact he'd gotten off one of the camera people while they were fixing Gray up for his time in front of the lens, and stepped in to repair the damage.

"Thanks." Gray lifted his chin, shutting his eyes.

Miller gently moved his boss's chin to the side with

a fingertip, and concentrated on getting an even blend with the compact's brush—something he'd learned from life with Samantha. "Someone could probably use it. But they need food, if there's any to spare."

"I'm keeping you people fed, right?" Gray asked, grimacing again, hard enough Miller had to tell him to relax before carrying on.

Miller thought before answering. "Luxuries are a little thin on the ground," he said, diplomatically. "But we're eating enough to get through the day."

"Good. Getting supply trucks through the city for the aid program is difficult, but the civilians don't come before my employees. I'm not going to fail the company the way Huck failed this damned country."

Was it the President's fault that exotic crop pests had crawled out of the ground after hibernating for tens of thousands of years? Miller didn't think that 'waking up an all-consuming ancient ecology' had appeared anywhere on the government's climate change risk assessments when it came to famines, but he could have been wrong.

Of course the amount of canned food that Gray had pulled out of distribution warehouses and moved into the Astoria compound's stockpiles could put any survivalist—or town full of survivalist preppers—to shame. The compound's refugee population needed a forty-foot shipping container brought in every day for bottled water alone, let alone food. Keeping them fed was a labour of Hercules. Providing aid to the remaining population of New York? Impossible.

"Tell Holly to find someone to take the furnishings away. Hell, give these people the trucks if possible—I don't want *anything* left for Stockman's goons."

"I'll tell her. Now can we please get your PR campaign moving again before Stockman arrives and takes you into custody?"

It took Gray two takes to make his grim pronouncement on the state of the world. His acid suggestion that Stockman's forces would do more good by assisting in reclaiming parkland for World-War-II-style victory gardens turned into a perfect soundbite. Once upon a time, a PR coup like that would have mattered. But the public was too busy surviving to listen, these days.

Thankfully, PR wasn't the only way Gray was fighting Stockman's 11th Infantry Division. "We need to slow that division down," Gray said afterwards, leaning in against the window while the helicopter whisked him away from the mucky reality of the world. "Literally slow them down, catch their feet in molasses."

Miller, back in his combat gear, M27 across his knees, the touch of cologne he'd applied under his jaw little more than a fond memory. "We can do that," he said. "Not with molasses, but we can do that."

"Good. I'll tell Harris to make it happen."

8

"WE LOST ANOTHER *drone. Re-pathing what's left to provide coverage...*"

"Third one in an hour. The 11th finally attacking, Northwind?"

"*Negative, Cobalt-2. Engine failure.*"

Miller edged in closer to the window of the building, squinting up at the sky to search for the failed drone.

There was a yellowish tinge to the light—maybe the after-effects of the dust storm—but no sign of any drones plummeting down from the heavens. They'd lost one to bird-strike earlier, or titan-bird strike, but the drones typically flew too high to be seen, let alone be interfered with by the new wildlife. It had to be those fungal particles that the storm had kicked up. Helicopter pilots were spending more time picking strands of pinkish-red gunk out of their air intakes than flying.

Well, in the event that Cyclops-Northwind lost all their drones, Miller and his team had a decent overwatch position. They were two-thirds of the way up a mostly abandoned apartment block. Fungal masses in the basement necessitated the use of gas masks while they'd been securing the building.

The local residents, thin and emaciated, ran for it the second they'd seen the well-armed Cobalt-2 team in the hallways. Miller had yelled that they were there to help, but the fearful survivors hadn't believed him.

He didn't blame them, not with the city's only remaining television channels broadcasting Swift's ranting tirades and carefully cut footage of corporate atrocities. There simply wasn't enough functioning bandwidth in the city to spread the now official story—that while the government strongly condemned the actions of a few out-of-control subcontractors, it supported Schaeffer-Yeager's larger humanitarian mission. And that the attempt to take control of the city under martial law by Major General Stockman were the actions of a mutineer.

Stockman's mutineers, advancing up the avenue towards Biogen's Upper West Side Laboratory, weren't wearing eye-patches and hobbling around on peg-legs, the mental image of a mutineer in Miller's addled-by-Hollywood imagination. They were rolling in sand-coloured Bravo convoys and wearing forest-green camos—using vehicles built for Middle-Eastern wars but never deployed, and wearing uniforms only ever intended for peacetime.

When was the last time America sent her troops anywhere that *wasn't* a desert?

Cobalt-1—Lewis, Hsiung, Mannon, and Crewe—stood ready to meet them in black combat gear and with weapons slung over their shoulders. Behind them, taking cover behind sandbagged roadblocks and inside Biogen's UWS Laboratory, were all sixty men and women of security team Switchblade.

Not much to meet the leading edge of the five or six hundred soldiers making up the 11th Infantry Division's Third Battalion. Schaeffer-Yeager's forces made up—what—two or three platoons?

Lewis stepped out in front of them all, holding up his hands at Stockman's advancing convoy. Thankfully, the lead Bravo slowed to a halt instead of cruising straight over him.

Behind it, two more Bravos turned in, blocking the head of the avenue with their slab-like armoured frames. The lead vehicle halted out front, while the rest of the convoy took the intersection's right turn.

From the fourth floor window of the building they'd commandeered, Miller picked up his binoculars, and murmured, gently, "The 11th are throwing a cordon up between us and Central Park."

"*I hear you,*" Lewis rumbled. He was still audible over the open com-link as he yelled at the convoy, "We're here to talk!"

Two of the soldiers who'd gotten out of the lead convoy vehicle, a captain and lieutenant, judging by the stitched in insignia at their collars, moved forward in near-lockstep. Two more, and the driver—all enlisted men, by the looks of them—were barely two steps behind. "I'm here for your surrender and the peaceful handover of that building behind you," said the captain.

Lewis's face didn't waver. "That's something we're going to have to discuss."

"Awful well armed for a *discussion*," the captain said.

"Right to bear arms is in the constitution," Lewis shot back.

One of Stockman's enlisted men piped up with, "Constitution weren't writ for *niggers*."

Lewis's already dark skin darkened further with a flush of red. "The *hell* did you say to me?"

It had been awhile since Miller had been in the Army, but he didn't think any private he'd ever met would butt into his commanding officer's conversation like that, no matter how heartfelt the racism.

The captain and his lieutenant didn't seem particularly shocked, however. In fact the lieutenant, himself an African-American, was nodding in vague agreement, as if Private First Class Klansman over there was the division's official historian. "Constitution *was* written long before the abolition of slavery..." the lieutenant said.

"Long before slavery," PFC Klansman agreed.

Another private chipped in with, "We own them now. Ain't that what the Major General said?"

The captain followed it up with, "It's what the Major General said."

"Did you not hear what your man just *said?*" Lewis demanded of their lieutenant, gaping at them.

The lieutenant shrugged. "He didn't mean me."

"That's right. You're a nigger, and Lieutenant Phelps is white. On the inside." PFC Klansman smiled crookedly. "I can see under his skin? And he's a person inside. You? You black as a tar-pit."

"So's she," the captain of Stockman's convoy said, pointing at Hsuing, a purebred Han Chinese. "Fuck. Are. all the ungifted like this?" he asked, boggling at Mannon. "Are they all so *empty*?"

Mannon clutched her belt just beside her sidearm holster 'til her knuckles were white.

From up in the building, Miller muttered, "They really are Infected. All of them. The entire division."

Doyle, sitting at the empty apartment's dining room table with his new rifle set up on top, eye to the scope, grunted. "Not exactly full of esprit de corps, are they?"

"Chain of command's *gone*," Miller muttered, using the corner window to get a look at one of the side streets. "There are civilians mixed in with the Army types."

"Volunteer brigades?" du Trieux asked, looking up from the ruggedized tablet she was getting a feed from Northwind with.

"Don't think so." Miller handed her the binoculars as she got up.

Bands of roving Infected, some wearing filthy bloodstained clothes almost ready to rot from their bodies, with inky, bruise-like blotches eating into their skin, were gathering to meet the troops at the far end of the cordon. And where they did, there were embraces, as if they were civilian girlfriends welcoming their boyfriends home with a kiss.

A soldier handed his rifle to one of the local Infected, and they all crowded back into the Bravo together.

"Great." Morland grunted from beside Miller's shoulder. He hugged his weapon to his chest—a custom 3D-print-milled monstrosity of blocky metal and polymer wrapped around an assault rifle and integral shotgun. "Why couldn't we be in a horror movie instead of this shit, eh? Zombies don't run around sharing guns."

"They're sick. Not dead." Miller patted Morland's shoulder.

"So they get to be a terrifying horde *and* we get to feel terrible for shooting back?" Morland glared at him. "I don't think bloody *Tasers* are going to work against the fuckin' *Army*."

"It's not going to come to that," Miller said with more confidence than he felt. "This is peacefully resisting arrest."

"Like *fuck* it is. That might be what Harris said to the media, but we don't have escape routes planned because this is peaceful."

Miller had to shake his impulse towards idealism. It was such an attractive lie, though—that peacefully resisting Stockman's 11th Infantry would cause them to simply leave them alone. The reality wasn't nearly so cut and dry, however.

Out in the avenue, Lewis and the Infected command squad continued to yell at each other.

"This here is *private property!*" Lewis shouted.

Stockman's captain squared his jaw. "We will not let you criminals destroy the evidence of the illegal chemical weapons BioGen has been producing. We are taking control of this facility with immediate effect, and you and your men will stand down immediately!"

One by one, the lieutenant and the enlisted men stepped forward, striking the same posture, wearing the same glare.

Step by step, Lewis and the rest of Cobalt-1 backed away, down towards the roadblock. "We don't want a fight! We're private citizens!"

"Tar-black citizens," PFC Klansman howled after them, joined by his African-American lieutenant's cry of, "Empty-eyed terrorists!"

"Just give us time to call our superiors and ask what to do, okay?" Lewis held up his hands peacefully, backing up towards safety behind the roadblock. "Nobody has to get hurt, here!"

"*You* do, you fucks—" "—terrorists—" "—company stooges—"

The rest of the convoy fell over themselves to join in shouting obscenities against Cobalt-1—'ungifted,' 'empty terrorists,' 'soulless'—the captain, struggling to keep up with his men, was pulled helplessly into the zeitgeist of the moment.

Miller swallowed, his dread growing. It was like the Parasite dug deep and brought up every flimsy wedge mankind had ever used to divide 'us' from 'them,' encouraging twisted prejudice in any way it could. Was that biological? He wondered. The stinking old justification for looking on anyone different with fear and hatred?

Like hell this was ever about *peaceful resistance.* Stockman's 11th Division seemed intent on finding incontrovertible evidence of Schaeffer-Yeager's wrongdoing, supposedly bound up in that BioGen lab.

Thankfully, Miller knew every computer in the building had been remotely wiped and filled with garbage random-encrypted files by Northwind's operators overnight. The labs were cleaned up and all equipment had been shipped out to some corner of the Astoria compound.

This whole charade was about putting up enough resistance to make the Infected *really* want the damn place, to waste their time holding onto it before they figured out there wasn't anything *there*.

It took time for the convoy captain to get back to his Bravo and start talking on the radio. He yelled bullshit into his radio, which seemed to Miller like it was a lot more important to the rest of his command squad than it actually served. It was minutes before the captain could sheepishly extricate himself and wander back as if organizing his forces was some dumb thing only a social pariah would ever do.

Lewis was back on the communication's circuit almost instantly. "*Give me some good news about that cordon, Miller.*"

Miller gestured du Trieux over. "Trix?"

"They've blocked intersections a block further east on Duffield than we expected them to, so there's a little room to play with, but you're locked in tight."

"*You inside the cordon?*" Lewis asked, worried.

She double-checked the drone footage on the

tablet. "No, sir. We're closer than expected to where they're blocking you in, but outside the cordon."

"*Good. Now plainly we aren't going to need you, because in about an hour Mr. Matheson's going to call Stockman and give this place up in exchange for our freedom, but you stay frosty up there. You're our insurance policy.*"

"Yes, sir."

"And remember," Miller said, looking at du Trieux, Doyle, and Morland in turn—though Doyle didn't look up from his rifle's scope. "If it happens, suppressive fire only. Get them to stick their heads down while our guys muscle their way out in their Bravos. No one has to be killed, here; this is about wasting their time—not taking lives."

So far as pep talks went, he could have done better. But Doyle looked up, at last, with a sceptical twist to his eyebrow, and Morland calmed down, nodding just a little too quickly.

"Yeah," Morland said. "Just make them keep their heads down."

Doyle ducked his head back to the rifle scope, biting his lip.

So far as Miller knew, Doyle hadn't yet fired his new rifle in anger. The weapon was one of the first out of the engineering section set up in the Astoria Peninsula. The frame came out of the printer/milling rig in three pieces that fit together perfectly, after a little sandpapering, pinned together around the rifle's barrel and internals.

Doyle had been using traffic signs across the East

River to get the weapon zeroed, and by the time he was finished he could hit the dot over the 'i' in 'FDR Drive' at a distance of half a mile. That's where Doyle's training lay. Putting holes in heads, not keeping them down.

Miller lifted the binoculars, and sighted in on the section of the avenue where Lewis had confronted the Infected command squad. PFC Klansman was howling away at the top of his lungs, hardly aware that he was alone, the rest clustered around their Bravo and its radio.

Other troops had drifted closer, enough of them dismounted to start forming a sizeable mob. The captain's interest in the radio looked to be dwindling bit by bit.

A chill sensation in Miller's gut mingled with unpleasant foreboding.

"Doyle?" Miller asked, voice barely a whisper.

"Mmm?"

"See the screaming private out front? Left and low from the command Bravo?"

"At about eight o'clock? Angry fellow. What about him?"

Miller hesitated. It was just a feeling. You didn't *kill* people on feelings...

"Target moving," Doyle reported, voice flat. "He's returning to the Bravo—they're all getting angry now."

The mob's mood rapidly twisted. The hard blush of anger on Private Klansman's skin flooded across his fellow troops, skin darkening, some looking around, mystified, unsure of *what* they were so angry at but willing to scream all the same. They were like emotional dominoes, Miller noted, primed and ready to tip over with a strong suggestion and a heavy dose of the Parasite's signal pheromones flooding over them.

Some of his troops might not have known what they were angry about, but the captain, trying to talk his way through the situation with his superiors, seemed aware of what the problem was.

A few minutes later another two of Stockman's Bravos pulled up, disgorging their troops and rolling forward to form a mobile barricade in front of Switchblade's sandbags.

"*Merde*!" du Trieux yelped. "Stockman's bringing in tanks!"

Miller cycled channels on his earpiece until he heard Northwind and Lewis.

"*—ow many?*"

"*Four M1A4 Abrams.*"

"*Just a platoon?*" Lewis rasped.

"*I, er...*"

"*Four tanks is a platoon—that's all there is?*"

"*That's what's moving into Manhattan. There were another eight that haven't crossed the river yet.*"

That added up to a tank company, and if they were on the opposite side of the river, in New Jersey, that could only be to provide covering fire. Miller checked with du Trieux, but the Northwind operator hadn't bothered tracking the other eight with the dwindling number of drones.

"*Goddamn,*" Lewis muttered.

Goddamn was right.

Miller listened in while Lewis called Harris for instructions, but while he did, Stockman's forces continued to move. The other checkpoints in the cordon were relatively calm, just following orders, but the situation around the command squad was worsening by the second.

More of Stockman's soldiers arrived. They got out of their Bravos, dragging their rifles with them, and were almost immediately swallowed by a growing mob of infantrymen. Within seconds they were red-faced and ranting too, spitting insults down the avenue. The only surprise when the first gunshot came was that it took so long to brew.

A soldier huddling behind the cover of his Bravo simply stood up, sighted down the avenue, and fired. Switchblade were sandbagged down, but enough of them were peeking over the top to leave a target—two security man went down screaming, and those screams, as much as anything else, ignited the infantry mob's bloodlust.

Miller knew soldiers never reacted all that quickly. Orders took time to sink in. Troops gathered up in position before making their move, and time got wasted waiting for one jackass or another to understand what was going on.

And in every simulated firefight Miller had been through in training, the rule of thumb was to walk or crawl towards gunfire. You only ever ran to get *away* from it.

But the Infected *exploded* down the avenue, toward the sandbagged security troops, sprinting like a wave.

Bravos lurched forward, set to rolling as mobile barricades. Troops fired from around the corners as soldiers ran from the moving Bravo to the next in a chain of screaming hatred that shed infantry at every speck of cover that could be fired from.

No orderly bounding overwatch here. Every single one of those soldiers were psychopaths racing through fire like men possessed, heedless of whether they were being covered or not, heedless of whether they were being shot at.

But the Switchblade unit were professionals. Behind their sandbags they had the superior position, but the Infected had numbers and willpower and a shitload more coordination. By the time Switchblade were ranked up against the sandbags in orderly firing lines, shooting back with the snap and crackle of automatic gunfire, the Infected were hurling grenades and following their grenades over the sandbags within a heartbeat of detonation.

They were overrun so quickly Miller audibly gasped.

Assaults did not begin that goddamn fast. They *couldn't*. And for every member of the Infected who was wounded or killed, dozens more flooded in from every direction.

"*We need fire support!*" Lewis shouted over the radio. "*Where the hell's that goddamn attack helicopter now?*"

"*Air support's taking off.*" The Northwind operator's voice was hitched, unsteady. "*They'll be there soon. It'll be fine.*" She clearly didn't believe it.

"*Miller! Insurance policy, now! We're pulling out!*"

"Roger that, Cobalt-1." Miller lowered the binoculars on the scene of Switchblade members desperately dragging their wounded back towards the WSU Laboratory's underground parking lot. "Doyle."

The sniper rifle filled the apartment with noise. The window Doyle had been sighting through blew out—more from the sheer force of the muzzle-flash's blast, than the relatively tiny .388 bullet crashing through the glass. If not for his earbuds, and the partial protection of their noise filters, Miller would have been deafened for life.

Not the suppression fire Miller had ordered, but the situation was beyond that.

Miller grabbed his M27 and charged downstairs with Morland and du Trieux.

There was plenty of cover in the streets, abandoned vehicles at the sides of the road, fuel-burners—either out of gas, or leaking bloody strands of the fungus that was breaking down what little was left.

Miller set his M27 on its bipod beside one of the abandoned vehicle, and sawed through its entire magazine in near continual streams of fire towards the two army Bravos blocking off the intersection. The rounds blew dusty hunks of brick from walls and tore paint from the Bravo's armoured hide, puffs of smoke wherever the rounds hit. He wasn't aiming at anyone, wasn't trying to *kill*, merely make a noise, draw attention while du Trieux and Morland made their way quietly along the street, heads ducked, walking at a near crouch.

One of the Infected infantrymen popped up over the back of the Bravo—Miller reflexively twitched the M27's sights over his face, pulled the trigger. It was a *reflex*, like firing at the range, no thought about it until ice flooded his veins and he realized what he was doing.

The face was gone. Between the roaring of the M27 and the brief blinding of its muzzle-flash, the face had disappeared and Miller didn't know why, or how that had happened. There were greyish smears on the Bravo's plating where bullets had torn gouges through the paint, but Miller didn't know, couldn't know, what had happened—only that the face was gone, ducked out of the way, and Miller's hands were shaking.

He was currently wearing the near-black urban camouflage pattern Schaeffer-Yeager had provided the Cobalt teams, but he'd once worn that same uniform, that same helmet as the faceless soldier. He should have been calling for a medic, trying to see if a friendly was down—but there wasn't, was there? That infantryman had just ducked down. Everything was fine.

Nothing was fine—a rifleman was at the corner of a building barely sixty or seventy yards away. Miller pulled the M27 over in time to accidently pour the last of his drum magazine across the building's side as something crashed into his chest like a mule-kick delivered in steel-toed boots.

Dead? Was he dead now? That was his first thought, scrambling down, struggling to breathe, diaphragm spasming in panicked wheezes, wind knocked out of him. There was even something damp on his fingers when he patted himself down, but his fingers came away smudged with grey-green gel—the flexshell vest under his combat webbing had stopped the rifle round. Its multiple layers— carbon-fibre/KevWeb composite weave, interlinked microcells of shear-thickening non-Newtonian fluid which hardened under impact, another layer of composite weave treated with ballistic resins—had done their job. But Miller couldn't breathe right. Something hurt under all that, and it hurt a whole hell of a lot. As he numbly picked at the vest, he found two smashed pieces of metal that must have been fragments of the bullet, but saw no blood.

He had worse problems than breathing—rifle rounds punched through the car he was sheltering behind, shattering its windows and boring straight through its plastic body-panels. The only real protection was the engine and underlying steel frame, thickest up front to protect passengers in the event of a crash, and Miller huddled down in that tiny space, spitting up phlegm in alternation between desperate gasps and a miserable retching as he tried to force air back into his lungs.

But now that Miller was the target, that opened

things up for du Trieux and Morland—and from their angle, the infantrymen had no cover at all.

Miller looked over just in time to see du Trieux lean into her weapon, her teeth gritting as she fired in quick double-taps—*blam blam, blam blam, blam blam*—Morland following her lead.

Chased away from their fire, two of the Infected bounded in the opposite direction. Behind them a civilian in ragged clothes scuttled past a dead soldier on the sidewalk and made away with his rifle, cackling as she ran off.

Another shot from above—Doyle—armour-piercing rifle rounds tore straight through the thinly-armoured roof of one of the Bravos. From Miller's angle, he saw a grenadier collapse out of the vehicle's door, 30mm airburst grenade launcher clattering across the street.

The first black-armoured Bravo, one of Switchblade's, made its appearance in the distance, cruising out of the cordon. It was taking fire from all directions from the Infected infantry at the intersection, and those behind it. Something exploded to one side of the vehicle, sending it swaying side to side, but it stayed intact. The Bravos were designed to survive IEDs at close quarters, massive explosions below or to the vehicle's sides. The thin roof was the only real weak point.

A second Switchblade Bravo followed it, then a third. By that time Miller was sucking down enough oxygen to move from his initial position, emptying out a fresh drum magazine at anything that remotely *looked* like cover.

The lead Switchblade Bravo thumped into the infantry vehicles blocking the intersection and sent them screeching apart. There were dead bodies behind them; Miller spotted one missing a face.

His hands shook, but that didn't matter too much for pouring suppressive fire into cover. He just had to keep his hands clenched tight, keep those Infected soldiers pinned down in a recessed storefront.

There was a flash, another explosion—this one tore through the door of one of the S-Y Bravos. Smoke coiled away from the impact as the vehicle slowed, and Miller dimly made out du Trieux screaming at him. "Rocket!"

He followed her pointing finger, and unleashed hell on a window spilling the tell-tale smoke of a SMAW's rocket launch, smashing through it and the wall for a six feet in every direction. Over, under, side-to-side—Miller's M27's 5.56mm rounds were unlikely to make it through a brick wall, but with enough of them, bricks would crack and shatter.

A second black Bravo pulled up beside the one that'd been hit, then a Switchblade trooper got out and took up the job of filling the SMAW window with bullets.

Miller switched drum magazines and ran for the wounded Bravo with du Trieux. The door that'd been hit had a neatly blast-cut hole in it. When they got the doors on the opposite side open, the smell of burnt meat and scorched plastic was unbearable.

Morland went in first, appearing as if from nowhere, hauling a still smoking body from the cabin and pushing them into the open doors of the next Bravo to stop. Whether the victims were dead or alive, it was hard to tell. The vehicle's interior was a mess of smoke and occasional twitching flames, surprisingly small, but there wasn't much left to burn after the sheer heat of the warhead's directed blast. It had thrown a high-pressure jet of molten metal ahead of the flame, and cooled copper droplets were scattered like jewels over the blackened flesh of someone Miller dimly recognised as Mannon. The rest of Cobalt-1 were nowhere to be seen inside, just members of Switchblade Miller didn't recognise. Two were alive, able to get out and stumble into another Bravo by themselves.

Howling, nearby. Human, loud, a roaring under the gunfire—Miller dared look back the way the escape convoy had come, towards the avenue. Soldiers and civilians ran in a rushing tsunami after the convoy.

"Miller!" Again, du Trieux screamed at him, and he found his way to her. She'd stolen one of the army's two Bravos, the keys stripped off a faceless corpse beside it. "We have to get out of here!"

Miller lumbered closer, one step, another. Twisting his head, ducking down behind the Bravo's frame. Morland was already inside, hanging out of an open door and firing off to the left.

"Doyle?" Miller said. He turned around, shouted it, "Doyle! We're leaving!"

"Pick me up at the door, would you?"

He'd forgotten all about his earpiece. Miller

pointed at the entrance his team had poured out of, and yelled at du Trieux, "There, go!" as he got inside.

She gunned the engine, slowed. Miller threw open the doors, and Doyle came sprinting out, pushing his rifle in ahead of him before clambering into the back bench seats. Du Trieux simply gunned the engine, momentum slamming the doors shut, and joined the escape convoy's tail.

Behind them, the signature boom of a tank cannon, and the wrenching, drawn-out smash of an exploding shell turning a building to rubble. Miller twisted around and spotted rising smoke far behind the mob chasing them. Rifle rounds splattered off the Bravo's hull behind him.

"The hell was that?" he asked, tapping over to Lewis's circuit on the earpiece.

"*Tank.*"

"Shooting at *what*, Lewis?"

Lewis sucked down a very audible breath. "*At us. Not all of us got out, son.*"

GETTING ACROSS THE East River was dicey. Stockman had just as many drones in the air as Northwind did, and Stockman's were armed. Every instant spent in sunlight on the bridge was an eternity, waiting for a hammer to fall on the convoy. But no hammer came.

The walls of the Astoria compound were a welcome sight, towering twenty feet above street level, higher where buildings had been integrated

EXTINCTION BIOME: INVASION

into its length. Windows were sealed off with sheet metal and search lights and cameras hung from every corner. A pair of heavy infantry, in exoskeletal harnesses, waved the Bravos through the armoured gate, clutching full sized machine guns in their fists.

Heavies would have been useful for dealing with the army cordon, but with hydrogen for fuel cells reserved for use in the Bravos, their exoskeletons were tied down to lithium-ion batteries and the compound's generators. After the empty streets of the city, lifeless without electricity, watching the flash of arc-welders being used to add a fresh strip of steel cladding to the top of the compound walls was an almost religious experience. This was home, where lights came on and electrical fire burned on the borders. Fungicides had stained some of the brickwork a harsh yellow-grey, but the sickly colour was preferable to the pink and scarlet fungus eating away at the city.

Fresh troops, members of Bayonet, surged out into the surrounding streets, taking up defensive positions both inside and outside of the compound wall. Miller took twenty minutes to himself and had the rare opportunity to clear his mind.

The gym inside the compound had been a luxurious place, once, but its machinery was breaking down under heavy use from the security teams and engineers. About all that reliably worked until the Boltman guys went on one of their fix-it crusades were the weights. The plumbing, on the other hand, worked just fine.

Before getting into his shower stall, Miller set out a dry hand towel and his cologne beside the washbasin with his straight-edge razor, and set the water running while he peeled off his gear and armour.

The bruise on his ribcage looked so bad that, for a moment, he thought the rifle round had made it through his flexshell vest. It was livid pink, a bloody colour. With some tender prodding at the ribs nearby, and a few careful deep breaths and coughs, he was convinced he hadn't broken anything. Just a bruise, and under the hot water, it hurt like hell before starting to ease.

He'd had worse.

No, that was a lie to bolster his self-esteem. In the army he'd been shot *at*—live fire training exercises, gunfire whizzing overhead—and he'd been in the vicinity of hostile gunfire in his time as a bodyguard, but he'd never been *shot*. Never had anyone specifically trying to kill *him*.

His strength fled him, and he clutched the shower cubicle's walls until he was steady on his own feet.

He saw that soldier's face, rising up from behind the enemy Bravo, and saw it vanish behind the muzzle-flash of his M27. He relived pouring fire into the window that SMAW had been launched from— for all Miller knew the walls were thin, the rounds had gone straight through. Then there was the faceless corpse du Trieux had stolen the keys from.

He'd worn that uniform. That same fucking uniform.

At last he punched off the shower's spray, wrapped himself up, set himself in front of the mirror, and picked up his razor.

He unfolded it, held it to his throat, thought better of it, and put the razor back down.

First no dry cleaners, now no barbers.

He ran the hot water faucet until it steamed, then doused the hand towel. It hurt to pick up, but Miller diligently did just that, spotting it with dabs of his cologne—the best substitute he had to hand for a barber's essential oils—before smothering his face in aromatic heat.

There were few pleasures in the world like a hot towel shave, and few so simple.

Rubbing the towel into his bristles, breathing in scented steam, Miller shut his eyes and did his best to forget, distracting himself with pleasant thoughts of ex-lovers he'd taught to do this, and the one he'd learned it from. He replayed a vivid memory of trying it on a laughing Samantha's legs, since she didn't have a beard.

He rubbed away tears, spat the sour taste in his mouth away when the image of that missing face came back to him, and went about carefully applying, then scraping off dabs of shaving gel with his straight-edge razor.

Feeling clean, aching, but purified, there was nothing he wanted more than to pull on his comfortable old suit and see if he could find the cufflinks Billy had given him, but it was all packed away, and Stockman's forces were on their way.

Fresh underclothes and a soft T-shirt to wear under his combat gear would have to do.

He emerged into the light of the end of days; not a new man, but at least a bruised and refreshed one.

SCREAMING SHAPES KNIFED through the air overhead, smaller titan-birds chasing down prey. A fresh coat of stinking fungicide had been laid down 4th Street, seeping into the asphalt and repelling the usual crowds of civilians looking for somewhere quiet to go.

Not that they'd find any.

The steady growl of generators was pouring in all the way from 1st Street. Miller hefted up his M27, and slipped his earpiece back in.

"Cobalt-2 Actual back on duty."

"*Join us at barricade six, son,*" Lewis said.

Miller made his way past piled car bodies that the Boltman engineers had stacked up for spare sheet metal, down an alleyway criss-crossed with old piping and new camera mounts, the shady space burned white in LED cones.

A kid chasing her ball stopped dead at the sight of Miller, and backed up against the wall as he passed. Her face was pale, almost unreadable as she hugged the ball to herself, running off the moment he'd gone by.

Before he was quite out of earshot, he heard her laugh. A child laughing, running along, being a kid.

In the middle of all this, with the internet and all its amusements effectively dead.

It felt good to hear something normal. Was this the new normal?

Some time soon the day would come when the children in this compound wouldn't remember anything different. Babies were born, children would grow up inside these walls. Miller wondered how many generations would be here, maintaining a twisted status quo, not recollecting how life outside had once been.

As it existed now, there were four refugee sectors pushed up against the inside of the compound's barrier wall, sprawling across streets cut in half by the wall, filling the buildings that had been incorporated into its structure. Shantytowns separated out from each other by chain-link fences with privacy strips woven into the wiring, to help contain any assaults that got over or through the wall—not that anybody had told the refugees that.

They weren't starving, but most of them had been, and the threat of famine was starting to loom large again. Trucks had stopped entering the compound that day, and in response, the warehouses of canned and preserved food had been broken open. Miller eyed the dwindling supplies inside one warehouse as he walked across the compound. It was shocking to see how much of a dent thousands of civilians had made in the stockpiles in just a few hours. It wouldn't last much longer at the rate they were going.

* * *

BARRICADE SIX WAS a spar of the compound wall that ran diagonally across 26th Avenue, jutting out an extra block to incorporate a string of row houses into the wall, their windows all welded over with steel plate scavenged from cars. Mounting pivots and armoured shields for heavy machine guns stood empty every six feet or so on the top, like a castle's battlements. Completing the medieval image, a rope ladder had been thrown over the top. A couple of workers below set up anti-personnel mines and IR trigger sensors in the streets outside.

Lewis and what was left of Cobalt-1, including a miserable-looking Hsiung sporting a glossy burn treatment bandage around her upper arm, were set up in a hole in one of the row-house rooves, a ladder leading down into an abandoned bedroom that had become a local command post.

The pungent aroma of mildew suffused the dark space, but Lewis didn't look too concerned about it, using a couple of screens set up on old bookshelves.

"Shouldn't we be under attack by now?" Miller asked. "Where's the rest of Stockman's convoy?"

"We ran into some luck. Here, look at this." Lewis made space for Miller at the screens.

Drone overflight footage showed M1A4 Abrams tanks with a crowd of angry-looking Infected beating on it. For a moment Miller thought the tank was under attack, but the crew were doing it too, flinging open engine hatches.

Abrams tanks had gas turbine engines. Not all that dissimilar to an aircraft's jet turbine. At the end of the day, the tanks were suffering the same way S-Y's drones had been. A couple of spores had gotten through the air filters, and now the Infected were tearing yard-long strips of soggy fungus out of the M1A4's engines. Miller didn't know how, or why, but the Archaeobiome's shroud fungus was capable of growing inches every hour on fuel oils and lubricants. Anything that wasn't electrically driven was at risk of getting gummed up, especially turbine engines that sucked down gallons of spore-laced air.

"Hmm," Miller mused.

Lewis nodded.

Miller looked back over at the refugee shanties and then across the wall as he grunted.

He sure as hell didn't *feel* lucky.

HOURS LATER, AFTER Miller had gathered up Cobalt-2 and spread his people out atop the barricade section, scattered reports came in of Infected civilians wandering through the area. But there wasn't a clear line between civilians and the military among the Infected. The 'civilians' started scattered firefights, the kind of unenthusiastic slow back and forth play of gunfire that kept everyone in cover that Miller had envisaged earlier, with few casualties but plenty of scares.

Lewis figured they were performing reconnaissance by fire for the military—shoot at shit until shit shoots back so you know what you're dealing with. They'd melt away the second one of the heavy machine guns mounted on top of the compound wall opened up.

Any attempt by S-Y's security teams to push out into the city were thwarted every time by the appearance of military assault teams, guided in by Infected civilians keeping watch. Occasional organized assaults fell back; the compound wall was too big, and too well defended, for them to hit without their heavy vehicles.

The stalemate went on into the night, but things slowed down. The company had enough night vision gear to equip every member of the security teams, and the Infected only had enough for the military. It looked like the Infected knew they wouldn't get anywhere under cover of darkness.

At eleven p.m., watchtower two exploded. Flames belched out of its base as the jury-rigged construction tipped over, only for another explosion to strike the ground directly beside it, gouging open the compound wall, a third, a fourth—six blasts in all, artillery shells, fucking *big* ones.

Miller and Morland couldn't leave their positions, bracing themselves against what felt like imminent attack, but they didn't need to. Major General Stockman's voice roared across the entire Astoria Peninsula, unnaturally warped by loudhailer systems that had to be only blocks away.

"That was a warning! You have twenty-four hours to surrender your illegal fortifications to us or I swear to God I'll tear it off the face of the earth with

my artillery. Any civilians who choose to remain under your protection at that time will be killed with the rest of you fucking animals!"

Morland cursed under his breath.

Miller shifted from his position and tried to conjure up his thoughts on Stockman's threat, but he felt nothing.

He rubbed the smoothness on his chin and closed his eyes and tried to imagine an end to this stalemate that didn't involve everyone inside the compound or outside the walls dead and faceless.

But no solutions came to mind.

9

"He can't be serious," Hsiung said, clutching at her hair. "There's fifteen *thousand* civilians in here with us."

"I don't think Stockman cares." Du Trieux's face was smudged in grey, something between mourning ashes and urban camouflage. She hadn't gotten any more sleep than Miller had—God alone knew when they'd get any, it was going on one a.m. and the day had no end in sight.

Cobalt's new break room seemed empty, compared to a few days before. The half-and-half coffee brew was so bad Miller skipped it, leaving it to Doyle and Morland. He left and joined Lewis in the attached briefing room, along with Jennifer Barrett and Robert Harris.

"Good, you're here," Barrett said, looking up at Miller as he came in.

Harris sat literally twiddling his thumbs, staring at his interlinked hands and fumbling one thumb over the other. "Don't see why I need to be here."

Barrett glared at him. "We still have procedures to follow, Bob. Security's still your purview."

"I already signed off on this," he muttered.

"Operation Wild Tarpan," Barrett said to Miller. "Lewis tells me you're the man to take it."

Miller straightened up, as if his career mattered anymore. "Yes, ma'am."

"You're taking Hsiung, too," Lewis interjected, hunching down over the table. "Mannon's dead, Crewe's in the hospital. I'm not pulling Cobalt-2 apart just so I have something to command."

"Hsiung's not going to like that."

Lewis shook his head, grinding his teeth. "You need the manpower if you're going to pull off this black ops shit."

Miller raised his eyebrows by way of answering.

"Operation Wild Tarpan is a carefully thought through response to Stockman's threats, not 'black ops shit,'" Barrett replied, snippishly.

Lewis turned tired eyes on her, and shrugged. "Whatever you say, ma'am."

"Stockman's made threats against us," she pressed. "With the correct reprisals we can prevent him from enacting them."

"He's going to blow us to shreds," Miller said. "I don't see a whole lot we can achieve with *reprisals*."

"We think he's playing for time as much as we are." Harris had switched over to toying with a loose pen. "Other than Bravos, every piece of heavy equipment available to him runs on hydrocarbon fuels. It's all bogged down with fungus."

"Until he develops a solution for the fungus problem," Barrett said, "and we don't think he can, his forces are spread out." She slid a file, a hard-copy paper in a cardboard cover, across the table to Miller. "That vulnerability is ameliorated by their communications network. Operation Wild Tarpan will deploy covertly into the city, dressed as refugees. The goal is to eliminate the electronic warfare and communications unit at the forward operating base the 11th Division's established in Harlem. You will complete the attack before ten a.m. today."

Miller checked his watch. It was barely two in the morning. He picked up the file and folded down the cover while he listened. The orders were handwritten— printers must have been in short supply.

"Without their local communications structure," Barrett continued, "not only will their dispersed forces be at a disadvantage, they will be cut off from local air defence radar stations. In conjunction with a projected drop in fungal particulate counts at altitude, the meteorological team's predicting a two-hour window for us to hit Stockman's artillery with our air assets."

Miller blinked at her. "What are we attacking them *with*? You might have StratDevCo's attack choppers, but Cobalt doesn't have any heavy gear, or explosives. The heaviest guns we *have* are fifty-cal machine guns."

Lewis folded one fist over the other. "I've been talking with StratDevCo's research and test service, they have the hardware we'll need."

"When did the Rats get to New York?" Miller frowned. StratDevCo's research and test service were nominally a field evaluations group. They assisted militaries around the world developing military gear. In reality, that meant a couple of platoons' worth of ex-soldiers and engineers with access to prototype weapons.

To Miller's thinking, this was good news.

"They're not here, yet. They're in Boston, fixing up an abandoned car ferry for their heavy cargo. But a few of them are coming in on pilot boats shortly before daybreak." Lewis gnawed on his lip. "They'll be bringing in an EMP device. That should take out the FOB's electronics, no problem."

"EMP weapons and running around dressed like civilians?" Miller muttered under his breath, paging through the file. "We're acting like terrorists."

"One man's terrorist is another man's guerrilla, Mr. Miller." Barrett's lips flattened to a thin line. "Asymmetric warfare is never entirely above-board."

Miller and Lewis shared a glance. 'Asymmetric warfare'? Black ops shit.

SO FAR AS private conversations went, Hsiung's 'just one word, please?' with Lewis wasn't private at all.

"But why aren't *you* in command? You run Cobalt!"

Lewis replied, voice too low to make out from the opposite end of the breakroom, causing Hsiung to explode with, "But *I* could run it for you!"

Miller very deliberately kept his eyes on his work, sticking trays of 5.56 ammunition into the loader, then using the loader, a box of plastic and springs and gears, to force them into his drum magazines, ten rounds with each pull of the loader's lever.

"So we're insurgents, now?" Morland asked, quietly.

Du Trieux, following Miller's lead, finished topping up one of her pistol magazines. "Not exactly."

Morland stared at Doyle. Doyle didn't rise to take the bait, even when du Trieux looked up at him, then Miller. They all knew who'd be on the trigger, if it came down to assassinating Stockman.

Doyle seemed entirely unconcerned. Part of his rifle's innards lay disassembled on the table, and he calmly applied a silicone lubricant that didn't provide a fungal growth medium.

He must still have a drug supply, Miller thought with a brief stab of envy. Doyle kept his addiction under control, even if he'd been expelled from his military career because of it. He'd never been anything but sober on duty.

Off duty? Entirely different story.

Whether it was drugs, a stern mind-set, or some kind of archaic upper-crust English thing about viewing everyone else as subhuman animals, on the surface Doyle didn't seem remotely concerned over killing.

If it was the drugs, Miller was going to corner Doyle and demand a share of his own.

"But—"

"But *nothing*, Hsiung. You're working with Miller—this one-sided grudge isn't relevant. You put it aside, understand?"

Hsiung shot Miller a razor-edged glare, biting her lip as she sucked down breath. "Fine," she hissed at Lewis. "I'm putting it aside."

Lewis nodded once, sharply. "Good. That's the end of it. Miller! Your team ready to move?"

He leaned back, grimacing. "It ain't even *three in the morning*."

"This isn't a football game—no time-outs. You ready?"

"The StratDevCo Rats said their boat's getting in at five with the device, then it's taking us over to Manhattan. Unless you think we can swim across the river, we're cooling our heels until it gets here."

"And here I thought you were some kind of bad-ass spec-ops ninja. Hurry it up, Miller, the second that boat's here, I want you across the river."

Miller nodded sharply. "Yes, sir. Understood."

Smirking as he shook his head, Lewis turned and left the room, leaving Hsiung standing by herself with a sour expression.

After a few more moments' sulking, she marched over and slumped down into a free chair, arms folded. "I should be doing your job," she announced.

Warily, Miller looked up. He felt the rest of the team's eyes on him.

Hsiung continued to glare.

"Okay," he answered her.

"*Okay?*" she hissed.

Du Trieux cleared her throat. "What's your problem with him, anyway?"

Hsiung shook her head as if the answer was obvious. "You don't *know*?"

"You want my job, fine, whatever," Miller said. "Career goals, I get it. But do you think I'm incompetent?"

Her eyes turned acid. The obvious response, the one he'd steeled himself against—that he *was* incompetent—didn't arrive. Instead she grit her teeth, and snapped, "You didn't earn it."

"How you figure that?"

"You walked into close protection for Gray with your pretty-boy face, then you took Cobalt-2. It all got fucking *handed* to you. Some of us"—she stabbed a finger into her chest—"put in the work and got *fuck-all*, because of you. That's my problem with you."

Doyle grinned. "You think he has a pretty face?"

Hsiung shook her head with a sneer.

Miller blinked, dumbfounded. "I... I'm sorry."

She was right. He *had* been handed things. Lewis seemed to have a soft spot for him, and after Miller had gotten along so well with Gray's children, it was hard not to have opportunities fall into his lap.

And here he was, underqualified and overpromoted into running an operation he'd never been trained for. Of course, neither had she. None of Cobalt were drawn from special forces. Hsiung's pedigree was strictly in private security and training. The closest the team had to black ops specialists were Doyle, with his ended-before-it-began military career, and du Trieux's adventures in liberating the Middle East.

Miller looked back at Hsiung as she angrily shuffled her arms across her chest, guilt gnawing at him. "Hsiung?" he said.

"*What?*"

"Thanks for helping us out. We could use someone like you on Cobalt-2."

There wasn't much less hate in her gaze, but the fire cooled, a little. She raised an eyebrow. "Flattery? Really? You think I can be swayed that easily?"

Miller shrugged. "It was worth a shot."

Hsiung rolled her eyes.

Sensing the worst had passed, Miller pushed the loader, empty drum magazines, and boxed ammunition across the table. "Here. Go ahead and do my job. Frees me up to get thirty minutes' shut-eye."

The table was silent, bar Doyle's amused snort.

"Oh, and don't forget to go down to quarantine processing to pick up our refugee clothes," Miller added, standing and stretching. "I got a few of the staffers to delouse a couple of boxes for us."

He felt the weight of Hsiung's glare as he drifted out of the room. After a moment, he heard her softly chuckle.

At least it was a start towards cooperation, Miller told himself. Before the famines, she'd have slugged him for pulling that.

10

"Peaceful, almost," du Trieux said from the railing.

Miller wanted to agree with her, but the boat crossing the East River felt more vulnerable than anything else. The sun wasn't quite up yet, but the eastern horizon was painted in blood and gold, a smattering of silver in the clouds. He thought he'd seen something churning around in the water under the Astoria compound's docks, like an oversized eel, and he wondered what the Archaeobiome had in store by way of marine life. The thought wasn't doing him any good. Neither was worrying about drones spotting the boat, alone on the water.

The pilot boat wasn't particularly big, a little like a converted tugboat, but it was more than big enough for a dozen crates of the Rats' gear, shipped down the coast from Boston. The captain had been happy to move Cobalt across the river before making the return trip home. It turned out that through a byzantine tangle of financial alliances,

Schaeffer-Yeager owned a controlling stake in the port authority he worked for. Not that he knew who Cobalt were, or what they were up to. With their guns wrapped up in rags, the EMP parts hidden in backpacks and satchels slung over their shoulders, and wearing the stinking clothes that had been stripped off refugees during quarantine, for all the captain knew they were just another group of refugees heading out to look for their families.

ONCE THE NEW Cobalt-2 team—Miller, du Trieux, Morland, Doyle, and Hsiung—had disembarked back onto land, Miller eyed the NYC skyline. It lacked the character of pre-dawn Manhattan, and wasn't at all what he remembered.

The new wildlife had settled in and taken ownership. The city's towers and skyscrapers shaded the streets to night black at this hour, a dark forest compared to the relatively open skies of Queens bordering the Astoria compound.

They hiked further into the city, huddling under high apartment blocks. The city's natural sounds— the blares of impatient taxi cab horns, the roar of constant foot traffic on the sidewalks—were missing everywhere they went, replaced by distant animal cries and the hiss of the wind.

It was like a wasteland.

With Morland and du Trieux on point, scouting corners before the others reached them, Hsiung and Doyle followed Miller, who checked every angle around him and covered the two in front with his M27. Miller's immediate concern wasn't military ambush, but being hunted by New York's wildlife.

Much of it had migrated into the city after the dust storm. Big animals, some Miller recognised and some he didn't. They'd scavenged on the dead left behind the storm, pacing along a few days behind its trailing edge, growing to monstrous size. They'd found safe haven within the city. And food. It didn't matter how many people the city had bled from famine, how many had fled Manhattan, there were always more hiding on some stockpiles of food, crowding the safer parts of the Bronx or Brooklyn, staying put and waiting in hopes that the aid trucks would come through. At night, anyone alone tended to wind up prey for the ancient predators trying their luck in the streets.

Biologists with any understanding of the Archaeobiome were in short supply, or at least outside of Miller's easy reach, but he knew enough to get the others to shine flashlights down alleys they approached, to keep weapons ready, if held low and close to the body to make sure that they weren't obviously armed at a glance.

They found a pile of discarded bones, probably human, around a cracked storm drain. They left it alone, though there was the temptation to roll a grenade—a gift for the rats-things—into the dark gap.

Central Park was a no-go area altogether, both to avoid military spotters and because of the shroud fungus steadily colonizing it. Wildlife in the park was doubtful. The stench of the fungus and its suffocating spores were obvious from three blocks away.

They needed to head north, into Harlem, but Lexington and Third Avenue were no good. Infected military patrols were taking the avenues south.

Near Park Avenue, du Trieux signalled she'd spotted a patrol, and they bunched up on the next corner.

Doyle tugged two pins from his rifle's frame, causing the whole blocky thing to fold near in half before he tucked it under his armpit.

They ducked their heads and shuffled across the road in single file, like the meek refugees they obviously were. The moment they were across the street, Miller swallowed the lump in his throat and pulled the rag-wrapped M27 up from beside his leg, ducking into a niche beside an abandoned news stand.

The team fell silent as the patrol Bravo hissed past, pressing themselves in against the walls, waiting... waiting.

But they'd faded into the background of the city. They were just civilians, at a glance.

Not that Miller wanted to risk more than a glance's exposure. Once certain the Bravo had no plans to double back, they continued on their way to the designated EMP detonation location, following the GPS Hsiung had tucked in her sleeve.

After thirty more minutes of fence-hopping and alley-shuffling, they arrived at a towering building near the outskirts of Marcus Garvey Park.

Breaking in was easy. Windows everywhere were smashed, and the smell of burnt bird shit was overpowering. Titan-birds were clearly using the building as a nest. They'd broken into rooms on the upper floors, and pale streaks of their droppings marred the facade. But someone, the military maybe, had made an attempt to burn the birds out with a flamethrower or something. The ash still smouldered in places, and the higher they climbed the building's stairwells, the more obvious the damage was. The army had cleared the upper floors with some kind of explosive shell. Metal splinters had chewed the walls to shreds.

As they neared the roof, du Trieux and Doyle held up their hands, signalling for silence.

Halting, Miller could dimly hear the creak of shoe-leather ahead.

It was too much to hope that the building was empty, but there weren't that many places that offered total overwatch of the park. It was natural that the military would have moved in first, after evicting the wildlife.

Silently, Doyle pulled a knife from within his ragged clothes, and du Trieux followed suit. Miller held a finger to his lips, and gestured Hsiung and Morland into covering positions. He slung his M27 over his back, and very cautiously unsheathed the combat knife he'd picked up from inventory.

He'd expected to use it for opening cans.

Du Trieux edged along the corridor and up against a doorframe, her knife gripped ice-pick fashion in her right hand, pistol in her left. Doyle was beside her, his rifle left leaning against the wall while he cautiously passed his slender dagger from hand to hand, thumb lightly against the flat of the blade.

Christ.

It was all moving too fast. Miller hadn't ever *killed* anyone, not like this. On the previous day, that had... that had been an *accident*. He couldn't picture attacking someone with a knife, slitting their throat—

He didn't have to picture it, in the end.

A soldier passed within striking distance of the door, along with two of his friends. The one closest shouted, "Hey!" and raised his rifle.

Not hesitating, du Trieux pushed the barrel aside with her handgun and stabbed him twice through the face. Once in the cheek, then again in the eye.

The soldier beside him probably never knew Doyle was there.

Pushing at the back of his head, Doyle glided the tip of that knife up the back of his neck and *in* before savagely twisting it left and right.

The third solider rounded the bend with wide eyes and ran smack into Miller.

Raising his knife, Miller slashed the air across and to the left, hoping to make contact with the soldier's throat, but he miscalculated the distance by millimetres, grazing the flesh and leaving a thin scratch.

The soldier grasped at Miller's hands, grabbing the hilt of the blade. The two of them struggled, fighting for control of the weapon and sliding deeper into the hallway, toward Hsiung and Morland.

Wrenching his wrists, Miller aimed the blade outward, at the soldier's soft underside to his chin, only to have his balance shift as the solider shifted his weight, and he lost the advantage.

The tip of the knife poked at Miller's cheek, drawing blood. He could smell the stench of the soldier's breath as he gritted his teeth and dug deep for added leverage.

There was a shot, and the pressure released.

The soldier's body flew back, then collapsed.

Miller, propped up only by the wall of the hallway behind him, gasped for a breath and looked behind him for an explanation.

Hsiung holstered her sidearm and frowned.

Doyle swore. "If they didn't know we were here before, they do now."

Morland stepped past them all and entered the room, flinging his satchel off his shoulder, and removing part of the EMP from the sack. "Better make this quick, then."

Still in shock, Miller eyed the bloody carnage surrounding them.

The soldiers took longer to die than he ever would have expected, gurgling where they'd dropped, shuddering. Du Trieux's victim spasmed against the floor while she pulled her knife free with a grunt and crunch of bone.

Doyle wiped the blood from his blade on his victim's pant leg.

Lying in front of him, the soldier who had fought Miller had a blast hole the side of a fist out one side of his skull.

Miller looked lamely at the knife in his hand. He pushed the back of his wrist against his mouth, forcing down another breath, and pointed at the bodies. "Get them away from the door," he managed to say.

Doyle looked up from his post-mortem examination of a flourishing rash on one of the dead men, a lurid, flaking yellow, and nodded. "Here. Hsiung, get the legs, would you?"

While the rest of his team moved the bodies, Miller knelt down and helped Morland unpack the device. The EMP weapon came in three parts: the antenna, the wave-guide, and the explosively pumped flux compression generator.

The antenna was a plastic-covered brick that plugged into the rest of the system with inch-thick cables. The waveguide needed to be set up around it, like a satellite dish, and set up on a tripod. Miller edged up to the nearest window, and glanced out at Marcus Garvey Park.

On the drone images, the Infected base hadn't seemed so *busy*, but upon further inspection, the place teemed with activity.

The park was the highest natural point in Manhattan, though some of the buildings around it were far taller than the central rocky hill. A baseball field beneath the hill had sprouted dozens of command tents. An outdoor pool had two or three hydrogen-crackers set up and pulling the pool water through their reactors to produce fuel for the Bravos lined up nearby. Two-man tents were strung up among the fungus-blighted remnants of trees, and rows of antenna-covered trailers occupied the summit of the hill, crowded together on the stone-tiled plaza.

Those were the key target, the electronic warfare and communications unit. There was a watchtower up there, too—something antique, an original part of the park—and it hosted a pair of snipers.

The military encampment had spilled out onto the surrounding streets, a pair of tanks waiting for repair while another was in the process of disassembly by a work-crew of Infected soldiers and civilians caught up in the ride. In truth, they seemed to be doing more to destroy the vehicle than repair it, frantically picking it apart piece by piece.

Bringing up his binoculars, Miller swept the park, searching for officers. Some were difficult to pick out of the groups wandering the FOB, but others were surrounded by guards. It looked like some of them were forcing their fellow soldiers away, using their guards to keep an area around them clear for thirty or forty feet. Those were easy to spot once Miller saw the pattern, like bubbles on top of boiling water, clear circles in the chaos.

Were they trying to retain their individuality amongst the mob? Keep from being overwhelmed the way that captain had fallen under PFC Klansman's influence the previous day? Miller couldn't be sure, but made note of it.

Putting down the binoculars, he angled the EMP device's waveguide to focus the beam's spread across the FOB, and centred it on the trailers. The final piece of the puzzle was the flux compression generator, the part of the device that made it a *bomb*. And a powerful one.

Miller wasn't entirely sure he understood how it worked. He'd only had a very brief introduction from the Rats who'd handed it to him. The flux generator's core was made up of coiled wire wrapped around explosives. By charging them with capacitors, the blast forced the coil apart, boosting the electric charge so high it dwarfed lightning strikes, and all that power was forced through the device's antenna. That, with the wave-guide, formed a focussed beam that would burn all electronics to slag, even military hardened gear.

Miller turned the mechanical timer's wheels to set it for ten minutes, and pulled the arming pin out of the generator. He'd asked how safe the device was, and had been told it was perfectly safe. The weapon couldn't hurt you. Unless you were anywhere physically near the thing when it blew itself apart.

"Doyle, you ready with the mines?" Miller called out the door.

"Nearly."

"Good. We're live," Miller announced. He twisted the last arming key on the antenna block, and ran through the checklist one last time as the clockwork timer's wheels rolled. "Ten minutes and counting. No need to rush this. We leave nice and orderly."

Hsiung gave the device a worried glance. "Which exit path do you want?" she asked, holding up her phablet and its latest download from Northwind.

Miller checked it, high-stepping over the puddles where the three they'd killed had fallen. "Second option. South out. Go the way we came a few blocks, then break east for the river. Unless there's something I'm not seeing."

Hsiung followed, flicking through views, muttering to herself while Morland and Doyle set up an infra-red sensor for their claymores in the corridor and stairwell.

"Trix?" Miller yelled.

She joined him in the corridor, a military radio—evidently stripped from one of the corpses—dangling from her hip. The earpiece cable was wrapped through her belt. She had it cupped to her ear, shaking her head. "Listen to this," she said, holding the earpiece out.

Miller took it, and came up against a wall of noise. At first he thought the system was jammed, too many channels lain over each other. This wasn't the mob's synchronized moaning chorus. These were conversations, words clear in the mess. But Miller could barely pick out individual voices.

"—*the mess tent's shut up again*—" "—*can't make an omelette without breaking a few eggs*—"

Nothing coherent. He couldn't tell who was responding to what. He was never all that good at eavesdropping in public, focussing on one conversation out of a dozen. He could just about listen to a friend over a table in a busy restaurant, but this… This wasn't just bad radio discipline, this was *impossible*.

Then, out of the noise he heard a trooper mention patrols near Marcus Garvey Park. Miller shook his head. "Fuck," he muttered.

Du Trieux's eyes narrowed. "Time to go."

The team followed Miller down the stairwell. They paused for just a minute near the bottom floor, waiting for Doyle and Morland to finish pasting another IR sensor to the wall and wiring it to a set of claymore mines they wedged into the stairwell corners. They were leaving the device alone for just a few minutes, but Miller wasn't taking chances.

Heads down, weapons low and camouflaged against their bodies, they shuffled around a corner a block up and ran directly into a band of troopers.

There were three soldiers in all: one in the driver's seat of the Bravo, twisted in his chair, talking to someone behind him, the third perched on the side of the vehicle, ripped fungus spores out of the fuel line.

Just as the driver's eyes squinted in confusion at the sight of them, the one at the fuel line shouted, "What were you doing in—?"

Then the twelfth floor windows blew out behind them.

In a flash Miller and the rest ducked down an alleyway, sprinting from the echoing shots as the troops' bullets popped from behind them.

No time for delay. The last thing they needed was a firefight in the heart of Infected territory.

Racing down another alley, and cutting across the street at breakneck speed, the group stopped short at an abandoned store front to catch their breath.

Once satisfied they had shaken the patrol, du Trieux checked her radio. It had fallen almost silent.

The EMP explosion, on the surface, didn't seem to have done much. There was no flash of thunder, no electrical sparking, no errors making the phablets crash. The wave guide had focussed the beam across the park alone. But if all had worked according to design, every piece of electronic equipment in the forward operating base, from wrist watches to Bravo control circuits, were now dead.

The only voices on the military airwaves now were a few scattered patrols screaming bloody murder, demanding to know what had happened, and where everyone had gone.

Du Trieux yanked the batteries and stuffed the radio into one of her pockets with a satisfied nod.

Miller fingered his earpiece as he followed the others back into the alley outside the shop. "Northwind, Wild Tarpan primary target burnt."

"*Understood and congratulations. Return to base and await orders.*"

"En route," he replied, jogging to catch up.

Morland, just in front of him, held open a chain fence gate, and Miller ducked through.

After another block they paused to blend into the background, staring like worried civilians as several Bravos rushed back to Marcus Garvey Park.

They then crossed the avenues towards the river.

Before they reached the shoreline a shooting star appeared in the midmorning sky, searing white as it streaked by. It exploded in a black spear of fire-dappled smoke, and another star appeared. A third, a fourth, all tumbling overhead and to the east, towards the Astoria Peninsula. They all blew apart, the blast-echoes reaching the team moments later.

"What the…" Hsiung shaded her eyes.

Morland stared gormlessly up like a child watching fireworks. Doyle knew what it was, so did du Trieux—it was up to Miller to break the news, as artillery shells tracked fire across the sky.

"Antiballistic DEW-CIWS." He said it the way his father, an Air Force man before retirement, always had. *Dewsie-Whiz.* Directed energy weapon/close in weapon system. Miller shut his eyes, and saw white spots dancing, burnt into his retina. "Defence lasers. They're burning artillery shells out of the air. Stockman's shelling the compound."

"But that's okay, right?" Morland gaped. "They're knocking them out of the air?"

"We only see what's the lasers are hitting. Not what gets through," Miller said, pointing at the horizon.

Dirty smoke rose from the direction of home.

IT WAS IMPOSSIBLE to get through to anyone at Northwind or the compound. They weren't burnt off the air like the Army, just not answering. Busy, Miller hoped.

They counted four out of the compound's six attack helicopters twisting into the air and slanting toward the barrage's source. Rotors twirling, side-mounted fanjet engines screaming for every last sliver of speed, the choppers chewed the air to pieces in their desperate sprint toward the attack.

And still the shells slipped through the defensive laser-web, hammering the compound below.

Northwind might not have been answering, but the Cobalt access codes gave them the feeds off the drones circling the skies over the compound.

They watched their phablets with mounting horror. The scene was pandemonium.

Within minutes, three breaches had been torn open in the compound wall. The northern sections, where engineers had already started concrete reinforcement, held up, but towards the south, near where Miller had stood at barricade six, sections had collapsed into rubble. Infected mobs, civilian and military both, poured through the gaps like medieval besiegers, running down side streets and into the sectioned-off refugee shanties before the heavies could arrive in their exoskeletons and hold the breach.

On infra-red, it looked like one man approaching the gates was wreathed in rat-things tearing him apart, but a second, longer look showed he wasn't under attack. The swarm was following him in, rushing past him like attack dogs, chasing a fleeing trooper down ahead.

Large sections of the compound had been walled off from one another in case of just such an attack, to help contain the damage. Members of the Rats moved in with flamethrowers, licking the streets with tongues of fire that caused as much destruction to home territory as the enemy did, but the Infected didn't dare advance, giving the civilians a chance to flee deeper into the compound's depths.

Shells continued to rain down, the Rats' DEW-CIWS systems only able to shield the most heavily populated parts of the peninsula. But even where the laser web was concentrated, artillery slipped through.

Miller watched in muted dread, chewing the inside of his cheek until he tasted copper. He watched as shells struck buildings he knew held civilians, refugees, and employees. Tiny dots scrambled on the phablet screen. People were running for their lives, trapped like fish in a barrel.

It seemed to go on forever, but eventually the air attack silenced Stockman's artillery. It had only been twenty minutes, but the damage was extensive.

Miller found an open relay channel and heard the cheers, but it was more than a minute before the shells already in flight finished landing on the peninsula.

Taking the opportunity, Miller and his team made it back overland, taking the footbridge over to Wards Island, and the Robert F. Kennedy Bridge back to Queens and the Astoria compound.

By THE TIME they arrived, the worst of the attack was over; but the city surrounding the compound had been reduced to smoking ruins, obliterated where the DEW-CIWS had simply let the shells fall.

Miller and the others pushed through the rubble. Climbing over fallen walls and hopping over piles of brick and concrete, they inched toward the compound too stunned to speak. The damage was immeasurable, the city unrecognizable.

And irreparable. S-Y hardly had the resources to reconstruct the damage to the wall and the infrastructure inside the compound, much less the surrounding areas outside the Astoria Peninsula. Manhattan was a ruin, and likely to stay that way.

As Miller ambled around a crater in the middle of

27th Street a surprisingly profound grief flooded him. To his mind, the heart of New York had just stopped beating. He kept his eyes ahead, looking directly at the compound gate a block away, trying not to see the details, but they were impossible to miss.

As he fought to gain control of his emotions, he heard the roar of a crowd.

On his left, a mob of Infected rushed in a screaming horde directly at them.

Civilian men and women in tattered clothes and in various stages of starvation shrieked and clawed the air on both flanks. Men in military uniforms ran at the centre of the mobs, armed and firing at Miller and the others.

Jarred into action, Cobalt-2 sprinted toward the gate with every ounce of strength they had left.

What was left of Switchblade guarded the entry. They exited the confines of the walls and maintained access to their entry point, randomly shooting to provide cover, but it was all for nothing.

Once the Infected had mobbed on the left, another approached on the right and Cobalt-2 were soon surrounded. They had no choice but to fight hand-to-hand and inch their way through the swarm.

Firing at will, throwing punches, Miller ran and shot, twisting on his feet, running a few metres, then smacking a civilian out of his path, only to come face-to-face with an Infected officer. Without hesitation he lifted his Gallican and put a bullet straight through the officer's eyes.

With a surge, the Infected civilians surrounding

that officer spilled out and away, into the street in scattered formation. Miller watched them recede and shouted to the others on the top of his lungs, "Take out the officers!"

Bullets pierced the air from all sides. With awful precision, Cobalt-2 and Switchblade drilled the soldiers to the ground. Most of the Infected civilians spilled away, but others did not, and those left behind, still trying to further the attack toward Miller and Cobalt, were soon mowed down.

Miller and his team killed, again and again, without respite.

It was a bloodbath.

Eventually, Cobalt linked up with the team from Switchblade at the gate, and fought through together. Once the entrance was closed behind them, Cobalt were ushered away from the front lines.

Miller heard the Switchblade commander order his troops to kill anyone in the vicinity of the compound wearing anything other than an S-Y security uniform. He was sickened with himself when he subconsciously nodded in agreement.

Just as he turned to count the heads of his team, three attack helicopters zoomed overhead. Miller understood now: with air support, the Infected assault would likely be fought back down to a siege and eventually stopped. The remains of Stockman's assault would slink back into the rubble of Manhattan like cockroaches and Miller would live to see another day.

He tried to be relieved.

* * *

IN THE AFTERMATH, and on the faltering bandwidth keeping the White House alive on the internet, the President addressed the nation and the world on a backdrop of S-Y workers picking through the wreckage of the refugee shanties.

"We are, today, a wounded nation. A broken nation. No matter what tribulations we face, our hearts bleed for our families, our friends, our countrymen in New York City today." Huxley Fredericks gazed down the camera lens with all the majesty a dozen sessions with Gray's plastic surgeons could bring. "This tragedy, this violence striking at the heart of us all has one origin behind it. The Archaean Parasite.

"But we cannot blame the Parasite alone. For those who wilfully pursue infection, who attack those trying to cure the sick, their own sickness cannot, will not, be a shield for them to cower behind. They are criminals.

"Major-General Stockman, and regretfully the entirety of the 11th Infantry Division, are criminals. Criminals against humanity, *war* criminals, for we are now at a time of war. Not only for survival, against climate change, ecological catastrophe, and famine, but against ourselves. This is a civil war against our country, and our enemy is within." The President stiffened, leaning in towards the camera. "As we all know, we are at a low tide, but American will and strength of heart are as strong as they've ever been.

So I call on you all, servicemen and women, citizens, our allies within NATO and our other friends internationally, to come to America's aid.

"The Archaeans *must* be stopped."

OPERATION WILD TARPAN was on hold, pending nightfall or a secured perimeter. Besides, they couldn't go after Stockman until Northwind had time to track him down. Right now, all drones were buzzing over the compound to monitor possible security breeches.

No time for a shower, this go around. Out of the refugee rags and poured back into combat gear, a plastic-wrapped mealpak and some water each, Cobalt were kicked out of the personnel halls and onto the walls, whether they were ready or not.

Doyle stood, body erect and face tired, rifle at his shoulder, shooting Infected who tried to swim around the wall's side and climb back onto shore.

Miller watched him at work, almost numb to the repetitive *bang, slap*, the bodies in the river, the gouts of blood and water.

He tried taking out one of his earpieces, but the rifle's blast hurt his ears, so he set it back in place and tried to understand why the Infected continued to doggy-paddle out into the river, one after another. There was a string of corpses floating in the muck. In fact, some were already being gnawed by black eel-like creatures downstream. You'd think that would have been clue enough that they should stop. But they didn't.

Miller didn't get it.

How could that kind of horde mentality be stopped? What was it even *for*?

Miller preferred trying to understand the Infected rather than trying to understand Doyle, who paused for a sip of water, then latched a fresh magazine into his weapon's stock and began killing over again.

Miller had lost count of the people he'd killed that day. Not because of the extent of the number—it couldn't have been more than six, including the fight through to the compound and the solider in the Marcus Garvey Park building—but because he didn't want to remember their faces. Didn't want to remember the sound and feel of his knife cutting into flesh and bone.

He wiped sweat from his face, and got up behind one of the sniper screens of heavily layered gauze across an armoured slit in the compound wall's upper lip. It was possible, just, to focus his binoculars through the rough weave to get a darkened picture of the streets below.

With their forward operating base trashed, the 11th Division were having trouble with Northwind's drones. The drones had been loaded with electronics jamming packages that could, now that the FOB's electronic warfare section was down, intercept and block almost all military communications within the city at will.

Trouble was, the Infected weren't *stupid*. They weren't using the radios anymore, even though each transmission tied down a helicopter sent out to drop a missile on them. But they *were* sending wretches out into the water for Doyle and the other snipers on the walls to hit, over and over.

Why?

Were the swimmers laying down a pheromone trail, like ants, and the Infected were helplessly chasing it to their doom?

The Infected were staying out of sight, mostly. Just recon by fire, two or three fighters popping their heads up from the rubble to make sure the machine guns were still working, to take pot shots and see what shot back. But they weren't throwing away their lives. So what was the difference?

It didn't take long, staring at the bodies being torn up in the river, for Miller to feel sick. So he put down the binoculars and pulled up one of the drone imagery feeds, hunting through the recent imaging map for clues.

The Infected in the river were emerging from between a set of buildings in good cover. Sheltered, shallow. There were a mass of soldiers nearby, hunkered down in an alleyway with a fire going, roasting a slab of flesh—Miller couldn't tell if it was human or something torn from one of the Archaeobiome's creatures.

Lured in by the scent of food, maybe, Infected civilians wandered closer in ones and twos. If there were any more than that, the soldiers lifted their rifles and made them come in one by one.

Flicking back and forth through the timestamped images and footage, trying to figure out what happened in the gaps, Miller couldn't understand why the Infected citizens who were accepted into the group then left to go into the water. None of the soldiers did it. It was only after watching a thin, bedraggled specimen going down to the water, then coming back, and repeating the trip until at last three soldiers came along and watched the poor civilian swim out into the open, that Miller understood.

The only Infected they sent out were sickly, thin, ravaged by famine. Almost all of them were covered in scabrous rashes, lichens and moulds blossoming on their skin. The healthy ones, the ones who could fight, were sent deeper into the city to join the fire teams and pick up weapons. The few sickly souls were left behind with dozens of single-minded soldiers around them.

They weren't being coerced. Not physically. Not tortured. Miller couldn't know for sure, not without being able to listen in, but it looked like the Infected were *peer pressuring* the sickly, those who needed help, into wandering out into the water for Doyle's gun.

If they didn't want to go, enough Infected brought them up to the shoreline that they couldn't think for themselves, and they fell prey to the group's desires.

Hell, maybe it was about *philanthropy*. This was about killing off the weak.

Racing through the other footage nearby, Miller also found a pattern in the boiling movement of the Infected through streets and alleyways. Here, there. A soldier being 'protected' from a larger mob of friendly Infected, a leader—often an officer—gathered up friendly faces to form a larger mob that swallowed up fire teams and spat them out at the compound wall for another round of recon by fire.

The Infected weren't *telepathic*. It was all pheromones and body language, the Archaean Parasite forcing them to respond.

Jimmy Swift was very nearly his old, smooth self when he was separate from the mob. On television, Major General Stockman had been his own man at the far end of a table from Swift.

Could the Infected be *controlled?* Not simply given orders by military leaders, but manipulated? Almost bullied into compliance, like those poor souls walking out into the water for Doyle?

"Doyle?" Miller said.

"Nngh?"

"They're using you."

"I know, suicidal little shits."

"Not like that." Miller showed him the footage, tried to explain.

Miller wasn't certain about it, couldn't be sure, but Doyle latched onto his half-theory, staring at an image of the soldiers around the fire with venom.

"Bastards," he growled. "Come on."

"Huh? We've got orders to hold the wall."

Doyle glared at him. "Did you never learn, in all the years of your Army career, how to interpret orders *flexibly?*"

It wasn't any particular demonstration of leadership, but Miller followed Doyle down from the wall, carrying his empty magazines and trailing along like a porter after the troublingly colonial image of Doyle the big-game hunter. Down onto the floating pontoons the Rats had set up as a temporary dock, and from there they could watch an unfortunate Infected paddling desperately through the water.

The eel-like creatures thrashing around the dead bodies were shearing flesh off her, piece by piece. Doyle ended that with his first shot, before even flipping down his rifle's bipod.

Without the Infected's screaming, just the watery rustle of the black serpentine lengths moving just beneath the surface, it almost felt like setting up for a peaceful day's fishing.

Almost.

It took a few moments, but the instant the Infected soldiers came to the alley mouth with the next sickly 'volunteer,' Doyle had one's head off. A second shot, maybe deliberate, maybe not, cut through a soldier's thighs, sending them down, bleeding and helpless, barely in the open, screaming for help.

Miller dimly watched as the Infected returned fire. White flashes followed by watery plops of bullets as they came up short and hit the water. The army's carbines, shortened assault rifles, didn't have the barrel length to take advantage of a rifle cartridge's full power. Compared to Doyle's custom .388, and at this range, it was like spitballs versus meteorites.

"Why the bloody hell aren't you shooting?" Doyle growled from the corner of his mouth, before the rifle.

"I, uh..."

"You aren't going to leave all the killing to *me*, are you?"

Raised on a steady diet of Hollywood violence, Miller thought the line had to have been a machismo-filled call to action. Like men comparing the size of fish caught. But it wasn't that. There was an edge of mania to Doyle's voice, an anguish.

Beneath the brittle glass of Doyle's enunciation, behind the words, Miller heard, *Don't make me do this alone*.

Miller's M27 had the range. Its lengthened barrel eked out every foot-per-second of velocity out of the same rifle cartridges the soldiers were using, sending the solid copper slugs in a hail across the alley-mouth, ricocheting down between the walls.

It didn't feel good. Pulling the trigger felt awful, like dragging a knife into himself. Look, point, kill, look, point, kill. Fighting wasn't supposed to work like that, but sending the sick and dying off to their deaths was *evil*. Killing those soldiers was right, wasn't it?

When the targets were all dead or hiding, and the last of the Infected sick had gotten away, Doyle got up and wiped his face with his hands in a very brief departure from cold decorum.

"Thank you," he said.

Miller swept his foot through piled bullet casings, sending them scattering into the river, and followed Doyle back into the compound.

"There are two kinds of snipers," Doyle said, as

they moved through abandoned refugee shanties to reach the wall. "The ones who count, and the ones who don't. The first kind... the first kind are psychopaths. The other kind don't last in the job as long." He shook his head, simply. "There's a fucking reason I gave up on trying to join the SAS and became a bodyguard."

"I... I'm sorry."

"It's not your fault. You need people dead. You need someone to kill them. That's the game, isn't it?" Doyle ducked into the shadows beside one of the ramshackle stairways up to the wall's walkway, and fumbled a small, torn-up square of paper from a pocket. He tore off a fragment, pushed it back into a plastic baggie, and chewed on the scrap, shaking his head. "Just..."

"Just?"

"Just don't use me to do things you wouldn't," Doyle said, voice shaking. "Alright? Don't force me to be the only one with blood on his hands."

"I won't," Miller promised. "I don't—" He hesitated. "I don't want that either. To be alone with blood on my hands."

"Good man." Doyle slapped Miller's back. "Smoke-break over. Hopefully no more swimming club." And with that, he climbed back up the stairs, face cold once more.

Miller watched him climb, and tried to understand the gallows humour that turned the Infected executions into a *swimming* club. And for that matter, why bother with swimming them into the river?

Marching them into the heavy machine guns over the gate would have been just as good, wouldn't it?

He hesitated. "Doyle!"

Doyle turned on the twist of staircase above, glancing down. "Yes?"

"You haven't seen any officers since we got on the wall, have you?"

"Been too fucking busy with the swimming club."

Miller had been able to pick them out on the drone footage. They were *everywhere*, barely behind the front lines, coordinating the siege. The open, half-eaten mealpak in Miller's waist pouch was evidence enough of how well that siege was going—the last food truck had gotten into the compound some time before Miller's last full night's sleep. He didn't expect to be issued any more food for the rest of the day.

The mob was coordinated, even with their radios down. They weren't drifting around the city, or rioting in the uncontrolled mobs that had swept the city in weeks past. They were *controlled*.

Miller knew the Archaean Infected mobs could flip their emotional state like a switch, just add the right amount of anger, the right amount of xenophobic fear. He'd hesitated before, and PFC Klansman had spread his hatred to his commanding officer. Could the Infected really *manipulate* each other like that? Use the sick and weak to distract snipers and let them hide in plain sight?

It was a question he'd already seen answered. The string of bodies being torn to pieces down-river were proof enough.

And Wild Tarpan had been put on hold until the perimeter had been secured.

"Doyle!" he called again. "Get down to the personnel hall and gather supplies for a full day outside the walls. Enough food and ammunition for the rest of Cobalt-2 and Hsiung. On my authority."

Doyle halted on the stairway, leaning out to look down on Miller. "But we've got orders to hold the wall."

"Y'all were the one talking about flexibly interpreting orders," Miller drawled.

JENNIFER BARRETT DIDN'T look happy being confronted in her office, or confronted at all, but she rarely smiled anyway. "We don't have the resources to support a push—"

"This *isn't* a push into the city." Miller bit his lip, angry at himself for cutting off the boss, but plunged on. "This is a five-man team."

"Our air assets are tied down, we can't push Bravos into the city. Everything we've got is being prepared to push the army off the bridges. It's the only way to get supply boats in safely. There's nothing left to provide any hope of support."

"We didn't have support in Harlem."

"If you just wait until nightfall..." She pinched at her nose, eyes squeezed shut.

"It needs to happen now. This is Operation Wild Tarpan over again, hitting their communications infrastructure, but the nature of that infrastructure has

changed. We need to capture or kill their Charismatics."
Miller leaned on Barrett's desk, and pushed his phablet
over to her. In a still image it was harder to pick out,
but the looping clip showed it clearly enough: the
Infected bubbled around individuals, protecting
them from the thickest part of the mob. Sometimes a
lieutenant, sometimes a private, sometimes collapsing
to outnumber a smaller band.

"Charismatics?" she asked, watching the footage.

"I don't know if there's a better term. Ones like
Swift, the ones skilled at manipulating the other
Infected. Or the ones so emotionally overcharged
they can swing the mob's mood by themselves."

"I think I see the ones you mean," she said, tracing
a path with her finger. "You think this might break
the siege?"

"It can't hurt."

"It can hurt *you*, Mr. Miller. We can't get you out
of trouble."

"The mobs forming out there aren't like the ones
during the riots, ma'am. This time they're not going
to wander home when they all decide they're tired
and shamble off in a group. We have to remove the
Charismatics from the equation."

Barrett's jaw tightened. "I thought you didn't
approve of 'black ops shit.' That *is* what you said
this morning, isn't it?"

"It's been a real long day, ma'am," Miller muttered,
bowing his head.

*   *   *

KILLING A MAN with du Trieux was one of the most intimate acts Miller had ever experienced. Like stalking deer with his father, like discovering he wasn't alone beside Doyle.

Something inside him had broken. He knew that. He could feel it bleeding away in the parts of his soul that had believed things would get better some day. All of Miller's faith in a brighter future had snapped into pieces and the brittle shards were grinding into the soft flesh of his throat, pushing him forward.

One step.

The thunder of his heart and blood in his veins.

A second step.

He still had the slashing blade on his thigh. It was useful, it had a can opener in the cross guard. But he also had an eight-inch long spike of a weapon in his right hand.

The 'Charismatic'—the label had an almost totemic, dehumanizing power, as if the man were a radio antenna instead of a living being—had moved between fire teams behind the lines for nearly an hour. Running like a messenger, in a stolen camouflaged shirt that hung loose over his bare chest, sweat visibly trickling down his back.

The procedure was easy for Miller. They came up with the worst scenario they could, as if they'd been protecting him as bodyguards, and picked their moment to strike.

Miller and du Trieux caught up with him between two buildings, leaping out like frenzied animals. Miller pushed him down from behind, fell to his knees with du Trieux, together stabbing down through the man's back over and over and the *screaming*...

Then they were off and running again, panting for air as the Charismatic died behind them, attracting a mob.

As they sprinted, a door opened in front of Miller and du Trieux. Doyle, Morland and Hsiung waited for them with open arms, and then the five of them hid like children, sweating and silent, in an apartment's middle corridor while patrols swept the streets around them.

Blood drooled from Miller's sleeve. His combat uniform's artificial fibres wicked it away as easily as any other stain, but he felt the blood even after it was gone.

Miller accepted the labels—Infected, Charismatic— and held them as tight to his chest as he could, gazing at du Trieux in wonderment.

At them all.

They'd committed the ultimate taboo.

They'd murdered, and there was no punishment. No anger, no recrimination. No one blamed one another, or hated each other for it. They simply waited for the Infected to move on from their search, no suggestion from any of them that what had happened was wrong.

It was a strange kind of love between them now. One built from the knowledge that every one of them had become the antithesis of what'd they'd once been.

Protectors had become assassins.

When Miller's hands shook, Doyle tore a scrap of paper from the sheet folded up in its plastic baggie, and handed it to him. Miller rolled it up and swallowed the drug-infused paper like a pill.

As his hands steadied, the anxiety did, too.

By nightfall they had assassinated dozens and called out other squads from the compound with the same orders.

Word of their efforts had obviously reached the Infected masses. In the darkness of their kills, the other Infected would sometimes run screaming, abandoning the Charismatics they were guarding, even before they knew what they were running from.

It was gratifying, in its way. But as the Charismatics fell, more Infected came looking for them, with bigger groups of guards surrounding them. Piece by bloody piece, Cobalt-2 and Shank, a hodge-podge squad of Rats members, Switchblade survivors and refugee volunteers with military backgrounds, worked their way up the chain. From corporals and street preachers to lieutenants and generals, from gangs of pipe-wielding thugs to full platoons.

The night progressed. Their killing spree continued. In the deepest part of the evening, their murdering shook a convoy loose from the FOB. A group of Bravos ran helter-skelter, including the officers, trying to hold the siege together.

It was partly luck, but killing everybody who worked for Major General Stockman had forced him into either abandoning his forces or pushing his influence on the troops directly. Stockman's Bravo ran straight into a pair of mines, and Miller's group slaughtered the guards who spilled out.

Stockman himself, so overpowered by the pheromones clinging to them, spilled out into the street, squealing in terror like a child as he gulped at the air, as if hyperventilating could bring his senses back.

For a brief moment, Cobalt watched him, dumbstruck at how such a powerful man had been brought to this by the very parasite he'd fought to spread.

Slowly, Miller left the protection of his position, and walked dead centre into the middle of the street.

The only indication that the wailing Stockman recognized the significance of the situation was when he met Miller's gaze. For a moment, the general's eyes were clear.

Without ceremony, Miller raised his weapon, rested the muzzle against Stockman's skull as if he were a rabid dog, and shot him in the head.

AT THE NEW dawn, for the first time since the artillery barrage, a boat made it safely into the compound's docks. Army units on the bridges had been set up with SMAWs and machine guns, leaving a small supply fleet baking away in the Long Island Sound waiting for safety, but a push by security team Dagger had cleared the way for them to arrive, at first in a trickle, then a rush that forced the Rats to deploy more pontoon docks.

The crewmen had wild stories of sea serpents, and Miller believed them. Snakes as thick around as garbage cans, coiling away in the deeps, didn't seem unlikely after watching those bodies get torn apart in the river.

No more Infected wandered out into the river for snipers to kill. Recon by fire slowed, then stopped entirely. The military fire teams broke down into armed mobs with a natural size that hovered between a dozen and twenty, agglutinating together into a mass of humanity that attacked vehicles and fled before the helicopters arrived.

For now the Astoria Peninsula was safe, and they had food. Meanwhile, engineers struggled to strip out and replace one of the helicopters' clogged fuel systems before the mob realized there weren't any airworthy helicopters left to chase them down.

With the Charismatics out of the way, the Infected were unfocussed, but not completely disorganised. Drone overflights of Manhattan and Brooklyn showed mixed groups of military and civilians foraging for food in the streets, hordes pulling down rhino-sized thug-behemoths with a mixture of brute force and firepower. What food they had was shared equally, fairly. But they weren't sending patrols along the main roads, the attack teams on the bridges had almost melted away in front of Dagger. The siege broke into dozens of separate groups.

Every so often another Charismatic leader would gather a larger mob, and whenever the next one arrived in the area, Miller was certain Cobalt-2 would be called on. For now, Miller was sharing a meal, in this case a can of creamed wheat, with his team.

The power was out. The generators were under repair after the previous day's damage, and the only light in the break room came from the alcohol lamp they used to heat their food.

Morland cleared his throat. "I can't believe we..."

One by one, they all stared at him.

He looked around, blinking, and ducked his head to his meal.

They weren't talking about it.

Shank were, however. Security team Shank had now formally swallowed what remained of Switchblade, along with a chunk of the Rats and as many uninfected ex-Army members as they could find from the refugee population. Miller had thought he might find some kinship with them, but when he'd visited, they were bragging to one another about how many Infected—*bug-brains*—they'd killed. Laughing, cheering each other on, like something out of a bad war movie.

They'd be collecting ears, next.

Miller hunched in on himself—slurping his soup—not bothering to look up when Lewis made his way into the break room.

The old man instinctively tried the coffee machine, but, without power, it was useless. Miller shuffled over on the couch to make space, and Lewis sat down, leaning forward to select a can from the random selection surrounding the lamp. He picked out some kind of stew, and Miller loaned him his utility knife—he'd never look at the damn thing as a weapon again.

Against the background noise of puncturing metal, Lewis said, "Hard day's work."

None of them answered him.

"I was always told," Lewis said, carrying on anyway, "that after action, heavy action, the best thing to do was to talk about it. Discuss our *feelings*." He snorted dismissively.

One by one, they stared at him.

"Never saw the point in pushing anybody, but if any of you need someone to talk to, I've done as bad in my time. Maybe worse, maybe not." Lewis set the open can over the lamp, and sat quietly, waiting for it to steam.

Still, none of them answered him. Not even Morland.

The can made tiny popping sounds over the flame.

Lewis picked up an old rag, and picked the can up with it. He dipped in a spoon, stirred... tasted. Grunted his approval, and got to his prosthetic feet. "You'll know when the time's right to talk about it," he said. "Or not." Then he left the room.

Miller stared into the flame. It danced. Alive, but not. The flame was blue, a dead colour, not red or yellow.

"They're attacking civilians now," Miller said.

"Hm?" Morland looked up.

"Barrett told me when she debriefed me." He poked his spoon into the bottom of his can. "Brooklyn, New Jersey. Further out on Long Island. The mobs the siege broke up into, they're killing uninfected civilians that resist."

"Resist *what?*" Hsiung asked sharply.

"Infection." Miller stared at the gelatinous glop at the bottom of the can. "The Parasite's in their saliva—they're biting people, spitting in their mouths."

No one looked up from the lamp.

"Good God," Hsiung gasped. "Even after all we did? I mean, we did good. Didn't we?" Her voice sounded soft all of a sudden. "Those Charismatics had to die. I don't see any other way we could have gotten to them either. But it's never ending. There's always going to be more of them than there are of us."

Du Trieux grunted her agreement as Miller shot her a look.

Hsiung's spoon stood poised over her can and her mouth sat in a thin, grim line.

It was true. The siege was over. The compound was safe, temporarily—the talk of trying to evacuate by sea had ended. They'd done all they could do.

But it was far from over.

Across the room, Doyle gave no reply. He chewed on whatever drug impregnated that sheet of paper and glanced at the door Lewis had left the room by.

Miller knew he should say something. He should get up. Talk. Encourage them, or something. Ask for help. Shouldn't he?

He did.

"Doyle?" Miller held out his hand. "Pass me a strip of that stuff."

The room remained silent, and for a little while, Miller sank back into peace.

OPERATION CASPIAN TIGER

12

THE EAST RIVER flowed backwards shortly after dawn. Miller had heard about it—the river, technically a strait, changed direction with the tides—but he'd never seen it before. He'd never been up at the ass-crack of dawn, waiting in line for ration packs, with nothing better to do than stare at the river.

Seagulls, part of the planet's old ecology, were clustered on a big, gelatinous-looking corpse in the river. It could have been one of the new animals—a small thug or bloated terror-jaw—or it could have been a pig, maybe an obese human being. The gulls' wings burned with an almost angelic light as they fought, flapping and graceless, over whatever it was.

First they were drifting left, but they gradually slowed and began to serenely drift back towards the right.

It was unlikely to be a human being, Miller reflected. The latest wave of famines had lasted months—the truly obese were a memory. Humanity, at least in New York, had been bled dry and left emaciated.

Say one thing for the apocalypse, everyone had their beach bodies ready.

Well, not exactly. Thinned limbs, sagging flesh, the unhealthiness of borderline malnutrition, temperature records still being shattered in the midst of a heatwave and its furious sunlight, respiratory ailments from fungal spores and dust... No one around Miller looked like fashion models. They looked broken.

The line shuffled forward a step.

Something in the river's depths surfaced. The birds tore away in terror, before the unseen creature dragged the carrion to the depths.

Miller was in the fast line; employees only. The refugee line, separated by a length of dirty chain-link fencing, hadn't moved at all. Some of the refugees sat slumped on the ground, snoring, back-to-back. Hopefully their line would move before mid-morning. The daytime temperatures at noon could kill the weak, and Miller sure as hell didn't see anyone strong on the other side of the fence.

He gazed at the ration cards in his hands. Mostly handwritten, to prevent forgery each one had been given a bar code label. Nobody had access to printers anymore. Bar codes qualified as key anti-forgery technology, now.

The wind brought an animal's howl from Manhattan across the water, a long keening sound. Too high pitched to be one of the thug behemoths, too long for anything not tough enough to take on all challengers for its territory. Miller didn't know what it could be, but whatever it was, it had one hell of a pair of lungs.

The line crept forward, and Miller trudged along with the others. There wasn't too far to go, now. The fenced-off lines all led to the main distribution warehouse, a converted building with its walls cut open on Fourth Avenue. The only people in the entire Astoria compound who looked halfway well-fed, and who weren't also members of the corporate board or major stockholders, worked behind its barred windows.

Another wait, and Miller lost himself in watching buildings' shadows sweep across Manhattan. Eventually, ahead of him, a welding technician handed over a handful of ration cards. She waited, looking back at Miller neutrally. Miller stared back, shrugged, and the technician turned back to take back her ration cards. Eventually she walked away with an open cardboard box, moving towards the docks, bulging with unsealed ration packages. Maybe... two and a half, three thousand calories for each person's ration card? A wealth, a goddamn fortune in food, but the welders were cutting apart the old oil tankers that had come in. Heavy work. Without food to fuel them, work would slow, and they were needed, expanding the Astoria compound onto barges in the river.

Miller's turn came, and he pushed the cards for his team—himself, du Trieux, Doyle, Morland, Hsuing—through the slot. The worker eyed his security uniform, the Gallican holstered at his hip, then the cards. He scanned the cards on a supermarket checkout with scratched glass, slid them back, and moved back into the warehouse's cool darkness.

Miller couldn't help comparing the warehouse worker's ass with the welding tech's, but his libido felt like the rest of him: tired, dried out, crumbling. In any case, he decided, receiving his cardboard box, his brief flutter of interest had only been over so much *food*. The warehouse worker glanced again at Miller's uniform, his sidearm, and said, sharply, "All sealed and correct."

Miller made a show of inspecting the box's contents. Sealed shrink-wrapped packages covered with handwritten labels. A thousand calories of canned goods, a thousand calories of candy bars, a thousand calories of dry pasta, a thousand calories... All sealed, unlike the welding technician's packages. Miller looked up, glaring.

"We ain't cheating you," the warehouse worker said, smiling, holding up his hands.

The barest *hint* of a double chin wobbled at his throat. Just a hint.

Miller took it all back. He understood how an obese human body could have gotten into the river, and right at that moment, he knew he was just about capable of having thrown another in.

"You tubby *fuck*."

"Hey, man. We don't mess with the security teams. We good?"

"You *moronic fuck!* When you start a food riot I'll fucking open the gate and *help* them tear you to pieces!" Miller snarled, jerking his head at the fenced off and unmoving refugee line. "Just give people their fucking *food*. Asshole."

He swept up his team's rations off the counter and stormed away, leaving the worker, pale and frightened, to his next customer.

Entering the fenced-in warrens of the compound's streets, covered to keep titan-birds out, Miller raged at himself. He shouldn't have gotten that angry with some jackoff stealing candy bars. It was uncivilized bullshit. A person didn't threaten to kill someone over *candy*. Not in the old, pre-famine world, anyway.

This new world, though. There were new rules, ones Miller wasn't adjusting to quickly enough. Maybe killing that corrupt ass for skimming calories off rations was *exactly* the right thing to do. But Miller had taken the rations and walked. He hadn't dragged that bastard out from behind the counter. And every step he took put him farther away from doing anything about it.

What the hell did it matter, anyway?

Miller brought the food back to Cobalt's break room. They had power today. The lights were on and an old television was hooked up to an even older Blu-ray player. Morland kneeled with a bottle of window cleaner and some rags, trying to clean up the discs and find at least *one* that worked.

Barely managing to avoid taking his own head off with one of the cables snaking around the television, Morland unfolded himself, his puppyish expression at odds with his imposing size. "Say we've got popcorn. I've got the sugar for it saved."

Miller's stomach rebelled. "Sugar? On popcorn?"

"Yeah. Oh, God. You don't like it *salty*, do you?"

"You put butter and you put salt on popcorn. What is *wrong* with British people?" Miller demanded.

Hsiung, draped over the couch, looked up from her perusal of the movie boxes they'd looted from the city. Slowly, glacially, her eyebrow lifted. "And Chinese people."

Desperately, Miller looked to the other half of the room for backup.

"You should try it," Doyle said, immersed in the guts of his rifle's firing mechanisms, oil and steel on the table in front of him. "It's good."

As one, everyone looked at du Trieux, minding her own business with Cobalt's weapons requisitions papers.

"Well?" Miller begged. "Salt or sugar?"

Her lips thinned. Bad news on the way. "Sugar."

"Just in France, right? That's just a European thing? What about Nigeria?"

"Both. Salt's bad for your blood pressure anyway."

"I'm going to get Lewis," Miller said, "and we're going to enact written orders that any popcorn this team gets hold of is doused in melted butter and salt."

"Americans." Du Trieux shook her head grimly.

"Salted isn't the end of the world. Not *very* good, but..."

"Shut it, Doyle." Miller pointed a finger at him. "Quit while you're ahead."

"Honestly. Just try it sweet some time." Doyle snapped a slender pin back into his rifle's firing mechanisms. "You'll like it. Like candy corn."

"Candy corn is a *whole* other thing. It's *candy*." Miller checked the requisition papers over du Trieux's shoulder, and stopped, leaning in. "*How* much ammunition did we use last week?"

"It's not quite that bad," she said. "We just don't have any *here*. A lot of it's in the caches."

They'd been going through a lot of ammunition all the same. Hunting down the city's Charismatics wasn't easy, even now that the main push of military organization seemed to have crumbled.

The Charismatics knew how to manipulate their fellow Infected into playing the role of bodyguard. A quick assassination or a single rifle shot could create a howling mob charging through the streets for their blood in an instant. Sometimes to get that shot, to kill an Infected Charismatic coordinating the others, they had to kill dozens, even hundreds. More than once Miller had barricaded Cobalt-2 into position, with a cache of ammunition and spare weapons, and fought like demons against the horde until none of the screaming Infected were left pounding at the doors and windows.

It went through a lot of ammunition. That was the comfortable way to look at what had happened. Maybe Miller could have viewed it in terms of circling the wagons, or drawn parallels with Rorke's Drift, a battle between savagery and civilization, in the kind of rhetoric beloved by white supremacists, neatly transforming himself into a conquering hero. But it didn't feel like that at all.

Afterward, Cobalt had used shovels to clear enough bodies from the window to get away before the big predators arrived to scavenge. Very heroic.

There wasn't enough soap in the entire compound to wash away the memories of how heroic it felt to crawl out over piled bodies, or how heroic it had smelled, or what kind of heroism a human being's face could be transformed into by a 5.56mm bullet.

The system worked, but it burned through ammunition, and if they didn't have the bullets, they'd be killed. Miller sat down beside du Trieux, pulling the ready forms over for him to sign. He had to ask stores for more bullets and equipment so he could walk his team out into the city and go through it all over again. So he could stumble on warm limbs, slippery with blood. Leave as the thug-behemoths started in on the bodies, shearing through limbs with gristly cracks of their beaked jaws.

Miller palmed at his face. "Pass me the pen."

She finished totalling how many quarts of fuel they'd need for the flamethrower they wanted for the cache in Queens, then slid the last form and the pen over to him.

The emotional impact had nothing to do with having to deal with paperwork, or what the paperwork represented—more killing in the future. The pen was so heavy in his hand because it amounted to *consent*. To putting it on paper that living through that kind of hell wasn't just something he'd suffered through, but accepted and repeated, willingly.

"Hey! There *is* popcorn in here!" Morland pulled a bag of microwave popcorn from one of the miscellaneous packs victoriously.

Miller pressed his fingertips over his eyes.

"Aw, bloody hell. It's pre-salted."

Well. That was a small mercy.

While his team struggled to figure out which discs worked and which didn't, or catalogued the day's rations into 'snacks' and 'real food,' Miller and du Trieux handled the rest of the paperwork. Miller couldn't understand why there was so much of it, but without programmers and a robust IT infrastructure, all the little things that used to be handled by automatically scanning your corporate ID as you walked into a room now had to be handled with paper. Thankfully, stationery didn't rot or go stale, so it was easy to scavenge and stockpile. The only trouble was the pens—they kept running out. It had never happened to Miller before, but in the past few weeks, he'd used up three.

Requisitions had eaten up one, the other two had perished writing reports—sanitized versions of what had happened in the field. He used to be able to type it all out on a word processor, but the internal security offices no longer had access to secure online cloud storage. It had to be on paper.

Filling out forms to a background of film-snippets, as Morland and Hsiung found working DVDs and Blu-rays, didn't cost Miller and du Trieux any blood, but plenty of ink. Without printers, they had to copy the form's grids and questions out by hand from a master copy they'd been given.

Who was going to read all this garbage, at the end of the day? The question kept distracting Miller. Some guy was going to glance over the paperwork, hand over a pallet of boxed ammo, and then the forms might as well go straight into the trash. It wasn't as though lawyers would be going over Miller's reports with a fine-toothed comb, subjecting him and his actions to legal scrutiny—there weren't any courts left. It was unnecessary bureaucracy, the dying, twitching remnants of a social structure that no longer existed. It let tubby bastards skim food off people, let the *real* atrocities slip by, and made Miller's fingers and wrists ache.

His penmanship was improving, at least. And there was salted popcorn. Something to look forward to.

He checked his wristwatch. It was just barely eight-thirty in the morning. "Don't start movie night until I'm back." Miller collected the loose sheets into something approaching a neat stack.

"We'll need to find a microwave first, anyway," Morland said.

Du Trieux turned her head, frowning. "Surely we can cook it in a pan?"

Miller drew in a deep breath. Improved penmanship, and burnt popcorn. Rolling his eyes, he gathered up the last of the documentation and left his team to their own devices, while he headed upstairs to see Lewis.

Lewis's office was, for now, part of the small suite of rooms assigned to Cobalt. Increasingly, though, since Mannon's death and the news that Crewe wouldn't be leaving a hospital bed, Lewis had ceased to be security team Cobalt's de facto leader. He was Gray's eyes on the ground, feeding Schaeffer-Yeager's CEO news from what qualified as the front line. He was Gray's voice, too—not that the CEO's new directive stopped security teams Shank and Bayonet from calling in with Robert Harris to confirm their every move. The old corporate hierarchy, with everything going through internal security first, held strong.

Miller knocked on the doorframe. Lewis's door was always open, but not as a matter of managerial policy—it was the only way to get any air-flow through the room in the day's oppressive heat.

"Give us a minute, son. Busy here."

A man with extremely dark skin, darker than Lewis's by a landslide, was sitting across the desk. Worn clothes, thin. Could have been a refugee, but refugees didn't carry guns—a battered, antique-looking AK variant Miller had never seen before. He glared at Miller with yellow eyes, seemingly jaundiced, and turned back to face Lewis over the desk. "Jolly promised shore leave to the men." His accent was foreign, but reminded Miller of the wide, flat tones of du Trieux's impressions of her Nigerian cousins.

"Not my problem," Lewis replied, going into a weary explanation of how there wasn't anywhere *for* shore leave. Areas were sectored out, refugees and personnel. The compound had no public spaces.

Miller wasted some time by following the breeze from Lewis's office door to a window at the end of a corridor. He stood, eyes half shut, letting the air blow past him. Maybe if he cooled down enough now, he'd actually be able to get some sleep at noon instead of waking up to helpless, muggy heat.

When the Nigerian asking about shore leave left, Miller stepped into Lewis's office, and set the stack of paperwork on the desk. "All good?" Miller asked.

Lewis finished jotting something down, and looked up at the stack without much enthusiasm. "Hell," he muttered, and pulled the pages over for a closer look.

Paperwork didn't really suit Lewis. He'd remained an NCO with the Marines as long as he could before taking retirement, and that was only because he was getting a little old to be jumping out of planes with a set of prosthetic feet. He'd taken work in the private sector as a bodyguard with the intent of staying active and on his feet well into his seventies. It didn't seem fair to Miller that circumstances had put Lewis behind a desk.

"I don't think I can get you this much ammunition," Lewis said, blinking at the page. "How the hell'd you use this much?"

"It's in the incident reports." Miller clasped his hands behind his back uncomfortably. "The short version? You remember that crowd of Infected the helicopter had to shoot to pieces?"

Lewis looked up, lips pushed grimly together. He nodded.

"Well, they mob up like that about a quarter of the time after we take out a Charismatic." Miller spread his hands in an awkward shrug. "Five of us with our asses in the fire doesn't rate air support anymore, what with the engine trouble the choppers are having, so we get ourselves out. That's where the ammo goes."

Lewis bowed his head, looking at the requisition forms. After a pause, he fished through the stack until he found one of the handwritten incident reports.

"So what was the deal with that other guy?" Miller asked.

"Nigerian pirate." Lewis turned a page over with a loud flick. "They're negotiating the sale of a hijacked oil tanker."

"Seriously?"

"Uh-huh."

"How about that. So that's where we're getting the tankers the welders are tearing up on the docks? *Pirates?*"

"Some of them. The company doesn't have enough big boats to spare for this floating farm thing."

Rumour was that with the compound jammed full of people, the plan was to string together boats and barges into the East River to find the space to start some kind of indoor farming effort. Couldn't start soon enough, in Miller's opinion.

"You kids okay?" Lewis asked, after putting down another incident report.

It wasn't easy to answer. The obvious answer, 'we're fine,' stuck in Miller's throat. At last he said, "Working the night shift isn't all bad. Not as hot."

"You know that's not what I mean."

"I don't know what you mean."

He pushed one of the reports across the desk and under Miller's nose. "If we were in the Marines," Lewis said, "you'd be due a psychiatric evaluation."

"Don't see why."

"Killing fucks people up, son." Lewis slapped down another. "In the world wars, the machine gunners went crazy. In mine, the drone operators. Basically, anybody who sits there with a trigger or a button and focuses on nothing but killing other human beings for days on end—they all come out mincemeat on the other side."

"Don't feel like mincemeat." Miller ducked his head.

Putting the rest of the paperwork down, Lewis kicked his chair back, lacing his fingers over his belly and staring. "Son," he said, "what I'm saying here is that I need you on your feet. Able to do your duty."

"Sure. No problem."

"If you and the kids start cracking up, we're screwed. You understand? Switchblade's gone, and Shank isn't any kind of replacement. They're good enough to keep terror-jaws from nosing around the breaches in the walls, but that's about it. The other security teams are barely in any kind of shape to get shit done. Cobalt's the only thing that resembles a flexible fighting force, and we're down to five of you. You have to take care of yourselves."

"Six, if you get out from behind that desk."

Lewis's face hardened. "The longer I can keep

you shielded from handling this bullshit and dealing with the board, the better."

"What do you want me to say?" Miller leaned forward. "We're tired. We're struggling. We're doing our job."

"You're getting put on crowd control until further notice."

Miller blinked. "What?"

"You heard me."

"What happened to speaking for the CEO? Your word is Gray's word?"

"Where do you think these orders came from? I speak with the voice of God because God tells me what to say. Gray and Harris are giving you until eighteen-hundred to acclimatize, and then Cobalt's on a regular guard rotation with security team Bayonet."

"We're on *down time*, waiting on ammo and supplies, we can't go back out until we rest and resupply."

"They want you on guard duty babysitting the refugees we've got canned up in fences like fucking prisoners of war," Lewis snapped. "And I agree with them. There's talk about evacuating to Boston. It's made people scared. Some of the refugees are even trying to escape into the city. I need you on this."

"So let them leave. Fucking let them."

"And then in a couple days we've got well-fed Infected outside the walls who know every nook and cranny of the compound—and who know exactly how many men and how much firepower we have left? Can't happen."

Miller clenched his fists. "We need rest, we need to put down the guns. We need to be *human* for awhile. Eighteen hours? That's a fucking joke."

"We're fighting a war against extinction here," Lewis kept on, his face reddening, "and you need to do your duty, which is to execute the orders I give you. I'll figure out how to straighten this out, but until it happens I need you to play along."

Miller stared at him, blinking. "My duty?"

"Your duty," Lewis said, evenly.

"I'm a fucking private employee. The terms of my employment contract don't say shit about guard duty, or mass murder, or assassination, or the fucking *end of the world*." Miller got to his feet. "If you can't straighten this shit out I'll go to someone who can."

"Miller!"

He looked back, once, before leaving. "You speak for God 'cuz God talks to you. *I* drive God's kids to school every day."

"Gray won't like this."

"Are you kidding?" Miller snorted. "Being compared to God'll make his damned day."

13

Holly Moulin didn't look up from behind her desk.

"Not even going to *try* and stop me?" Miller asked, reaching for the office door.

"It never works, Mr. Miller."

He smiled, a thin veneer of levity over his foul mood, and let himself into Gray's office.

L. Gray Matheson's den had grown even more opulent, by the compound's standards. A functioning air conditioning unit hummed beneath one of the windows, banishing any idea of heat. It seemed somehow unfair, but that was how capitalism worked, even now. Big glossy desk, fresh bagels baked out of flour from God-knew-where, real coffee...

As Miller neared the desk, and Gray behind it, he realized that the dainty plate wasn't covered with the crumbs of a fresh-baked breakfast snack. He looked at Gray quizzically, and pointed towards the stubby, flat triangles on the plate.

Rolling his eyes, Gray eased back in his seat,

clasping an antique corded telephone to the side of his face. He nodded, waved for Miller to take one. "Yes. I know none of the shareholders are happy. Nobody's happy, Ben."

Taking care not to smear the plate with the rapidly cooling sweat covering his fingers, Miller picked up the daintily cut quarter of a DG-12. Cautiously, he tasted it. The bread, purportedly identifying the DG-12 as a sandwich against all other evidence, swelled as it drank the saliva off his tongue. Chewing transformed his mouth into a wonderland of filthy, clinging gobbets. Somewhere in the midst of it all, rubbery strips of something that had been soy, up until a team of industrial chemists had taken a crack at making their mark on history, slithered between his teeth and eventually down his throat.

The DG-12 was not a sandwich. It was a way to preserve food for decades, most likely by the time-honoured tradition of rendering it inedible by both macroscopic and microscopic life.

"I understand that," Gray told the other end of the line, "but if they leave the cove, we can't provide them with support. Any kind of support. The security teams are too busy holding the compound."

Miller took another bite, because, fuck it, you didn't turn down a meal. Not anymore.

"Ben, do me a favour. Before you try and threaten me with a suggestion like that, actually try and *hire* private security. It doesn't exist anymore." Gray laughed. "That's why you need to stay with us. I'm not hardballing you. There really *isn't* any other option. Thank you. Yes, that's fine. We'll pick this up later. Goodbye."

Miller sank into one of the two visitor's chairs opposite the desk, and gestured with the remains of the DG-12. "Ran out of caviar?"

"Getting a preview," Gray said, fumbling with the old phone, trying to fit its pieces together the way it was done in old movies.

"We aren't even feeding the refugees this old stuff yet." Miller turned it over. The last time he'd had one was as a hazing exercise in the Army. The DG series rations were long-term storage, last-ditch meal items. The kind of thing they started stuffing into bunkers after the Russian Federation started stockpiling nukes again. "There's no way in hell you don't have a source on the fresh stuff."

"That's the problem, Alex." Gray smiled thinly. "I felt I needed a dose of the reality we'll be living through if I screw this up for us."

"What's Ben's problem? You torturing the rest of the board with this stuff?"

"Something along those lines. What can I do for you, Alex?"

One last bite, but only one, and Miller balanced the remnants of the DG-12 on the plate's edge. "Cobalt's being put on guard duty."

"Yes?"

"We just got in from the city this morning. You can't put us on guard duty."

"I was told that you had the time. That you weren't doing anything for the next two days or so?"

"We need down time," Miller said through gritted teeth.

Gray hesitated. "How much?"

"Honestly? A lot more than eighteen hours."

"Alex, come on. We're short-handed. This is crunch time. We need you twenty-four hours a day, here. I know what it's like, I've been in the office overnight too. But you can't shirk responsibility..." He trailed off, staring at Miller's expression. "I'm sorry. I know how that must have sounded."

"Do you?" Miller asked, his face feeling hot. "What kind of late shifts have you pulled at the office lately? Did you hit your quota and kill a couple dozen people before you got home?"

"Alex..."

"Because that's what I had to do to get back to the compound. I haven't slept yet. I don't know if I'll be *able* to sleep."

"You know I didn't mean..."

"I know you didn't *think*," Miller said. He leaned back until the chair squeaked. "We're not software developers. You can't push front line combat troops like that."

Silence stretched out until Gray pinched at the bridge of his nose. "Bob assured me it'd be fine."

"*Robert Harris* never held a gun in his life. You don't put armed soldiers fresh from battle in front of civvies. We're too hopped up and on edge. It'll be a disaster," Miller all but pleaded.

"I think you under-estimate yourself and your team."

"Look, I'm not saying we have PTSD yet, although I'm not saying we don't. But after doing what we just did out there, our judgement is shot. I mean, killing seems normal right now. Everything feels like a threat, *everything*." Miller got to his feet. "You really want a group of armed, hyper-sensitive, shell-shocked troops to babysit a panicky crowd? How is that a good idea? You can't mix in the wolves with the sheep. It's a slaughter waiting to happen."

"Okay," Gray said, gently. "Okay. Your team needs down time. I get it. Harris didn't know what he was talking about. Any suggestions for how we get the job done?"

"Which job you talking about? Keeping the refugees pinned behind their fences?"

"That's the objective," Gray nodded.

Miller could barely believe his ears. "What happened to keeping the Infected out? Or stopping them from infecting people unchecked? What about making this city safe?" Miller gazed out Gray's window at Manhattan across the river. "Wasn't that the *objective* last time I looked? Isn't that what Cobalt's been *doing*?"

"It's getting out of hand. We need to keep the refugees in check."

"Do we?"

Gray bowed his head and steepled his fingers. "That's what I've been told."

"What do you think me and my people are out there for? Killing the Charismatics?" Miller turned to face Gray and gestured out at the window. "We're buying you time, and time for what? What the hell have you been doing? Dicking around with turning boats into floating islands?"

"The farms—" Gray began.

"Cutting up a few oil tankers and turning them into hydroponic farms is pissing on a forest fire, and you know it. You won't be able to grow anything fast enough to make a difference. There isn't any food *now*."

Gray got to his feet. He looked older than he should've—older than anyone Miller had ever seen—as he took slow, heavy steps to stand at the window.

"The population of the United States must have been cut to a quarter over the past six months," Miller continued, "but nobody knows because there aren't enough of us left to count. What happened to saving humanity? Giving your kids a future?"

Gray only sighed.

"We fought back the Infected," Miller kept on, "we pushed Stockman off us, we bought some time. Great. But now the Infected are unopposed in Jersey and Queens and the Bronx, going after everyone left. And you want to put your best squad on guard duty? Here, sit tight and starve while we build a farm—from scratch. Why?" He slapped the glass. "What the *hell* is it all for, Gray?"

"Harris said—"

"*Fuck* Harris." Miller glared at his boss. "Stop listening to Harris and start telling *him* what to do."

The air in Gray's lungs escaped in a long, helpless breath. "I can't."

"You're the most powerful man in the world. You're used to dealing with money, with whole industries, with people's livelihoods. The stakes haven't changed. You pick up a phone, you give the wrong orders, people die. Same was true before. If you screwed up that government contract for BioGen, famine would have hit us six months earlier. If you screwed up the merger five years ago, two hundred *thousand* people would've lost their jobs, their health coverage, their homes, everything. You've got to step up, Gray. I mean, you have an annoying nickname for the President and you use it to his *face*, for God's sake. Surely you can stand up to *Harris*."

"Huck's not an annoying nickname."

Miller raised an eyebrow. "It annoys the shit out of *me*."

Laughing despite himself, Gray stepped in against the window, gazing at the compound below. "I don't know shit about this situation, Alex. If I let the refugees leave when they want, they're going to get eaten by some monster, or get infected. If I don't, we risk riots. And more of them are coming in every day. You know that? People think it's *safe* here."

"I've been out there. You don't appreciate how safe it really is."

"Maybe not." He shook his head tiredly. "The board's leaving."

"Directors or shareholders?"

"Shareholders," Gray said. "All this belongs to them as much as it does to me, and they're not happy. Too crowded, too many strictures on what they can and can't do. They want me to give them aircraft and security teams to ferry them to private boltholes. Holiday homes, ranches out in the middle of nowhere, that sort of thing."

Miller made a face. "Being out on a ranch won't do them much good."

"Probably not," Gray said. "I'm losing their trust. They like what Harris has to say. For my part, I agree with you. He wants the refugees bottled up and the compound expanded. He doesn't seem to know what he wants to do beyond making himself a very comfortable little fortress. But that's what the board wants, and they think he's responsible for stopping Stockman."

Miller raised an eyebrow. "How'd he do that while he was hiding in his fortress?"

"He's head of internal security, Cobalt's in his wheelhouse..."

"*I* killed Stockman," Miller said, a dangerous rumble at the edge of his voice. "Killing the Charismatics was my plan. Harris didn't put a bullet in *anyone*."

"All the same," Gray said, "they think the victory's his responsibility. Not mine."

Miller pushed out his breath in a frustrated sigh, and leaned on the window, joining Gray to look at the compound below.

Even in full daylight, the flashes of arc-welders were obvious from ground level. Patching the barrier wall, cutting into the ships tangled together around the docks. The sprawling refugee sectors were neat, fenced-off squares covered in checkered brown and grey patterns of prefab housing and tents wedged into spaces too small for either to be effectively used. Even the white tiles of the Cove's luxury plazas were now overflowing with refugee encampments.

A small kingdom, cut off from the mainland by a perilously thin fortress wall, but a kingdom all the same. Miller was glad he wasn't in charge.

"What the hell do I do now?" Gray whispered.

"Put the board on the boat," Miller said, pointing at a white wedge amongst the oil tankers. A cruise ship, bigger than the tankers, higher over the water. "That's what it's for, isn't it? A floating bolthole?"

"Harris had me bring the *Tevatnoa* in as an emergency power supply." Gray sighed, tiredly. "Now he tells me it can't leave, it's essential infrastructure."

"*Tevatnoa*. What is that, something in Hawaiian? Samoan? I preferred it when it was the *Sea-Star*."

"Neither of those. And *Sea-Star*'s a name for trying to sell fusion reactors. It had been an attempt to convince the Navy to switch to fusion from nuclear—a demonstrator for all the essential technologies. Desalinating and cracking sea-water into hydrogen, long mission endurance technologies, the works. *Tevatnoa*," Gray finished, "is a better name for an ark of hope."

"So we pack it all up. Load everyone on that thing, set sail for somewhere better. Europe, maybe."

"It's an option," Gray said, pressing his lips together tightly. "One of several I'm holding in reserve. But it's infrastructure now—can't tear it out anymore. And besides, there are too many refugees to fit aboard."

"So what then?" Miller asked.

"For now, go back to your people," Gray said. "We stay the course."

"But—"

Gray interrupted Miller, this time. "An organization this size is like one of those boats. They don't turn fast. This is going to take time. Besides, you have to know where you're going before turning the ship around."

Miller nodded, bitterly. "Fine," he said. "So long as you don't push us too hard, I guess I can't complain." He turned for the door.

"Alex?" Gray held his hands behind his back.

"Yeah?"

"Thanks for getting my hand back on the rudder."

14

In the end, orders came down from above: no more chasing the Charismatics across the city. If it didn't directly impact operations at the compound, it was to be ignored. The bright side was that their replacement duty was cushy, and kept them away from anyone who didn't understand. As Doyle put it, keep dogs with dogs, cattle with cattle. Mix the two up and neither would be happy.

These dogs were ride-along escorts on the food trucks. There was a lot of time to sleep, waiting for the trucks to arrive or snatched between Infected ambushes and wildlife attacks. Generally Miller and the rest of his team didn't even have to dismount—the heavy lifting was handled by a pair of armed Bravos. Their remote turrets, mounting an automatic grenade launcher and .50 cal machine gun each, could clear the road no matter what was in front of the convoy. Sure, ammo was scarce, but five rounds in a thug-behemoth's ass got the thing moving along pretty damn quick even if it didn't seem to slow the carnivorous rhino bastards down any.

What the hell were those creatures built from, if a burst off the .50 was the equivalent of a sharp swat with a newspaper? What was it going to take to stop them? Maybe the 40mm grenades could do it, but they didn't have enough of those to waste.

Anyway, didn't matter. Wasn't Miller's—or Cobalt's—problem. The trucks never stopped long enough for them to dismount, so Miller never had to wake up. If he had trouble sleeping he could always call on Doyle and his drugs, but the occasional burst of gunfire and the jolting ride didn't bother him.

It had been a long, long time since Miller had caught up on his sleep. But now he was sleeping eighteen hours a day, making up for the madness in the weeks before.

He listlessly hung, trapped between day-dreams and sleep, picturing his ex-girlfriend Samantha sitting down with one of her self-help books and explaining, reading aloud section by section, that he was actually depressed. And bit by bit, though he might have claimed she was way off the mark, she'd work through the checklists in her books and get him to open up until he admitted that, yes, he missed the Army, and civilian life was taking a lot of getting used to. Maybe this time she could have gently pried at him until Miller blurted that with enough of Doyle's drug-drenched paper strips in his system, killing people in cold blood didn't seem all that bad. That *nothing* seemed bad, that everything was just fucking copacetic.

His memories of the killings were an unpleasant, intrusive tangle. But they felt like something that had happened to someone else, mostly, and that seemed like the best possible situation. So he shut his eyes and concentrated, hard, on the hum of the truck's wheels, curled up in one of the three bunk-beds behind the driver's compartment. He let conversations between du Trieux and the driver wash through him and vanish, and he thought about nothing in particular. Just pushed everything out of his head and slept, waiting for the next cycle to complete, the truck looping into the city to the compound and back to the checkpoint in New Jersey, where they'd switch to a fresh truck coming in.

He woke to the ebbing, back-and-forth oceanic roar of humanity. He jolted straight, almost banging his head on the bunk above his. The driver was rolling down his window, while Morland, now occupying the passenger seat, was twisted round to look back.

"Miller!" Morland pointed out front. "It's a riot."

"The Infected don't *riot,* they *attack,*" Miller snapped, scrambling off the bunk in time to catch du Trieux's foot in the face. She swore, pulling herself back up on her bunk, while Miller grabbed his M27 and pushed up against the back of Morland's seat.

"It's not the Infected..."

It wasn't a riot, either. But it could turn into one.

The late afternoon light burned across the barrier wall, pouring across the open gates and illuminating a rectangle of the crowd filling the motor pool. It wasn't the Infected. It was the refugees, tired and sweaty but washed clean of color, their clothes faded white by the delousing regimen. They were chanting, words clear—nothing like an Infected chorus.

"Hell, no! We won't go! Hell, no!"

None of the unified purpose of the Infected, either. Most were there to protest the rumoured evacuations to Boston, while others were scrambling through the crowds, passing backpacks along in fire-gang fashion, rushing out as the gates slowly rolled back, trying to escape into the city before a guard on the streets outside barked at them to stay put. Hell— even the lead Bravo's turret swung to cover the now terrified would-be escapees.

The truck stopped halfway through the gates, a few feet from the back of the crowd instead of driving through—something Miller half-expected to see, memories of pulped bodies briefly distracting him, before he ordered the dismount and climbed last out of the truck.

Hsiung, who'd been riding along in the lead Bravo, was already outside and waiting for them, shrugging helplessly, as if this were her fault. "No one told me, there wasn't anything on the drone footage..."

Why would there be? Northwind was keeping an eye on the land routes into the Astoria compound, trying to keep logistics going. Civil unrest wasn't on their dance-card, or Cobalt's.

The motor pool's guards were the only ones there to handle the crowd that had broken into the parking and repair zone, just about the only open space *left* in the compound. The wall guards were taking turns staring at the crowd, making sure the machine guns facing the city were all manned.

"Hey! *Hey!* Clear a path, we need to get the convoy in!"

Miraculously, a path didn't appear. An impulse to lift his M27 and *make* one, filling the air with bullets, was the first Hollywood solution to present itself. But that wasn't how the world worked, or even the way it was supposed to work. Miller knew that much, through the red fog of frustration. He tried yelling again, but it fell on deaf ears.

He marched back to the lead Bravo and leaned into the cabin. "Turn on the siren."

"*What* siren?"

The driver, one of the guys from Bayonet, clearly hadn't spent any time in the Army. Miller reached past him and flipped a mode toggle and punched commands into the driver side screen. The Bravo screamed like a cop car on bad methamphetamine, and the crowd backed away from it, covering their ears and hurling their slogans at the vehicles shouldering their way in. The stragglers trying to get out, or who didn't get out of the way, Morland and the Bayonet team pushed aside.

At last, Miller and Hsiung dragged the gate shut, bracing it at either end with swinging sets of steel bars. The crowd eyed the truck hungrily, but as members of Bayonet shepherded it through the press to the cargo dock, nobody did anything more than eye it. The refugees were hungry, sure, but they were being fed. They didn't open a path up as easily for Cobalt. Fighting through, pushing along through the crush, Miller froze in place, staring, searching.

The past—so much *better* than the present—was on Miller's mind, sure. That's what was going on. Miller hadn't actually spotted Samantha in the crush. Had he?

It was impossible. She was one of the Infected, probably. And her light brown hair—impossible for him to match, Miller's highlights always taking him to dirty blond—simply wasn't anywhere he looked. Had he seen her? Or had he just *wanted* to see her?

He kept twisting around to look, until du Trieux reached out of the crowd and grabbed his shoulder. "What's wrong?"

Miller wet his lips to answer, but he couldn't. He shook his head, and meekly turned to shoulder through the crowd after her.

THE REFUGEE PROCESSING office hadn't heard of Samantha. Their files were a mess, though—boxes of unsorted refugee forms waiting for processing mixed in here and there, and not an electronic device in sight. All handwritten. It was possible she'd been processed and her form simply wasn't where it should have been in the files, but Miller wasn't entirely convinced he hadn't made it all up, anyway.

At the checkpoint outside the city, curled up on his stretch of bunk in a repurposed truck stop office while they waited for the next truck in, all he cared about was the privacy he had between the wall behind him and his phone in front of his face.

Getting a connection to the wider internet, any kind of connection, was more through luck than any kind of skill with the phone's menus. Eventually he connected to a public network, so choked of bandwidth that not even the user icons loaded on his social media pages. And every few profile flips, he had to reconnect. Not that he could *use* the site, no one could. The friendly cartoon dog that failed to properly load at the top of every page continually informed him, in a small pop-up window, that the site was down for maintenance and available in a read-only mode. Maintenance would be over in a few hours, Barker the dog explained, and had been explaining since the spring.

It was all more than three months out of date, but he continued to page through each and every profile for 'Billy R.' in Los Angeles he could find. Without pictures, and without being able to log on and directly access his contact list or view last names, it was slow going.

A lot of people named Billy had been very cranky about food, all those months ago. Some had stopped posting months before the site froze, some had the public discussions on their pages filled with 'miss you' and 'rest in peace.'

Not his Billy, though. Miller was sure Billy wouldn't be so unfortunate as to starve in a famine. Billy was smart, resourceful. Had... marketable skills, Miller realized, a traitorous feeling in his gut as he thought about it.

He thought he found the right Billy. Lots of friends—not that Miller could log in and see the list, just the total: a number value for Billy's grace and charm. Lots of smiling emoticons, lots of cheerful, upbeat little updates. About how he and his boyfriend were packing to leave the city.

More traitorous feelings bubbled up in Miller. It had been a long, long time since he and Billy had parted ways. Visiting him three weekends a month hadn't been quite enough to hold things together after Miller was hired by Schaeffer-Yeager. And he'd been too busy to chat with Billy, or send messages back and forth, or play games together. A bodyguard wasn't much good if he spent his time thumbing at a phone like a kid in love, even if that's how the bodyguard felt.

Leave the city, Miller thought. *You leave the city, Billy, and get the hell away from anything or anyone dangerous. And make sure that boyfriend of yours is the practical macho type you loved, the type you claimed I was, someone who can live off the land with you on some beach in Baja.*

Of course there wouldn't be anywhere Billy could get ahold of cheap, sweetened liquor now. That was Miller's mental image of Billy, maybe the one he'd have to hold onto forever: Billy on a deck chair on the beach, holding a pair of drinks with ridiculous names and a dozen colours and their own little paper umbrellas to keep the sun off the ice.

Miller let himself wallow in the desire to be the guy keeping Billy safe for a little while, then tried his other friends, his parents. All of them were as he'd left them months before, when the phones still worked. Dad using the public part of his page to discuss how to get pot-luck meals around to the neighbours, dozens of miles away from the ranch but still the closest human beings around. Mom's page seemed similarly practical, filled with updates on far-flung members of the family. Even an update on 'Alex staying busy in New York.'

Busy. Right.

He tried old acquaintances, friends of friends, until his eyes burned with fatigue and he couldn't put it off any longer.

He put in a search for Samantha L. of Philadelphia.

Philadelphia had, almost, been convenient. Forty-five minutes on the fastest direct train. It was entirely possible for him to stay at her apartment and get to work on time, or, as she often preferred, for her to get back to her job and classes in leisurely time from his studio-apartment in the city, rather than having him disentangle from her at five-thirty every morning.

It had been good until the question of their future arrived. She'd been a little unhappy when he'd told her that he didn't consider himself straight, but she'd gotten over that. The question of kids had, for Miller, been one he'd tried to keep distant. Samantha hadn't liked that, been impatient to move in together more formally. He'd forgotten her favorite kind of flower three times over, turning his make-up bouquets into fodder for fresh fights.

Maybe she was right.

Maybe it was unfair for him to have entered into that kind of relationship with her when he knew full well they wanted different things out of it, stringing her along with vague promises that more commitment would be on the horizon. All he'd really wanted was someone he could be happy with, in the now, and all she'd really wanted was someone she could be happy with for the rest of her life.

Once in a while she turned it around to his bisexuality, sometimes asking if he didn't want to commit because he still wanted to be with men, or if he was actually *gay*, and those conversations always left him feeling hurt and misunderstood. But it was easier for Samantha to believe the issue was one of sexuality, than that her confident, strong, gun-toting boyfriend had been too much of a coward to admit that kids, a family, a future, *responsibility*, scared the shit out of him.

If only, if *only* they could have been on the same page about things. Surely this Archaean water stuff could help them figure it all out? Her latest self-help books *all* said it worked, all of them. And that ended it.

The most likely Samantha L. of Philadelphia's last activity had been six months earlier, slavishly reposting a string of protest posts affirming that the Infected— the *gifted*—had the right to refuse treatment.

He scrolled back as far as the page's archive went, but he couldn't find *his* Samantha. The Samantha who could sit him down and patiently work through the issues until he finally admitted, both to her and to himself, that he was afraid of committing. Afraid of taking the next steps. So afraid, in fact, that he needed to get away from her. Maybe, if he hadn't, and if she hadn't terrified him with the Archaean water, she could have sat him down and gently pried the truth out of him. That walking out on her had been a mistake.

But that Samantha was gone. That whole chapter of his life was gone, and nothing he could do would get it back. The world had changed too much.

Miller paged through, curious, to Alex M. of New York. Another long list to search through, but he could recognise the condensed search result more easily for his own profile than he had for Billy or Samantha's.

There were unanswered messages on the public part of his profile. He didn't log on very frequently, too busy with work, not enough friends. Some dating site spam bot had gone wild just before the site had frozen into its eternal maintenance—a string of messages, all repeating, 'We should get back together, call me.'

Eventually, scrolling down in search of something an actual human who cared about him might have said, he found the first message in the spam bot's chain.

From Samantha L.—We should get back together, call me.

Miller's stomach turned cold.

15

GRAY'S CONTROL OF the corporation, his hand on the rudder, was all but invisible down on the ground. Miller and the team had received new orders that barred them—barred any security team— from operating further from the compound than absolutely necessary.

It was a mistake, and Miller intended to tell Gray as much. For such an obvious mistake, though, it looked pretty good from where Miller was standing. He'd taken his team into civilian country, and it was a pleasant place to be.

An impromptu market had dropped out of the sky and landed in one of the refugee runs overnight, in one of the semi-public covered walkways that gave the refugees their only freedom to move between sectors.

More specifically, a titan-bird had been hit by machine gun fire while it was flying low, and the corpse had tangled up on the wire loops overhead. The civilian refugees cutting it down and repairing the fence also had a barbecue running on the side, roasting hunks of the beast's flesh over barrel fires until it was blackened, then selling it right there. Folks were laughing, bartering, water was flowing freely and a little distilled moonshine not so freely.

Miller stood huddled in a shadow like a teenager too nervous to join in, watching his team have a good time.

He hadn't ever been much of a wallflower. Not in high school, not in his Army years, not even as a bodyguard. When he hadn't been seeing anyone, he'd been *happy* to be seen. Get dressed up, get his hair done, find some new bottle of cologne or attack his drawers for an old favourite, and go out on the town. But now, past the end of civilization, he found himself awkward and untalkative.

His hair was growing out. He wanted to get his highlights back. He told himself that was the problem, not the way he glared at the refugees after stilling the urge to raise his M27 for the dozenth time to point at some vaguely threatening movement in the corner of his eye. It wasn't as though anyone around him could see the bloody thoughts jabbing for attention in his skull, the swallowed fear, the prickling between his shoulder blades—all irrational. He was *inside* the wall.

It was true, the compound's barrier wall was no longer the imposing, impenetrable edifice it had once been. Stockman's artillery had blown sections down, those as yet unrepaired patched with wire fences that members of Shank on extermination duty used to display their kills—decaying juvenile terror-jaws with their heads pushed through the fence weave, dangling limbs and heads of larger creatures strung up as effigies against the new ecology.

It all looked *wrong* to Miller, the dismembered bundles of flesh dangling from paracord belonged in a scene from a horror movie, not New York.

All the same, it kept the smarter predators away, or so the Shank team members said. But half of them were ex-Army volunteers young and old, and Miller knew what kinds of men wound up in the Army. More specifically, what kinds wound up as *ex*-Army. There had been a domestic terrorist in his battalion—a full-on white-supremacist who believed that if white people weren't going to make an effort to outbreed every other race in America, at some point there would need to be a culling. How the hell that guy had slipped through the screening process Miller had no idea. Apparently the home-grown militias and domestic terrorist organizations made an effort to send their best through the Army to receive free training. Gangs, too.

Miller eyed the distant stretch of fence he could make out from the midst of the refugee run between sectors two and six. The dark shadows of the hanging bodies—almost familiar enough to look like cats and dogs in silhouette—made Miller wonder just how Shank's volunteers had got booted out the Army.

"How much money do you have on you?" Morland asked, just barely in Miller's peripheral vision. Morland had picked a perfect angle to make him flinch and clutch his rifle.

Miller did his best to settle himself back down, and reached for his back pockets, not his sidearm. "Hundred and fifty?" Miller ventured, checking his wallet. "Two fifty-ish. You want beer money?"

"Nah, that ain't remotely enough. Don't you have any other cash?"

He shrugged. "Spent most of my cash already." On getting his suits dry cleaned and pressed, not that he was ever going to wear them again.

"Come on, you've got to try t-bird steak! They're starting to figure out how to cook it decently, so the price is getting *extortionate*."

"So long as they're not cooking it rare—fuck knows what kinds of bugs are infesting those things."

Morland waved off Miller's concern. "When they tried that, it tasted of piss."

Miller allowed himself to be dragged away from his patch of shady wall, and joined the rest of his team goggling at the barbecue cook attacking the lopped off bits of titan-bird with a couple of cleavers. The bird was a big one. There had to be more than a hundred and fifty pounds of its stinking guts alone. One wing still flopped over the fencing overhead, providing impromptu shade as stretches of its other wing were hacked up, skinned, and fried. Even at the rate the cook was working, it'd be a long, long time before they had to drag down the second wing.

The trick, it seemed, was to avoid the beast's flight muscles. A few hunks were drooling blood into a gutter nearby—there was a forlorn hope that draining the creature's blood would improve the flavor—but the wing's relatively scrawny flesh could be cooked immediately.

Du Trieux wafted a shrivelled, scorched scrap of meat clinging to a chipped piece of yellowy bone under his nose; it smelled better than anything. Maybe it was the spices—some kind of dry rub rustled up out of rations.

"What?" Miller pleaded, trailing after her. "You're not going to let me try a piece?"

Du Trieux grinned and darted back out of reach. "At the prices they're selling for? You're crazy!"

It took two loops of the little knot of people, his team, and a couple of friendly refugees, including a woman a little younger than du Trieux but with a smile that was far more captivating for her availability. Plus, she was the one handling the money and selling beer.

"How much?" Miller asked, gesturing at the cooler behind her.

She looked him up and down. "How much you got?"

"Two hundred fifty or so."

"Eeeh..." She looked back at the cooler. "I guess I can give you a beer for that."

"And one of the wings?" He jerked his head toward the barbecue.

She laughed. For a moment, just a moment, Miller wanted to try and live in a world with laughs like that again, but he couldn't help thinking about what he'd done to earn that world.

Memories flooded his mind. The violent pang in

the back of his head—the sensation of punching a knife's tip through bone.

It just wouldn't go away.

He was glad she was looking back at the barbecue, and then at his M27—not at him. Glad he didn't have to meet her eyes, or cross the fence between soldier and civilian to be a barbecue cook, have to handle a cleaver. He wouldn't have to touch *anything* like that until it was time to kill again.

"What calibre's that gun?" the seller asked.

"Five-five-six," Miller said without thinking about it.

She squinted, and called back to the cook, "Jeff? Five-five-six's the same as two-two-three? Was that right?"

"Uh-huh. That's right, Honey."

It wasn't, not exactly; Miller's dad had blown out a perfectly good .223 rifle with Army surplus 5.56mm rounds. But he didn't point that out when she turned and flashed her smile at him again. It had lost a little power through 'Honey.' Miller was as likely to make a move on her as he was on du Trieux now, but it was still a very good smile. Especially for a saleswoman.

"A four-inch piece for ten bullets," she said. "Or, you can have an eight-inch piece for fifteen."

He blinked at her. "You're selling food for ammunition?"

"Money ain't worth much anymore," she said, shrugging with a smile. "And if those guys kick us out to Boston"—she jerked her head in the direction of the Cove's shining towers—"we're going to have to protect ourselves somehow."

Miller looked up at the window he'd stood at with Gray not that long ago, and bit his lip. "Guess so," he said, wondering if Harris and the rest of internal security had *any* idea that the refugees were stockpiling guns and ammunition. Wasn't his problem, though. He pulled the drum magazine from his M27 and stripped fifteen rounds out for her, setting them in her outstretched hand.

She bobbed daintily, went back to the barbecue and got him his spiced up piece of titan-bird. Big one. And then all the cash he had left over, for a beer, too.

Other than the sellers—it looked a *lot* like Doyle was making some kind of illicit drugs trade with a scrawny refugee to one side—Cobalt and the civilians surrounding the barbecue didn't mix much. But the atmosphere was good. No fear of a food riot, no hammered-in oppression. Just the surprisingly tangy flesh of the titan-bird's wing, crispy on the bone, lovingly smothered with dry-rub so it tasted of mustard and pepper. Mouthwatering, and good with the beer.

Bit by bit Miller drifted to the edge of the Cobalt group, joining in on a conversation between du Trieux and one of the refugees, laughing about how extortionately priced the barbecue was.

"First of all," the refugee laughed, "the meat's a literal fuckin' windfall. Second of all, they're overcharging. There's gonna be plenty of food once those oil tankers get turned into floating farms, y'know? This is artificial scarcity. Someone'll rustle up some rabbits or something. We'll feed them on oil tanker lettuce, barbecue every weekend. You'll see."

"There are chickens somewhere around Massachusetts. Get about thirty, forty fresh eggs in a week," Miller said, chipping in.

"That's for the ivory tower boys, right?" The refugee laughed. "Well, at least there are still living chickens *somewhere*."

"And there's still flour coming in. Trouble with the sacks, though. I've seen it coming in through barrels." Du Trieux shifted her weight from foot to foot thoughtfully. "What's it like in the black market?"

The refugee bit his lip, eyeing Miller. "Well," he said, noncommittally. "Not that I'd *know* about that."

"If I cared about the black market, I wouldn't be standing here letting *that* happen," Miller said, nodding towards the barbecue. "You don't have to worry about me."

That got a *very* twisted smile out of the refugee. "Nothing to worry about anyway—it's all stuff people trade out of their own ration packs, right?"

"Right," Miller said, thinking about that bastard with the rations at the warehouse a few days before.

"But you can get a lot, a *lot*, for powdered milk." He continued staring at Miller and du Trieux, as if through their company connections they could produce live cattle with a snap of the fingers. "You guys seen any fresh milk?"

"...Month ago?" du Trieux ventured. "Maybe two? Before the compound wall was finished, anyway."

The refugee didn't seem entirely convinced. Surely the corporate bastards had all kinds of stuff hidden under their combat uniforms, right? He gnawed his lip a moment, then blew out a wishful sigh. "Well. There've gotta be safe farms somewhere. Maybe up in Canada, y'know? Someplace it's too cold for all those bastards," he said, gesturing up at the partly-dismembered titan-bird.

It'd have to be pretty far north to be that cold in midsummer, now. But maybe. Not everywhere was as hard-hit as New York, anyway. There wasn't much news available about what was going on in the rest of the world—collapsing governments made surprisingly little noise when they pulled the media and journalism apparatus down with them.

"They've got some good ranches up there. Saskatchewan, Alberta, around there. Probably some smart guy moved his herds north," Miller ventured. "Could happen, easy."

"Hope so. A steak. Big, fat and juicy. That'd really hit the spot. Maybe if they start letting civilian traffic in and out of the compound, we can get some stuff in from Canada—then we'll see about a *black market*, huh?" The refugee laughed. "Maple syrup, that's what I'm talking about. You know Canadians use maple syrup for barbecue? That'd be something to try..."

Later, after Miller and the rest of the team had blown a firefight's worth of ammunition on getting themselves fed—ammunition, its supply, and whether or not the refugees were armed was Harris's problem, and *fuck* Harris—Miller stood back with du Trieux, leaning in the shadow of a wall, ostensibly watching the civilians haul the butchered pieces of the titan-bird away, leaving its bloodstains on the paving.

Miller gazed across the refugee run at the moving profile of Doyle's jaw. In an official capacity, Miller was pretty sure he was chewing gum. In a social capacity, he was pretty sure he was just interested in scoring another hit of something beautifully numbing off Doyle.

His gaze flicked to the moving civilians, the now-unattainable seller he knew as 'Honey,' women too old or too young for him, men he felt uncomfortable thinking of approaching without the social lubricants of alcohol, loud music, and clothing that signalled something other than 'I'm a soldier' or 'I'm a refugee without easy access to water.' He felt longing, but not desire.

Miller glanced down at the bottle by his foot, but he'd finished his beer long ago. "Trix?"

"*Oui?*"

"You've done this kind of thing before. How do you transition between fighting and being human?"

She leaned back, her eyes drifting nowhere in particular. "Fighting the Daesh wasn't like this."

"No?"

"The fighting was short, decisive. Nothing like what happened in the bank."

The bank office had been reasonably secure. A

logical place to fortify. Miller would have done anything to go back and change that decision now.

"The difficult parts were not what we did, it was what we saw," du Trieux went on. "The aftermath."

Miller shifted uncomfortably, thinking of the aftermath of what he'd done.

"Miller?" she asked.

"You think they've got a future?" he said. "This new society we've built?" He flicked his gaze toward the refugees making their way between sectors.

"Perhaps." She sounded wistful. "A better chance than many have had."

"And for us?"

"How do you mean?"

He slouched down. "How do we fit into whatever future they've got? We're why they're stuck behind the fences."

Gunfire rattled in the distance. They both looked up, but didn't see or hear anything else. It wasn't an unfamiliar sound, probably someone taking potshots at another titan-bird. Du Trieux watched the sky for a moment before answering. "I don't know."

"How do we wake up knowing we committed mass murder so Joe Average over there can sell t-bird hotdogs?"

"Well," she said, "he can take the safety to do that for granted. We can't do that—you can't—but what you did gives them the option to quietly get on living their lives without fear."

Without fear? Lucky for them. What about him?

The gunfire returned, and then there was the

distinctive chained rumble of a burst of 40mm grenades going off. It wasn't someone taking pot shots at a titan-bird, it was one of the escort Bravos. Within seconds, the emergency response alarms shrilled across the compound.

So much for freedom to live without fear.

Didn't seem to Miller that he'd done a good enough job for the refugees to have that.

16

THE REFUGEE RUNS weren't designed for a combat team to get anywhere in a hurry. They were designed to keep the civilians moving along like well-behaved cattle.

Miller hit the fence a second ahead of Doyle, launched himself off it back along the hairpin turn. He grabbed and pushed down a civilian—Miller didn't see them as anything more than a dirty brown shirt—and charged through the now-unoccupied gate. Metal rang behind him. Hsiung trailed him, but the whole team was on the move with the same coordination they'd used out in the field hunting the Charismatics. This time, though, they were on home turf and they were seriously disadvantaged.

Dystopian prison architecture and hundreds of miles of chain-link fence was the least of their problem. There was motion everywhere. People were everywhere.

With a quiet roar of footsteps, the mob crashed

around a corner, chasing Doyle towards the bank. Miller followed a few metres behind.

Then between them a titan-bird landed above, coming down on the fencing looped overhead *specifically* to protect the refugees from the titan-birds. It was a little one, twenty-foot wingspan or so—a silent mass of stretched skin and bony wings. It hobbled around above on its knuckles, wings folded, and it jabbed down, trying to break the fencing. Its teeth snagged and caught on the weave as it wailed, beating its wings in an attempt to free itself.

Miller shot it on the run. It screamed, tearing at the overhead chain-link fencing, so he stopped and shot until the thing stopped moving. Chipped remnants of its skull poured out through the fencing along with its brains and splattered onto the ground below.

The *human* screams bore into Miller's head. Human screams felt like a threat. Like a mob. But the Infected lunged at him, *hated* him, the refugees cowered away into the corners of the run like terrified animals. He had to shake his head just to clear his mind, remind him of where he was, what he was doing.

He gave his M27 a shake—the drum magazine was light, too light. "If we run out of ammo," he yelled over the ringing in his ears, "because of *barbecue*, you are all in *very* big trouble!"

"Why us?" Morland asked, stepping around the spatter. "You were the one paying for everything."

"You should have stopped me," Miller snapped back—more vicious than he meant to be.

They got into refugee sector six, one of the holding pens, and immediately pushed through the clusters of shacks, tents, and prefabricated buildings clustered around the old tower—a dilapidated structure with a dozen floors packed to the brim with refugees.

More titan-birds clawed at the wire fencing overhead.

Parts of it had privacy screening woven through to provide shade—but now it provided the titan-birds solid footing to scrabble and claw at the weak points where lengths of fencing had been wired together.

Miller lifted his M27 to fire on instinct, then saw Hsiung doing the same, following his lead. "Hold fire!" he yelled. "Check background, check background!"

He hadn't seen what he was doing until he saw Hsiung doing it. They were pointing their guns at the titan-birds—and at the tower behind them. The tower filled with civilians.

"Leave it!" Miller started moving again. "We have to get out of the civilian section!"

Miller came to a halt at the abandoned sector gate. It was supposed to be locked—refugees were fleeing through, fighting to get deeper into the compound and away from the walls—but there weren't any guards.

Du Trieux and Doyle seemed to be having a similar thought. Doyle picked up something that looked a lot like the lock and chain and showed it to du Trieux. The chain had been neatly shorn apart with a pair of bolt cutters.

In the chaos, Miller tried his earbud again. The security channel was broadcasting the same order it had been since the alarms sounded. *"All staff report to emergency stations! Attack is imminent or underway. All staff report—"* Miller snapped it off, flicking through channels as quickly as the limited interface on the earbud let him.

"Problem on the boulevard."

"That fucking thug-behemoth?"

"Think they killed it, but some asshole just shot the truck driver."

Guards on top of the wall? Miller tried another channel, racing after his team towards the motor pool.

"We're under fire! Under fire! No, I don't know from whe—"

The channel went quiet but for the crackle of nearby gunfire. If whoever the speaker had been talking to was on another channel, Miller couldn't hear them.

Miller tapped du Trieux on the shoulder and moved up. They pushed ahead in short bounds, covering each other. Doyle lagged behind, lugging his .388 custom rifle with him.

Miller didn't have to give the order—the refugees had thinned out and things were scarily quiet as they approached the motor pool. They reached the compound wall in no time.

The path ahead was one long alley of high fencing on the other side, open to the sky, a straight shot with none of the twists of the refugee runs, but there were no security personnel in sight. Not on their feet, anyway.

Four from security team Bayonet were down, but Miller couldn't cycle through to a command clear channel to report it.

Du Trieux crouched by the first body, then skipped ahead and checked the second while Miller searched the sky and the refugee sectors on either side of the fence, but he saw no obvious threat.

"Small calibre," du Trieux said. "They were shot with handguns from behind, I think." She lifted one of their heads, twisting it to show Miller the surprisingly neat hole in the back of the neck. No real exit wound.

Someone had ambushed them—from *inside* the compound.

Miller crouched down and gestured Hsiung over to cover him while he got out his phone and flicked through the communications channel lists. The earbud was shit for cycling through channels, but if his phone could load the menu he could just *select* a channel straight to Northwind and—

Something happened; Miller didn't understand what. He had been holding his phone and it was gone. His hand was empty. He was on the ground. The asphalt. Something was hot. His face was hot. He touched it, fumbling to his feet. There was blood. His blood. He'd scraped open his nose. How?

He looked up, confused, vision blurry. There were flames. His head hurt. His chest hurt. Everything hurt. He'd fallen. How had that happened?

The fences behind the team were now crushed flat, torn apart. Pieces of them lay on the ground. They'd been blown to literal shreds. A twenty-foot section of the compound wall had been blown out, one of the weak sections that was just a skin of sheet metal.

Miller could see the city outside. The shanties behind the fence were gone, or on fire.

A bomb?

Miller didn't remember a bomb. He didn't remember anything.

He struggled onto his hands and knees, then his feet, and immediately fell back onto his hands, scraping them on the asphalt. He puked. Acidic glop. No blood in it he could make out. Not until his bleeding nose started to drip into the puddle. He struggled to breathe until he felt arms come in under his shoulders and lift him up. Du Trieux sounded very far away as she shouted at him, but he heard her.

"Are you hurt?"

He tried to speak, but his throat was raw. He'd had the wind knocked out of him, that was all. He wheezed down a breath and tried again. "Artillery?" he croaked.

Du Trieux shook her head. "Satchel charge. Doyle—"

"Doyle!" Miller spun round, struggling. Doyle had been behind the team, Doyle had—

She grabbed his shoulders hard before he stumbled off his feet. "Doyle's fine!"

"He was *behind us!*"

"He's chasing the attacker, he's *fine!*"

Miller swayed on his feet. Morland and Hsiung approached from the far side. He palmed blood off his face and stared at the blood on his hand. "What attacker?"

"Someone threw a satchel charge at you over the fence from the refugee sector while you were trying to contact Northwind. We all got clear—it detonated while you were still running. Are you *hurt?*"

"Phone," Miller mumbled. "Was holding my phone..."

"I don't know where it is." She held up her fingers. "Miller! *Alex*. How many fingers?"

His vision was blurry, but not doubled. "Two," he murmured. "I'm fine, got to warn command—contact Northwind, attackers in the compound—" He couldn't stop wheezing. He took one step from du Trieux and doubled up, hands on his knees, retching, but nothing came up.

"What's wrong with him?" Hsiung asked, while Morland swung his gun at the gap in the wall.

"Concussion," du Trieux answered.

"I'm fine," Miller croaked, taking a step unaided. A second, unsteadily. He was relieved when the ringing in his ears turned out to be the emergency response alarms blaring away. He got to the nearest section of fence, still upright. He must have gotten pretty damn far on his feet before the detonation. "Don't leave Doyle *alone!*" he snapped. "Hsiung, Morland. *Go*. Me and Trix will be fine."

Morland backed up a step uncertainly, then followed Hsiung as she accepted her orders with a professional nod. They jogged over the collapsed fence and into the refugee sector, while Miller struggled to breathe.

"Miller?"

He looked up at du Trieux unsteadily. "Am I hurt?"

"Eh?" She looked him over worriedly. "No. No pieces of fence sticking out of you."

"My face?"

"Your face is a mess."

He winced. "Am I ugly?"

She laughed, soothing despite the fear, and she upended her water bottle over him. He spluttered through the liquid, but the lukewarm splash helped him feel human. She poked and prodded at his nose and cheek about as professionally as anyone could. "Grazed. Doubt it'll scar—probably done worse to yourself shaving with that straight edge."

"I'm careful with the straight edge," he muttered unsteadily, clinging to the fence. "Thanks."

He couldn't have been out long. He gave himself another thirty seconds to feel sorry for himself, then had du Trieux lead him through into the refugee sector after the rest of his team.

As they jogged, more detonations exploded across the compound, inside and outside the wall. None of them were artillery shells, Miller noted— no airbursts, and no direct strikes. The bombs left smoke coiling over the compound, blocking out the light for minutes at a time as they searched.

Miller had no idea where his phone was. He

resorted to tapping at his earbud, following du Trieux, listening to chaotic radio chatter until he thought to check his pocket—the first place he would've put his phone. And there it was, an unexpected gift. He connected to the Northwind channels he had on file, but those were all jammed with requests for support, overwatch, everything. Northwind was fully aware there were attackers inside the compound, at least. Whether this was the food riot Miller knew had been brewing for days or not, they knew. He didn't have to report shit.

He switched back to Cobalt's private channel in time to hear Doyle murmur, "*He's gone round the back there. Yes. Stop there.*"

Step-by-step, under Doyle's direction, they converged on an alley filled with shanty huts built from plyboard and corrugated iron torn from roofs. Dark, miserable. Crowded. Doyle had line-of-sight on the far end. Hsiung and Morland waited at the edges. Miller and du Trieux found their way to the near end, shuffling along an old building's wall until it gave way to the improvised construction leaning against it. Another step, and Miller looked down the alley. It was dark, and damp, and full of people.

For an instant, just an instant, he thought he was looking at a commune. But the frightened people gathered up in clusters and inside their overcrowded homes weren't moving with the coordination of the Infected, but with mutual fear as gunfire continued to crackle nearby. Too many people. Too many targets. And too many of them moving to get away.

The first who reached Hsiung at the far end got shouted down to their knees—far enough that Miller heard her challenge as echoing tones, not words—and a half-dozen approached Miller and du Trieux's end.

"Who's the attacker?" he quietly asked over the private channel.

"*Mid-twenties male, messenger bag, black tank top, dirty jeans, yellow-soled trainers,*" Doyle responded instantly.

Miller spotted the attacker the moment Doyle finished the description. The guy had a weary expression. Tired, set in stone. Something like the thousand-yard stare Miller had seen in older veterans, but it was a gaze born from fear and determination.

The bomber looked like everyone else. A little scruffy—there weren't a lot of showers to go around, not much hot water—but reasonably clean. He'd shaven more recently than Miller had, looked thinner. He had bags under his eyes, and probably hadn't slept much lately. Who could, carrying around a bomb big enough to hole the wall?

"Trix?"

"*Oui?*"

"Cover me while I do something stupid," Miller said, and stepped out into the alleyway.

He locked eyes with the bomber immediately. The bomber had nowhere else to look, and an armed man was pretty damn obvious amongst panicked civilians. Miller held his M27 out to the side by the barrel, and dropped it. The bomber watched it topple and fall, his eyes wide.

The nearest refugees backed away into their hovels, turned straight around and made way the other end of the alley.

"Easy!" Miller yelled. "Easy, pal. You ain't going anywhere, you're trapped. But we can talk about this."

The refugees around the bomber scattered, halting and falling to their knees as du Trieux hung behind him, weapon up. The bomber himself stood still, frozen, half-tensed to run, but they all knew that wasn't going to happen.

The bomber relaxed. Staring at Miller as if he were looking at a piece of furniture. He tilted his head, slowly, and looked down at the messenger bag hanging under his arm.

That's when Miller realized he'd made a mistake. The guy had another bomb.

"Don't," Miller said, slow and reasonable.

The bomber hesitated, straightening up. He bit his lip, taking a slow, hard breath, gazing cautiously at Miller—like a cat unexpectedly caught with a mouse in its mouth.

"Just put it down. We can work this out, get you anything you need. Better food rations, clothes, safe passage to Boston. Whatever." Miller took one cautious step forward, another. "We know the refugees have problems, terrorism isn't the way to fix them, we can talk."

The bomber cocked his head to the other side,

almost reptilian. "Those aren't my problems," he said, and thrust his hand into the satchel.

Miller snatched the Gallican from his hip and fired.

He'd heard people talk about time slowing. It wasn't like that when he fired his weapon. More like everything sped up. It went too fast for Miller to comprehend.

Fumbling his Gallican up, the warmth of the steel in his hand, thumbing off the safety, pulling the trigger almost before he'd drawn it out, the way it jerked in his hand, forcing it in both hands in front of him as the second shot, the recoil and sound, reached him... he was slow, and everything else was fast, and he knew he'd made the decision to kill the bomber, or some other human being, long before now. Maybe days before, maybe years, long before he'd even known he'd have to kill anyone, and his body was finally going through the motions, late.

Blood fanned behind the bomber's head onto the asphalt, his body limp.

The satchel was smoking, a smouldering plume of smoke, and one of the nearest refugees was crying.

Miller fell to his knees, having covered the gap without realizing he'd taken the steps, and pulled open the satchel.

A piece of fuse cord sizzled down towards something that might have been a detonator. Fleshy looking blocks of some kind of plastic explosive, and a fuse cord that burnt about an inch a second. There was a loop of cord from the improvised friction striker—a matchbook stapled around the fuse cord—to the detonator.

In theory, Miller had a minute or so to deal with the problem. It wasn't a complicated bomb. He could take his time, be calm.

In reality, he tore the fuse cord out so fast he burnt his fingers on it, stripping it away from the bomb and stamping on the sizzling length like a dead snake.

By the time du Trieux came up behind him, Hsiung and Morland corralling the crowd in front of them as they approached, his shoulders shook and his breath came in uncontrolled gasps. Her hand, on his shoulder, was strangely solid and warm.

"You got it. It's out."

Miller shook his head, and found he couldn't stand up. In the end, he needed du Trieux's help just to stumble away.

17

Du Trieux sank down awkwardly onto the couch across from Miller. "I don't think this is healthy," she said, putting a mug of tepid water down on the table, and pushing it toward him.

The sunlight danced strangely on the bottom of the mug, a shaking, twisting oval pulled out of shape by the water's surface. Miller picked it up, and held his hand out to Doyle. "Give," he said.

Doyle tore a strip out of the sheet of thick paper, and placed it into Miller's palm. "He's right. Possibly. There were studies on treating PTSD with immediate drug use."

Du Trieux glared at him. "I doubt they used whatever the hell you've got."

"It was some antidepressant or other." Doyle shrugged. "Close as."

Miller's hands shook as he swallowed down the scrap of paper. The filthy stuff left his mouth bitter and coated in a chemical tang. He gulped the water down to force it into his system and clear his mouth.

He didn't know why he was shaking. Not for sure. Was it from killing someone? He'd done that, he'd killed. Was it from nearly getting blown to shreds? He'd come close to death, too. The past months had been a real learning experience. Maybe he was shaking because there was something wrong with him, because he wasn't cut out for this kind of work, never had been. Maybe—

"The other thing they used to do," Doyle said, "was talk about it afterward. Debriefing. With people who understand what it's like."

Du Trieux's expression softened, a little. "That sounds a little more sensible."

"Everyone gets nerves," Doyle said, voice slow, reassuring. "Everyone. You know I do. You know du Trieux does."

Miller shrank in on himself. His head went down, his shoulders up. Hands trembling, he gripped the mug against his face. "I lead."

"So?"

"I can't talk about it with you. It'd erode authority."

Doyle squinted. "What authority? We're your friends, or the closest thing that's left."

"He does lead," du Trieux said, eyes all ablaze again. "He has authority."

"Cut it out, Trix." Miller set the mug down, and held his face. "You don't have to protect me from Hsiung. She isn't fighting for my job quite so hard anymore."

"That's not the point..."

"There's authority," Doyle said, "Lewis-style

authority-with-a-capital-A, and that's what isn't happening here. Miller's not that kind of authority. You don't think you're *his* kind of authority, do you?"

Miller managed to shake his head. He wasn't much of anything, to tell the truth.

Raising his hands peaceably at du Trieux, to forestall another interruption, Doyle plunged on. "Miller's down in the trenches with us. He keeps us on course, he makes the calls, he leads. Saying this erodes his authority is absolutely absurd. He's one of us." He leaned forward, ducking his head to make eye contact with Miller. "Authority isn't the point. Trust is." Doyle seemed entirely serious.

"How the hell do you figure that?" Miller asked.

"Don't know. You got put in charge because you're the best at being in charge, not because you've got a badge on your shoulder. That's all."

"You could show... deference," du Trieux hissed.

"I could? What about you? You're closer to him than I am, been that—"

Morland slammed open the door, pale, frightened. He seemed too big to act like a scared child, but there it was. "Have you heard? Have you heard?"

There was too much news. Too much rushing through Miller's head. The attack was over. There had been a total of seven bombs. Most had originated inside the compound. Someone had attacked an incoming food truck, the compound's security teams were pulled thin responding to both. They'd had to let the attackers escape with the truck in order to protect the breaches while some *very* large predators were nosing around and trying to get in. Thugs that *earned* the name of behemoth, eight and nine feet high at the shoulder. Bigger than rhinos, now.

"What now?" Miller asked, clutching his head.

"They did an autopsy on the bomber. The guy you shot? He's Infected. He's also full of Firbenzol—and he was *still* Infected. The parasite's immune to anti-parasitic drugs. Firbenzol doesn't work anymore."

THAT ONE PIECE of information knocked a ton of weight off Miller's shoulders, and he felt like a bastard for it.

The suicide bomber was Infected—wasn't human. Oh, he *looked* human, would have been human if the refugee population had been given some other anti-parasitic drug, but the concentration of parasites in his hastily-autopsied brain proved it. He wasn't human, he was Infected, and just like that all thought of the bomber as someone with the right to a life vanished from Miller's mind.

He didn't like the change the news had brought about in him, but he felt relieved.

Sure, there might have been another history with the Infected if the slaughters—both that first one with the helicopter and the Charismatic killings—had never happened. If Harris had never tested NAPA-33 on an unwilling population, or if the company hadn't pressured the population into taking anti-parasitic drugs. Maybe with some alternate history of cooperation there could have been peace.

Maybe.

But those things had happened, and none of it was *really* his fault. Miller told himself that, instead of listening to the briefing that took place at the far end of the boardroom table.

"They *knew*," Harris growled down the length of the table. "Someone's feeding the Infected intel on our every move. They have attacked *prime* strategic targets!"

Miller pawed at a glass of water unsteadily, and dragged it over the table toward him. Across from where he sat, one of the guys in charge of Shank—some volunteer named Hannesy—stared disapprovingly. Miller didn't care.

The heads and upper staff of all remaining security teams—Cobalt, Bayonet, Stiletto, Dagger and Shank—had been dragged into a room along with representatives from the StratDevCo Rats and the Blue Bolts emergency relief teams, to listen to Harris rant. Lewis sat beside him, stony-faced. So much for Lewis's words from God. They apparently didn't allow him to interrupt.

But Miller, of course, had driven God's kids around. He sipped unsteadily and croaked up the table, "How the hell is *food* a prime strategic target? They're just hungry, everyone's fucking hungry..." He still wasn't sure that this whole mess wasn't somehow because of the food situation. Some kind of food riot? Maybe refugees were working with the Infected.

But that idea got battered out of his head in two hammer blows.

The first was Harris's cold reply, "As I said

earlier. The truck was transporting key indoor agricultural equipment: lighting, power supplies and hydroponics. We can't do without them for the oil tanker conversions. It was also carrying other need-to-know essentials. Which you would know if you had been *listening*, Mr. Miller."

The second hammer blow fell from Lewis's lips, a harsh whisper that carried all the way down the table. "Go easy. Boy nearly got killed by one of the bombs."

Harris grunted.

Miller remembered pointing a gun at the man. He debated pawing up his Gallican and doing to Harris what he'd done to the bomber, but the mood around the table wasn't quite right for that.

The other team heads were looking at him like a liability, a useless appendix. Cobalt was the smallest security team by a long shot, despite its former glorious role. Interrupting hadn't won him any points.

Miller smacked his lips closed and leaned back, alternately holding his head and refilling his water glass from the jug on the table as Harris went on.

"We *will* develop the tankers into factory farms. This delay will not slow us down. We will not allow the Infected to set the pace of engagement. Now, as it's clear that there is a strain of the parasite which is immune to the anti-parasitic drugs being distributed to the refugee population, based on the body recovered—"

Body. Not bodies. *Body*. Miller's team had nailed the only known attacker within the compound. There had been an escape—almost a hundred and forty civilians ran out through the breaches—but no one knew how many of them had been Infected. Maybe none of them.

Miller couldn't blame them for wanting to get out.

"—it seems clear that we have more quislings in our midst. We will find them and we *will* exterminate them. The only barrier between us and our rightful ownership of this city are the Infected. They are stupid and they are violent. They are our *enemies*. Little better than animals. There must be no compunction in killing them, even when they appear to be our friends and allies..."

Miller made eye contact with Lewis, and shook his head ever so slightly. It'd come to that, had it? Sanctioned extermination?

Lewis nodded back.

The worst of it was when the other security team heads, following Hannesy and the other Shankers' leads, started smiling, nodding. A few even applauded before Harris could finish his hateful oration. No plan, no solution, no *direction*, but hate and murder. The purge was called Operation Caspian Tiger.

"We will root them out from every corner," Harris promised. "Every uncooperative refugee will be checked, every staff member who fails to carry out their duty investigated. We will *cleanse* ourselves of the Infected."

Miller poured himself another glass of water, and wondered if Doyle had anything stronger than anti-depressants.

18

COBALT MIGHT HAVE been the smallest security team, but that came with advantages. Not for Cobalt themselves, of course. Wherever Harris—and increasingly Harris was calling the shots—needed a small team for an errant task, rather than break up Shank or Bayonet, he could just pick on Cobalt. Day to day, they were plucked from whatever they were settling into, with very little recognition of anything they might need, and sent on a new wild goose chase.

One day it was escorting a team of medics armed with a new set of saliva tests to try and find the new, drug-immune Infected within the executive staff. The next it was hiking out into the city to try and track down what was left of escaped civilians for 'interviews.' Miller wasn't sure if it was appropriate to feel joy at finding no trace of them beyond torn backpacks and a single abandoned shotgun, but there would be no interviews, Harris would go unsatisfied, and Miller was happy enough with that.

And that was Operation Caspian Tiger. Pansy-ass bullshit. Snatching at straws.

They were getting enough sleep, at least, and they were largely away from the killing fields. Regular movie nights and a supply of moonshine bought off the refugees with more ammunition kept them comfortably numbed, able to heal a little. But the jobs were getting weirder.

One day they were sent to secure the compound's septic tanks and wastewater outflow. The sewage went straight into the East River every day when the tides pulled it most quickly out into the ocean. That had been an odd one, just quietly walking in and taking the keys and holding the local staff in place while medics showed up.

Then there had been the hunting trip. They'd dumped a bunch of dead rat-things in the middle of a city street and killed everything that came in to feed. Harris had them taking blood samples out of each new monster.

Today, they were bringing home a small convoy. That was all that they'd been told before being sent out before dawn in two Bravos, one turreted, the other a salvaged ex-Army vehicle sprayed over in corporate black.

As du Trieux drove, stone-faced, Miller sat in the passenger seat of the front-most Bravo and eyed the city as the convoy zipped through what was left of the streets. He brushed away a brief moment of nostalgia as they rumbled through an area that used to be Brooklyn. Now, it wasn't anything.

The animals ruled now. Not just titan-birds in the sky, but rat-things and terror-jaws swarmed every foot of the ground. The thug behemoths were scavenging for something under the concrete. What the big creatures were looking for, Miller couldn't say.

The thugs, big enough to push even super-predators off their meals, stood smack dab in the middle of the roads in packs of two and three, and rooted their massive front tusks into the concrete, shearing away chunks of the street and sidewalks like it was nothing. He had a brief memory of when pigs used to root up truffles for fancy sauces in high-end restaurants, and almost smiled.

They were making the mission trickier than it needed to be, though, and his smile fell before reaching his lips. Du Trieux kept changing course, making sharp turns down alleys and side streets in order to avoid the things, not wanting to waste ammo or time in herding them out of the way.

There must have been at least twenty in a ten-block radius. The Bravo and following transport zigzagged and doubled back to avoid them, and the fungal blooms that piled up across the streets like snowdrifts. At times it felt like they were traveling in circles.

Miller said nothing. Du Trieux was giving the thugs a wide berth, which was for the best, lest they think the Bravos were competition for whatever it was they were searching for under the concrete.

From the back seat, Doyle suggested the thugs looked like a pack of hippos had gotten randy with a shark, but Miller didn't laugh.

As they passed the famous Park Place brownstones, now in ruins, doubt gnawed at the back of Miller's mind.

What a waste of time.

These missions were starting to get to Miller. It was as if they were being kept away, or, at least Miller was; pushed to the outskirts of the inner circle. He supposed he should be glad of the break—it certainly beat the shit out of murdering Charismatics or chasing down bombers—but something was off. It just didn't sit right.

No sense in stewing about it, though.

If Lewis or Gray knew what the grand scheme in all Harris's plotting was, they weren't about to share it with the likes of Miller, and even if they were, Miller wasn't certain he wanted to know—not when there was a job to do, bombs to dodge, staff to keep alive, and monsters to evade. Although throwing him to the monsters could have been the whole point, he mused.

He wouldn't be much trouble to Harris if he were dead.

Du Trieux whisked the Bravo around another sharp corner, sending Hsiung, who drove the transport behind them, to the airwaves to complain, again, but before anyone bothered to respond, du Trieux slammed on the brakes and screeched to a stop in front of what looked to be an abandoned four-story office building.

Down a half a block from there sat two transport vehicles: a big rig and a passenger van.

Miller tapped his earpiece. "Cobalt to transport: Rumor has it you need a lift?"

"Oh, thank God," a feminine voice responded. "Not a moment too soon. We can't manoeuvre the rig around these behemoths and there's a pack of terror-jaws down that alley to our left, and they look hungry."

"Sit tight," Miller answered. "We'll clear out the alley and then get you and the cargo out of here."

"My hero," the woman responded.

Du Trieux's eyebrows popped high as Doyle snorted from the back seat.

"Shut up," Miller said.

"I didn't say anything," du Trieux smirked.

Outside in the alley, the terror-jaws were stripping the corpse of a baby thug, which was still as big as a full-sized hippopotamus. Once Miller, Doyle, and du Trieux cleared them out, Hsiung and the others set to work moving the cargo from the rig to the smaller transport vehicle, while Doyle and du Trieux watched the perimeter for more terror-jaws.

Miller went to meet the female voice from the radio, which belonged to Dr. Gwen Davenport, a serious-looking brunette with a clipboard tucked under her arm. She climbed out of the big rig and shook Miller's hand harder than necessary. There was another scientist, an older gentleman who climbed out of the passenger van with a few technicians, and the two drivers, who looked more like delivery men than soldiers.

Upon Miller's arrival, the drivers held back, covering Hsiung and the others as they unloaded barrels and crates from the back of the rig. Meanwhile, the techs gathered around the Bravo as if waiting for permission to enter.

Miller couldn't shake an odd feeling in the base of his skull. "I'm going to need to see a copy of your inventory," he said, nodding toward the clipboard tucked under Davenport's arm. Technically, he should be escorting her to the Bravo, but that odd feeling wouldn't go away.

Her congenial smile fell and she adjusted the clipboard with her free hand. "Food supply gear," she said, eyeing Hsiung as she ambled by with a crate.

Now that wasn't suspicious at all. "Uh-huh," Miller said, pursing his lips. "And where did you come from again?"

Davenport swallowed then shifted on her feet. Her boots looked clean and hardly broken in. They creaked as she altered position. "Boston."

"What facility in Boston?"

She scratched her cheek. "Does it matter?"

Miller raised an eyebrow. "No. Not as much as what's in the inventory."

"Look, they tell me where to go, I go," Davenport said, her face reddening. "I don't have a beef with you, okay? Can we just go? We've been stuck here for hours and if I see another one of those terror-jaws ever again in my life, it'll be too soon."

"You don't have terror-jaws in Boston?" Miller asked, knowing full well the answer.

She sighed. "Of course we do, but I don't usually get out of the lab much. Can we go?"

"The 'food supply gear' lab?"

"Oh, for fuck's sake," she burst, thrusting the clipboard into Miller's hand and stalking off toward the Bravo. "Go ahead, Linus!" she bellowed. The older man and the other technicians scrambled inside the vehicle like children.

Miller held up the clipboard and frowned.

From his left, du Trieux appeared and squinted at the paperwork. "How are we supposed to read this chicken scratch?" she asked.

"Says here, 'Food Supply Gear,'" Miller said. "But I doubt it. They're too jumpy."

"Wouldn't you be jumpy, stuck out here for three hours?" Shrugging lightly, du Trieux walked back toward the Bravo and climbed into the driver's seat.

Doyle called the drivers from the perimeter and, eyeing the thugs in the distance, barked at Miller, "Let's roll."

Undeterred, Miller walked past the Bravo to the transport, where Hsiung and the two drivers were getting inside.

Hopping up onto the back bumper, Miller leaned over the railing and examined the cargo. There were six metal barrels, each painted black. Next to them were four wooden crates, which were nailed shut.

Why would they transport food supply gear in sealed metal barrels?

Miller jammed the edge of his thumb under the lip of one of the barrels. Pulling upward, he popped the top off. His stomach lurched.

Inside were clear acrylic cylinders, labelled with a

strip of paper secured by a single strand of browning masking tape. The label read, 'Engineered yeast.'

"Supply gear, my ass."

"Put the lid back on, the seal is supposed to be air-tight," Davenport said from behind him.

Miller rammed the lid back on the barrel, punched the edge down with the side of his fist. "You want to explain to me why my men have put their lives in danger so we can courier *yeast?*"

"Get in the car, cowboy," Davenport frowned. "I'll explain on the way."

Du Trieux punched the accelerator and the Bravo lurched ahead, turning around to head back the direction they came.

Miller turned from the passenger seat and eyed Davenport. "Okay, now do you want to give me that explanation?"

Davenport sighed from the seat beside Doyle in the back and cleared her throat. "The yeast in those barrels was originally created at a perfume company some years ago as an attractant pheromone."

"Gwen!" snapped the older man.

"They have a right to know, Linus."

"We're transporting *perfume?*" Doyle scoffed.

"It's not perfume," Davenport corrected him. "I assume you've heard about the wasps? Well, this yeast combats their hibernation cycle in the Infected. We've made some headway back in Boston, so they wanted a sample of it here."

"That's more than a sample," Miller interjected. "You've got half a dozen barrels of it back there."

"Yes, and those crates are filled with samples of a breed of wasp—a larger, nastier one from South America, which was originally trapped using the same pheromone, as it turns out. But you didn't hear any of this from me," she clarified.

"Hold up," du Trieux interrupted. "They're experimenting on the Infected in South America? That's what started the whole mess here."

Miller kept his mouth shut.

"How else would you have us defeat this?" Davenport snapped. "Desperate times call for desperate measures. It's certainly had better results than anything BioGen and Schaeffer-Yeager has done."

"By experimenting on people?" du Trieux spat.

"They don't think they're people, remember?" Miller grunted. "Besides, I thought the Infected were drug-resistant?"

Davenport's eyes widened then narrowed in one swift fluid movement. "This is different. We're not fighting the Infected with anti-parasitics. We're attacking the wasp's gestation period inside the Infected hosts."

"Sounds lovely," Doyle snapped.

"So much for reversing the effects on the Infected, then. Is that it?" du Trieux asked, swinging the Bravo into a hard left and sending Davenport's lurching against the door. "Sorry, another pack of thugs just ripped up Alabama Avenue."

"Better buckle up," Miller said as Davenport

struggled to regain her seat and Hsiung cursed from the airwaves.

"I wouldn't say we're giving up on saving the Infected," Davenport said. "Just that our focus has shifted. Oh, stop giving me that look, Linus. We're all on the same team."

"I have a feeling there's a hell of a lot we don't know," Miller said. Reaching up, he rubbed his throbbing temple and turned his eyes back to the road.

Another herd of thug behemoths came around the bend and stampeded in the opposite direction.

Du Triuex pitched the Bravo around another sharp corner, tires squealing.

"What the hell are these thugs after under the concrete?" Doyle asked. "Won't be long before we can't bloody well drive anywhere."

"I don't know what they're after," Davenport confessed, snapping her belt across her shoulder and peering out the window. "But you're not wrong. The planet's not ours anymore."

"I'm not sure it ever was," Miller said, still pressing on his temple.

His whole mind ached. It felt to him like the pieces of the puzzle were all there, lying before him. But his head hurt, and his eyes ached, and the answer remained just outside comprehension. He peered out the window at the remains of Brooklyn and suppressed a sigh.

No doubt the landscape was shifting, again, even from the start. Phase two of the planet's adjustments had begun. Roads were gone. Buildings were overrun with creatures and fungus. New York City had gone wild, and there was nothing anybody could do about it.

If there was one thing you could count on, it was the planet's adaptive ability. Miller only wished humans came by it as naturally.

THE BOARD ROOM was climate-controlled and well stocked with padded chairs and cool water. Compared to other, less hospitable, portions of the compound, this was a veritable paradise. Still, Miller couldn't get comfortable. He'd crossed and uncrossed his legs at least a dozen times in the last half hour, trying to settle in. It wasn't going to happen.

Lewis seemed to be having the same issue. Seated beside him in the corner of the room—in two chairs propped against the wall as almost an afterthought—Miller noticed Lewis reach down and scratch at the stump of his left knee, a nervous habit of which Lewis was clearly unaware.

Honestly, Miller wasn't surprised they were both so distracted. Harris was on another tangent and had been droning on for a good ten minutes. Miller was doing his best not to listen, but failing miserably.

"There is no reason to delay. The order has been given," Harris was saying calmly, and a little too coolly for Miller's taste, considering what he'd just announced to the board.

"In case you forgot," Gray said, sitting halfway

down the table from Harris and looking perturbed, "you've already tried NAPA-33 and there was some question as to its effect on pregnant women and children. Not the mention the ethical question."

"That data was inconclusive," Barrett said, her fingertips cradling her head at the temples. She sat across from Gray, not making eye contact with anyone. "With no practical evidence of that, there's no reason *not* to try."

"The only reason the data was inconclusive," Gray argued, "was because the Infected found out he'd used it on them without their permission and started a revolution. Let's not make the same mistake twice."

"I think it's a bit late to try and prevent a revolution," Lewis muttered.

Only Miller caught the comment. He grunted quietly by way of reply.

"The only mistake that was made," Harris went on, "was when the Infected discovered the air traps before we could fully understand the effectiveness of the formula. Now that they've mutated and built an immunity to the anti-parasitics, we have no choice but to further the NAPA-33 treatment, taking advantage of the larger breed of wasps, procured by Dr. Davenport." He gestured to the end of the table, indicating the woman on the far side.

She'd showered and pulled her hair back since Miller had last seen her, but she looked strung out, as if she was still staring down terror-jaws in the alleyways of Brooklyn.

Davenport nodded toward the older gentleman sitting beside her—the one she'd called Linus. "We've uncovered no major side-effects in women or children with use of the wasps in Boston," Davenport said. "Although, yes, the data on NAPA-33 itself is inconclusive. But the means of transmission affects everyone the same. All the wasps do is interrupt the parasite's genetic replication, which should slow spreading of the parasite."

"And since the Infected are already under attack via the smaller breed of wasp, there's nothing we're doing to them that wouldn't happen anyway," Linus stated.

Gray spread his fingers across the conference room table, his fingertips glowing white. "It doesn't negate the fact that we're experimenting on a population of people…"

"That depends on your definition of the word 'people,'" Harris said to him. "Besides which, as I said, the order has already been given. We're not here to debate this. We're here to inform you of what's been done."

"Have you already launched the wasps?" Gray asked.

"Preparations have been underway since Dr. Davenport's arrival. The air drops will begin tonight at oh-nine-hundred."

Gray's voice deepened to a husky timbre, his brow furrowed. "The board didn't vote on this."

"There was no need to hold a vote," Harris insisted, his calm exterior showing no sign of decay. "NAPA-33 was approved long ago."

"By *you*." With a burst of spite, Gray turned away from Harris toward Barrett. "Did you know about this?"

She lifted her head from her fingers. "No. But I would have voted for it even if it had come to the board. We have to do *something*, Gray. We can't just sit here. The compound will not survive another direct assault like Stockman's."

"Speaking to that," Harris butt in, "we have another matter to discuss…"

"Are we going to actually discuss it or are you just going to tell us?" Miller asked.

The room quieted and all eyes turned toward him.

"You're here as a professional courtesy," Harris snapped. His cool exterior was starting to crack.

Good. About time.

"Plans for Operation Atlas Lion," Harris kept on, puffing out his chest like a deranged peacock, "are underway."

Gray's face had paled. "What the hell is Atlas Lion?"

"After consulting with leaders of the security squads…" Harris began.

"Really?" Miller interrupted. "Which ones? Because I wasn't in that meeting."

Harris ignored him outright. "…We've devised a plan to permanently prevent the Infected from overrunning the compound."

"This should be good," Lewis commented under his breath.

"Using pheromone attractants derived from a yeast extract procured by Dr. Winters and Dr.

Davenport, which has been highly effective on the Infected in Boston, we plan to lure the Infected to Lawrence Point, two miles from here, where they will be exterminated using a nuclear weapon."

For just a fraction of a second, the words hung in the air. Eyes widened or blinked rapidly, mouths fell agape. Then the room erupted into shouting.

"Are you out of your mind?" Lewis demanded.

Barrett: "What the hell are you talking about?"

Miller: "How the fuck did you get a nuclear bomb?"

"You crazy bastard, you'll kill half the people in the compound with radiation poisoning!" Gray yelled.

"Don't be an idiot," Harris shouted back. "We've a line on a nuclear-equipped tactical surface-to-air missile from North Korea. It's point-five kilotons. The fallout will be minimal."

"Says who?" Lewis asked.

"Just what do you mean, you 'have a line' on a SAM? How did you plan on paying for it?" Gray burst.

"It's already done. It's on the way here."

The room fell silent again.

For just a moment, all Miller could hear was the shuttered breathing of a panicked room.

Panicked, save one.

Harris stood at the end of the conference table, arms crossed. "There's a shipping route between China, Europe, and the East Coast—the missile should arrive within the week."

"On whose authority did you purchase a nuclear weapon?" Gray seethed. "On whose authority?"

"On *my* authority," Harris snapped sharply, his façade of control finally breaking. "I am the only one willing to take the necessary steps to procure safety for this compound. While you sit on your *ass* building farms, I'm the one *fixing* this infestation. Me."

"How is setting off a *nuclear bomb* two miles from the compound supposed to make it safer?" Miller asked.

Harris reeled on him with a vengeance. "It's going to get a hell of a lot more done than running around like a pack of deluded ninjas, killing one Infected Charismatic at a time—for all the fuck that did." Twisting on his heel, he let loose on Gray. "Farms, Gray? Really? As if cows and chickens are going to stop the Infected. We're in the middle of a war. Drastic measures have to be taken, and somehow, I'm the only one with balls enough to take them."

"You cannot and will not circumvent the authority of this board by making rogue decisions of this magnitude without our consent," Gray seethed. "We will not authorize use of a nuclear weapon." Pounding his fist on the table, his face coloured to a bright purple. "And if this Operation Atlas Lion is to ever take place, it will do so with the unanimous vote of this board—and nothing else. Until that happens, I am ordering Miller and the Cobalt team to commandeer the missile when it arrives from North Korea. Is that clear enough, Harris? Did that have enough balls for you?"

Harris pushed his shoulders back. "We cannot continue to occupy the same island with a mob of Infected militants without expecting more to arrive. We must make an example of the remains of Stockman's men and remove any chances of them re-amassing."

"With a goddamned nuke?" Gray shouted. "The fallout alone could wipe out the entire compound…" He gestured toward Dr. Davenport and Winters, who looked just as dumbfounded as the rest of them.

"Technically speaking," Dr. Winters said, "if we're looking at a point-five kiloton surface blast, the fallout radius would only be about a half-mile."

"More than enough breathing room," Dr. Davenport added, a hint of irony in her tone.

"The casualties would be in the thousands," Miller said, standing from his chair. "Tens of thousands."

"Not to mention any civilians who may still be holding out in the blast radius," Lewis said.

"The populous is minimal at this point. I'm willing to lose a couple hundred in collateral damage if it means saving the thousands inside this compound," Harris said.

"This *will not* happen," Gray insisted. "I don't know who the hell you think you are, but you are not the one calling the shots around here."

Harris's expression hardened as his jaw set. For a moment, Miller expected him to dive across the conference table and smack Gray across the face. Instead, he inhaled sharply and said, "We'll see about that."

Harris stormed out of the room, his footsteps echoing down the hallway.

Miller let his breath out and unclenched his fists.

The remaining people in the room looked shell-shocked. The doctors excused themselves awkwardly, and Barrett slapped her phablet into the palm of her hand and stalked out.

Lewis, sensing the tension between Gray and Miller, patted Miller on the shoulder and limped out of the conference room with instructions for Miller to come to his office later.

Gray ran both hands through his hair and pulled his face tight. "I don't even know where to begin."

"If the warhead arrives within the week, we have only a few days to get ahead of this. We can contact the vessel, turn them back."

"You think Harris is going to tell us how to get in touch with the ship?" Gray shook his head and scooped his phablet off the conference room table. "I should have listened to you."

"When? I've been right more than once."

Gray shook his head, his face gone slack. "You told me to keep a tighter leash on him. You knew he was going to pull something like this."

"I never imagined *this*."

Gray's eyes locked on Miller's and his mouth thinned to a fine line. "We should have left when we had the chance. I never should have let him build this fortress. Now he's willing to blow up the rest of the city to save it."

Miller nodded, the weight of his shoulders making him feel heavy. "And whether it *would* save anything is a whole other debate."

Gray stood to leave the conference room, speaking over his shoulder as he walked away. "That crazy son of a bitch won't be happy until we're all dead."

OPERATION SEA MINK

19

NIGHT FELL IN the remains of New York City, plunging the Astoria Peninsula into gloom and sending the refugees inside the Schaeffer-Yeager compound scurrying to their shanties like skittish rabbits.

A robust wind from the south scattered fungal spores into the sky, making the air thick, red, and difficult to breathe. For better or worse, the winds had delayed the launch of Operation Elephant Bird by two days.

That was time enough, Miller thought, for Gray to prevent Harris's dicey plan—but the order to cancel, much to Miller's disgust, never came.

Preparations for the mission proceeded with or without the weather's cooperation, or Miller's approval. The payload was packed and loaded, the choppers were fuelled and prepped, and when the wind calmed on the third day, it was time for lift off.

The spore count was wreaking havoc on the machinery, however, causing unplanned additional maintenance and slowing the process. With the red wind, fungal blooms erupted around the chopper quicker than maintenance crews could remove them.

This was not in any way how Miller wanted to spend his time.

He watched the chopper pilot and the technicians on the helipad as they reached into the air intake valves and fuel lines, pulling out strips of pinkish-red fungal gloop, and realized that he would rather be doing anything else on Earth.

What the hell was he doing here? He was so utterly sick and tired of this compound, of this city, this planet—of the constant feeling of rolling a boulder up a slippery slope, sliding downhill as fast as he climbed.

His thoughts searched for comfort and turned to Samantha, to Billy, and then to his parents—who probably had long run out of supplies on the ranch—and he felt worse, wondering how they were all faring, or if any of them fared at all.

His gut twisted. He should be there, with his folks. He should be packing them into Dad's truck and getting them to safety—not here, acting as Harris's stooge.

But where would he take his parents, if he were with them? There was no such thing as a 'safe place' anymore. Even inside the compound, the concept of safety was wishful thinking. Safety didn't exist.

Standing on the helipad, Miller yanked the gas mask off his face and coughed into the thick, hot wind.

How did he end up here—doing Harris's bidding? Of all the idiotic things to do. If someone had told him—after Harris had announced to the board that he planned to release a super-wasp laced with

NAPA-33 to the Infected communes around the compound—that Miller would be implementing said plan, he'd have laughed in their face.

Why would he do *anything* that psychopath wanted?

Robert Harris operated under the delusion that he ran the whole world—and Miller, who knew the full scope of Harris's delusion included nuking the shit out of the Infected population only two miles from the compound's flimsy walls—hated that he had to babysit this operation.

It was a joke. Miller was a pawn in a fucked-up power play between Harris and Gray, and somehow, Miller was supposed to make sure everything happened as it should. One man.

"I'm counting on you," Gray had said when he'd asked Miller to spearhead the wasp drops, minutes after storming out of the conference room in a rage.

Miller had only agreed to do it because deep down, under the resentment, exhaustion, and suspicion, he agreed the operation needed heavy oversight—and not by one of Harris's gun-blazing cowboy brigades, but by him.

Still, when he asked, it felt as if Gray had ordered Miller to eat a shit sandwich—and to smile while doing it.

"PILOT SAYS FIVE minutes," du Trieux said, coming up beside Miller on the helipad and resting her hand on the strap of her Gilboa.

Miller swiped the sweat from his forehead with the

back of his hand and let the perspiration drip from his fingertips. It had to be over a hundred degrees, even at this hour. The air was so thick with fungus the stars were obscured. Even the moon looked red. "Payload on board?" he asked.

She nodded. She didn't appear to be any more thrilled to be there than he was, but at least she was talking to him again. When he'd informed Cobalt of Gray's instructions, she'd protested, then gone quiet and hadn't spoken to him since.

"THIS DOESN'T MAKE sense," she'd said. "We're missing pieces of the puzzle."

Miller looked away from the faces of his team, and around the break room, nodding. Sparse, dim, and filthy around the edges, the break room was hardly that anymore. Half the furniture had been commandeered and moved elsewhere. Even their silverware had gone missing. Miller would bet his rifle that one of the other security teams had raided the place, but not wanting to start a rivalry with no point to it, he'd kept that thought to himself. Although he was sure his team had had the same thought. "I know," he said.

"All we went through with the Charismatics, and now they want us to spread *more* bugs?" Morland piped in, visibly confused.

Du Trieux mumbled something in French.

Doyle, sitting in a lopsided folding chair, sipped his coffee-flavored water with a slurp. His feet were propped against a broken cabinet door he'd ripped from the wall and set on top of some old paint cans—their new table. "Does the right hand know what the left is doing?" he asked. He made an obscene gesture and Hsiung coughed.

"Doubt it," Miller said. He glanced at du Trieux and she frowned, deeply. "There'll be five choppers in the air," he explained to them. "One man each, aside from the pilot. We scout communes, drop payload, and come back in less than half an hour, which is about how long the fuel lines last before they clog with fungus. Any longer than that, payload or not, you bug out. We do this until the wasp samples run out. Rumor has it, that'll take a few days. Any questions?"

"Why are we dropping wasps on communes again?" Morland asked.

"It's a special breed. It's supposed to stop other wasps from laying eggs in the Infected's brains, and interrupts their 'genetic replicating.' Don't ask me how."

"I don't get it," Morland said, "are we *helping* the Infected now?"

"No," Miller answered, a little too quickly. "Well, sort of. Yes. But no. It's more to stop the parasite from spreading."

"Why stop the wasps at all?" Hsiung asked. "If they lay eggs in the Infected's brain, and then the Infected go nuts and find ways to die, like with the swimming club"—she gestured at Doyle, who grunted in reply—"then why are we stopping them? The Infected are dying. They're literally killing themselves. I say let them. Less for us to do."

"Now there's an idea," Doyle said.

Du Trieux shook her head.

"Look, I don't make the orders," Miller said. "I just relay them. Gray wants us to do this so he knows it's done right, and quite frankly, I agree with him—at least on that point."

"Doesn't makes sense to me," Morland said.

"No argument here," Miller agreed. "Now, get loaded up and be ready. We lift off once these winds die down."

Doyle stood and slurped one last gulp of pseudo-coffee. "No rest for the wicked."

Miller didn't bother to comment.

TWO DAYS LATER, out on the helipad, du Trieux stood with her back against the breeze, her gas mask slung around her neck as she eyed the crews scooping fungus. "You sure this is a good idea?"

Miller frowned. "Taking the choppers out or dropping the wasps on communes? Take your pick."

"Both."

"I don't know," he answered honestly. "Apparently, they've had success with this method in Boston. Those two doctors we picked up have the data to prove it. If this slows things down as they project, perhaps we can finally get ahead of the parasite. Maybe it'll keep things from getting out of hand."

Du Trieux raised an eyebrow.

"...more out of hand," he corrected himself. He had meant Harris's plans for nuking the Infected at Lawrence Point, but he didn't clarify.

"Well," du Trieux said, "when you're ready, board. Looks like the crew's done cleaning out your bird."

"You be careful up there," Miller said.

There was an odd hitch in du Trieux's face as she nodded and turned away. "You too."

MILLER ADJUSTED THE night vision goggles on the top of his head and watched the phablet's infrared display.

Searching for communes at night was risky, given the unreliability of the helicopters' equipment—not to mention the wildlife.

Since titan-birds were believed to be diurnal, and rarely seen after sunset, Miller hoped the airways were clear, for now. What happened to the days when you didn't have to worry about being swallowed whole by a colossal lizard with wings?

"Twelve minutes on the fuel lines," the pilot said.

"Copy that."

Miller scanned the phablet display. It was surprisingly sparse down in the depths of the streets. Either the Infected were doing a better job of hiding their communes, or there were fewer of them. The majority of movement came from wildlife. On the display, large red blobs of heat slunk up and down alleys—which had to be terror-jaws—while larger, titan-bird-sized blobs crowded rooftops and upper levels of skyscrapers. Out on the avenues and streets, enormous heat signatures—thug behemoths—crowded in clusters but stayed still, most likely keeping in herds to protect their young at night.

In all that confusion, it was difficult to find batches of human heat signatures at all. In fact, so far, he hadn't found any.

If he didn't find one soon, this whole trip would be for naught. Miller didn't want to waste the compound's dwindling supply of chopper fuel, and frankly, didn't fancy sitting next to the wasp containers on the way back, either. Their buzzing and movement inside the cardboard containers was unnerving. Hell of a prize inside *this* cereal box, Miller thought.

Movement on the phablet screen caught his eye.

"West," Miller said into his earpiece. "Thirty degrees."

"I saw it, too," the pilot said. "Swinging back around."

The chopper banked and Miller reached out, unthinkingly grasping the wasp containers to keep them from tipping—before whipping his hand back with disgust.

He went back to examining the phablet, trying to ascertain where best to drop the boxes.

Given the size and dexterity of the heat signature he saw dart between two buildings, it was human— or Infected, given how many of them bunched around one another. It joined a faint cloud of body heat clumped into what Miller could only suppose was the lobby of a building of some kind.

They were three blocks east of 34th and 12th— and from what he could tell from the readings, a pair of titan-birds had taken control of the top of the building, forcing the commune down into the lower levels. The only evidence the commune was there at all was because they seemed to be on the move— their heat fading right before Miller's eyes.

Wait. Fading? Why would their signatures disappear like that?

Down. They were occupying basements, Miller realized. Moving underground as he watched.

The subway system was probably teaming with communes. That was why they were having such issues finding them on infrared.

Miller switched his earpiece to the all channel. "Aim for the subway entrances, they've gone underground."

"No wonder we can't find the little blighters," Doyle said. He almost sounded impressed.

"Drop payload near or into subway stairwells and get back to the compound ASAP," Miller said. "The wind's picking back up."

"That's like dropping a ping pong ball into a coffee mug from a hundred meters away," Morland said, a hint of a whine in his voice, "while standing on a surfboard in the ocean."

"Just do the best you can," Miller snapped. He switched back to the internal channel and urged the chopper pilot to descend.

"Any more and I could clip the side of a building," he said. "This is the best I can do, sir."

"Alright, here goes nothing," Miller mused, twisting in his seat. He peered at the darkened ground below, and released the lever that held the wasp containers in place.

Picking up one box at a time, he pushed the containers out the open side of the chopper, working down the block and hitting any subway staircase he was able to spot. Three. Five. Ten. Finally, when there were only a few left, he slid the wooden pallet with a hard shove, pitching the remainder over the side.

Miller held tight as the chopper bucked from the loss of weight and watched as the containers dropped out of sight into the darkness below. He listened for the sound of ground contact, but knew he'd never make out the noise over the thump of the helicopter's rotors.

"Bugs away!" the pilot cheered, pulling the chopper up and banking toward the left, back toward the compound.

Miller held tight and glared at the open end of the attack chopper, the second passenger seat and door had been removed to make room for the wasps.

He listened over the all channel as the other teams made their drops and announced their return toward base.

It was a victory—technically. Payload was delivered, and they'd go back at it the next evening, although it would be days, maybe even weeks, before they'd know if the super-wasps were doing their job.

Still, Miller felt the familiar twist in his gut as his eyes trailed up and outside the chopper, resting on the red glow of the moon. He wondered if there was such a thing as safety up there.

20

"WHAT THE FUCK is the Tartarus Protocol?" Miller barked.

Brandon Lewis stood behind his desk and shifted his prosthetic legs, rocking back on his heels.

"And why do you need me to do it?" Doyle asked from beside Miller.

Both stood on the opposite side of Lewis's desk, facing him, their backs to the door and their arms across their chests.

Miller's skin felt sticky. He and Doyle had just returned from another bug drop, and stunk to high hell of fungus and chopper fuel. If it had been up to him, they would have been enjoying a hot shower or getting some shut-eye, not reporting to Lewis's office in the wee hours of the morning.

Besides, there wasn't much point to this meeting, as far as Miller was concerned. Given how Lewis's hands were tied, he wasn't sure what the man's role was within Schaeffer-Yeager. If the orders came directly from Harris, what was the point in having Lewis give them?

Still, this latest development required immediate interference, even if Lewis was only Harris's parrot. Miller hoped he would side with him in the matter— for all the good it would do.

Lewis nodded, as if agreeing with the question. "They need a sniper," he said. "And you're the best in the compound."

Doyle snorted.

Miller frowned. "Who gave the order?" From Lewis's expression, he already knew the answer.

"Who do you think?"

Miller ran his hands through his hair and scratched his scalp.

Doyle drummed his fingers against his arms but said nothing.

"There are only five Cobalts left as it is," Miller said. "And technically Hsiung is on loan from your old squad. You can't strip me of one of my best men..."

Doyle coughed. "One of?"

"...my *best* man, and not give me a reason except the name of some covert protocol I don't have clearance to know about. It's bullshit. Doyle reports to me. How can he know what he's doing and I can't? Besides which, I don't take orders from Harris, and neither do my men. We take orders from Gray."

"He knows," Lewis said, sitting in his rolling office chair and grasping the desk's edge. "Gray's signed off on the transfer."

"I find that hard to believe."

Lewis reached across his desk, dug through a pile of papers, and flicked one across to Miller and Doyle.

Doyle snatched up the paper before it hit the floor and handed it to Miller, who read the order and grimaced.

The sheet was headed *Operation Caspian Tiger: Tartarus Protocol*. Sure enough, Gray's signature was scrawled across the bottom of the hand-written document. He handed it to Doyle, who took it and grunted.

"This still doesn't explain what the hell Tartarus is," Miller said.

"That's on a need-to-know. Even I haven't been told everything," Lewis said, his face grim. "All I can say is that it has something to do with the results of those mouth swabs we took a while back. They're separating some people out based off that."

"And why do they need a sniper?" Doyle asked.

Miller could hardly believe what he was hearing. "They're separating people *inside* the compound? What kind of McCarthyist bullshit is that?"

Lewis held up his hands. "The order came from Harris, and Gray's done nothing to combat it. Look, son, this is between them and neither you nor I can do anything about it. There's no sense in putting yourself in the middle."

Miller dropped his arms and pressed his fingers onto the edge of Lewis's desk. "I'm in the middle of it whether I put myself there or not. And now they're playing poker with my *men*."

"In case you haven't noticed, we're not running this show," Lewis reminded him. "We're soldiers. They point, we go."

"I'm not a soldier, I'm a fucking bodyguard. I never signed up for this shit, and Doyle didn't ask for this either."

Lewis pressed his lips together. "You cannot *make* Gray stand up to Harris. He has to do that all on his own. In the meantime, we follow orders or desert and run for the hills. Nobody will stop you."

Miller shook his head, his face hot, blood boiling. "I don't like this."

"Welcome to the club, son."

"I get him back when it's done," Miller said. "Whatever the hell it is."

"Understood," Lewis agreed. "Now get out of my office."

OUT IN THE hallway, Miller and Doyle stalked toward the break room. The whole ordeal stunk to high hell, the worst of it being there was nothing Miller could do to remedy that.

"What should I do, boss?" Doyle asked.

Although Miller hardly considered him a subordinate, Doyle continued to relinquish command to him at every opportunity. He bit the inside of his cheek, thinking. "Report as ordered," he said.

Doyle arched an eyebrow. "What did I tell you about orders?"

"Better yet," Miller said, lowering his voice.

"Report as ordered and then tell me what the hell the Tartarus Protocol is."

Doyle smirked. "Roger that."

THE BRAVO RUMBLED down the remains of 18th Street like a bulldozer in a library.

It was fascinating to Miller how much the streets had changed, even a week since their last drive outside the compound. The thug behemoths had decimated the roads almost in their entirety, making the trek more of an off-road excursion than an actual drive.

After the latest windstorm, the fungal growths had taken control of the skyline. Blooms wrapped around the buildings in thick coils all the way from foundation to tip, in and out of the broken windows, and blocking doorways.

Evidence of human existence was less and less apparent. It now made more sense to Miller why the Infected had retreated underground. Above, there wasn't room left for people.

Du Trieux maneuvered the Bravo through the terrain while Miller rode shotgun, grabbing the support bar above the window for balance. Hsiung and Morland sat in the back, bouncing around as if on a trampoline.

"We can't go any farther," du Trieux said, slamming the brakes and careening the Bravo to a full stop. "The roads."

"We'll have to hoof it from here," Miller said, snatching up his M27.

Du Trieux nodded and grabbed her Gilboa—snapping the clip tight and pocketing another magazine from the Bravo's console. Hsiung and Morland poured out the back and came around to meet them.

They advanced on alert, du Trieux on point. Dirt and crumbled cement crunched underfoot. The noise echoed across the boulevard, bouncing from one broken building to the next with deafening clarity. From their vantage point, the area looked deserted, although the rat-things scurried in corners and crevices, skittering and squeaking.

The building on their left had a blue wooden door that was boarded up tightly with splintered two-by-fours. On the right, the entire glass storefront of an old laundromat had been shattered. The shredded strips of the laundry's awning fluttered in the wind—whispering into the hot fungal breeze.

If their mission perimeters were correct, not far from their position a group of researchers had gotten stuck—for reasons unspecified—and had requested escort back to the compound. Lewis had sent them out to retrieve the civilians with a casualness Miller couldn't help but distrust. He'd just stripped them of manpower, and now he was sending them back out into the wild. It was hard for Miller not to resent his old mentor.

They rounded a curve in the road and the air turned putrid. The stench was so bad Miller felt the inside of his nose burn.

"There," Morland whispered.

Miller swung around. To the right, sitting on what was left of the curb, sat a medical cooler, half opened.

Swinging the muzzle of his M27 toward it, Morland nodded and approached the container. Using the edge of his combat boot, he tipped up the lid. "Shit!"

"What is it?" Hsiung said, facing south to cover their backs.

"It's shit," he repeated. "Literally. Petri dishes of the stuff."

"The researchers were collecting samples from the Infected," Miller informed them. "They can't be too far."

Without much by way of working sewers, finding and sampling faeces—which was generally disposed of a reasonable distance from the communes—would be the best option for testing the Infected to see if the latest dispatch of NAPA-33 was working.

The whole idea seemed repulsive to Miller, but he was curious to hear if Harris's latest scheme would bear fruit, and with no other way of telling, he supposed there was purpose to the nauseating exercise.

That didn't deter from the fact that by coming to escort the researchers, Miller and the remains of Cobalt had found themselves in the middle of an Infected septic tank. The stench was overwhelming. Miller's eyes watered as he turned full circle, catching Hsiung, who walked with her arm covering her nose.

Du Trieux, a meter ahead, had put on her gas mask and held up a fist.

Freezing in position, the four strained their ears. Aside from the echoes of the rat things, movement and whispers could be heard inside a brick building on their right. They approached, weapons drawn.

A woman's voice said, "If you go after him too, then I'll be left here alone, and I'm not leaving until the cavalry arrives."

"We can't stay here," a man's voice answered. "We have to go after Lester."

"No. We don't. Let the escort handle it."

"But..."

"Just shut up, Linus."

Despite himself, Miller grinned. "Dr. Davenport?" he called softly.

From the building's interior, they heard more shuffling and whispering—panicked movements made as if someone had been caught with their pants down.

"Wait!" the man's voice said. "How do we know it's them?"

"They wouldn't know my name, Linus. Honestly, for a man with doctorates in microbiology and immunology, you can be so dense."

Dr. Davenport appeared. Looking disheveled and covered in what Miller hoped was dirt, she cautiously peered out from a crack in a boarded-up window, saw him, and smiled. "We really have to stop meeting like this," she said.

Miller laughed and felt himself blushing.

Du Trieux approached the entrance, a broken wooden door with peeling green paint. It looked as if someone had punched a hole through in order to open it. "Are you all here?" she asked, an edge in her tone. "We should go."

"What about Lester?" the man said. From beside Dr. Davenport, Dr. Winters appeared, also covered in splotches of dirt and road dust.

Miller slung the strap of his M27 over his shoulder and gripped Dr. Davenport's hand to help her out of the building, Dr. Winters following. "Lester Allen is with you?"

Davenport shook her head as Dr. Winters nodded. "He *was*," he explained. "He took off—that way." He pointed east. "Then our guard called for backup and went after him. That was almost an hour ago."

"What do you mean, he took off?" Morland asked.

Dr. Winters cleared his throat. "I don't know, he just..."

"He ran," Dr. Davenport interrupted. "He started ranting and raving about how the 'corporation' shouldn't be experimenting on the Infected. How we didn't understand their *gifts*, and then he bolted. Ditched his cooler and then—gone."

"He said *what?*" Miller exclaimed.

"It drew a lot of attention from the animals." Dr. Davenport said. "We had to barricade ourselves inside that building to keep them from getting at us, but I guess after a while they gave up. Thankfully."

"What about your guard?" Hsiung asked.

Dr. Winters shook his head, but Davenport answered. "He hasn't come back—yet."

Miller turned to du Trieux. "Trix?"

"*Oui?*"

"Get them back to the Bravo. I'm going to sweep the area and look for Lester."

"Negative," she said. "We both go. Too wild out here to solo."

Miller considered disagreeing with her, but saw no point in it. She was right.

"Fine. Hsiung?"

"You got it," she answered without hesitation. "Come on, docs."

As Hsiung lead the two doctors back down 18th, du Trieux and Miller went in the opposite direction. After a solid ten minutes of silent searching, they turned up a terror-jaw, a school of rat-things, and one thug behemoth giving birth—but Lester Allen was nowhere to be seen.

"*If* we find him, this could go poorly," Miller told du Trieux.

She gave no immediate reply, only pushed through a destroyed back alley, and stepped over the remains of a half-eaten terror-jaw. "He was *hesitant*," she said carefully, "the last time we took him into custody. I'm not sure why we're going after him now."

"Lewis told me he didn't want any well-fed, well-informed people from the compound giving information to the Infected."

"So, we're not here to find him. We're here to silence him?"

"I didn't say that."

"Didn't have to," she replied, tapping the sheath of her hunting knife on her thigh.

He hoped it wouldn't come to that. They'd taken Lester Allen into custody by force once before, they could do it again—even if he had to pistol whip him and drag him by his hair.

This time however, they didn't have the comfort of pulling him into the back of a transport vehicle or a dose of anti-parasitics laced with sedative to keep him complacent. They were exposed, even worse now than they'd been at the time of the helicopter massacre—and they both knew it.

Up ahead, a thug behemoth pack had taken residence in the middle of the road. Turning a corner to avoid them, they walked down the center of what had once been Astoria Boulevard. Miller eyed the remains of a Cuban restaurant opposite a beauty shop. Straight ahead, a hardware store lay open and desolate; through the shards of the storefront window, Miller saw movement—the profile of a man slunk out of sight.

"One o'clock," Miller said.

Crouching low and coming in fast, Miller bounded toward the storefront, his M27 feeling heavy in his hands. With du Trieux just behind, they entered the store and swung around, eyeing the corners and checking the shadows. The sound of something dropping caught their attention. Rushing toward the source of the noise, they saw him.

Wide-eyed and wild-haired, Lester took one glance at du Trieux and panicked. In a blur of flannel and corduroy the scientist bolted like a shot—zipping from the store's back door and disappearing down an alleyway, squealing like a frightened pig. He was gone before Miller could get out more than two words.

"Stop! Wait!"

Out the back door and down the alley was a chain-link fence and another store, an abandoned apartment building from the looks of it. Miller and du Trieux searched the apartments, but came up empty. It was too late. Lester had disappeared— again. It was as if he'd evaporated.

"Dammit," Miller fumed. He stalked his way back through the apartments and the hardware store to Astoria Boulevard.

"Should have put a bullet in him the moment we saw his face," du Trieux said.

"Could you have done that? Just shot him for no reason?"

"We had a reason. You said so yourself. Lester Allen was an asshole, but he also knows every inch of the compound, including the research Davenport and Winters are doing with NAPA-33 and the super wasps. If he joins a commune, we're fucked."

Miller sighed. "Let's hope not."

"I don't know whether to pity your optimism or admire it."

"Six of one, half a dozen..." He didn't finish his sentence.

Ahead of them on 18th Street, just around the bend from Astoria Boulevard, huddled a pack of Infected.

Dirt and cement crumbled underfoot as du Trieux

and Miller skidded to a halt. Miller's first instinct was to open fire. Shouldering the M27, his finger brushed the trigger. It was only when he saw a familiar face that he stopped.

Samantha?

She stood to the left of the group—her long brown hair braided to the side, her face gaunt but relatively unchanged. She wore the remains of a long, wide sheath dress with thinning yoga pants underneath. Her head tilted to the side.

His chest tightened and the M27 dipped in his hands.

Du Trieux didn't lower her Gilboa, but she didn't fire either. Her face shot back and forth between Miller and the Infected. Rocking on her heels, she took a step backward, then reset her feet firmly in the crumbled cement.

The mob, unlike every other Infected horde they'd ever encountered, stood perfectly still. They weren't running at them, trying to tear their limbs off their torsos. Nor was there a Charismatic in the center of the group, or odd fungal growths budding across their faces and skin. They had rifles slung over their shoulders or loosely clutched in their palms. Their clothes were ragged, but not completely filthy. They were just a gathering, a group of people, as if out for a stroll. They looked almost human.

"Sam?" Miller breathed. He wanted to go to her. The relief at seeing her was immediately replaced by a dull dread. She was Infected, obviously, yet—

"Hello, Alex," she said.

The sound of her voice hit him hard. He swallowed the lump in his throat and shifted his fingers on his rifle.

Samantha's dark eyes trailed down to his hands, then back up to meet his gaze. "Aren't you going to shoot us?" she asked.

"I'd rather not."

Du Trieux altered her stance. He could hear her breathing. To her credit, her rifle never budged an inch.

"Were you, by chance, chasing that man?" Samantha asked.

"What man?"

Samantha's eyebrows raised. "Do we look stupid to you?"

"He's one of ours," Miller answered her.

"Then why was he running away from you?"

He didn't bother to answer that.

Her eyes narrowed. "Don't worry. We'll take care of him for you. Just like we take care of all our own kind."

The group around her nodded their agreement and Miller's stomach roiled.

"I think you and I have very different opinions on what it means to take care of each other," he said.

"That was obvious from the beginning," she answered. "Wasn't it? Now, is she going to put down her gun, or is this going to get nasty? You're outnumbered, two to one."

Miller raised his rifle again. "Thanks, but I'd rather die than become Infected."

Samantha laughed.

The sound struck a chord in the hollow of his belly. He'd heard that laugh before, early in their relationship, before things had turned south and she'd come to resent him. He hadn't realized he missed it until he heard it again.

"Why would we bestow our gifts upon you?" Samantha asked him. "You're doing more for our benefit from your little compound than you could do in our ranks."

Miller blinked.

"Oh, come on now," she continued. "Haven't you noticed? There are different variations to how a host reacts to the parasite. That's why some of us are immune to your pathetic attempts at distributing anti-parasitics." She shook her head at him like a disgruntled schoolmarm. "And here we thought you were smart. You haven't put the pieces together yet?"

"Enough to know I don't want any part of it," he admitted.

"Have your compatriot point her weapon down, and we'll go into more detail."

"I like it just where it is, thank you very much," du Trieux said.

"That's not very hospitable of you," Samantha scolded her. With the slightest flick of her wrist, the Infected surrounding her snatched up their weapons and pointed them at du Trieux.

Miller's trigger finger flinched but stopped short of pulling.

"Put your weapon down, Alex," Samantha said.

"And we won't shoot her. In fact, we'll even promise to let you both go."

"I don't believe promises from the Infected," Miller said. "No offense."

"Smart man," she said. "But unlike you, we follow through on *our* promises—so when we say we'll let you go, we will. Isn't that right, everybody?"

The group surrounding Samantha all agreed.

Miller glanced around, searching for an escape. If they ran back to the hardware store they could jump the chain link fence in the alley behind it and disappear in the labyrinth of backstreets, just like Lester had. But they couldn't outrun a bullet.

"Put it down, Trix," Miller said, lowering his M27.

"Are you mad?" du Trieux snapped.

"If she wanted us dead, we'd already be dead."

Du Trieux reluctantly lowered her Gilboa.

Two of the Infected ran forward and collected Miller and du Trieux's rifles, as well as their sidearms and knives. It was like being strip-searched at a prison—humiliating and dehumanizing. Not to mention the smell. Even if they were a different kind of Infected, as Samantha claimed, they still stank the same.

After they were disarmed, the group of Infected surrounded Miller and du Trieux on all sides, turned them around, and walked them back toward the hardware store.

Samantha came up alongside Miller. Given the look on du Trieux's face as she glowered at her, he wasn't too glad to be standing between the two women.

"Did you know that it's impossible for the gifted to kill another gifted?" Samantha asked him.

He shook his head. Actually, he suspected as much, but playing stupid might get her to divulge information he *didn't* know.

"It's true," she said. "If we get within just a few meters of each other, our subconscious becomes one."

"Sounds like hell."

"It's a beautiful experience, actually," she said, smiling slightly. She ran her palm down the length of her braided ponytail and he fought back the urge reach out and touch her hand. She was Samantha—that was true. But she wasn't.

She'd changed, even from the time she'd become Infected and left him. Her sharp wit, the way she would wink at him when she caught him watching her, the intelligent gleam in her gaze: those were all gone, vaporized by the parasite. What remained of her now—the almost placid facial expression; the slow, deliberate steps; the dull gleam in her eye—they mirrored the other Infected surrounding her in an unnerving way.

He wanted to ask her questions, to find out what her life had been like since she'd left—but he feared the answers would only agitate her, and hurt him, so he chose to remain quiet. Whatever her plans were, disturbing her and the other Infected wouldn't benefit anyone.

"We're so glad we found you before the others did," Samantha said. "We're not like Swift's bumbling gaggle of drones."

"You all smell the same to me."

"That's where you're wrong," she explained. She walked past the hardware store and the group continued down Astoria Boulevard—in the opposite direction from the Bravo and the rest of Cobalt.

Du Trieux glanced behind her and then turned her attention to the Infected. She was probably devising an escape route just as he was. The farther Samantha walked them in that direction, the harder it would be to get back.

He hoped Hsiung and Morland weren't waiting for them. If packs of Infected were patrolling the area, they had best get the doctors back to the compound as soon as possible.

"We're the Archaeans," Samantha said. "We're a separate group of the gifted from Swift's. We had nothing to do with the assault on the compound, if that's what you're wondering. In fact, we've been working to devise ways of eliminating his Bishops, but haven't been able to get close enough to them without bonding."

"Bishops?"

"The leaders of Swift's groups. The ones you've been killing?"

Miller shook his head, not following. He'd killed too many to keep track.

"Bishops surround themselves with Pawns," she explained. "They've been most troublesome to our group, but as I explained, we've been unable to eliminate them because of the pheromones. But, as you always somehow do, you became helpful without even trying. Did you know that? That we've been your back-up out in the field?"

"What the hell are you talking about?"

"The Bishops," she said, her tone becoming more impatient. The group around her shifted with agitation. "We've been herding them in your direction. After you'd eradicate one Bishop, freeing his Pawns, we'd set up the next group to send your way, and pick off any stragglers you'd missed. You didn't honestly think you'd survived all those attacks on your own, did you?"

"Bullshit," he said. "I would have noticed if there was a pattern."

"Of course you'd think that," she said.

They continued down Astoria Boulevard and stopped at the front of an old food market. The group of Infected stood closer to one another, side to side, closing in around du Trieux, Miller and Samantha, looking blank.

"Why have you stopped the attacks, Alex?" Samantha asked. "It was *working*. Swift's ranks were disbanding. Without the Bishops, he was losing power. All this violence could end. You want that, right? You want the killing to stop?"

He looked at her dark eyes and her frayed, frizzy ponytail, and wondered why the hell he hadn't shot her the moment he'd laid eyes on her. What the hell was she talking about? Was she implying that Stockman's siege was actually orchestrated by Jimmy Swift?

"Of course I want the killing to stop," he snapped.

This wasn't Samantha, he reminded himself. It wasn't the woman he'd known.

She reached up and touched the buttons of his uniform, and his chest clenched.

"We want to thank you," she said, voice almost a whisper. "You've done an amazing job with the Bishops. You need to keep it up."

"I don't make my own orders, Sam," he told her.

Her head tilted to one side and as she did, the group surrounding him and du Trieux did the same. A chill ran up his spine.

"And here we thought you were your own man," she said. With that, she pressed her palm against his back and lightly shoved him toward the empty market.

The Infected surrounding them parted. The frontmost two walked a few meters ahead, then dropped the M27 and Gilboa at the market's sliding glass doors.

"It was nice seeing you again, Alex. Keep up the good work," Samantha said.

One of her Infected knocked on the cracked glass. Then like a pack of spooked gazelles, they sprinted off in the other direction.

Du Trieux ran forward, snatched up her Gilboa and the M27, and tossed it back to him. She took aim at the backs of Samantha's herd as they scattered, but didn't take a shot. She lowered the rifle and glared at Miller so fiercely, he actually blinked.

"What the fuck..." she began.

Just then, the market doors slid open and there stood three more Infected. It took a matter of seconds for Miller to realize these were different from Samantha's group. Their eyes were wider, glassier, even more distant; and they had a rash of fungus growing up each of their arms and veined across their faces.

With a violent surge the Infected thrust forward, reaching with their fungal-infested hands toward du Trieux's face. With a quick burst, Miller opened fire and shot them down.

At the noise, three more spilled from the opening. Du Trieux used the butt of her rifle to knock them back, trying to get far enough away to open fire. Without their hunting knives or sidearms, they pulled back quickly, shooting at will as a horde of Infected spilled from the building.

Only after the Charismatic entered the street and returned fire did Miller realize that Samantha had led them straight into a trap.

Shouldering his M27, Miller aimed and fired, hitting the Charismatic between the eyes, and sending the surrounding horde into a panic.

"Trix!" he bellowed.

"*Oui!*" she answered at equal volume.

And, together, they turned on their heels and ran.

21

MILLER PACED THE confines of his cell, spun around, and stalked back in the other direction.

What utter and complete *bullshit*.

He did not punch and shoot his way out of an Infected commune and come all the way back to the compound—*on foot*—through the wilds of New York City, fighting terror-jaws and slapping away packs of hungry rat-things, just so they could throw him in quarantine like a dog that had gotten off its leash.

He was so angry that when they came to take a tissue sample from his mouth, he almost bit the swab in half.

Not to mention the way they had treated du Trieux.

It made his fists clench to think of it. How they wrenched her arm behind her and pushed her off and away from him as soon as they'd crossed the compound's threshold. As if she were under arrest. As if she were resisting, which she wasn't.

He understood they thought they'd been infected. He got that. But didn't they understand that if he and du Trieux had been infected, they wouldn't have been *able* to come back to the compound? They would have already communed with the others and the pheromones would have kept them with the Infected.

Did they really not understand how that worked by now?

Of course, there had been that bomber. He'd been an Infected inside the compound. Why hadn't the pheromones kept him with his commune? But still, he was an unknown refugee, a stranger amongst the masses. Miller and du Trieux were members of the security team—a part of the inner workings of the compound—and shouldn't have been treated like common terrorists.

Miller shook his head at his own logic. There was no sense in spinning his wheels until he knew what they wanted, or why they were putting him on ice.

The only explanation that made any sense to him was that they must have known how they'd been held by Samantha, and they wanted to know what he'd said to her, and vice versa.

But how could they know that, though—that'd he'd seen her? The security forces at the gate had 'arrested' them seconds after their return. Miller and du Trieux hadn't even had the chance to tell them what had happened.

Had Morland or Hsiung seen them get taken by the Archaeans?

Maybe, but unlikely. Neither of them would have left the doctors to go after Miller and du Trieux in the first place—but if they had, they'd surely have intervened.

Losing steam, Miller unclenched his fists and sat on the floor, resting his back against the concrete wall of his cell.

There was no sense in guessing. He just had to wait and see what they wanted. Either that, or he had to wait for Gray to spring him. He knew there was no way in hell Gray would let this fly for long.

Miller blinked, closing his eyes against the glare from the lamp that hung from the ceiling over a table and two chairs. He couldn't bring himself to sit there. Not yet. It felt as if sitting in one of the chairs was admitting they'd been right to quarantine him— that they had a right to question him. He couldn't concede that.

The cement felt cold against his back as he rested his head. God, he needed a shower, and for more than just to get clean. A shave would feel great, too. There was a bucket of filth in every pore of his skin.

Images of angry, starved, thrashing Infected flashed in his mind's eye, and then Samantha's hands stroked her long braided hair and he popped his eyes open, lifting his head from the wall to blink away the memories.

He didn't want to re-live that escape. Not yet, probably not ever.

Where was Doyle with his magic paper when you needed him?

He got back to his feet with the intention of continuing his pacing when the door unlocked and a man entered.

Miller knew him as Paul Kimball, a leader from Shank. Short and broad-shouldered, Paul struggled to find a uniform that fit. His biceps were so large they bulged against the seams of his shirtsleeves. He eyed Miller up and down, then nodded toward the table and chairs.

"Miller," he said.

"Kimball."

Kimball sat at the table and waited for Miller to do the same.

Begrudgingly, he did. He rested his hands on the table and glared directly into Kimball's eyes.

The man's face barely moved. If Miller wanted to intimidate the captain, it wasn't going to be easy.

"Why am I in quarantine?" Miller asked. "I'm not Infected."

"We had to be sure."

"And?"

"You're clean."

"Of course I'm clean. What about du Trieux?"

"She's clean, too."

"I could have told you that. Have you let her loose?"

"Yes. But she won't leave until you are."

"So?" Miller's eyes widened. "Why am I still in quarantine?"

"We have a few questions. Things we'd like you to explain."

Here it comes, Miller thought. The third degree. The proverbial thumb screws about Samantha, about his loyalties, about what he knew of the Archaeans. He braced himself while simultaneously trying to appear calm. "What questions?"

"We found some odd behaviour in your search at the refugee processing office."

Miller rubbed at his earlobe and fought back the urge to laugh in Kimball's face. What the hell was this now? What searches? Miller wracked his mind, filtering through memories of battles, blood, and bombs and tried to recall anything to do with the refugee processing office—and then it came to him: when he thought he'd seen Samantha.

A few weeks back, after the bomb explosion, he'd gone to the refugee processing office and searched their mess of unfiled, random stacks of forms to see if she'd been brought into the compound. She hadn't—at least, not as far as he could tell. But he'd asked several of the staff if he could browse through their paperwork, and apparently he'd made an impression.

Fuck. If he'd known they kept records of who looked through the files, maybe he would have kept his suspicions to himself.

Were they asking him because they knew about Samantha and the Archaeans? He doubted it. If they did, they'd probably be shooting him in the head for treason after having met up with her again, or ripping out his thumbnails for information.

This had to be about something else. Sometimes

the best defense was a good offense. He clenched his jaw. "Yeah. So, I checked the records? What of it?"

"We want to know why. What were you looking for?"

"Who is *we*? Is Lewis asking why I accessed the refugee paperwork? Is Gray? I have a feeling if either one of them knew you were asking me this, they'd rap your knuckles like a Catholic nun."

Kimball's eyebrow twitched. He wasn't taking the bait, yet, but Miller'd struck a nerve. "Why did you access confidential files?" Kimball asked. "For what purpose?"

Miller tipped back his chair. Stretching like a cat, he forced a yawn. Then, with a slam, he tipped the chair forward and let the *crash* echo throughout the cement cell. "I'm the fucking leader of the Cobalt security squad, Kimball. *That's* why. A bomb had just been detonated in my face. I had concussion, for Christ's sake. And who the hell are *you* to demand answers from me? Do *you* even know what's in those files? Do *you* have security clearance to access them? And since when do I not? When did you outrank me, Kimball? I must have missed that memo."

"Who is Samantha Hernandez?" Kimball asked sternly. His face had turned red and he looked about ready to bash Miller's face in. "Why were you searching for her records?"

"I'm not sure you have security clearance to know the answer to that question. Maybe you should get your superior officer. Oh, wait. I'm sitting right here."

"If I didn't have clearance, I wouldn't be asking. Quit dodging the question."

"Which question? You've asked three, and I can't remember which one was first."

Kimball's left eyelid twitched. Miller suppressed a smirk.

"You think this is funny?" Kimball asked, his eyes bugging slightly.

"Not at all. Funny would be if you were wearing a clown costume instead of your uniform. Of course, the way yours fits..."

Kimball stood abruptly. "You son of a—"

Miller grinned as Kimball reached forward and snatched his uniform collar with his fist. His first instinct was to head-butt the asshole, but over his shoulder, the door opened and in walked Harris.

Kimball whipped around, Miller's collar in one hand, the other hovering in the air.

"Put him down, Kimball," Harris said, looking only mildly concerned.

Kimball dropped Miller back into his seat. The veins in his massive arms were visibly pulsing.

Harris pointed his finger in Kimball's face. "Do you have any idea who he is?"

A flash of confusion flickered across Kimball's brow, but he said nothing.

"How dare you speak to him in this manner? Or lay hands on him? You're dismissed."

With an angry flash, Kimball stalked out of the cell, leaving Harris and Miller alone.

Harris turned and faced Miller, his face a façade

of concern. It was so artificial that Miller almost smiled.

"Are you all right? Did Kimball hurt you in any way?"

Reaching up, Miller adjusted his uniform. "I think my collar may need ironing."

"What happened? Why was Kimball so angry?"

"Like you don't know."

Harris's demeanor shifted slightly. His concern morphed into an expression of concern and friendship.

Miller sighed. Did he truly think he was this stupid?

"I apologize on Kimball's behalf," Harris said. "As I'm sure you understand, our security forces are under a tremendous amount of pressure. I want you to know that if any of the men give you any further problems, you can come see me straight away. After all, you and I—we want the same thing, don't we? We're in this together."

Miller pursed his lips.

Harris blinked in orchestrated confusion. "Miller?"

Standing from his chair, Miller walked toward the door. "Mr. Harris," he said, as if saying good-bye. He twisted the handle, which was unlocked.

"Miller? I hope you see how sincere I am," Harris said, stopping him in his tracks. "I think you and I could work well together, and I would hate for something as silly as an unauthorized search of classified information to tarnish a record as exemplary as yours."

Miller's smirk faltered as he felt himself flush. "I thought you didn't know why Kimball was upset?"

Harris's façade cracked. "Are we understanding each other, Mr. Miller?"

Miller pulled the door open and stepped out into the hall, but thinking better, he leaned back inside and glared at Harris. "What I *understand* is that we have a mutation amongst the Infected due to some asshole experimenting on them with secret air bombs full of anti-parasitics—and I *understand* that by playing God, this jerkwad has made things worse. That's what I understand, *Bob*."

Miller slammed the door before he could hear Harris's reply.

Du Trieux stood a few feet ahead in the hallway. She'd obviously heard every word, given her expression.

"Making enemies?" she asked, waiting for him to catch up so they could exit the cell block together.

"Only when I have to," Miller grunted in reply.

22

MILLER ENTERED L. Gray Matheson's office without bothering to knock.

Lewis stood beside the desk, looking dejected and tired. A pair of binoculars were up to his eyes as he peered out the window. The air outside looked thick with dust, which gave the horizon an ominous red glow. Miller didn't know how Lewis could see anything through the film caking the window.

The air conditioner that normally hummed by the window sat in the corner, unplugged. The office was as stuffy as a sauna.

Gray sat as his desk wiping beads of sweat from his brow, looking grim.

"What's the emergency?" Miller asked. "This have anything to do with my being detained?"

Gray's confusion spoke volumes. "What? When were you detained?"

"Never mind," Miller said. Turning to Lewis, he asked, "What's happened this time?"

"The ship's arrived," Lewis said, not turning from the window. "The one from North Korea."

"Harris's payload." Miller nodded.

Lewis handed him the binoculars.

Miller took them and searched the East River, eventually spotting the tail end of the ship to the south, past Roosevelt Island. A Paramax freighter, approximately three hundred meters long, sailing *away* from the compound.

Miller couldn't see any disturbance from the engines. The vessel floated freely—even crookedly— drifting down river like a ghost ship.

"Where the hell is it going?"

"It went right by us and picked up speed once it passed Ward's Island," Lewis said. "No radio response or contact since it entered the Strait of Gibraltar. We're not sure who's in charge of the ship, or if there *is* anybody in charge at this point."

"Dangerous cargo for a ship to be floating free down the East River," Miller said. "It had to have steering capabilities at some point. They never could have navigated this far without them."

Gray nodded. "Can you imagine if the Infected got a hold of that ship? The losses would be catastrophic."

"'Catastrophic' doesn't do it justice, sir. It would be the end."

Gray's face paled. "We can't lose the cargo, Alex. Harris was a fool to bring it here, but now we have to make sure nobody else gets it. And we can't send any of the other security teams—they'll take it to Harris and he'll blow all of Manhattan to ash." Gray rubbed the stubble on his face with a soft scraping noise. His eyes were bagged and bloodshot. Miller wondered when he'd slept last. He looked like hell.

Come to think of it, they all did.

"I've got sign-off from the board," Gray continued. "Operation Sea Mink."

"We've only just—"

"You have to secure that cargo," Gray said. "Whatever the cost."

Miller turned toward Lewis. "Do we even have a plan?"

The commander shrugged. "Take a chopper and secure the ship. Repair the thrusters and steering. Get that ship back here asap."

"I want Doyle back."

"No can do." Lewis shook his head. "He's with Dagger squad on a mission outside the compound."

"You want me to secure a three-hundred-meter freighter with only four men?"

"Yes, and you'd better get moving. You're in the air in less than an hour."

"How many men can you spare from Cyclops squad, then?"

Lewis glared at Miller with an expression he suspected meant there was more, but he declined to comment. "None. They've been sent outside the compound, too, to clean out a commune of Infected encamped too close."

"On whose order?"

Gray and Lewis didn't bother replying. They only shook their heads.

"Besides," Lewis added. "We can only spare you one chopper. No room for any more men."

He didn't like it, but it seemed he had no choice. "Fine," Miller grunted.

"And Miller..." Lewis said as he turned to leave.

"Yes, sir?"

"You be careful, son. Something happened aboard that freighter. We don't know what you're walking into."

"Understood."

THE HOT WINDS over the East River stank of dead fish. Miller could just make out large eel-like creatures below the waves, breaching the water's surface and splashing polluted mist like a rotten perfume.

Beside him sat Morland and Hsiung. Scrunched together in what should have been a four-man chopper, they'd removed the center console in the front to make room for a jump seat. Hsiung, the smallest of them, hadn't looked happy when she strapped herself in.

Du Trieux and the pilot, a ruddy-faced man who called himself Smitty, sat comfortably in the back row of the attack chopper. He and du Trieux discussed wind current and air flow while the three in the front sat crammed together, giving no voice to their discomfort.

Miller hoped it would be a quick trip. With the additional weight, they'd need to conserve fuel for the return trip.

It was a miracle they'd gotten off the ground at all. Smitty and the launch crew had needed hours to clean out the chopper's fuel intake and air filters, so they were already behind schedule by the time they got into the air.

The ship, which had been floating just south of Roosevelt's Island, was now far down the East River near the Williamsburg Bridge, and dangerously close to striking land as the currents grew more irregular. There was no telling how it would get past Governors Island without thrusters.

As the chopper approached the freighter, Miller listened over the headset to du Trieux and Smitty chitchat and gripped the muzzle of the M27 nestled between his knees. It wasn't until the nose of the chopper dipped and Smitty swore that Miller checked out his window and peered down at the freighter.

There were bodies on deck—and not just human bodies.

Along with the human corpses—at least a dozen of them—there were also several massive walrus-like beasts lying on deck. Some were obviously dead—missing flippers, heads shattered, bleeding rivers of blood which pooled on the deck—while others took a break from gnawing on the bodies to look up at the chopper.

"What the heck are those?" Morland asked.

Hsiung, stuck in the jump seat, couldn't see, although that didn't stop her from straining against her belts, trying to get a look. She grunted in frustration.

One of the beasts opened its blood-soaked mouth

and bellowed at the chopper. Miller couldn't hear the noise over the rotors, but the other pinnipeds on deck waved their heads in response and opened their massive jaws, exposing rows of sharp teeth and two enormous tusks that rose from their bottom jaws.

"Let's call them tusk-fiends," Miller said.

Hsiung smirked. "Did you just pull that out of your ass?"

"Works for me," du Trieux said.

"Anybody bring armor-piercing rounds?" Miller changed the subject.

"No," Morland answered, still looking out the window.

Hsiung shook her head.

"I did," du Trieux answered from the back seat. "But I didn't bring enough to share."

"Alright," Miller said as the chopper continued to descend towards the freighter's deck. "Trix, you're out first. Take head shots with the armor-piercing mag and then swing around so Morland and Hsiung can exit the other side."

"Copy."

"I'll be right behind you." Miller unlatched his belts and an alarm sounded in the cockpit. "I suspect body shots won't do shit to these things, given how much blubber they've got," he said. "Head shots and eye shots. You all got that?"

They all responded in the affirmative.

"Okay, Smitty. Take us down."

"What the hell does it look like I'm doing?" he barked back.

The chopper banked hard to the right and hovered lower. Below, the tusk-fiends scattered. Then, as if thinking better of it, the animals stopped their retreat and surged forward, flopping headfirst in ripples of blubber with remarkable speed toward the helipad.

The chopper was quickly surrounded by the creatures, and a number of the fiends disappeared directly underneath them. Smitty cursed over his headset and pulled back on the stick, raising the chopper back into the air.

By way of reply, du Trieux unlatched her restraints and opened her door, turning the interior of the chopper into a storm of wind and dust.

Taking aim at the creatures on deck, du Trieux hung out the chopper door and took several shots with her Gilboa. The first two grazed a pair of fiends, but she hit the third—a mist of red splattering into the wind as the armor-piercing round struck brain matter. After another two kill shots, she'd cleared a space on the right near the bow of the freighter by the mast head.

"There!" she pointed.

Smitty yanked the stick of the chopper, banking hard and tipping du Trieux in her seat as she dangled out her door.

Du Trieux and Miller exited the chopper seconds after touching down, bullets flying.

The tusk-fiends lurched backwards away from them, while the creatures on the other side of the chopper surged forward. Working her way around the helicopter, du Trieux took shot after shot, wounding some of the pinnipeds—which Miller finished with his M27—and killing others with a single shot through the eye.

Once the deck was sufficiently cleared, Morland and Hsiung exited the bird, swinging around to the back to prevent any of the fiends from running into, and possibly damaging, the tail rotor.

When the onslaught of creatures finally slowed, Smitty shut down the chopper and joined du Trieux and Miller on the right, wounding stragglers with his sidearm and cursing like a sailor with every shot.

As the rotors slowed and the echoes of gunfire ceased, Miller counted the heads of his team and lowered his M27. He'd gone through an entire clip of ammo, but they were all still upright and the fiends had stopped coming. That had to count for something.

Once the main deck was deemed secured, Miller, Smitty, and the team searched the bodies for survivors. There were none. Given the look of them, some hadn't even had their weapons drawn. It stood to logic that the tusk-fiends had climbed aboard the freighter and surprised the crew. Their bodies were crushed, and most were missing limbs and chunks of flesh, as if the creatures had grabbed them by the arm, and flopped right over the top of them, crushing them under their two-meter-long, multi-ton bodies, and then had a nibble.

After the team swung around the perimeter to remove any more tusk-fiends, they headed up the iron stairwell toward the bridge, but just past the chart room, a different kind of corpse blocked the walkway.

The thing was enormous. Just slightly shorter than the fiends, the animal looked half-hippopotamus and half-dog, with a pronounced underbite. Miller had never seen a creature like it before—although the tusk-fiends obviously had. It looked as if the fiends had torn chunks from this corpse, too.

"Never seen these before either," Morland said, looking over Miller's shoulder. "Anybody want to name it before Miller does?"

"It doesn't look like a predator," du Trieux said. "But there are bullet holes."

"Doesn't have to be a carnivore to be dangerous," Hsiung said. "Suppose it went after the crew?"

"How about we call it a colossal cow?" Smitty suggested.

All eyes turned toward him, except du Trieux's, who was having a hard time hiding her impatience. "Can we go around it?"

To backtrack across the deck would waste valuable time, and Miller was already anxious to get to the bridge. The farther the freighter floated downriver, the longer it would take to get back to the compound.

Slinging the strap of his M27 over his shoulder, Miller climbed over the stinking creature. It was blubbery and wet, and with nothing to grasp onto it was slippery, but Miller ungracefully ambled over the corpse and encouraged the others to follow suit.

Once they'd cleared the body, Hsiung announced

the name of the animal to the others. "It's a goliath brute," she said.

Morland looked confused but du Trieux nodded. "*Oui.*"

"Works for me," Miller said.

They continued on, up the last flight of stairs to the bridge. When they arrived, Miller tugged at the steel door, but it was locked. People were visible through the round cracked window, however, so Miller waved.

A short, skinny kid, no more than a teenager, noticeably relaxed as he opened the door. He introduced himself as the first mate and quickly explained in a mix of Korean and broken English what had happened aboard.

From what Miller could understand, the freighter had lost control of its steering and thrusters someplace near Riker's Island when they'd been thrashed by a group of pseudo-whales. Once the ship was dead in the water, tusk-fiends and goliath brutes had swarmed the deck, taking out the masthead and radio antennae.

The captain had sent a squad to secure the deck, but that had failed. He then sent another squad below to the engine room to check on the engineering team and to repair the thrusters, but they'd lost contact with them almost immediately.

Frustrated, the captain had gone himself with the last squad to secure the cargo hold—but they'd disappeared as well.

The first mate and what was left of the bridge

crew had considered abandoning ship, but the pseudo-whales had surrounded the freighter, and getting to the lifeboats through the tusk-fiends and goliath brutes would have been suicide. Instead, they'd barricaded themselves inside with a stash of provisions and hoped help would come, or that they'd strike land, enabling them to abandon ship without touching the water at all.

Miller looked over the frightened bridge crew and chose his words carefully. "With the steering damaged, there's no point in fixing the thrusters, gentlemen. You're floating dead out here, and the longer you float free, the farther away from the peninsula you get. I think our best course of action would be to secure the cargo and use the chopper's radio to request aid for you to evacuate the ship. I don't see anything else for it."

The first officer sighed heavily, but looked relieved. He spoke with his crew in rushed Korean, and then in broken English told Miller they agreed.

Miller turned to his team. "First priority is to radio the compound. Smitty, stay here with the crew. We'll be back."

Smitty frowned, his pink face growing more crimson. "You're going back out there with those things? What if you don't come back?"

"Then wait for the aid to come."

"Assuming it'll come," Smitty mumbled.

"Don't worry," Miller said. "Worst case scenario, they'll come for the cargo and take your body back with them."

Smitty's frown deepened. "Nice."

"What?" the first mate asked, his eyes wide. "He's joking, right?"

Miller patted the panicking first mate on the shoulder, nearly knocking the skinny kid over.

THE CARGO HOLD was dark, dank, and smelled of blood and oil.

Miller walked down the stairwell, the hairs on the back of his neck standing on end. Behind him followed du Trieux, Hsiung, and Morland, in that order.

Now that the call for aid had been sent from the chopper, it was time to secure the cargo. With any luck, they could load the missile onto the bird and lift it back to the compound before the aid arrived. Miller wasn't one-hundred-per-cent certain of who'd arrive when, or if, aid came. If a squad of Harris's men showed up, things could get complicated.

Miller's hands slid down the stairwell railing, then quickly dropped off once he reached the first landing. He activated the search light he'd mounted to the side of his rifle, flashing it around him.

There would have been a reason why the captain and his squad had disappeared trying to secure the cargo, and they'd probably had ten men. Miller had four. His palms felt slick with sweat, but he proceeded, allowing the remainder of his team to follow.

The lights in the cargo hold were non-functional

when Miller tried to toggle the switch. Overhead, long rectangular fluorescent fixtures hung dark and lifeless.

From what he could see using his mounted light, there was a one-meter-wide walkway, without a railing, that went around the perimeter of the cargo hold. A center catwalk led across the middle to the other side. The pathways were narrow enough to maneuver around the hold, but Miller and his team could only advance in single file.

The walkway itself was clear of debris, but the mouth of the cargo hold below housed crates upon crates—stacked several meters high, reaching up and toward the ceiling and creating a maze-like labyrinth.

How Miller was supposed to find one crate amongst all these others, he had no idea. Not to mention how he and his team were going to get to it once they located it. There didn't appear to be any ramp or stairs leading down.

A loud crash sounded to the left.

Swinging around, Miller led the group down the walkway and toward the noise. At the tip of the hold, Miller stopped and angled his mounted light down toward the cargo.

Below, a stack of wooden crates had been smashed opened. There appeared to be leafy greens inside. Lettuce, spinach, and some variety of purple kale. A pack of a half-dozen goliath brutes were making a meal of it.

They didn't take too kindly to having the sharp

glare of the lights flashed into their beady black eyes. They growled and, with surprising speed, scattered into the maze of crates like cockroaches.

"Shit," Miller breathed.

"Over there," Morland said, shining his light farther into the center of the cargo hold, near the middle catwalk.

With Morland in the lead, they returned from the direction they came.

The bodies of the captain and his crew were strewn along the floor, crunched between crates and crushed into bloody pulp. Some had been disembowelled; their entrails lay splattered against the hold floor.

"They don't have flashlights," Morland said, shining his light on the remains.

"So the lights worked at some point," Hsiung offered.

"Think we can get them back up and running?" Miller asked du Trieux.

She shined her light across the ceiling, following the electrical cords from the light fixtures to their origin, a panel in the wall housing a circuit breaker of some sort. "I'll see what I can do."

"How are we supposed to know which box is the one we're looking for?" Morland asked.

Hsiung shone her light near the center of the cargo hold. "It's right there."

"What?" Miller twisted around to see.

"See that long crate right there? It's the only box labelled in English," she explained, "and the captain and his posse's bodies are surrounding it. They were trying to protect it. They'd already rigged a pulley system to that crane over there. Are you all blind?"

"It's dark in here," Morland said.

"Uh-huh."

Miller signalled the others to follow suit as he reached across and grasped the dangling rope attached to the rectangular crate. Taking hold, Morland and Hsiung pulled along behind him, with Morland at the tail end.

The crate rose, the ropes groaning under the strain.

Below, a brute appeared amongst the bodies of the crewmen. Lurching forward, the goliath bumped the crate, causing it to swing to the side and crash into another stack of crates.

The rope slipped in Miller's sweaty hands and dropped a foot before Morland howled and leaned back, stalling it before it completely slithered out of their grasps.

"Trix?" Miller grunted.

"Morland, watch your six!" du Trieux shouted.

"What the..."

The rope reeled from Miller's grasp, slipping through his fingers. The crate dropped, but stopped just short of smashing to the floor.

Gripping the rope tightly, his palms burning through his gloves, Miller heard Morland shriek and checked over his shoulder.

A brute had climbed atop another stack of crates and bounded onto the center catwalk. Morland swung around and dodged the goliath's first attempt to bite off his arm, but the beast swung its massive head back around and knocked Morland clean off the platform.

Miller released the rope and reached for his hunting knife, but couldn't reach the brute.

The crate lurched to the floor, sending Hsiung, still holding the rope, into the air.

Miller faced the goliath brute as it lurched forward, snapping the air in front of it. Swinging his blade, Miller caught the beast across the face, slicing a deep ribbon of flesh just under its tiny black eye.

The creature roared in protest and backed off.

Shots rang out.

Below, Morland had regained his footing and fired upward, hitting the attacking brute in the face and sending it slipping over the edge.

Just then, the hold was flooded with fluorescent light as the overhead fixtures illuminated the carnage.

Brutes on all sides of the group, on each side of the walkway, roared and sprinted back into the depths of the hold in search of darkness.

Du Trieux came up behind Miller and grabbed the rope. Together they pulled Hsiung down from the ceiling, where she was dangling like a worm on a hook and spitting what Miller could only guess were expletives in Chinese. When her feet finally reached the platform, she, Miller, and du Trieux wrenched up the cargo crate, Morland dangling precariously beside it.

*　　*　　*

BACK ON DECK, with the crate safely secured to the chopper, Miller waved to Smitty on the bridge, and waited with the others for the pilot to return.

If all went as planned, they'd have a response to their distress signal and could bug out of there, take the crate back to the compound, and maybe sleep for a week or two.

It was dark out now and the team was exhausted. The blazing sun had set and Miller took a moment to marvel at the depleted New York City skyline. It was all dark, save for a bright beacon of yellow in the distance which came from the Astoria Peninsula.

Within minutes, Smitty arrived. He climbed into the cockpit and checked if their distress signal had received a response. There was none. When he exited the chopper, he eyed the crate they'd attached to the landing gear and scratched his head. "We don't have enough fuel to fly back to the compound with that," he informed them. "Even if we lost the additional man aboard. We spent too much circling the freighter trying to find a safe spot to land."

Miller ran his palm against the leg of his uniform. "Then we wait for rescue. In the meantime, we'd better secure the rest of the freighter."

BACK UP ON the bridge, Miller watched as the first officer released the controls. He hadn't been too keen on the idea to begin with, but after Miller had convinced him the freighter was a lost cause, he willingly dumped some of the ship's fuel into the water.

Miller glanced outside to the edge of the deck and could just make out du Trieux as she fired a flare into the slick. The oil burst into flames and set the water ablaze.

Even from the bridge, Miller could hear the pseudo-whales and surrounding animals squealing as they burned.

"Pull up a chair," he said to the crewmen as he eyed the scorching ocean. "This could take a while."

23

MILLER FELT A slap on his knee and slowly opened his eyes.

He'd been dreaming of Billy; of the day that he'd taken him to buy his favourite Armani suit. Miller could still smell the wool and leather inside the outlet store. He could still see Billy frowning when Miller had tried on a Hugo Boss three-button pinstripe and realized his build was all wrong for the cut.

"You look like a linebacker wearing skinny jeans," Billy had said with a sparkle in his grey eyes. "Just *no*."

Miller shook the image from his head.

Seeing the look on du Trieux's face, he briefly worried he'd said something embarrassing in his sleep, but she nodded toward the first officer.

The first mate gripped the communications microphone in his palm, his knuckles white. He was yelling at someone in a mixture of Korean and English about evacuating the crew, but the line went dead and he turned pale and sweaty.

"What's going on? Has the aid arrived?" Miller asked.

"Not exactly," du Trieux said.

"He's not listening," the first mate said, turning around, looking panicked.

It'd been two days since they'd been trapped on the freighter with the crew. The current had pushed them around Governors Island, in the end, and they'd floated right past the Statue of Liberty their first night, and were heading towards the open Atlantic. Scanning the land to the west, Miller guessed they were someplace just south of Delaware.

Each time the wildlife had attempted another onslaught they'd burned the sea and pushed them back. But the fuel supply was dwindling, and Miller wasn't sure how many more times that would work.

Morland and Hsiung had spent the better part of the day before clearing out the cargo hold of brutes to get proper food and provisions, but their ammo was dwindling. An evacuation couldn't happen soon enough.

Given the reaction from the first mate, who'd introduced himself as Ryung, Miller didn't think an evacuation was what the approaching boat had in mind. The modified tug boat they'd used to transport the EMP from Boston for the operation against Stockman's comms was coming in quick off the port bow. The men aboard were wearing S-Y security uniforms.

Miller borrowed Ryung's binoculars and peered out the bridge window.

"He said no crew, only to give him a special cargo," Ryung said. "That you'd know which one he meant. I asked him, 'What about my men?' He said again, 'No men. Only special cargo.' That wasn't our deal, Miller. No evacuate my men, no cargo."

Miller adjusted the binoculars and focused on the crew of the incoming boat. He spotted Kimball—that asshole who had questioned him about researching Samantha—one of Harris's men. "Oh, boy," he mumbled under his breath.

Du Trieux nodded, glumly.

Taking the communications mic off the bridge console, Miller pressed the side button and cleared his throat. "Kimball, you old dog. How you been? Long time no see."

Through the binoculars Miller watched as Kimball smirked, then spoke into his own mic. "Miller. Good. Is our cargo secured?"

Miller released the button and turned to du Trieux. "Have the team bring up those crates of greens from the cargo hold and have Smitty warm up the chopper."

Du Trieux nodded, then disappeared out the bridge door.

"What's going on?" the first mate asked.

"Just give me a second, Ryung," Miller said. He hated where this was headed, but didn't see any alternative. "Cargo is secured," Miller said into the mic. "Are you our ride back to the compound?"

"Not quite," Kimball said. "Our orders are to retrieve the cargo, and nothing else."

"That's funny," Miller said. "Those aren't my orders, and I got here first."

"Situation's changed since you left," Kimball answered.

Miller watched the boat through the binoculars as Kimball put a hand on his hip and shifted his weight. The small vessel came to a sliding stop several meters away from the freighter, just far enough to give the surrounding oil slick a wide birth.

"Gray Matheson has relinquished his position as CEO of Schaeffer-Yeager, and Robert Harris is in charge," Kimball said. Miller almost dropped the mic. "There's nothing you or Cobalt can do about it, other than to get out of our way."

Miller swallowed, his mouth suddenly bone dry. "I'm going to need verification of that information, Kimball. You'll forgive me if I don't take your word for it."

"Verify all you want, but I'm not waiting for my cargo much longer. I'll give you ten minutes."

Miller handed the mic to Ryung, and patted him on the back. "I'm sorry, kid."

"Sorry? Why're you sorry?"

Leaving the bridge, Miller made it out onto deck in record speed.

Coming up the stairwell from the cargo hold were Morland and Hsiung, lugging a half-bashed-in crate of limp lettuce and soggy spinach.

"What do you want with this?" Morland asked.

"There's a boat off the port bow. On my go, chuck that on top of it."

Morland pursed his lips. "You got it."

At the chopper, du Trieux and Smitty cleaned fungus out of the fuel intake and the air filters.

"Wish I'd had more of a heads-up," Smitty said, as Miller approached. "Without a full crew to help, this could take a while."

"Do the best you can," Miller said, hopping inside and booting up the communications array. After a brief delay, Miller tapped into the Northwind network, but immediately received an error message and was unable to connect. Clicking again, he got the same result. If he didn't know any better he'd think the network had been disabled, but that would give credence to Kimball's fantasy that Gray Matheson had stepped down as CEO, and there was no way Miller could believe that.

After everything Gray had gone through to get that far? Why would he walk away now? It didn't make sense.

No, until he heard otherwise, Miller was proceeding as ordered. Besides which, if Harris was indeed in charge, did he really think Miller would simply relinquish control of a nuclear warhead because his lackey told him to? Harris was smarter than that.

Or, perhaps that had been Harris's plan all along— to set Miller up for a gunfight and eliminate Cobalt? That was a real possibility. Either way, they couldn't stay aboard the freighter, and they couldn't outgun a boatful of soldiers, not with their diminished supply of ammo. Flight was their only course of action.

Miller hopped from the chopper and inspected du Trieux and Smitty's progress. There was still a film of fungus on the fuel intake, but there wasn't much fuel to begin with. It would have to be enough.

"Start the engines," he said, ignoring Smitty's look.

Miller tapped his earpiece. "Dump the greens, light the slick again and get aboard the chopper asap," he ordered Morland and Hsiung.

"Roger," Hsiung answered.

From the helipad, Miller watched as Morland and Hsiung tipped the remains of the crate overboard. Meanwhile, du Trieux, sprinting to the edge of the freighter, dropped a lit flare onto the oil slick and bolted back.

All three reached the chopper simultaneously, hopping into the bird just as the rotors picked up speed. The engines struggled to ignite the fuel not consumed by fungus in the gas tank, but fired up, giving them lift off.

"And we're off!" Smitty yelped, yanking back on the stick and gunning the twin turbo-shaft engines.

As they rose above the freighter, Miller gazed at the action below. The animals, kept at bay by the oil fire around the freighter, attacked the greenery aboard Kimball's boat—one of the first brutes aboard knocked a solider into the water.

Bullets pierced the sky. The chopper lurched to the side and alarms blared—they'd been hit on the right side but had managed to get some distance between them and the freighter. They flew over open ocean, away from Kimball and the jump boat.

"What the..." Smitty cussed, swinging the bird hard to the left. More bullets zipped in their direction.

"They're firing at a fucking nuclear missile!" Morland gaped, rushing to attach his safety restraints.

Out his window, Miller could just make out the action aboard Kimball's boat. Soldiers hacked back a trio of goliath brutes as Kimball aimed his assault rifle at them. It wasn't until Miller saw the outline of a soldier on the boat's pilothouse hoist a long tube up onto his shoulder that he felt a rush of panic. "Smitty!" he bellowed. "Anti-aircraft missile incoming!"

The chopper banked harshly to the left again, tipping sideways over the wretched ocean, nearly twisting in a full circle.

Smitty howled as he twisted the stick. The engines sputtered and fought, losing thrust as chunks of fungus clogged the tubing.

On the right, coming in hot, was a trail of smoke straight at them.

"Miller!" du Trieux shouted.

In a rush of heat and smoke, the helicopter was struck.

Miller braced his body for impact as the chopper spun wildly, whirling out of control. With a crash, the chopper dove headlong into the rancid ocean below.

24

THE SMELL OF putrid salt water and smoke filled Miller's nostrils as he choked.

Opening his eyes, he blinked away the darkness clouding his vision and forced himself to focus. He was up to his hips in sea water. As his sight and hearing cleared, the picture came into view. The helicopter alarms were blaring and it was sinking fast.

To his left, Hsiung lay slumped in the jump seat. Past her, Morland was conscious but struggling as he sawed through his restraints with a utility knife, his elbow rapping the cracked glass of his door as he worked.

Miller reached up with shaking fingers and detached his safety belts. Then, twisting in his chair, he unlatched Hsiung and caught her as she pitched away from him.

Morland, finally free, rotated in his seat and slung one of Hsiung's arms over his shoulders. "Go!" he barked at Miller, jerking his head toward the door behind him. "Go up!"

Miller pushed off his feet and shoved his shoulder into the chopper door. It opened with a snap, rushing more water, smoke and stench into the cabin.

Climbing out of the doorway, Miller jumped into the tainted seawater.

Morland, climbing out of the chopper just behind him, quickly activated the flotation device in his combat vest. The collar of his vest bloomed up and around his neck, giving him instant buoyancy in the thick, steaming water. Morland then reached around and pulled the release on Hsiung's vest. Grabbing the unconscious soldier into his arms, Morland pulled her tiny frame into his massive chest, then rotated onto his back, kicking and floating both of them to safety, a few feet from the sinking chopper.

Miller rotated his arms, barely keeping afloat as water gushed over his head. Two safe, two to go.

Swimming back toward the sinking helicopter, Miller reached into the filling cabin, searched with his hands under his seat and found an air canister. Shoving the device into his mouth, he activated the airflow, then sucked in a breath of oxygen, before diving deeper into the muck toward the sunken tail.

His eyes burned in the putrid salt water. Ignoring the sting, he kicked his legs and arms. When he reached the chopper, the door was closed. Inside the fogged glass he could just make out the sight of du Trieux as she struggled to free an unconscious Smitty from his restraints.

Miller pounded on the window. Du Trieux turned to him and mouthed something, but Miller couldn't make it out. Finally, he pounded again and the door opened from the inside.

Reaching in, Miller yanked du Trieux out. She'd already activated her flotation vest, so she popped out of his hands and rose toward the water's surface immediately.

Sucking in another breath from the air canister, Miller dove into the submerged cockpit to free Smitty. The pilot's eyes were wide open, and unblinking. His mouth was agape and slack.

Pulling another breath from the canister, Miller sliced through Smitty's safety restraints with his knife, unlatched the buckles of the pilot's vest, and removed it from his slack body. Leaving Smitty to his watery grave, Miller climbed out and around the helicopter's shell in search of the crate.

By the landing gear, strapped in with three restraint buckles, the nuke was still attached to the chopper.

Miller cut the buckles loose and tugged on the crate—but he was unable to move the heavy box from the sinking chopper.

The whole contraption, Miller included, was getting sucked deeper into the ocean. All he could do was hold on until they struck bottom.

Finally they touched the ocean floor. Finally able to move without fear of losing the crate, Miller pulled another breath from the canister and wrapped Smitty's vest around the edge of the box, pulling the tab. The vest's flotation device expanded, partially raising the crate on one side—but it wasn't enough.

Thinking better, Miller unlatched the buckles on his

own vest, wrapped it around the other end of the crate, then pulled the tab. With this added buoyancy, Miller was finally able to lift the crate free of the chopper, but it still wasn't enough to float the heavy container to the surface, no matter how hard he kicked.

Holding his breath, Miller released the crate and swam to the surface. Breaching the water, he spotted Morland, du Trieux and Hsiung, floating just a few meters away.

Swimming arm over arm, he clutched the air canister in his fist and shouted at the trio. "Give me Hsiung's vest!"

Without question, Morland held tight as du Trieux unlatched Hsiung's straps and chucked the vest at Miller.

Miller swam toward the vest, snatched it, then swam back. Re-inserting the air canister into his mouth, he dove again, kicking toward the sunken chopper.

On reaching the bird, he lashed the additional vest to the center of the crate. The extra lift was just enough for him to raise the box from the chopper. He strained and pulled, hauling it upward, struggling toward the surface.

Du Trieux dove down, meeting him halfway, and helped lug the crate toward the light. They broke surface—panting and kicking to keep afloat—du Trieux gasping to catch her breath.

Using the floating crate like a buoy, they met up with Morland and the unconscious Hsiung. They pumped their legs and swam toward land for what seemed like an eternity. Finally, when Miller thought he couldn't kick one more time, they reached a rocky beach.

Morland swam onto shore first, and left Hsiung's unconscious—but breathing—body a safe distance from the water. He then returned to the water, and assisted du Trieux and Miller in dragging the crate up past the breakers and onto the rocks.

. Every inch of Miller's body ached. His head pounded, his chest pulled tight with each breath, and his eyes, swollen from the foul salt water, burned. He flopped down on the rocks beside the crate with a grunt, and coughed with gut-wrenching hacks.

Du Trieux, lying on the rocks beside him, gasped for air and spit out phlegm from her throat. She turned toward Miller and whispered, "Smitty?"

He shook his head. "Gone by the time I got to him."

"*Merde*."

After a few moments of rest, Hsiung stirred and awakened, mumbling in Chinese. She coughed violently a few times, then sucked down a jagged breath; her eyes opened and focused on the orange sky above. "Oh, fuck," she muttered.

Morland, lying beside her, pushed himself to sitting and helped her do the same.

The four of them climbed to their feet and stood on shore, dripping like wet dogs. In the distance, the freighter sat, floating crooked and diagonal across the Atlantic. What they couldn't see was the Shank jump boat, which undoubtedly was still on the far side of the freighter.

South from them, resting on the beach in the

remains of the day's sunshine, lay three goliath brutes. They gave massive, honking cries, echoing across the ocean waves.

"That's our cue to leave," Miller said.

Not willing to waste any more time, or risk an encounter with the brutes, they dragged themselves and the soaked crate up shore, inland.

Just above the beach, a stone wall edged the remains of a greenway. The area, which had probably once been a manicured lawn, was now covered in overgrown trees and weeds, looking wild and desolate. Beyond that was what looked to be a residential area running up and down the shoreline, followed by a two-lane highway and more beach on the other side.

Morland crawled over the wall first, balancing the crate on top, while the others pushed it from the other side.

With Morland in front, du Trieux and Hsiung on either side and Miller at the end, they walked the crate north, up the highway toward—Miller wasn't sure.

What the hell was he supposed to do now?

He needed a plan, fast, but his head was still swimming and he swayed as if he were still on board the freighter.

His M27, slung over his shoulder by the strap, continually rapped against his hip and dripped water on the ground as he struggled to keep hold of the crate. A shiver ran up his back as he pressed his lips together.

He took a long hard look at the remnants of Cobalt—they didn't look any better than he felt, and he was genuinely surprised Hsiung was on her feet at all—and a sense of foreboding stirred his gut.

This isn't going to end well.

"The sun's setting," du Trieux said. "We can't walk all the way to New York City like this."

"Why bother going back at all, if Harris runs the compound?" Morland asked.

"What if he doesn't?" Hsiung snapped, rubbing her palm across her forehead. "We can't trust what those assholes said."

"Let's see if we can't find a deserted house and camp for the night," Miller suggested.

The neighborhood was a risk, but Miller saw no other option. If they were lucky, they would find a house they could pillage for food, water, and shelter. The temperature had dipped dramatically. If they were unlucky, they'd find an Infected commune and be ripped to pieces, unable to fight back a horde in their weakened condition. Either way, walking in the cold, wet of night, with wild creatures abounding, while drenched in stinking seawater, was not a viable option.

After crossing the highway and entering the neighborhood, they soon learned that it was infested with rat-things and a handful of terror-jaws—but the larger predators, the titan-birds and the thug behemoths, seemed to prefer elsewhere.

Du Trieux released hold of the crate, and took point, leading the team through the quiet streets and clearing a path free of varmints—kicking and slapping them out of the way, since her ammunition was still wet.

There had, at some point, been some sort of an anti-Infected resistance in this community. There was evidence everywhere—old banners across garage doors and balconies that read *No Infected*, and graffiti like *Parasite-Free Only*. Ammunition casings littered the sidewalks and roads, and a handful of houses had been shot up or burned. A skirmish had happened here. The only question was, how had it ended?

Given their own experience, Miller knew none of Cobalt were expecting to find a community of non-Infected humans welcoming them with open arms. If anything, they lugged the crate holding the missile with looser fingers, ready to drop and draw their weapons at the first sign of a mob—or run for their lives.

Not wishing to delve too deeply into the neighborhood, they found a tiny two-bedroom cottage close to the shore and not far off the road. From the outside, it didn't look too damaged. Once they secured the residence, they placed the crate near the front door, barricading it closed, and then scavenged the pantry, coming up with a few cans of condensed soup and canned vegetables.

Mercifully, the gas was still operational, although the water and electricity were not. Miller placed the cans on the gas stove and heated them while Hsiung raided the closets and found dry clothes and blankets. Meanwhile, du Trieux unearthed two large five-gallon bottles of water hidden behind the ironing board in the mud room.

As fortune had it, there was a stack of firewood by the back door, which Morland used to make a tiny fire in the main room's fireplace. After eating, wearing dry clothes and wrapped in stiff woollen non-functioning electric blankets, they warmed themselves by the fire, drank lukewarm water, and took turns sleeping until the sun rose.

In the grey of morning—dry, somewhat rested, and with enough food in them to keep moving—they checked the cottage's detached garage for supplies and found an old gas-guzzling four-door sedan.

The old, late-model Ford was locked. After popping the window out and attempting to hot-wire the monstrosity, they found the battery was long dead, and the gas tank empty.

A check of the adjacent houses failed to find any viable cars. It would seem that the resistance had cleared out—having taken the best-functioning vehicles with them, after draining the others—and gone off to find an Infected-free area, if such a thing existed.

This didn't bode well for the surrounding houses being commune-free, Miller figured, so the four of them walked back to the highway, lugging the crate by hand, and continued their sojourn north— dejected, discouraged, and saying little.

After a good hour, Hsiung stopped walking, jarring the four to a quick stop. "There's smoke coming out of that chimney," she said, pointing to a large, mansion-like house with a shingle roof. Further up the beach highway, the house was at least a mile or more away, but any sign of life, Infected or not, was a chance at a vehicle.

They approached with caution. Miller directed

the group off the main highway and back into the residential area, which allowed for some coverage as they advanced toward the target. This proved a smart move, as the closer they got, became evident that the house was an Infected commune.

One block from the smoking chimney they found the commune's 'septic area.' A greenway with a running gutter was stacked high with faeces and waste. In the distance, they heard voices, along with the low roar of a working truck, or van.

Sneaking closer to the mansion, they spotted it. A white, fourteen-passenger van, rusted in some places, but operational and ambling down the residential street at a decent clip.

Quickly taking cover behind some shrubs, they watched from a distance as a dozen Infected scrambled out of the van, eyed the mansion in trepidation, then hugged, kissed, and greeted those standing out front of the house as if they had long anticipated their reunion.

The greeters, looking slightly less threadbare than the new arrivals, encircled the recruits and ushered them inside, leaving only two left at the van—the driver and an armed guard.

The guard, a tall lanky man in a dirty overcoat, had a sawed-off shotgun in one hand, and was glancing around the area as if sensing Miller and the other's presence. Then, feeling the coast was clear, the driver and the guard hopped into the van, slamming the doors behind them.

"Miller?" du Trieux whispered.

"Morland and Hsiung, stay with the crate. Du Trieux, you're with me."

"*Oui.*"

Crouching as he ran, Miller booked it toward the idling van—du Trieux just behind him. Coming up to the driver-side window, he yanked open the door and thrust his hunting knife deep into the driver's ribcage, angling upward toward his heart.

On the passenger side, the guard barely had time to raise his shotgun before du Trieux stabbed him in the ear and twisted her bowie knife free for another jab at his carotid artery.

Spilling the corpses out into the street, they hopped inside, closing the doors quietly, and Miller shifted the vehicle into drive.

After swinging around to pick up Morland, Hsiung, and the crate, Miller pulled the van out onto the beach highway, and shoved the gas pedal all the way to the floorboard.

It wasn't until they were many miles away that he felt his hands relax.

Bloodstained, and gripping the steering wheel so tightly they ached, Miller wiped his bloody palms on the pants of his uniform and let out a slow, hot breath.

Morland laughed from the back seat and Hsiung yipped with excitement.

They were on their way home, Miller thought, his grin quickly fading—whatever was left of it.

THEY TOOK SHIFTS driving through the day and got as far as Secaucus, New Jersey. There, on the I-95 north, just west of the Lincoln Tunnel, the van sputtered to a stop and died—right smack in the middle of the highway. Fungus had clogged the fuel lines, or they'd run out of gas. Either way, they were fucked.

"Bollocks," Morland sighed, tossing his weapon onto his shoulder and moving to the back of the van to open the tailgate.

Assuming their prior positions lugging the crate, the four of them took to the road, opting to head east through the Lincoln Tunnel, into the city. If all went well, they'd be able to walk through Hell's Kitchen, cross the Queensboro Bridge and arrive at the Astoria Peninsula in about three and a half hours, but Miller was too realistic to hope for that.

For one thing, they had no food. They'd filled their canteens with water at the cottage, but that wouldn't last long and it was already dark. For another, if NYC Infected communes were living underground, they stood a real chance of running into one inside the tunnel. But with no other viable option, and being unable to radio for help—the batteries of their short-range radios were long dead, and besides, there was no help to be had—and having slim chances of finding another vehicle to boost, they trudged on: alert, exhausted, but steadily moving.

The tunnel, at first glance, appeared empty. Fearing to hope for a bit of luck, the team pressed forward, passing the empty toll booths and entering the tunnel on the far right. The lights were out and the tunnel was pitch black. Disregarding the walkway on the left, Morland snapped on the light mounted on his rifle and they walked in the center of the road, using the single beam of light as their only source of illumination.

That there'd been a past commune was obvious from the smell. Mixed in with road tar and the years of exhaust that permeated the walls, the stench of body odor, waste, and burning rubber filled the two-lane channel to the point of choking. Piles of blankets and the ashes of extinguished campfires lay scattered throughout the underpass.

The only sound was their boots echoing off the concrete walls. The temperature, a good ten degrees cooler than it had been at the opening, made the tunnel seem almost tomb-like—desolate, dangerous.

At the midway point, as expected, they encountered a small band of Infected—three of them, huddled around a campfire and starving to the point of collapse.

Miller and the others armed themselves, ready to dispatch them if they got aggressive, but the Infected merely lay on the ground and watched them amble by, bug-eyed, covered head-to-toe in fungal growths, mouths gaping as if they didn't even have the energy to ask to be put out of their misery.

One of them, a woman of indeterminate age, raised a skeletal hand a few inches into the air as Miller and the others walked by—but she said nothing.

There was no helping them, and no one wanted to risk going nearer.

A bullet to the head would have been the kind thing to do—unfortunately, none of them had a bullet to spare. Instead, they skirted to the far side of the tunnel and walked right past them, hands on their sidearms.

As they neared the far end of the tunnel, the customary light at the end of the path proved non-existent. Instead, more darkness loomed. They exited the underpass with sighs of relief, and made their way to the left, toward the darkness of Hell's Kitchen.

It wouldn't be long, Miller hoped. The worst was surely behind them.

WHAT SHOULD HAVE been a three-hour walk turned into three days.

They searched for food and water the first night,

dodged communes the following day, only to come across a pack of terror-jaws the morning after that, and swooping titan-birds that same afternoon. Before long, Miller and the others found themselves out of ammunition, still miles from the compound, with swollen feet and sunken bellies, disheartened and beyond exhausted.

The closer they came to the compound, the more swarms of large, aggressive wasps attacked around every bend. Gas masks seemed to keep the wasps at bay, although the obscured visibility made navigating the treacherous streets all the more perilous and didn't stop them from being continually stung.

Whatever plans Harris had had for the super-wasps seemed to have gone awry, Miller surmised. He highly doubted they'd included flocks of venomous wasps attacking people's faces at random. Hell, maybe they had. Miller couldn't imagine that the NAPA-33-infused bugs had done what they were supposed to have done. It was like walking into a huge hive.

Closer still, and Infected communes seemed to multiply. Skating around them, hiding in buildings as gangly-looking squads of Infected passed, slowed Cobalt's sluggish trek even further.

Finally, their fingers blistered and raw from carrying the crate across the city, they arrived at the compound's southern refugee processing gate—only to discover that it was shut. Chains with padlocks secured the gate and with no guards to protect them, it looked outright abandoned.

Miller peered through the chain-link, but soon the wasps were at him and he had no choice but to put his mask back on. Even with the naked eye, he couldn't make out anything inside the walls, other than deserted shanties and cold, fireless barrels where people had once stood to stay warm.

They had better luck at the central gate, several blocks to the north. Two guards stood at the entrance, which had once been the station for a half-dozen soldiers.

"Oh, thank God," Morland breathed.

Miller, sensing there were probably more than the two guards, left Morland and Hsiung in a nearby alley with the crate and took du Trieux with him.

As they approached, both guards, wearing gas masks as well, eyed the advancing pair and raised their weapons. "Halt!" they shouted.

Miller stopped cold.

"Identify yourselves!" the guard on the right bellowed.

"Hands in the air!" the other barked.

Carefully, Miller and du Trieux held their hands in front of them. Miller wasn't surprised they couldn't identify who they were: their uniforms were practically falling off them. It was probably the only reason they hadn't been shot on sight.

"Identify yourselves!" the first guard ordered again.

"Who's in command here?" Miller demanded. "Who is your commanding officer?"

"We asked you a question," the guard snapped.

Miller's eyes scanned the guards. There were no insignias on their lapels, no security squad identifiers. "What squad are you from?"

The guards, with the lightest of motions, lowered their rifles. "Who are you?"

"We've been out in the field a while," Miller explained. "Who's your commanding officer?"

The second guard lowered his rifle. "How long you guys been gone, man? Didn't you hear?"

"Hear what?"

"There aren't any squads anymore."

Miller felt his face go numb. "Since when?"

"Since Harris is running the show. Where the hell have you been, dude? Under a rock?"

Beside him, du Trieux shifted on her feet.

"Hey!" the first guard interjected. His rifle now shaking slightly, jerked in his arms as he swung it around. "Don't move!"

"Easy, now, easy," Miller said, his hands still raised. "Nobody has to get hurt here."

"Hey, is that a woman? Has she been registered?"

"Registered? Why would...?" Miller didn't finish his sentence. In a rush of understanding, his hands bunched into fists and he backed up, ever so slightly.

Women were being registered. Wasps were running rampant. Harris was in command, just as they'd feared. The compound looked empty. And the guards, faced with two armed soldiers, hadn't asked once if they were Infected.

Miller's worst fears were realized—the compound was a lost cause.

Gray and Lewis were probably dead, or in the brig, if they were lucky.

The wasps, he suspected, had wiped out not only the Infected, but the uninfected, too. Women were being registered, presumably for breeding. The survivors, no doubt, were under lock and key, someplace 'safe' inside the compound, hidden from the outside world, trapped like laboratory rats.

Walking into the compound, at this point, was suicide. Especially considering the cargo they'd lugged all the way from the Atlantic Ocean.

Miller continued backing up. His M27 was out of bullets, but he had about ten rounds left in his sidearm. He'd been saving them for an emergency.

Carefully, he lowered his hand to the holster on his hip. The first guard, sensing the movement, jerked his rifle back toward him, and aimed right at Miller's head.

"Both of you," the guard spat, "stop where you are! Who are you? What're your names?"

"Can't help you, kid," Miller said. "I'm under orders to report to my commanding officer."

"Oh, yeah?" the second guard said, raising his rifle again. "And what would Harris want with you?"

Miller slid his thumb over the Gallican's safety. "I'm really sorry. I'm really, really sorry." Then whispering to du Trieux he said, "I've got the left."

The second guard frowned at Miller. "What?"

Miller raised his sidearm just as du Trieux dropped to one knee and drew her pistol. In an instant, shots rang out and both guards slumped to the ground, a single bullet in each of their foreheads.

Miller sighed. He wished he could feel something about what they'd just done, but he was numb to guilt now. "Let's go," he said.

As the alarm was raised behind them, Miller and du Trieux sprinted down 27th Avenue, jumping over blast holes, skirting around piles of crumbled concrete, and cutting down an alley off 18th. They picked up Morland and Hsiung and kept going. The crate jostled and clanked in their hands.

Cutting across one building and leading the team into another, Miller hooked a sharp left, catching the others by surprise.

"Where are you taking us?" Hsiung breathed, gasping for air.

"There's an old cache of ammo and supplies stashed ahead, from Wild Tarpan. We should stock up and go for help."

"Help?" Morland burst. "If we can't go inside the compound, who the fuck is left?"

"I have an idea," Miller said, kicking down the door of an old donut shop and pulling the tarp off a pile of ammunition boxes.

"Care to share?" du Trieux asked, bending down and stuffing the pockets of her combat vest with clips and magazines.

"We find the Archaeans."

"The who?" Morland asked.

"The other Infected. I know somebody on the inside."

Hsiung's eyes were practically bugging out of her

head. "We're going to the Infected? Are you *insane?*"

Miller looked over at du Trieux. She looked pale, but resigned. She nodded and jammed two fresh magazines into her Gilboa.

Miller slung a fresh canteen over his shoulder and stuffed food pouches in his pockets. "Probably," he said, ripping open a packet with his teeth and sucking down the processed vegetables in a single swallow.

OPERATION ATLAS LION

26

HUMANS WERE AN endangered species in New York City. Alex Miller wasn't sure how they were faring in other parts of the world, but from where he stood—in the bowels of the city's streets, holding a can of spray paint—wildlife was flourishing. Thug behemoths bred out in the open, terror-jaws had evolved to almost twice the size they'd been since he'd first laid eyes on them, and titan-birds had easily tripled their numbers, as far as Miller could tell.

Humans? They weren't doing so hot. In fact, with each passing moment, they were harder and harder to come by.

Miller shook the can and sprayed the cement again. At least there were fewer angry mobs of Infected to fight. What communes he and Cobalt squad had found in the four days since their return to the city were starved, dying, driven to mindless aggression by the wasp larvae growing in their skulls—even worse than before, if that could be believed.

In the hysteria that followed when a den of Infected was discovered, it was clear the Charismatics couldn't maintain control over the masses anymore—they scattered as soon as the first bullet flew. The packs—whole communes—were disorganized, weak and easily destroyed. It almost felt unfair.

But truth was, in the days since they'd returned, Miller hadn't seen any uninfected humans *at all*.

Bad sign.

Miller cramped from pressing the spray paint nozzle, but he pushed down harder, squeezing out the last drops.

Du Trieux, standing guard at the curb, eyed their surroundings, her Gilboa held low. "You done yet?"

Miller nodded and dropped the empty can. It rolled, slid down the sidewalk, and landed in the gutter. "Yeah." They walked away from the abandoned museum, back toward the temporary camp they'd established a few blocks east.

They'd moved camps twice already, just to be safe, but Miller was beginning to wonder if this was why they were having such a hard time finding Samantha and the Archaeans. Maybe if they kept to one place, they would find them?

Then again, Miller reasoned, maybe the Archaeans weren't responding to the tags because they'd moved out of the city to avoid the wasps. He certainly wouldn't blame them. Samantha had said they liked to keep on the fringes, avoiding violence when they could. The wasps had spread, covering every square inch of the city like a blanket.

The wasps were why he'd eventually led his group out of Astoria and across the Queensboro Bridge. They were in Mid-town now, by the Museum of Modern Art. He'd been painting pictures of a straight-edge razor all over any flat surface he could find, in the areas surrounding Astoria, Hell's Kitchen, and now Mid-town, then gone back the next day to see if there'd been any sort of response from Samantha.

So far—nothing.

Maybe she didn't understand the reference?

"This isn't working," .du Trieux said. "We need another plan."

"I'm open to suggestions."

She fell silent.

Miller listened to their crunching steps on the broken asphalt of West 53rd Street until she found her words.

She sighed, then said, "What about a covert operation? You and me find a way inside the compound and we stick Harris through the ear with a blade. Simple, *non?*"

His first inclination was to laugh, but she wasn't kidding. "Without knowing what's inside the compound now," he said, "we have no idea what we'd be walking in to. There's only four of us. I'm not risking even one without some sort of plan."

"I thought that *was* a plan."

He raised an eyebrow at her. "A better one."

"How are the Archaeans supposed to help us with that?"

"I'm not sure yet," he admitted, "but at least there will be more than four of us."

She stopped in the middle of the road. "I don't trust them. I know you have a history with that woman. But she's not who she was. This is beyond risky—it's reckless."

"I know. But truth be told, I don't know what else to do."

They turned down the Avenue of the Americas, passing an old hotel and skirting by an empty car at the curb teeming with terror-jaw pups. The sound of shuffling footsteps made them both freeze.

Down the block, on the east side of the road, an Infected approached alone. Shuffling their feet, the person moved forward, their head hung low, their arms swinging loose.

"Not another one," du Trieux said, sighing deeply.

Miller drew his sidearm, although he suspected there wasn't need for it. Lone Infected weren't typically aggressive. In truth, Miller wasn't sure if they should be considered Infected at all. They were finding them quite frequently since their return. More often than not, a single Infected wandering the streets, upon inspection, would be found in some sort of catatonia—unresponsive and blinded by the super-wasps hatching out of their eyes.

As if unaware of the wasps crawling on their face—or even of Miller pointing a gun to their head—the Infected would continue shuffling forward, barely able to put one foot in front of the other. They merely stumbled on, unresponsive to everything until they were attacked and consumed by some predator, or collapsed in a heap and stopped breathing—wasted away like a spent cocoon.

Miller and du Trieux watched the Infected pass them on the other side of the street, ignoring them both.

He holstered his weapon. Why waste the bullet? This one, from the looks of him, would be dead within the hour—especially since he was shuffling straight toward the terror-jaw pups they'd passed not five meters behind them.

Unmoved, they continued back toward camp, saying no more on the subject. There was nothing to say. With no way to help the catatonics, his only course of action was to move ahead with his plan, such as it was, and hope a solution would present itself. That was, if the Archaeans were still around and hadn't been lobotomized by wasps.

Miller frowned. The number of ways his plan could go wrong were not lost to him. Doubt riddled his thoughts. There were times his misgivings crippled him.

What if the Archaeans wouldn't help? What if they couldn't? What if they *did,* and it led to Cobalt's destruction?

Perhaps du Trieux was right, and they should attack by stealth. If you couldn't trust anyone, surely keeping your numbers small was prudent?

Just as the wasps had claimed the island of Manhattan, doubt had commandeered Miller, and with each passing day—as Cobalt's food rations dwindled, and Morland developed a hacking, phlegmy cough—it grew worse.

How was collecting caches of ammunition stashed around town doing any good, if there was no one left to use them? What difference could four people make against the compound security forces—even if they were a quarter of the size they once were? Cobalt was outnumbered, outgunned, and outmatched. If there was ever a lost cause, this was it.

He knew they should walk away, save themselves. Maybe they could travel to Boston or Washington DC and find an Army base and join forces with a troop or squad there—try to make a difference. Or, maybe he should finally desert his position like the majority of the armed forces had and attempt to find his folks back home. It would be so easy to simply stop fighting, tuck tail, and run.

People were dying whether they were inside or outside the compound walls, he was certain—the wall didn't protect anyone anymore. The super wasps he'd helped Harris distribute knew no boundaries.

And that was partly his fault, but mostly Harris's. Harris was the true madman. He'd tried once to procure a nuclear weapon, intent on blowing the Infected sky-high—and anyone caught in the way— and if not stopped, he'd probably try again.

If Miller and Cobalt weren't there, who would stop him next time? What were the chances Miller *could* stop him again? For that matter, *should* Harris be stopped? Who was to say they shouldn't blow up the whole of Manhattan island and let it burn?

There wasn't anything left worth saving.

And what good were they—four starving soldiers—against all that? Against a wild army of Infected? Against hordes of mindless drones marching toward collapse?

Miller's mind looped in an endless cycle of doubt and depression, but kept coming back to the same point, no matter which way he turned, over and over again.

Why didn't he just leave?

Because there was no one else left who could stop this.

Because there were people still inside that compound. Doyle, Lewis, Gray, Gray's children—James and Helen—and the surviving refugees.

Would Miller be able to sleep at night, ever again, knowing he'd walked away from the only innocent people left on that forsaken island?

MILLER KICKED THE gravel under his feet and sighed. He was about to speak when another movement caught his eye. To the right, near the intersection on 50th, a small band of soldiers were on patrol.

Miller pulled the strap of the M27 off his shoulder and crouched behind a hunk of broken concrete as he watched their approach.

Du Trieux got low, following suit.

The soldiers wore the black security uniforms of former Schaeffer-Yeager team Dagger and Cyclops-Northwind, but Miller was savvy enough to be suspicious. They could be decoys. They could be Infected.

"Got any eyes on you?" Miller asked.

Du Trieux wordlessly handed him a pair of compact binoculars from her vest. Adjusting the focus, Miller zoomed in on the approaching patrol and searched the oncoming faces for signs of fungal infection. There wasn't any he could see—although most of the troops wore gas masks, despite the wasps being fairly light in this part of town.

"They look clean," he said, handing the lenses back to du Trieux, who took a look for herself. "But I can't be certain."

"They've got a rocket launcher," she said. "The tall one with the neck tattoo in the back row."

"I saw."

"We could use that," she said. "Especially since we have a missile in want of a launcher."

"We do. But I have other plans for that." Without going into further detail, he swatted a wasp from his face and squinted at the approaching men.

There were about a dozen in the squad, maybe more. He knew he should do something, anything—establish contact, at least, and determine if they were hostile—but doubt left his feet cemented to the ground.

"Suppose we can break them up, take them in smaller groups?" he asked du Trieux.

She gave him a funny look, then held out her hand. "Hold on..." she said, still peering at the advancing patrol. They'd turned at the intersection, and were now coming directly toward them. Just their luck. They would have to move in the next few seconds.

"Lewis is with them," du Trieux said.

"Let me see."

She handed him the binoculars.

"Where?"

"Look at the legs," she said.

Miller focused and swore. Lewis *was* with them. Walking near the middle of the squad, his Uzi-Pro poised for action, he limped along on two battered prosthetic legs, the straps of his gas mask tight across his shaved head.

Miller shifted behind the concrete slab, but still failed to rise. Du Trieux nudged him with her elbow, but he remained down. Sweat beaded on his brow and dripped to the tip of his nose.

Was this was a trap? What if Harris sent Lewis out of the compound to draw Miller out?

He scoffed at his own logic. How would Harris know he had survived the helicopter crash?

Peering over the debris, Miller continued to watch the patrol approach, debating with himself.

When Infected troops marched, they were scattered, disorderly. These walked in formation—but that still wasn't a guarantee they were safe to contact.

He couldn't be certain that Lewis wouldn't take a direct order from Harris. Maybe he was on patrol for the compound? He *had* given him a speech about following orders. Or maybe Lewis had gone rogue?

Miller hated his uncertainty, but it didn't matter

anymore—they'd missed their window. The squad would spot them no matter what they did now.

He shook his head and, gathering his bravery, stood. "Only one way to find out."

Du Trieux frowned. "What?"

Advancing toward the squad, Miller raised his M27 to his shoulder. "Halt! Identify yourselves."

Twenty assault rifles all swung to point at him— luckily, none fired.

"Hold fire." Lewis pulled the gas mask off his face and gaped up at Miller with an expression of pure awe. "Well, I'll be damned. Miller, you crazy son of a bitch. I'd given up on you."

"Masks off, everybody, I want to see your faces," Miller demanded.

"Whoa, there, son," Lewis said sternly. "We aren't the enemy here."

"No offense, sir, but if it's all the same to you, I'd like to see who I'm dealing with. The wasps are light in Mid-town. It's safe enough."

"We've got twenty guns pointed at you, what makes you think you're in any position to ask us to do anything?"

"Du Trieux?" Miller shouted.

From the opposite side of the squad, du Trieux popped up from behind a dilapidated car, her Gilboa raised. She'd flanked them in a matter of seconds. "*Oui?*"

Lewis eyed du Trieux and sighed. Still looking unconcerned, he nodded at his men. "Go ahead. Just for a minute."

In rapid succession the soldiers pulled off their gas masks.

As far as Miller could see, no one appeared Infected. And nobody had shot him on sight, so it was probable they weren't working for Harris either. Cautious but sure-footed, Miller met Lewis at the front of the squad.

"You're a sight for sore eyes, son," Lewis said, slapping him on the shoulder with a little too much force.

Miller clenched his jaw. "It's good to see you too, sir."

"Where the hell have you been?"

"Getting my ass back from the Delaware coast, sir. Shank attacked the freighter."

Lewis nodded slowly. "I'd heard. Glad to see you out and about. Were you able to secure the cargo?"

"That depends, sir. Who are you working for?"

Lewis's eyes went wide, then narrowed. "What the hell kind of question is that?"

"Are you out here on Harris's orders," Miller asked, "or in spite of them?"

Lewis ran his tongue along the edge of his teeth. "You haven't heard, then?"

Miller's palms grew slick with sweat and he took a step back, ready to run if he had to. He doubted there would be a need—or that he would get very far with twenty rifles aimed at his head—but still, Miller wasn't sure he could trust his instincts anymore.

"Right before you left," Lewis explained, "Dagger and Cyclops were sent outside the compound to clean out some Infected communes nearby."

"I remember you saying."

"Except there weren't any communes."

"Come again?"

"It was a setup," Lewis said, "an excuse to get Gray loyalists out of the way so Harris and Shank could stage a coup and assume control of the compound."

Everything Miller had feared. "Fuck."

"When the squads reported back to the gate," Lewis continued, "Shank opened fire. These few were able to escape, but not many." He stuck a thumb over his shoulder. "Gray confronted Harris, but the bastard was one step ahead of us the whole time. He'd taken Gray's ex-wife and children into custody, and demanded Gray step aside as CEO."

Miller felt his hands clench on his M27. They weren't his kids, but the thought of James and Helen in Harris's custody was enough to make Miller's skin crawl.

"It was a matter of time before they came for me," Lewis said. "I tried to get Gray to come with, but he wouldn't leave the compound so long as his family was still inside, so I grabbed what and who I could, and we shot our way out. It was bloody. Those of us that are left have been living on the outside. We've tried assaults on the supply trucks coming in and out, but we don't have the numbers. We've assisted a handful of refugees who've managed to escape the compound, getting them to safer territory, and we even tried to track the transports, but lost most of them once they crossed the bridge."

"Transports?"

"Harris is sending busloads of survivors out of the compound. We can't tell where they're going, or why. My guess is he's sending the sick and dying away so he has less mouths to feed."

"Good God."

"From what I can tell, most of the survivors from the wasp attacks are still inside, but have been moved indoors. Rumor has it Harris is registering the women and assigning breeding couples to maintain the population of uninfected—at least that's what the escaped refugees are telling us. Those unable to reproduce, or unwell, are sent out on a transport or into the shanties to keep the wasps fed—but they don't last long, and it just means they're breeding faster."

Lewis shook his head slowly. "The ones the wasps get to? They walk, but they don't talk. They're like mindless bodies, until they get eaten or fall over and croak. It's grotesque. We found the best solution was to burn the bodies once they give out—it kills whatever's hatching in their brainpans."

Miller's stomach roiled. "We've seen them. What about my man, Doyle? He was supposed to be with Cyclops or Dagger. Do you know if he got out of the compound?"

"Couldn't say," Lewis said, sympathy in his eyes. "He's not with us. Maybe he got out on his own."

Miller frowned. "Yeah. Maybe." He lowered his rifle.

"You going to answer my question now?" Lewis asked.

Miller forced his eyes away from Lewis's intense glare. "Yes, I have the cargo. Lost the chopper and the pilot."

When Miller looked back, the older man's face had fallen slack. "Sorry to hear that. What condition is the cargo in? Is it operable?"

"No idea, sir. We've not opened the crate. The damned thing could be leaking radiation for all we know. We don't have a Geiger."

"I think Moore has one." He turned around and shouted at a guard a few rows back with salt-and-pepper hair and a black beard. "Hey, Moore? You still got that Geiger?"

"Yes, sir," Moore responded.

"Bring it here," Lewis said.

"The question remains, though," Miller said, "what am I supposed to do with the cargo? I can't leave it here. I can't take it into the compound or Harris will get it. I'm not sure what to do, sir. The responsibility. It's—overwhelming."

"How many people know what it is?" Lewis asked, taking the Geiger from Moore and handing it to Miller.

"You, me, and my team." Miller clipped the meter to his belt with a snap.

"Have any of Harris's squads come into contact with you since you left the ship?" Lewis asked.

"No. There have been a few scattered patrols, but we've avoided them."

"So, for all Harris knows, you and the cargo went down with the chopper."

"I suppose."

"Good. We can use that."

Miller thought of asking Lewis to clarify, but let it drop. For now, he wanted to enjoy the feeling of not being the lone leader. His doubt, as thick and all-consuming as it was, dissipated slightly.

"What's with your fingers?" Lewis asked, nodding toward the spray paint stains on Miller's hand.

"Trying to find allies, sir."

"By finger painting?"

Suddenly, in the face of his commanding officer, Miller's plan felt childish and foolish. "I've been leaving tags, sir, all over town in an attempt to contact assistance."

"Tags?"

"A straight-edged razor. It's an inside joke," Miller said, his face hot. "Come to our base camp. I'll show you the cargo and we can check for leaks. I'll explain the graffiti on the way."

Lewis slapped his shoulder again as they pulled their masks back on. "It's good to see you," he said, voice muffled behind the mask. "Best news I've had in days."

Miller nodded and walked beside Lewis. He wanted to stay reassured, but the feeling evaporated with each passing step. The news was nothing but bad and Miller couldn't shake the feeling they were facing a fight they had lost long ago.

27

THE ALLEY SMELLED of piss and something else that Miller couldn't quite identify. If he didn't know any better, he'd say it reeked of blue cheese.

Two brick buildings lined the alley on either side, while the rising sun scorched his back. The asphalt, cracked but still mostly intact, had a river of something red and vile running down the center that pooled over a blocked drain.

After talking through most of the night, Lewis had reluctantly agreed to give Miller's strategy another few days. If no progress had been made reaching the Archaeans by then, alternate plans were to be made on how to infiltrate the compound.

Miller and Cobalt had set out as usual the next morning to check the tags for replies—but he hadn't expected this: the image of a woman's leg. It had been spray-painted underneath the tag he'd made of the straight-edge razor.

Samantha, even as an Infected, was still a smart ass.

Miller caught himself grinning.

What came after the leg, however, was the confusing part. Beside it, she'd added two additional images.

"Are those dogs?" Morland asked, coughing and spitting a wad of phlegm onto the pavement.

Du Trieux peered at the wall and frowned. "I think they're lions. They have manes."

"You're both nuts, it's a two-headed dragon," Hsiung said. "See the tail?"

"What the hell is it supposed to mean?" Morland asked.

Miller shrugged. The image on the wall had to mean something—but just what, he couldn't say.

"They're lions. Look at the claws," du Trieux said.

"Dragons have claws," Hsiung offered.

"Why would she paint two lions on the wall?" Miller asked.

Du Trieux just looked at him, the hint of amused appreciation playing at the corners of her mouth. "It's a location."

His face went slack as the realization came to him. "Well," he said, nodding, "isn't she crafty…?"

A FEW HOURS later, after checking in with Lewis and walking down Fifth Avenue, they came to the Beaux-Arts grandeur of what had once been the New York City Public Library. Miller sat under the marble entry overhang and leaned his back against the right-side alcove. Eyeing the two—now broken but still recognizable—marble statues of lions on either side of the courtyard entrance, Miller grinned to himself.

Clever girl.

His amusement was short-lived. A flock of titan-birds were on the hunt above. The half-eaten carcass of an over-sized terror-jaw lay rotting at the curb, clogging the gutters and creating a stagnant pool of rancid meat. On occasion, a titan would swoop down, rip a chunk off the corpse, and then take flight again, in search of a fresher meal.

Miller pressed his back harder against the alcove. Best not to give them a target.

Hopefully, Lewis wouldn't get impatient and barge into the area, blowing the whole operation. When Miller had told him about the response and the planned meeting, the old lieutenant had been hesitant.

"I still don't like it. It's sleeping with the enemy," he'd said, rubbing his palm against the receding stubble on his scalp. "We're just asking to get fucked."

Miller raised an eyebrow. He didn't disagree—the whole plan left a bitter taste in his mouth—but there was no other alternative that he'd been able to find, and there was no going back at this point. He had to see the meeting through at the very least, even if nothing came of it. The way he saw it, they had nothing to lose.

To the left of his position, behind a patch of dead trees, movement caught his eye.

A pack of thug behemoths moved up West 40th Street—four, maybe five. To his utter astonishment there were riders perched on the mammoth creatures, like some sort of prehistoric cowboys.

Samantha rode in the front of the herd, her long

side-braid looking just as ragged and unkempt as in their prior meeting. She wore safety goggles, like the kind used in construction work, and a bandana over her nose and mouth.

Stopping at the base of the courtyard, Samantha scanned the stairs up toward the library entrance and rested her eyes on Miller.

He stood and walked toward them, not looking at du Trieux, covering him from across the street, or Morland and Hsiung on either side.

Samantha casually raised her arm and the behemoths followed her stopped. While they waited in the middle of Fifth Avenue for him to reach them, Samantha jumped off her mount, pulled down her bandana and propped her safety goggles up on her head, then walked to meet him.

"Alex," she said. She looked thinner than last he'd seen her. Her sleeves had been torn away, her dress slit up the side and knotted on her hip. He assumed the adjustments had been made to allow her to straddle the behemoth, but he couldn't say for sure. Her yoga pants had holes worn in the knees.

"Samantha," he said, trying not to stare. She looked like a wild woman—tanned, with sinewy muscles on visible bones. A hunting knife was strapped to her thigh with two thin strips of leather, and a rifle hung casually over her shoulder.

"What do you want?" she asked, looking impatient. "You went to enough trouble to find us."

"I need to talk to you."

Her eyes barely moved, but she nodded quickly as

if expecting as much. "I'm not coming with you."

He blinked a few times. "What?"

"You're about to evacuate the island, and you want me to come—don't you? I'm not leaving my people, Alex. I thought I made it clear the last time we spoke that we aren't on the same side. Although we're not on opposite sides either."

"What makes you think we're evacuating New York?"

She narrowed her eyes at him. "There are convoys full of people coming out of the compound almost every day, and hardly anything going in."

"That's not why I need to speak to you."

She ran a palm across the bristles of her braid and pursed her lips, waiting.

When she didn't speak, Miller continued. "I need to get into the compound—me and my men. I'm willing to bet you know how to get us inside."

Her nostrils flared. Behind her, the Infected—two men and two women, still astride their behemoths—bristled as one of the mounts grunted and moaned. "And why would we help you do that?" she demanded.

"This can be a mutually beneficial arrangement. I'm willing to offer our assistance in any way that you might need, in exchange for passage inside the compound."

"What makes you think we can get you in there?"

"I'm willing to bet you already have people inside—am I wrong?"

She didn't answer straight away. "I don't think getting inside is possible anymore. Certainly unwise."

"You let me worry about that. Can you do it or

not? Don't tell me you haven't gotten inside before, because I'd know you'd be lying."

"For the record," she said, her face—and the faces of those behind her—reddening, "we've taken no part in any of the attacks on the compound. Swift's Bishops and his Pawns—they're the ones who attacked you, not us. We Archaeans believe in adapting to our new world and building an existence of peace and planetary harmony."

"Are you telling me you're pacifists? Because you said yourself you helped dispatch some of Swift's lot."

"Self-defense is one thing, an assault on the compound is something else. We aren't looking for a fight. We keep to the periphery and don't want any part of what you're planning. We keep to ourselves— but we do what we must to survive."

"That's all I'm trying to do, too."

"How does breaking into your own compound help you survive? If you've been banished, then you'll no doubt be greeted with gunfire upon your return. How will that benefit your survival?"

"Like I said, that's my concern."

Samantha jutted her chin. "Why go back at all?"

"Because there are people inside I care about."

She nodded, and for a moment the veil across her eyes lifted—she looked alert, but sad. "You have an over-developed hero complex—you know that, right?"

For a brief moment, she sounded like herself— argumentative and wickedly sarcastic—but with the suddenly saddened faces of the Archaeans behind her, the illusion of individuality disappeared.

"And what do you offer in exchange?" Samantha asked.

"As I said, assistance with anything you may need. You said yourself my crew was handy in clearing the area of Swift's goons—surely, there's a commune someplace causing you trouble?"

She stopped and thought a moment, then turned and looked to her group. They said nothing to each other, but seemed to be having a debate using only their facial expressions. After a few awkward moments, she turned back around, her eyes shining with emotion. "I don't think it would be possible to smuggle anyone into the compound on foot," she said. "The refugee processing gates are sealed fairly tightly. But, if you're determined to get inside, I may be able to help you obtain a vehicle. You'll have to take it, though."

"You want to run that by me again?"

"The compound moves cargo in and out on supply trucks," she explained. "Not as often as they used to, but about once a week trucks come in, while the transports go out. A few months back, we obtained a supply truck. You could drive in, pretending to bring supplies."

Miller didn't think that would work at all, but kept his thoughts to himself. "How'd you get a truck? I thought you said you weren't looking for a fight."

She gave a light shrug. "Who are we to stop a pack of terror-jaws from ripping open a supply truck and eating the crew? We don't control nature, we're a part of it."

Miller pursed his lips. If the Archaeans were communing with wildlife—as was apparent, given their thug behemoth mounts—and sharing common emotions and thoughts with the animals, it was probable they could convince a weak-minded terror-jaw to do their bidding. All they'd have to do is tell the jaw to take out the driver, while others handled the guards, and the supply truck would be ripe for their taking.

If this was true, the Archaeans were more dangerous that he'd thought. Perhaps a deal with them *was* a bad idea.

"What was on the truck?" Miller asked, trying to keep the suspicion from his face.

"It was labelled 'Agricultural Gear'—but we didn't get a chance to verify that. The camp where the truck was stored was soon thereafter attacked by wasps. We couldn't risk entering the camp for fear of communing with them and becoming Exiled ourselves."

"Exiled? You mean catatonic? Like the Infected you see wandering around?"

"Yes. The dead ones who still move. If we commune with them, we're a wasp hive waiting to happen."

He nodded.

"If you want a vehicle," she continued, "it's the only one I can offer. That is—if you're able to enter the camp and get by the Exiled, and the nesting wasps."

Miller chewed on the inside of his cheek. "Let me get back to you."

Samantha blinked at him, her eyes wide. She waved a hand in front of her face to shoo a wasp away.

"Meet me at on the corner of Third Avenue and 33rd Street tomorrow at sunset if you want the truck."

"Understood."

Miller watched as Samantha put her goggles back on and covered her face with the bandana. With a smooth gait, she strode back to her thug behemoth and climbed aboard, swinging her leg up using a rope stirrup lashed to the beast.

As they rode away, the lining of Miller's stomach twisted with unease.

Her proposal had the potential to go badly, very badly—but it also had the potential to be exactly what he'd hoped for. Either way, it was a lot to digest and he had a great deal to consider, not to mention Lewis to convince.

When the Archaeans had gone from view, du Trieux and the others came up from their positions and met Miller in the middle of Fifth Avenue.

"Did I hear correctly?" du Trieux asked, gazing north in the direction of the pack. "Agricultural gear?"

Miller nodded. "How much you want to bet the 'agricultural gear' is labelled as accurately as the 'food supply gear' we escorted with the good doctors?"

Morland twisted his face in confusion, then coughed lightly, but Hsiung's expression brightened.

Miller heard du Trieux chuckle as they marched back to base.

"*Oui*," she said. "Let's hope so."

28

THAT DAY, BASE camp was set at the old Wyndham, just north of Madison Square Garden. The abandoned hotel had running water, although the color left much to be desired. Even after boiling it for an hour, they were still unsure what parasites and bacteria they were ingesting. Truthfully, they didn't have a choice. There were only twenty-five of them, but finding enough food to feed even a squad of that size was proving difficult.

Hunting parties were sent out to capture game and scrounge for supplies, but each soldier was barely eating enough to function. Whatever they were going to do, they had to do it fast. Time was running out.

Inside the lobby they'd built campfires. Miller found Lewis sitting before one. The older man lifted a dented pot of water from the flames, and set it on the floor to cool as Miller sat across from him. "Give it to me straight, son. Will they help us or screw us?" Lewis asked.

Miller pressed his lips together and shook his head. "They've got a line on a truck, but we have to clear out a commune of those zombies—Exiles, they call them—to get to it. So, to answer your question—both?"

Lewis leaned his back against what was left of the concierge desk and adjusted his prosthetic limbs with a grunt. "All the makings of a trap."

Miller didn't disagree with him.

"You're sure about these Archaeans?"

Miller picked up a slab of wood from the pile beside him and tossed it on the fire. "As far as I can tell, they're more like Labradors than Dobermans. It doesn't seem like they're the type to turn on us—they're almost... reasonable."

"Hmph," Lewis grunted, pouring a cup of hot water from the pot into a cracked hotel mug and slurping it while it steamed.

"Labs can be useful on a hunt," Miller added.

Lewis gulped loudly and hissed through his teeth. "I feel better already."

THE RED SUN burned bright on the horizon, casting the corner of Third and 33rd in an orange hue so blinding, Miller had to shield his eyes with the crook of his arm, even with his gas mask on.

The wasps in the area were thick, moving in swarms like clouds of scorching mist. Standing between two buildings to hide from the sun, Miller and Cobalt found themselves under siege by bugs.

Miller had already been stung twice just standing there.

Waving his arms defensively in front of his face, he walked down the alley toward the road to check for signs of the Archaeans. He was stung three more times.

Just as the sun disappeared over the compactly stacked buildings, Miller caught sight of a herd of thug behemoths one block north. Samantha, in front of the pack, still wore her construction goggles and bandana. She dismounted and waved; Miller pushed his way through the cloud of wasps and went to her.

"There's a parking structure," she said, pointing down 33rd Street, to the north side of the block. "Inside there's an encampment. The truck is in there."

Miller eyed the street. It was an old commercial boulevard, complete with small businesses on the first floor, and tight apartments a few levels above. Halfway down the road a parking sign hung on a chipped red building with a stoop to the left. The windows of the building were completely obscured by tendrils of fungus blooms.

"Is there another entrance?" he asked.

Samantha shook her head. "Not that I'm aware of. You'll have to check."

Miller swatted a wasp from his sleeve, feeling the burn of its sting as it pierced his skin and scorched his blood stream. "Can we count on you to come with us?"

"We can't," she said. "The pull of the Exiles is too strong for us to resist."

"How do I know you aren't sending me into a trap?"

She twitched, but kept her face neutral. "You contacted *us*, remember? The risks you take are your own."

Miller frowned. He didn't like this in the slightest, but there was no turning back. This was their only chance of success, and given their supply situation, there wasn't time to orchestrate another strategy.

He stared at her a moment, contemplating. It was now or never.

Leaving her there with minimal words, he made his way back to the others.

Du Trieux, Hsiung, and Morland stood by ten of Lewis's men in the alley between two buildings, beside an arched entry to an old café. The remaining ten men, along with the aging commander, had stayed behind at the base camp to keep an eye on the infamous cargo crate, which turned out *not* to be leaking after it had been checked with the Geiger.

When Miller arrived back, the bulk of them looked to him for explanation.

Morland was the first to speak. "Are they coming with us?"

"No," Miller said, taking up an M20-B flamethrower that rested against one of the walls. He handed the other to Morland, then slung the pressurized fuel pack onto his back.

"Good," Hsiung said, swiping a wasp from her sleeve. "At least I'll know the bullets aren't coming from behind us."

Miller snatched up the hose attached to the igniter

on the flamethrower and tightened his grip. "Let's do this."

The weapon, developed by Schaeffer-Yeager some five years ago, had been used—as far as Miller knew—for agricultural purposes. It was by some twist of luck that Lewis had managed to snatch a pair while he fought his way out of the compound.

They'd have to be precise in using them. The two tanks—one cylinder of compressed nitrogen for propellant and the other filled with petrol, laced with a thickener—only allowed for a few seconds of burn at a time, since it guzzled fuel so rapidly.

Miller only hoped it would be enough to scorch through the wasps and keep whatever else was brewing in the parking structure at bay long enough for them to jack the supply truck—leaving aside whether or not the truck had any fuel in it, or keys, for that matter. They'd have to figure that out as they went.

Miller led the way toward the opening of the parking structure, Cobalt and the others trailing behind him. He activated the igniter's wire coil in the nozzle and waited outside the entrance for the coil to heat.

The garage loomed ahead, ominous and foreboding. It was dark inside, with large tendrils of fungus blooms spilling out the door and windows, creeping up and around the entry like tentacles of the kraken. The smell reached him all the way outside on the street—*with* a gas mask. He couldn't imagine how bad it would smell inside.

Just then, beside him, du Trieux popped a flare from her belt, burst the end and rolled it into the garage opening. A flurry of wasps audibly frenzied and buzzed—spilling out of the garage and swarming the soldiers in the street.

Even wearing his mask and STF vest, Miller felt panic rise. The stings pierced the seams of his armor plating with ease, cutting him twice in his left arm, once on his scalp, a half-dozen times on his legs.

Soldiers all around him weren't faring much better. A chorus of cursing and dramatic arm flailing erupted throughout the squad as they fought through the cloud of wasps. Finally, when Miller's vision cleared and he'd become accustomed to the throbbing pain of the stings, he flooded the reservoir of the flamethrower and compressed the spring-loaded trigger, igniting the system.

Flames burst from the weapon, burning the wasps in front of them and cooking the fungal blooms across the front wall of the garage. Fire crawled up the tendrils, burning hot and fast, and left charred husks of ash in its wake.

Miller knew the fungus would burn out quickly. He had no intention of finding himself, or the others, trapped inside a burning inferno, especially if the truck proved to be a long way inside the parking structure.

As the fire spread up and out across the building, the group advanced—swatting at wasps while compressing their ranks to four rows of three. Miller and Morland marched in front with the flamethrowers, burning a path ahead.

The first floor of the parking structure had ten parking slots, mostly empty, and a ramp at the back that led down to the other levels. At first glance, the first floor appeared devoid of warm-blooded life.

Three dead cars sat rusted in the first, fourth, and sixth spaces. They were almost entirely absorbed by fungal blooms, cascading from the fuel tanks. The tendrils had grown up and around the walls, ceiling, and floor of the garage, closing in the confined space—making it feel even more claustrophobic.

And the place stank.

Even through the gas mask's outlet valve Miller smelled the putrid stench of burning blooms, and tasted the metallic toxins from the wasps that coursed through his body and swelled his tongue.

The wasps, slightly abated by the fire, were easier to see and get through, although every few moments Miller felt a new sting pierce his skin.

Passing the vehicles and making their way to the back of the first floor, they marched down the back ramp toward the lower level.

There were five cars on this floor, also fully encased in a massive growths of fungal blooms—but still no truck. Here as well, the wasps polluted the air like a shifting haze.

Miller and Morland lit up the room, burning a path, but they didn't get more than a few meters into the second level before they heard squealing and stopped in their tracks.

Behind them, a burning terror-jaw pounced on a soldier's head near the rear of the group. Chaos erupted. Bullets rang through the air as more terror-jaws, fleeing the flames, attack the squad. There were at least five of them, ripping through the formation and scattering the soldiers like toys.

Du Trieux and Hsiung, just behind Miller, twisted around to help shoot down the creatures while Morland and Miller burned forward, leading the way down.

Three-quarters of the way through the second level, Morland stopped his advance, coughing violently, bent at the waist and heaving. He gasped and fought for air, his entire body rocking as he strained to catch his breath in the stench and flurry.

Miller halted in place, the tip of his flamethrower momentarily cooling. "Morland?"

The large man held up a finger as if to say, 'One minute.' Then, after a few more phlegm-filled coughs, he recovered, stood upright, and re-ignited his flamethrower. Pushing forward, Morland scorched a car packed with terror-jaw pups, frying the little beasts as they spilled out the window and attempted to gnaw on the soldier's shins.

Turning back to the task at hand, Miller burned a swarm of wasps in front of him and eyed the ramp at the back of the second level.

A figure stood there, watching.

Miller squinted through his mask, but didn't hesitate long. The individual was human, or had once been. Now, she was blank-faced, seemingly unaware the room was in flames. She shuffled forward on limp legs, her arms bent at odd angles and her shoulders slumped to one side. She was barely upright. Wasps visibly crawled over her face and arms as if she were a living, moving hive.

Miller lit the woman ablaze. As the flames blackened her clothes, caught her hair, and blistered her skin, she continued to approach. The wasps scattered like fireflies and singed out, sinking to the floor in wisps of ash.

Miller watched in mounting horror—bile rising in the back of his throat. Eventually, the Exile dropped to her knees and face-planted on the garage floor. It sickened Miller when he felt a rush of relief, but the sentiment didn't last.

More Exiles appeared behind her, five of them, drawn to the noise. They advanced up the ramp, straight for the squad. With terror-jaws at their back and Exiles at their front, Miller's squad had to act fast.

Morland shifted to the right and lit up the Exiles, while Miller concentrated on the left of the pack. Like a fiery wave, the burning people continued their slow, mindless approach, inching toward the squad and threatening to set the entirety of the garage ablaze.

Unlike the fungal blooms, which charred quickly, the humans were taking longer to burn out, spreading the fire to the ceiling and the parked vehicles, raging out of control.

Soon, having gotten the terror-jaws under control, the soldiers behind Miller stepped to the sides and opened fire on the burning humans, dropping the Exiles like fiery sacks of bones.

Miller stepped over the blazing corpses and made his way toward the ramp down to the third level. He spotted more Exiles ambling toward them from below, a half-dozen or so. Three of them were covered from head to toe in wasps, like the one they'd seen above.

Miller set the lot ablaze, then stepped aside for Hsiung and du Trieux to shoot the walkers down.

They stepped past the bodies onto the third level. On the left, parked in one of the bays, sat a Schaeffer-Yeager supply truck, partially consumed by fungus—with a gaping hole on the side clovered over with blooms.

Miller went to the truck and quickly burnt away as many of the blooms as he dared, then dropped the flamethrower hose and started ripping the rest off by hand.

Beside him, Morland did the same, his cough returning in force. Several times he had to stop— bent over, gasping for air, barking like a dog—but each time Morland regained himself and went back to work. As they laboured, the remaining squad cleared out the Exiles.

Just as Miller pulled a chunk of fungus off the truck's driver's side door and wrenched it open, Morland dropped to one knee, a hand on his mask as he choked and hacked.

"Morland—no!" Miller shouted, but it was too late.

Morland ripped off his mask, coughed wetly, then spat a bloody chunk of phlegm to the cement floor. He was immediately swarmed with wasps. Up and across his face, into his mouth and up his nose—the wasps blanketed Morland's upper body in a flash.

A bellow erupted from Miller's chest as he ran to his friend and swatted at the insects, wiping them away with his hands and ignoring the innumerable stings piercing his gloves.

Morland's screams echoed throughout the garage, bringing du Trieux and Hsiung to his side. All three worked to clear the bugs off the man as he collapsed onto all fours and shrieked holy hell.

In the meantime, the remaining soldiers finished clearing the blooms from the supply truck. By the time Miller and the others had cleared the wasps from Morland's face and gotten his mask back on, the truck was ready to move.

Miller almost yelped with joy when he heard the motor roar to life. With Hsiung at the wheel, du Trieux, Miller, and the other soldiers threw Morland's flailing body into the back of the truck, and with a grind of the transmission and a burst of gasoline, the truck slammed into reverse, then lurched up the ramp. Crunching over the burning corpses of the Exiles, they burst through the remaining floors of the parking garage, and shot out of the front entrance like a bat out of hell.

Outside, on 33rd Street, the soldiers gripping the sides of the truck jumped off to cover the entrance of the garage, waiting for stragglers.

"Right! Turn right!" Miller shouted to Hsiung.

Without hesitation, Hsiung shifted the truck and barrelled down 33rd, toward the intersection at

Third, where Samantha and the Archaeans waited with their thug behemoth mounts.

Hsiung slammed on the brakes a mere meter from the pack.

Outside the truck, the wasps were dense in the air, swirling and swooping like the funnel of a tornado, spun into a frenzy by the chaos inside the parking structure.

The behemoths reared back, moving away from the truck.

Without thought, and with Morland's shrieks of agony spurring him on, Miller threw open the back of the truck and jumped out the vehicle. He ran straight toward Samantha and the retreating thugs.

"Sam! One of my men! The wasps!"

For a moment, behind her bandana and goggles, Samantha looked high, her eyes rolling back into her head. Then she pounded against her skull with a fist and yelped at the pain. "What is that smell? What *is that?*"

"Sam! The wasps are in his head!"

Snapping out of it, Samantha looked to a woman behind and to her right, and held out her hands. The woman rummaged in a saddle bag draped across the back of the behemoth, and tossed a plastic zip packet to Samantha.

"Show me!" she said, swinging her leg over the beast and sliding from her mount.

He brought her around the back of the truck. Half pushing, half helping her inside, he followed her, slamming the door behind them.

Inside, Morland lay sprawled on the truck floor,

his feet toward the cab. Thrashing and screaming bloody murder as if he were still being besieged by the insects, he pounded his fists against his head, clawing his skull with his fingernails.

Du Trieux and Hsiung were doing their best to keep him from gouging out his own eyes, holding back his arms from his face, but the two were no match for the sheer size of Morland's arms, which flailed and whipped like the branches of a possessed tree.

"What is that smell?" Samantha repeated. She inhaled sharply, ripping the bandana and goggles from her face. Her eyes rolled back into her head as she swayed on her feet.

"Sam!" Miller shouted at her.

Her mouth dropped open. A trickle of saliva dripped from the corner of her mouth. "That *smell*," she mumbled.

Gripping her by the shoulders, Miller shook her. "Sam!" he shouted into her face.

Her head shot upright. She blinked rapidly a few times as if coming out of a trance. Her eyes lurched around the truck interior and rested on three metal barrels sitting at the front, near the cab. Then she focused on Morland, who continued to flap and yowl holy hell on the floor. If nothing else, Miller reflected, he was learning a few new British swear words.

"Hold him down," Samantha said. She opened the zip bag in her hands and pulled out a long length of plastic tubing. "Hold him!"

Miller jumped into the fray, taking off his gas mask and straddling Morland across the chest. He buried his knees into the man's shoulders to hold him down. It stopped him from bucking, giving du Trieux and Hsiung enough time to attach straps to his wrists. They looped the straps around support beams on either side of the walls and pulled his arms back and away.

"What is she doing?" Hsiung asked, horrified.

Samantha clambered over Morland and straddled his head. "Keep him still," she said. She held the tubing in her hands, the tip pointed downward. It couldn't have been more than a millimeter thick, but it looked long and ominous as she held it over Morland's face.

"What is she doing?" Hsiung asked again.

"I'm saving him," Samantha said. Then getting down and close to Morland's face, she pressed the tubing into the corner of his right eye, and pushed it in.

"What the fuck!" Morland shrieked.

"Hold still," Samantha said. "Look up. Don't move your eye. This is important!" She tilted her head to one side and drew a deep breath. Steadying her hands, she pushed the tubing deeper into Morland's eye. He shrieked but kept still.

She met resistance and stopped pushing the tube, then reached around to the plastic bag and pulled out a clear plastic bottle. Sloshing inside the container was a thick orange liquid. She inserted the tip of the bottle into the other end of the tube, and squeezed, sending the fluid down the tube, and straight into Morland's eye.

The team watched, confounded.

"*Mon Dieu*," du Trieux breathed.

"What is hell is that?" Hsiung asked.

"Oil of orange extract," Samantha said, squeezing the tube until it was empty. "The wasps hate it."

When the bottle was empty, she dropped it to the truck floor, then pulled with both her hands, inching the tubing out of Morland's eye.

"What the fuck! What the fuck!" he whispered.

"When I say," Samantha said, bending down and talking into his ear, "blink."

The tube came free. An orange glob of extract came out of his tear duct and collected in the corner of his eye.

"Blink," she said.

Morland did. The extract dripped down the side of his nose, then cascaded down his cheek, dribbling onto the truck floor with a sick plop. He sniffed and coughed once, twice.

"Hold still," Samantha urged him.

The pool of orange gloop in the corner of his eye was now mixed with blood in streaks of crimson.

"Blink again," she said.

He did. The extract ran down his face. "It burns!"
Plop. Plop.

The whites of his eye turned orange as Morland grunted, pulling against the restraints.

"Okay everyone," Samantha said. "Here they come."

If Miller wasn't watching it himself, he never would have believed it. From the corner of Morland's eye, tiny legs, then the head of a wasp emerged—

birthed from his brain in embryotic orange extract. It crawled out of his tear duct and sat on his eye, stunned and slick with oil.

"Holy shit," Miller breathed.

With her bare hands, Samantha reached forward and plucked the wet wasp from Morland's face, then slapped her hands together and squashed it with a splat.

"Blink again," she said.

He did.

Plop.

Another wasp.

Samantha dispatched the next one, then another. Eventually the wasps stopped coming. Samantha leaned over Morland, took his neck in her hands and tilted his head to the side. The oil dripped from every orifice. Morland coughed violently, then hocked a chunk of phlegm-laced orange extract to the floor of the truck.

"Is that all of them?" he asked in a hoarse whisper.

"We won't know for sure," Samantha said. "We can repeat the process tomorrow."

"No, thanks."

"It's better than ending up an Exile," she said, her eyes resting on Miller. "Now," she added, standing to her feet and sniffing toward the front of the truck cab. "You want to explain to me what's in those barrels?"

ONCE ALL THE parts were in place, it was go time. The preparations had taken two days, including planning and getting Lewis and his men in position. If even one part of the plan failed, the whole scheme was in jeopardy. There were too many pieces to the puzzle.

Back at the library, Miller offered Samantha his hand, which she took. Putting one foot onto the truck's step, she jumped up into the driver's seat and strapped herself in. Another Archaean, an older man wearing shreds of a three-piece suit, was sitting in the passenger seat. He grunted his greeting as Samantha adjusted the mirrors.

Her eyes met Miller's, and for a brief second, her expression glassed over. With a concerted effort, she scrunched her lids tightly, then shook her head.

"Are you sure you can do this?" Miller asked.

Samantha's face reddened. Gripping the steering wheel with white knuckles she looked away, through the cracked windshield. "Of course we can. We're people, not animals. If we make a decision, we can stick to it." There was a hitch in her voice, then she added, "Mostly."

"If you can't handle having the pheromones this close, I can get one of my men to drive the truck."

"A deal's a deal. We can do it."

"This is important, Sam," he reiterated. "I can't have you and your kind wandering off into the streets. I need you to focus if this is going to work."

"We understand our part."

Miller frowned. "Right. And you're sure the remainder of Swift's Charismatics and communes will trail after us?"

Samantha pulled in a deep breath and squared her shoulders. "I can't guarantee anything, Alex. No one can. But given how much the pheromones affect us Archaeans, I doubt Swift's weak-minded kind will be able to resist. You'll get what you want, and then some."

Miller sighed. "All right." He stepped away from the truck so she could close the door. "I'll be in the back with my men. Once it starts, get down in your seat until I tap the side three times. After that, get the hell out, pick up the rest of your people, and drive the truck as far away from the compound as you can."

She tilted her head to one side and narrowed her eyes at him through the dirt-encrusted glass of the window. "You've said that three times."

"After this we're square." He adjusted the heavy pack on his back and gave a half-hearted wave. "Good luck." Turning on his heel, he marched toward the back of the truck.

"Alex?" she called, opening the door and leaning out to speak to him.

He turned to face her.

The look she gave him was one he couldn't quite place. She was pale, face slack. Could that be fear, or sadness?

"Goodbye," she said.

Miller swallowed thickly, unable—unwilling—to process the rush of emotions. "Yeah. Take care of yourself." He moved quickly and jumped into the back of the truck.

Inside, du Trieux, Hsiung, Morland, and a couple of Lewis's squad sat crouched on the floor, the barrels of pheromones in front of them.

Du Trieux blinked at Miller as he crouched near the door and propped it ajar. "All right," he said. "Open them up."

The truck roared to life and grinded into gear.

As the others worked to open the barrels, Miller kept his eyes focused outside the truck, and surveyed the ruins of the city. Old hotels. Crumbling storefronts and cracked and broken stoops. Dirt and gravel roads weaved across the ground, surrounded by mountains of mushrooms and strange alien animals. As the truck pulled away and picked up speed, a city he hardly knew as Mid-town rushed by.

One way or another, all this was going to end.

29

GETTING THE SUPPLY truck was one thing. Getting it from Mid-town to Astoria proved to be something else. The roads, such as they were, were far more dangerous than any of them had thought possible. They had expected it to be bad; what they got was nothing short of impossible.

Once the barrels of pheromones were opened, Infected from across the city flocked toward the truck like locusts. Men, women, children—hordes of them—starved, withered, desperate, and volatile. Entire communes emptied the subway stations and flooded the streets like rats to the Pied Piper when the truck drove by.

With every bump in the road, every U-turn, every time they had to double back or move a pile of cement debris blocking their path, it slowed the truck and brought the advancing horde inches from grabbing hold of the open tailgate. More than once, they did—leaving Miller and those riding in the back no alternative other than to knock the Infected off with the butts of their rifles, or shoot them down.

In some areas of the city the truck took fire as some of Swift's armed groups tried to shoot out the tires, and Miller and the others had to hang on for dear life, hunkered down behind the barrels while the vehicle bounced over the treacherous, rocky terrain.

Then, the animals got into the action, following the truck, too. Thug behemoths, terror-jaws, scurrying packs of rat-things, even titan-birds high above. Traveling in small groups, the creatures chased after the truck and mowed down Infected and Exiles to clear a path to the vehicle.

"Pick it up! This is getting out of control!" Miller shouted.

Samantha screeched back from the driver's seat. "No shit, Sherlock!"

Eventually, after they'd ploughed through a commune blocking the road, they managed to cross the Queensboro Bridge toward Astoria. By then, the flock behind them had reached the thousands.

Miller had no idea the pheromones would be that powerful. He'd figured on a few hundred, maybe. But *this?*

It was awe-inspiring and disturbing, all at once.

There was no room for doubt now—they were committed.

THE TRUCK LURCHED forward and sped down the rocky roads of Astoria, winding around debris and crashing over and through pot holes and craters. At this speed, on roads this bad, they'd be lucky to remain upright.

Coming up 14th Street, the truck spun a hard left onto 12th Avenue and drove full throttle toward the compound's barricaded front gate.

"Here we go!" Samantha bellowed. Slamming on the brakes, she yanked the truck hard to the right and skidded the vehicle across the gravel to an abrupt stop.

Miller and the others inside were tossed against the wall. The barrels, open and exposed, spilled pheromone packets—which looked like tea bags—spreading them across the back of the truck along with the people.

The truck immediately took on fire. Bullets whizzed straight through the side of the vehicle—through the gaping fungus-covered hole on the side. One of Lewis's men took a bullet to the head and died in an instant.

"Go, go, go!" Miller shouted. Rolling the barrels out of the truck, they all spilled into the street and rolled the cylinders across the area in front of the entrance, scattering the pheromone packets far and wide.

Miller pounded his fist on the side of the truck three times. Gravel spit at his face as it quickly accelerated and roared away down 12th, fading from view.

He and his squad crouched behind the barrels in front of the compound's gate. Miller raised his M27 and took out two guards at the entrance as bullets pierced the air around him. The shooters stood on the towers at the ends of the wall. They'd fortified the entrance since their last attempt to enter.

Behind him, a handful of Lewis's troops, who had been lying in wait for the truck's arrival, rushed the gate and took up defensive positions amid the rubble and mortar craters.

When Lewis's second line came, a rattle of machinegun fire ruptured the air. The advance was stopped cold, the majority of them dead before they reached cover.

Miller spotted the gun mounted on the edge of the wall to the left, but he couldn't see who was manning it. Pulling the pin on a hand grenade, he tossed it toward the tower. Over-shooting by several meters, the grenade flew over the wall and exploded in the air, someplace inside the compound. He heard a voice, some asshole laughing.

A head popped out behind the machine gun: Kimball, the jerk who'd interrogated Miller after he'd returned from meeting the Archaeans and Samantha for the first time. The asshole who'd manned the assault on the freighter.

Kimball stood to the side of the machine gun, a shit-eating grin on his face as he re-loaded a magazine. Without hesitation, Miller raised his M27, aimed, blew out his breath calmly, then shot the prick straight through the face. Kimball dropped.

With a sickening sense of satisfaction, Miller lowered his rifle. His only regret now was that Doyle wasn't around to witness the shot. He didn't have long to revel in his ego, however—just then Morland stood, ready to advance on the deteriorating troops inside the compound gate. Miller heard the undeniable sound of mechanized footsteps.

"Morland! Get down!"

The big guy barely had time to take cover behind a mound of rubble before four exoskeleton machines stomped through the gate. They ripped through the scene with double-barrelled submachine guns, pinning Miller and the others to the ground.

A shell erupted from an under-slung grenade launcher and blew up in front of Lewis's position, scattering shrapnel and rubble over the Northwind guys' heads; if they didn't take out the suits quickly, they were toast. Miller chanced a look behind him and caught sight of the advancing stampede of Infected, who had finally caught up to the pull of the pheromones.

Soon, every inch of the gate would be swarmed with parasite-ridden people and animals, bringing chaos in their wake. If Miller was going to do something, it had better be now, or he and Cobalt would be swallowed by the rush.

He heard du Trieux holler in protest. Just left of the gate, she was scrambling out of the way of one of the exoskeletons. She dove out from behind a barrel of pheromones and crouched next to the wall. Bullets hit the dirt at her feet; cornered, she had no other choice but to close on the mechanized suits.

To Miller's utter astonishment, she vaulted off the barrel on one leg and catapulted herself onto the closest exoskeleton suit's arm. Clambering up the suit like a spider, she skirted around to the rear of the arm that held the machine gun, dodged the driver's attempts to snatch her off with the other arm, and crawled up the spine of the suit, toward the top. Then, bracing herself on the driver's shoulders, she jabbed her pistol into the suit's helmet ventilation fan and fired a single round into the driver's head.

They both dropped like a bucket of bricks.

Taking her lead, Miller got up, pushed off the barrel with one leg, and jumped onto the arm of another exoskeleton suit. For a brief second, Miller locked eyes with the driver. The soldier glared back, looking utterly shocked and horror-stricken at having a man attached to his machine.

"Get off!" the driver bellowed. "Get off me, you dumbass!"

Instead of reaching over with his free hand like the other driver had, this operator shook his arm as if trying to dislodge something sticky.

Just as the horde of Infected and parasitic animals thrashed the gate entrance and scrambled toward the barrels in a living tsunami, Miller gripped the exoskeleton's arm with his arms and legs, holding on for dear life as it bucked and jostled him. The heavy pack on Miller's back crushed his spine with every sway, until the pack shifted and he lost balance.

Slipping, Miller rolled sideways on the mechanical arm. His hands fell loose and he hung, upside down, gripping the submachine gun with his thighs.

Locking his feet at the ankles, Miller reached up and grabbed the underside of the mechanical arm just as the driver stretched over to grasp at him with his other hand and narrowly missed.

Miller held tight with all four of his limbs and twisted to one side. Using the force of the pack and his body weight, he wrenched the submachine gun free of the suit with a loud crack, and then fell to the ground.

In the dirt—surrounded on all sides by Infected, animals of all sizes and shapes and Exiles, clogging and complicating the scene—Miller scrambled to his feet, the submachine in his hands.

Pulling back on the drum loader, he injected a grenade into the chamber and launched a shell straight into the face of the unarmed exoskeleton, blowing it to pieces.

Miller swivelled around, reloaded and launched another shell into the exoskeleton standing by the gate entrance.

On the opposite side of the horde, du Trieux was doing the same. She hit the fourth and final exoskeleton in the chest and sent pieces of it careening backwards.

With all four exo-suits out of the way, Miller raised his arm into the air, and swung it toward the entrance.

Then, in a rush, Cobalt and the remaining Northwind troops rose from their defensive positions and swarmed the compound gate.

30

MILLER BROKE THROUGH the compound barrier and shot down two guards behind the gate without hesitation. The massive submachine gun in his arms felt heavy and was difficult to maneuver, but the mere sight of it rendered some of the guards dumbstruck. They gawked in pure terror as he showered the entrance with rounds.

Sandbag bunkers had been constructed in a ring around the compound gate. Each foxhole was manned with a handful of the stunned soldiers, as well as a gunner behind either an M203 submachine gun or a rocket launcher. Some returned fire, but the majority of the men did not, stunned by the onrushing swarm. The Exiles, Infected, and parasitic animals poured through the gate like a flood of destruction, climbing over the sandbags and swallowing the area like a disease.

Several of Harris's men ran. Others took aim, but with too many targets and no apparent leadership, they were quickly overpowered and consumed by the horde of bodies.

Du Trieux was to Miller's left with the other commandeered exoskeleton gun. She wasn't hesitating at all. Laying waste to anyone who crossed her path, she mowed down the stunned bunkers, screaming in a mix of fury and anguish.

The other two members of Cobalt pushed past him with a body of Northwind troops, making a mad dash toward the refugee storage facility. It was only then that du Trieux released the trigger of her gun and tossed the empty weapon to the ground to follow.

With plans of his own, Miller dove through the multitude and pushed his way toward the cove. On his left were the abandoned shanties and camps, desolate and swarming with wasps. On his right, a chain-linked fence surrounded an area full to the brim with Exiles from inside the compound.

The mindless bodies of former Schaeffer-Yeager employees and city refugees hammered and crowded around the flimsy barrier, straining to break free of the barricade. It held for now, but it was a matter of time before they broke through and added to the mayhem.

Picking up speed, he ran down 27th Avenue, then sprinted to the right up 9th. Ahead, the darkened cove sat quiet and ominous. Many of the windows had been boarded and blocked by corrugated steel or overcome by fungal blooms. A small band of guards stood at the front entrance behind sandbags, watching Miller approach. They debated among themselves and two ran off. A third shot at Miller and grazed his arm, sending him back a few steps but only slowing him for a moment.

As Miller picked up speed, he carefully activated the submachine gun's drum loader and injected a grenade into the chamber. Barely slowing his steps, he launched the shell at the building's entryway.

The guards took off running, deserting their post. The blast hit, sending sand and debris in all directions. Miraculously, no one was hurt.

The doorway was wide open. Faced with no opposition, Miller ran forward, hurdled over what was left of the sandbags, and entered the cove unabated.

Inside the darkened entry hall, two groups of Shank soldiers stood in clusters, jumbled and in disarray around the elevator and stairwell. They stopped shouting at each other long enough to stare at Miller.

"The compound's lost," Miller barked at them. "Get the survivors to the ships. Go!"

A handful ran past him, back out the door. Two others stood in a state of befuddlement, still uncertain what to do. Miller raised his submachine gun at them and took aim, waiting only a heartbeat for them to decide. They ran after the others.

Once satisfied that the entry was clear, Miller dropped the submachine gun in the corner and yanked open the door to the stairwell. Bounding up the steps, his breath echoing through the gas mask and reverberating off the walls in his own ears, he snapped a fresh magazine into his M27 and unlatched the safety on his Gallican, sliding a round into the chamber.

Thankfully, the wasps were scarce in the building. Miller yanked down his mask and huffed his way up four flights, his lungs burning. When he reached the landing— gasping, choking—he had no choice but to grip the wall and wait for the dizziness to clear.

Adrenaline could only take a person so far. He'd been on starvation rations for weeks, and had burned out to the point of collapse. He had no energy left to give. Once the black spots cleared from his vision, Miller found what strength he had and pulled open the door in the stairwell, entering the fourth floor and forcing his eyes to focus.

The hallway was dark. Down the corridor and past several empty offices, Miller rounded the bend and came up to the corner suite. No guards stood at the door.

He twisted the knob and entered Gray's office, then immediately bent to the side and got to one knee, his rifle raised to his chest.

Those in the room froze. The kids, James and Helen, sat beside the makings of a homemade fireplace, built out of chunks of cement and cinderblock. A make-shift chimney led up and out the side panel of the large window. They blinked at Miller through tired eyes, their faces lighting up at the sight of him.

Gray and his ex-wife were on the other side of the room. Barbara sat up from a pile of blankets that had been tossed over sofa cushions on the floor. She opened her mouth as if so say something, but instead looked to Gray, who sat slumped in his office chair behind his desk, as if he still had a kingdom to rule over.

Gray's drooped eyes squinted at Miller through the smoky office. "Alex?"

"My god, you look like hell," someone said in a drawling English accent.

There were two guards in the room. Behind Gray, leaning casually against the wall, stood Doyle and one other—one of Harris's men. Doyle had his arms crossed over his chest, but the other guard had his rifle in his hands. Neither one of them moved—yet.

For a brief moment, Miller and Doyle only stared at one another. Then the other guard's face contorted, his mouth opened in abject rage. "It's Miller!" he cried, raising his rifle to his shoulder

A shot rang out.

Almost every person in the room, including Miller, jolted.

The soldier dropped to his left, gripping his ribs with a bloody palm, aghast. His mouth gaped, "What the—what the…"

Doyle pulled his crossed arms apart and revealed a handgun in his right hand.

He reached down, disarmed the wounded soldier, then nodded at Miller. "I've been waiting for you, boss."

Miller lowered the tip of his rifle and got to his feet. "Is that right?"

"And by the way, the Tartarus Protocol was bollocks."

"So I heard."

"Thank God, Miller," Gray huffed, standing from his desk with effort. "Have you taken control of the compound?"

Miller balked for a moment, then shook his head. "No one has control of the compound, sir. I'm here to evacuate you."

"But…"

"What's the plan?" Doyle asked, crossing the room and helping James and Helen to their feet.

Helen gave Miller a look beyond her fourteen years. "I knew you'd come for us."

James eyed Miller's bloody arm and frowned. "You're hit."

"Just a scratch." He shook the boy's hand, working hard to hide his grimace, and turned his attention back to Doyle. "Take them all to the ships. Du Trieux, Morland, Lewis, and Hsiung are evacuating the survivors. Launch as soon as they're aboard."

"But what about the compound?" Gray asked.

Miller felt something inside him break. Heat flooded his face. "Staying here was a mistake," he said. Gray opened his mouth to protest but Miller put up his hand, stopping him mid-breath. "We should have left the moment the ships arrived. The super-wasp hasn't stopped the parasite from spreading. On the contrary, it's done nothing but make it *worse*, no matter what Harris intended. And he's turned the company into a twisted dystopian monster. Breeding programs, Gray? What the *fuck*?"

"We could rebuild…" Gray offered. "Surely there are enough survivors. We have power, water… The infrastructure of the compound is still sound. Isn't it?"

Miller gritted his teeth. "Look out the window. What survivors? There are hardly any. And those promises Harris made about the refugees getting treatment after they were exposed to the super-wasps? Total horseshit. The wasps are eating people's brains inside out. You should see them, Gray. There's no treatment for that. They're fucking zombies."

"For now," Gray admitted. "But if we just did some research, surely we could come up with something…"

"You want to experiment?" Miller burst out, losing all patience. "On people?"

Barbara's face twisted in pained revulsion. "Oh, Gray."

"You'd be no better than Harris!" Miller shouted.

Gray's face went pale. He gripped the back of his office chair, his eyes rimmed in red. "All that work that went into securing this position, our survival. And you just want to run away? To where? There's nowhere left to go!" He squared his bony shoulders. "I'm still the leader of this facility…"

"The hell you are," Miller barked. Coming forward, he pointed a sharp finger at Gray's chest. "I hate to break it to you, but nobody runs anything in New York City. The *wasps* rule. We've lost. Your 'leadership,'" he sneered, "is a fucking joke."

"Hey, I've made mistakes, but we can't just—"

Miller threw his hands in the air, all patience lost. "Admitting you've fucked up doesn't mean you can take us further down the wrong path." He inhaled, making a concerted effort to calm himself. His blood was pumping so hard, he could hear his heartbeat echoing in his ears. "We disembark within the hour with whomever we can save," he told Gray. "End of story."

Stunned into silence, Gray blinked at him, his face pale.

Miller almost felt sorry for him. He'd been a good leader, once. He'd believed he was doing the right thing—even if he had been completely wrong. Somehow, somewhere along the way, Gray had gotten lost and managed to pull the whole of New York's humanity with him. It was a hefty price. Ultimately, he'd been outsmarted by Harris. But a good leader relied on those he led as much as they relied on him, and it was time for Gray to trust Miller. It was something he'd had to learn himself from hard-won experience. Miller couldn't be a leader without du Trieux, Doyle, Hsiung, and Morland. And Gray couldn't be a good leader without him.

He saved the speech, though. It wasn't the time or place.

Instead, he raised his rifle back to his chest and turned to Doyle and the others. "Gather your things. Stay clear of the Infected, and get to the ship. Now!"

He turned to leave. With one hand on the door, Doyle shouted after him. "Where are you going?"

He shot his words over his shoulder while he exited Gray's office. "I've got one last thing to do."

31

MILLER BOUNDED UP the cove's stairwell, his lungs once again protesting the effort. Blood from his grazed arm seeped into the fabric of his uniform, staining the cloth a deeper shade of black and warming his skin as his blood pressure rose. With every step the pain pulsed down to his fingertips.

It may be more than a graze, but it was nothing compared to the ache that throbbed in his head the moment he'd left Gray's office.

The realization of what he was about to do had settled into his bones, weighing his feet. His legs slowed; flashes of light forced his eyes closed.

Good God, how had it come to this?

He knew what he had to do. It was planned. Everything they had worked for in the last several weeks led to this moment. He couldn't afford to have his body give out just when he was nearly there.

Miller pushed his palm against the wall of the stairwell, his knees shaking. His backpack felt a thousand pounds, pulling him into the hollows of the earth and threatening to blow his psyche to pieces.

All the mistakes that Gray had made, and Miller could very well be making the biggest misstep in all of history.

He was a nobody—a burnt-out bodyguard who'd gotten caught up in the most horrendous fight of human history; how could he, of all people, make a decision that would affect the lives of everyone on the planet?

Miller opened his eyes and forced one foot in front of the other. Up the stairs he continued, his body protesting with each move.

There was no time for regret now. The path had been laid.

When he reached the sixth floor, Miller entered the hallway and chanced a look out the windows, his mind whirling.

Below, in the pandemonium of the compound, the Northwind and Cobalt troops—and strangely enough, some of Harris's troops, too—were leading a small pack of survivors from a warehouse and hacking through the Exiles and Infected toward the docks, where the *Tevatnoa* sat, waiting.

The massive ship looked rusted and decrepit at the docks, but there was a flurry of activity on deck. Half the crew pulled up the cables mooring the ship, while the other half detached the power lines connecting it to the power station farther down the dock.

Satisfied, Miller continued down the hall toward the master suite. He rounded the bend and spotted two guards at the door. They glared at him in shock, looking anxious and sweaty.

His hesitation only lasted a second. Raising his rifle, Miller opened fire, hitting both stunned men in the face. The rounds cut clean through them, throwing them against the wall with a splatter of blood that sprayed across the cracked paint.

Bile burned the back of Miller's throat, but he swallowed it down, adjusted the pack on his back, and stepped over the bodies toward the door. Inside the office he heard shouting.

"Who authorized you to start the chopper's launch sequence? We are *not* evacuating. Not after all we've done to secure this compound!"

"Sir, you must go—we're under siege!"

"Seal off the gates. No one gets in or out."

"Sir...!"

"Don't give me excuses!"

Miller had heard enough. Pushing through the door, he immediately cut to one side and squeezed off several rounds, hitting one unsuspecting soldier in the back and the other in the side.

There were at least three more guards. Miller dodged a shot by diving into a side roll, his heavy backpack off-setting his balance. He landed with a flop, then scrambled up, coming up behind a padded chair and unconsciously grabbing at his throbbing arm. The pain blinded him for only a moment, but it was enough time for the guards to shoot off several more rounds. One of the bullets pierced the stuffed chair and hit the wall behind him. Miller shook off the discomfort, raised his M27 and blindly shot a few more rounds, taking down another guard.

Two left.

Bob Harris stood behind his desk, looking clean, well-fed, and aghast that anyone would have the gall to enter his office and shoot at him. "What the hell are you waiting for?" he bellowed. "Take him out!"

The remaining guards opened up, ripping the area around Miller to shreds with a dozen rounds each. Stuffing from the chair exploded out the back a few more times. Miller felt a round hit the ground at his feet and tucked his leg in. When there was a break in the bullets, he came around to survey the scene.

The two guards stood on either side of Harris's desk, the man himself between them.

"Ha!" Harris burst. "Not so tough now, are you Miller?"

Shaking his head, Miller grabbed at his vest, pulling out a hand grenade. Biting the pin from the top, he rolled it across the floor, between one of the guard's feet.

"Grenade!"

As the guard bent over, using his body as a shield, Harris and the other soldier dove for cover.

The explosion was loud, making Miller's ears ring, but it was mostly contained by the guard's sacrifice. Using the distraction, Miller stood from behind the shredded chair and took out the other guard before he could regain his footing.

Harris made a mad dash for the door; Miller took aim and shot out his kneecaps.

The old security head bellowed in agony as he hit the floor, his chin striking hard against the ground. He rolled onto his back, gripping his smashed knees with shaking, stubby fingers. "Miller—you son of a bitch."

"Sticks and stones, Bob," Miller said.

"What the hell have you done? You've ruined everything—condemned us all, all of humanity."

"*I've* condemned us?" Miller wrenched Harris to his feet, then propped up the battered office chair and sat Harris down in it. "I'm only here to finish what you started." Pulling a length of rope from his vest pocket, Miller tied Harris to the chair, binding him around his arms, across the chest and ankles. "If anyone threw our humanity away, it was you."

"Miller, please. You have to listen to me. Don't do this."

Miller tightened the last of the rope, then bent to remove his backpack. "This is your mission, Bob. It's Operation Atlas Lion—just like you wanted." He pulled open the pack's zipper and spoke through clenched teeth. "Right outside your window, the compound is swarming with every parasite-ridden creature within a ten mile radius." Opening the pack, Miller pulled the surface-to-air nuke from the bag, and with both hands level, brought it over to Harris.

The man's eyes widened in horror. Miller felt sick at the satisfaction that expression brought him.

"We're going to cleanse New York City of the Exiles," he said. "Hope you don't mind, but I improvised a little."

Gingerly, Miller slid the nuke between Harris's knees and used the rope to anchor it to his thighs. Harris struggled, twisting his hips in an attempt to escape, but between his shattered knees and the ropes binding him to the chair, there was no place for him to go.

Bending down, Miller activated the control panel on the side of the missile, set the timer for a half hour, then bent upright.

Harris's eyes had filled with tears. "You don't have to do this," he blubbered. "Just give the wasps time to spread NAPA-33. If we can maintain control of the compound, I know we can beat this."

Miller shook his head, not bothering to reply. He dug into his vest and tossed a handful of pheromone tea bags into Harris's lap.

"What would be worse, do you think? The terror-jaws finding you first, or the timer running out? Good-bye, Harris." Turning on his heel, Miller slung the strap of his M27 on his good arm, and crossed the office.

"Miller! You can't leave me here like this. Miller! This won't solve anything. We can still save New York. You just have to listen to me. Miller! Miller, get back here!"

But he was already out the door.

32

NEW YORK CITY was bleak and dark and much reduced. With power lost at the compound, there were no lights visible anywhere on either side of the East River.

Miller gripped the top of the captain's chair on the bridge of the *Tevatnoa* with white knuckles, his eyes never leaving the darkened city, awaiting the execution.

As the burden settled into his chest like a fungal infection, he sighed and felt the weight of a hand on his shoulder.

L. Gray Matheson patted his bandage, then stopped when Miller winced.

Aboard the *Tevatnoa*'s bridge, Miller, Gray, and Lewis stood silently, watching the Astoria Peninsula. The East River was running fast, whipping them down past Roosevelt Island. It would take only a few minutes to reach the open water of the Atlantic Ocean.

They couldn't see the carnage at the compound from that distance, but they knew. Someplace on that pocket of land, the last of New York's humans were fighting against a horde they couldn't possibly beat.

"How long?" Gray asked.

Miller checked the timer on his watch. "Three minutes."

Their eyes turned back to the peninsula.

Lewis cleared his throat. "You could say that Harris is about to get what he wanted."

Miller didn't speak. He'd thought the same thing, but his throat felt tight.

"I think when we enter Boston, that's the story we go with," Gray said.

His tone was matter-of-fact. Miller looked up in surprise.

"Story?"

Gray raised his eyebrows and gave a half-hearted shrug. "Don't be so eager to take the fall for this. You want to be known throughout all of history as the man who nuked New York City?"

"But I *am* the man who nuked New York City."

"No, Harris is. And it's not as if he's going to be around to deny that story, is he?"

"Sir, I'm not sure..."

"Alex," Gray said, looking a little like his old, controlled self. "Remember me saying that a good soldier needs something of a sociopath in him?"

"Yes."

"Well, that can mean doing the wrong things for

the right reasons," Gray continued. "It can also mean shifting blame onto someone too dead to object."

Miller shot Gray a quick look, then turned his attention back to the skyline. Maybe he was right. Maybe not. Honestly, it was hard to think straight. Exhaustion and the depletion of adrenaline was making Miller feel sluggish.

Lewis grunted. "He's right, son. It'll stay between us. No one else need know."

But Miller would know. It was a weight he was unsure he could forget he was carrying. But he nodded slowly. "If you two think that's what best."

Gray frowned. "We do."

The bomb went off.

From their distance, there was no sound, but clearly visible from the ship's bridge, there was a flash of light. A large cloud of dust puffed into the air from where the compound had once stood. The plume darkened the sky, covering the stars in all directions, hanging on the horizon like a black curtain.

Lewis's shoulders slumped. "That's it, then." He turned away from the window, his eyes passing over Miller's stricken face toward Gray. "What comes next?"

Gray shook his head slowly, his mouth thin and compressed. "I suppose we adapt."

Lewis snorted. "And how do you propose we do that?"

Gray rubbed his chest with the butt of his hand. "There are rumors," he said. "I hear the Russians are attempting to get back into space. There have been discussions of a colony off-planet."

"Good God," Lewis breathed. "Could they even...?"

"And the French have devised plans for some sort of mega-bunkers to house survivors—to try and wait this whole thing out," Gray added.

"What about us?" Lewis asked.

Gray cocked his head. "First, Boston. Then after that...?" He shrugged.

Miller said nothing, the tightness in his chest making it hard to breathe. He had a feeling the survivors of New York were condemned to a nomadic life, for now. It would be tough, but traveling could buy time for the world to settle down. A new normal would have to be found aboard the ship. Maybe for a generation, perhaps two.

He wasn't sure what the new beginning was, but Miller tried to feel it like a rebirth. Every expectation of what the world was, or would be, or had been, was now stripped away.

Miller watched the dust cloud of the Astoria Peninsula in the distance and swallowed the lump in his throat.

For here on out, anything was possible.

MILLER STOOD ON the dock in Boston Harbour, the pier swarming with activity around him. Behind him, the *Tevatnoa* sat moored, creaking like an old rocking chair before its departure.

The trip from New York to Boston had been

difficult. Once the survivors had been medically treated, fed from the hydroponic farms aboard, and informed of what had happened to the compound— or a version of what happened—the mood aboard fluctuated between stunned silence, mourning, and cautious hope.

They were the new pioneers, Gray told them. They were the next settlers of the new world, and they would explore this evolved land and find their place with all the strength and tenacity of the first colonists at Plymouth.

"We will rebuild!" Gray had preached, standing on the deck of the *Tevatnoa* like their savior.

The survivors had cheered, clinging to each other as if their faith would keep the large ship afloat.

Meanwhile, behind Gray and surrounded by du Trieux, Hsiung, and Morland, Miller had hugged his M27 to his chest.

He wanted to believe it would be that easy, but he knew history didn't always remember the hardships the first colonists had faced. They were in for a battle, the kind his M27 wouldn't always fix. But at least they weren't in it wholly alone.

The British Royal Navy, or what was left of it, was rumored to be doing the same thing. Several of their own frigates had been converted into floating cities. Lewis had mentioned there were plans to converge with their vessels and embark together in search of new land—joining forces and resources would be a wise choice. The greater their numbers, the greater their chances for success, Lewis had said.

Before beginning their trans-Atlantic cruise to meet with the Navy and to try and pick up more gear and more ships in other parts of Europe, the *Tevatnoa* collected supplies and passengers in what was left of Boston.

Some survivors opted to stay there—to try their hand at living on familiar territory. Others never left the ship, concentrating on building infrastructure and living quarters inside the depths of the boat.

Miller wasn't sure who would fare better. He wasn't certain of anything anymore.

Now, on the dock, the *Tevatnoa* waiting for him, Miller's uncertainty resurfaced. Where did he belong? He wasn't sure. He wasn't even sure of who he was—what he had *become*.

The old Miller, the bodyguard who had risked his life to protect others—he was long gone. He'd died at the beginning of all this shit; the moment Harris had ordered the attack helicopter to slaughter the Infected during the extraction of Lester Allen.

Even the Miller who had fought against the Charismatics, and teamed up with the Archaeans to liberate the compound's survivors—even he didn't exist anymore. He'd died in the mushroom cloud, blown to ash with all the Exiles and Infected of New York City.

How many times had he been reborn? How many versions of himself had he discarded to come this far?

He wasn't certain someone like him *belonged* on a ship full of humanity's hopes and dreams.

The weight of his old phone made his skin itch. He turned it on, flipped through his photos, trying to feel something familiar, something good. His family's smiling faces stared back at him with such innocence, such life—it made his eyes water. He kept flipping, his calloused thumb scraping across the scratched screen. Photographs of Billy, Samantha, of all the members of Cobalt, many lost and gone forever. The ache in his chest made him look away.

Quickly, he pressed the power button, shutting it down. He pulled his arm back—to toss the phone into the water, be done with his past forever—but he stopped himself.

Footsteps approached from behind.

Turning around, he spotted du Trieux ambling up the dock. She carried a wooden crate of supplies in both her hands, her vest exchanged for a T-shirt and a headband. No gas mask; there weren't too many wasps here.

She grinned at him, eyeing the phone in his hand and his pitcher's stance. "Cleaning house?" she asked.

Miller dropped his arm to his side, phone still tight in his palm. "Yes. I mean, no. I—hell, I don't know."

She nodded, then skirted past and lugged the crate up a ramp leading to one of the cargo holds. "We disembark in a few minutes. Wouldn't want to leave without you." She stopped mid-step then looked at him kindly. "You ready?"

Miller pocketed his phone and wiped his palm against the leg of his pants. "I'll be up in a few."

She pursed her lips and nodded. "Okay." Then, still carting the crate, she disappeared into the ship.

For a moment he just stared after her.

He walked toward the ramp, the phone weighing heavily in his pocket. This was a new beginning for all of them: for all the survivors, for the remains of humanity. For Cobalt, for du Trieux. For him.

Who he was, what he'd done—when the *Tevatnoa* pulled away from Boston's docks, that man would be left behind, just like all the others.

As he bounded up the ramp into the cargo hold, he squared his shoulders.

Had to start someplace.

EPILOGUE

SAMANTHA HERNANDEZ LEANED her shoulder into the stilled subway car door and shoved it open the remainder of the way.

Inside the car, the smell of death hung thick, billowing out and filling the station behind her. She pulled her bandana back over her mouth and nose.

She squinted into the darkness, but nothing moved. She reached behind her and was handed a burning torch, then stepped inside the subway car and looked around in the glow of the torchlight. It was a distasteful scene. Bile gathered in the back of her throat.

The support of her friends filled her mind with reassurance. She was protected, there was nothing to fear.

She *knew* this.

She swallowed the bile and with a calm assurance, stepped further into the subway car, the strength of her people filling her.

The car was full of people, too—but not of the living. Skeletal remains from the Infected lay slumped together in groups, as if connecting with their dying commune had been a source of comfort near the end.

Sidestepping over the bodies, she pulled strength from her family members waiting in the station, and made herself walk deeper into the train, changing cars and slowly making her way toward the front where she knew *he* would be.

She could smell him.

Anger flooded her mind, but she was experienced enough with the sensation to recognize the anger she felt was not wholly her own. The Archaeans were angry with *him*—to the point of riot. But allowing a riot would undo the growth the Archaeans had achieved over the last year, so she had made the decision to come alone.

She would handle this.

If anyone could identify their own emotions in the swell of the Infected, it was Samantha. Between the pheromones in the truck, and the emotional turmoil driving the horde of the Infected stampede, it was Samantha who had driven the truck to the compound and picked up the Archaeans, who'd led the caravan to the outskirts of New York and safety.

She hadn't known what Alex had planned—but she knew him well enough to heed his warning. She was glad they were long clear of the city when the bomb blast hit.

There would be fallout; perhaps for decades. But

the Archaeans were used to adapting to a changing environment. If the radiation caused mutations, they would meet them just as they had met every evolution the Archaean parasite had brought them—with love, respect, and acceptance.

It was only because of *him* that she'd had to return to the city so soon. He was a source of conflict that needed to be quelled—permanently, quickly.

At the head of the train, she found him, just where she knew he would be.

Jimmy Swift looked nothing like the charming, assured newscaster he had once been. Now, he was crouched in the corner of a death-filled subway car like a scared, mangy dog—bald, bleeding, and in tatters.

He'd clearly been topside when the blast had hit: he was covered in radiation sores and breathing in short, hurried, shallow breaths. His eyes were yellowed. His head rested on the floor. His hair, eyebrows, lashes—everything—was gone. His eyes went wide at the sight of her and his breathing increased. He opened his dry, cracked mouth.

She felt the pull of his fear, and the depth of his despair, but she also felt the anger and hostility of the Archaeans back at the station, and she said nothing—only watched Swift struggle for breath. Mixed in with his fear and the crowd's anger, she felt her own sense of satisfaction.

"H-how you…?" he whispered.

"How are we not covered in radiation sores?" she asked.

He nodded, barely perceptibly.

"Because we knew better."

He swallowed, lips wide open, although she doubted there was a drop of saliva left in his mouth.

"H-help me," he begged, panting faster still. "P-please."

She felt his flicker of hope and her heart swelled at the power of it. It took effort, but she was able to push it down, away from her mind, so that she could concentrate on her own words—her last shard of individuality.

"I can't help you," she said, honestly. "But I can't kill another Infected either, even if I wanted to. All I can do is tell you that you've lost. The whole of New York City is lost. You didn't win the city away from the humans like you fought to. All you did was give them no choice but to destroy it. And now, those of us who are left, we will be better off without either of you."

"N-no," Swift gasped, fighting for air.

"You will be dead soon," she said, enjoying the primal fear that radiated off him in a panicked wave. "And the world will be better for it."

"N-no, it w-won't," he whispered. "Worse," he added. "M-much, m-much worse."

With a hiss, his final breath escaped his lips.

She felt his relief like a blow to her gut. There was an instant release of pain from him that flowed through her, and then nothing.

His open eyes gaped at her, his mouth still open as if searching for one last breath or word.

Satisfied, Samantha turned from Jimmy Swift's body and began the trek back to the subway platform, and to her people.

From deep within, she felt a dull sense of dread, but she pushed it away and fabricated a triumphant bravery, forcing it to the surface. They *would* be better off, she insisted. They would thrive.

They had to.

When she reached her people on the platform, she vowed—stepping over the bodies of the Infected—she would do so with a conquering smile.

ABOUT THE
AUTHORS

Extinction Biome is the creation of jungle warrior, revolutionary, counter-revolutionary and outdoorsperson **Addison Gunn**. But who is Addison Gunn? Addison's too damn busy to answer that. Instead Gunn's wrangled some of the best new talents in the genre to pen this exciting new series...

After writing for children's television, **Anne Tibbets** found her way to writing novels by following what she loves: books, strong female characters, twisted family dynamics, magic, sword fights, quick moving plots, and ferocious and cuddly animals. Anne divides her time between writing, her family, and two furry creatures that she secretly believes are plotting her assassination.

Malcolm Cross lives in London and enjoys the personal space and privacy that the city is known for. When not misdirecting tourists to nonexistent landmarks, Malcolm is likely to be writing. A member of the furry fandom, he won the 2012 Ursa Major Award for Best Anthropomorphic Short Fiction.